BLOOD & TACOS

The Beginning

edited by
Johnny Shaw

Blood & Tacos
The Beginning

Edited by Johnny Shaw

ISBN 978-1894953-900
First printing September 2013

This book is a collection of the stories published in the first four issues of Blood & Tacos Magazine, ISSN 1929-011X.
www.bloodandtacos.com

Published by Creative Guy Publishing
Victoria, Canada
www.creativeguy.net

Cover art by Roxanne Patruznick, ©2013 Roxanne Patruznick

BLOOD & TACOS

The Beginning

edited by
Johnny Shaw

CREATIVE GUY PUBLISHING
VICTORIA | CANADA

CONTENTS

INTRODUCTION by Johnny Shaw	1
FOREWORD by Brace Godfrey	3
SUNSHINE: STRIPPER ASSASSIN in G-STRING GUNDOWN	7
APACHE BLOOD in A GOOD DAY TO DIE	21
THE SILENCER in THE SILENCER STRIKES	35
TIGER TEAM BRAVO in BONDS OF BLOOD	51
FATHER DUKES in DOPEHOUSE INFERNO (ABRIDGED)	73
BLOOD & SWEETGRASS in THIS REZ IS MINE	93
BROWN SUGAR BROOKDALE in TITTY TITTY BANG BANG	107
THE ALBINO WINO in LONGHAIR DEATH FARM	124
DEAD EYE in END OF THE RENAISSANCE	137
CHINGÓN in BLOOD AND TACOS	153
VIPER in SHADOW SISTERS OF SHINJUKU	164
A.R.V.N. presents NEVER SAY GOODNIGHT IN SAIGON	181
STUDS WINSLOW in THE BITCHES OF THE FIFTH REICH	205
BATTLEGROUND U.S.S.A.: TEXASGRAD	224
THE CHEMISTRATOR in DRUG CITY, USA	245
BASTARD MERCENARY in OPERATION SCORPION STING	256
THE SANITIZER in THE POTOMAC PENETRATION	270
THEY CALL HIM CRUEL in BURN IN	290
L.A.N.D.B.O.A.T. (THE BOAT THAT GOES ON LAND) in L.A.N.D.B.O.A.T. (THE BOAT THAT GOES ON LAND)	305
MAJOR MCCALL AND THE WIFE in FRAGGED	326
AUTHORS	343

INTRODUCTION
by
Johnny Shaw

IT'S HARD TO BELIEVE that *Blood & Tacos* has put out enough stories to fill a book. From a silly idea to four issues, a podcast, a phone app, and a book imprint, it has grown well beyond what I first imagined. And I have the writers and readers to thank for that.

Blood & Tacos all started with a story—the story that would eventually become the Chingón tale in this anthology. I wrote it with a hoax in mind. The idea was that I would claim to have "found" a book and put a sample chapter on my blog. My wife would paint the cover. And I would get a few crime writer pals to "remember" reading Chingón when they were teenagers, or to brag of having a few of the paperbacks in their collections.

That was the idea. But that seemed like a lot of work for little reward, and anyway, why should I get to have all the fun? As soon as I mentioned the premise to other writers, they wanted to play in the same sandbox.

Call it satire, homage, parody, or tribute—these stories embrace the men's adventure stories from the 1970s and '80s that inspired them. I encourage every reader to seek out the books and stories of the authors in this collection. Without them, there would be no *Blood & Tacos*.

A huge thanks goes to Cameron "The Albino Wino" Ashley and Gary "The Silencer" Phillips. These were the first two authors I told about *Blood & Tacos*. And instead of laughing at me, they immediately pitched stories, as if they had been itching for something like this to come along. Without their enthusiasm and support, I probably wouldn't have pulled the trigger on this project.

I also thank Bart "Father Dukes" Lessard, who not only fixed all the commas and did the incredible graphic design for the covers but wrote one of my favorite stories.

Speaking of the covers, I would be nowhere without *Blood & Tacos* artist-in-residence (literally—she's my wife) Roxanne Patruznick. Her one-of-a-kind oil paintings give *Blood & Tacos* its unique look. To have that kind of talent at my disposal is crazy.

And I thank Pete Allen, the mastermind behind Creative Guy Publishing, the publisher of *Blood & Tacos*. The amount of creative control that he gives me over this project is ridiculous. I hope that he never realizes how irresponsible a decision that was.

Finally, on behalf of both Pete and myself, I thank all of our readers and supporters. We would be writing our explosions and punches in the dark if it weren't for you crazy people.

Now on to the action. And remember, if it's too cheesy, it's a quesadilla.

Johnny Shaw
Portland, Oregon
2013

FOREWORD
by
Brace Godfrey

LET'S GET ONE thing out in the open. I am writing this under duress. Johnny Shaw is a bastard of monumental proportions. The world needs to know that.

The only reason I put pen to this foreword is because on the day Johnny came to see me at my local tavern, the Spittoon, he happened to witness a few things that I would rather the Stockton PD not know about. He might be a monobrow hack with the talent of a prize pig on a carnival midway, but from one bastard to another, I reluctantly have to respect his moxie in resorting to blackmail. Long story short: if he ever goes into a lengthy digression about me, a woman named Frank, and a panel truck full of stereo components, it's all lies.

And while my inclusion in this anthology was of no interest, not to me anyway, after I leafed through it, I realized how good a thing it was that I got a chance to set the record straight.

Some of these stories were written by contemporaries (not equals) of mine. More than once, I'd even gotten historically, world-class drunk with Mal Radcliff and Guy Rivera. But it wasn't until now that I actually read any of their stuff. And when I did, I was surprised at how familiar it was—all of it. That's because these stories, they were all stolen from me. Every last one. Each and every newsstand emission squirted into the pages of this book is just a cheap swipe of one of my modern classics.

The evidence is overwhelming. For example, Father Dukes, the clergyman who purges the ghetto of drugs, is nothing more than a thinly veiled rip-off of my character Fist Priest. If you can find a copy of *Hell Comes to Helltown*, you'll see what I'm talking about.

The same screaming sense of déjà vu rings loud and clear in the characters Albino Wino, Apache Blood, and L.A.N.D.B.O.A.T. (the Boat That Goes on Land). If you can't see the obvious parallels with my heroes Ginger Ninja (*Night of the Alopecians*), Billy Jacque (*Wreck in Quebec*), and Auto Pilot, the Car with Wings That Make It Fly (*Coffee, Tea, or Die*), then you're in a coma or huffing paint.

Blood & Sweetgrass's adventure is so close to my story *Injun Trouble*, featuring Brave & Squaw, that it barely requires a connection of the dots or the feathers.

The Chemistrator and the Sanitizer, two mavericks on the run who use science to defeat threats to the American way of life, are pretty much straight counterfeits of my character The Sciencer. Like a three-dollar bill, if you catch my drift.

The most blatant of all is Studs Winslow. I've got my lawyer on the phone as we speak (mostly for the aforementioned panel truck full of stereo components, but I'm a bulk buyer). If that character isn't a sham of my character Woods Stinslow, I'll eat a dog turd with mustard. Just pick up a copy of *Woods Stinslow on Ass Mountain* and try to call me a liar. It's physically impossible.

Battleground U.S.S.A.: Texasgrad is my story *Red Dusk* from my Futurecide series, right down to the colon and the mushroom cloud. Sunshine, Stripper Assassin? My own Sister Afro. They Call Him Cruel? Vicious Sid. The list goes on.

But the one that brought a tear to my eye (to be honest, I was about nine whiskey sours in, and when I'm that drunk, I get weepy if someone blesses a sneeze) was the A.R.V.N. War Chronicles, which admittedly didn't pinch from any of my stories. No, instead it was all yanked directly from my self-published autobiography, *Brace Yourself: The Brace Godfrey Story with Recipes*. That's right: even my right to my own life story isn't held dear. You weren't there, man!

Johnny calls these stories hidden treasures, lost to newer generations by a lack of interest or curiosity. I say good riddance to bad rubbish. Some treasure should remain buried. After all, isn't pirate gold little more than stolen loot?

Still if you bought this book, I suppose I should thank you. I do have a story in it. First royalty check, I'll name a fart after you.

Brace Godfrey
Stockton, California
2013

SUNSHINE: STRIPPER ASSASSIN
in
G-STRING GUNDOWN
by Walter Himes
(discovered by Josh Stallings)

HEY BOSS, somebody sent you a strip-a-gram."

"Send her in."

Sunshine O'Shay trembled as she walked across the marble floor. She never thought she'd be in an honest-to-god mansion and yet here she was. Dressed like a sexy cop, showing as much cleavage as tape and a push-up bra could generate. Over her shoulder she carried a garment bag.

She entered a den that was larger than her entire home. A fat man in his mid-thirties sat in a club chair in the middle of the room. He had on a shiny gold velour track suit. He looked Sunshine up and down twice, slowly examining every inch of her coffee and cream skin. "They sent me a negress. Now that's a spicy meatball."

"You ready for this?" She was eighteen and fighting to sound so much older. "I hear you been a very bad, bad boy."

"Oh yeah, I been bad, officer. Ha, take me in." He put his wrists out, practically drooling at the thought of what was coming. Pauly stood at the door smirking. Jimmy didn't need to tell him twice to get the hell out, guard the door in case Gina got home early. Now that would be a massacre. The closing door covered up the sound of the cuffs snapping home.

"Damn girl, that pinches. What are those, real cuffs?"

"Sorry baby." She leaned down, kissing his wrist and giving him a look down her top at her breasts.

"Mmmm, they little, bitty things, but I still love to suck on those dark cherries. I hear the darker the berry..." That was the last thing he ever said. The blast from the twelve-gauge took his face off. He didn't scream. His wide eyes showed life, but how does one scream when he is missing his lower jaw and most of his throat?

Pauly burst in, gun in hand. He saw his boss fighting for life and a dead stripper at his feet. What the fuck had happened?

Pauly ran to his boss hoping for some whispered information or instruction. As he stepped over the dead stripper, Jimmy's eyes went huge. He was gurgling, fighting to warn Pauly of something. From the floor the shotgun fired between Pauly's spread legs. The blow lifted him into the air and dropped him five feet back, blood pouring from his groin.

The bloody stripper stood over Pauly. "Yo cracker, you got any idea why I'm here?"

"No, none, I swear."

Wrong answer. Flame and smoke engulfed Pauly's head. When it cleared he was nothing but a stain on the carpet.

Sunshine walked to the boss. She pushed his ruined face with the shotgun barrel. "You, I bet you know why I'm here. Huh, smart man? Too bad you can't tell me." The shotgun rocked and Jimmy became a smear.

Sunshine dropped her blood-splattered cop's costume. Dropped her bra and g-string. Crossed to the bathroom, where she took a hot shower. She soaped and removed the gore. She even washed the shotgun. She had hoped she would feel better afterwards, what she felt was numb. Clean, she slipped into the starched white maid's uniform she had carried protected in the garment bag.

Careful to leave by the back door, Sunshine became invisible on the sidewalk. Just another brown-skinned maid heading home. Beverly Hills was full of them. Climbing onto the crosstown bus, she dropped in a dime and took her seat. She'd be back in Compton before they even found the bodies. Maybe she would feel better after the next on her list.

Caesar Cavasos was a big, bald Mexican. He ran Pussycats striptease club in East LA. He also ran the cribs behind it where a man could get his sexual needs serviced for a small price. He was known as an evil man. Now he was a dead man. Crabs crawled in what was left of his skull.

Detective John Stark stood on Santa Monica Beach, looking down at the corpse. "What are you doing so far from East LA, Caesar?"

"Hope you aren't waiting for him to answer." Leroy Jones was Stark's partner. Salt and Pepper, the other cops called them, but only behind their backs.

Stark tossed the waterlogged wallet to his partner. Jones let out a slow whistle. "Well, well, looks like Caesar's having a bad day."

"Any idea who wanted him dead?"

"Shoot, Stark, might as well round up all of East LA. Truth, can't think of many who wanted him alive."

"What's in his hand?" Stark knelt down. The dead man's hand was frozen into a fist. A tuft of glitter shone through his fingers. With a pen he pulled the fingers open . Lifting a round half dollar-sized strip of lamé, a red tassel was attached at the center. He held it up to Jones. "Now all we need to do is find a stripper missing one pasty."

"Case closed."

"What's up, little soul sister?" Ronnie leaned on his Chevy Bomb by the front door of Pussycats. James Brown's "The Payback" thumped through the wall. Ronnie bopped his head to the beat. He was cholo cool, khakis and a wife beater, Pendleton top button closed.

"Boss in? I needs to speak to him." Sunshine wore Chuck Taylors, a pair of hip huggers, and a crop top that showed a healthy amount of skin.

"Ain't you heard? Found his dead ass in Santa Monica Bay."

"What?"

Ronnie tilted his head toward an unmarked police car. "The man's inside asking questions. Better skip out if you done it." He kept a straight face for a moment then burst out laughing.

"What? You don't think I could've done it?"

"Chica, you couldn't kill a rat with a scattergun." He was still laughing to himself as Sunshine entered the club.

The two detectives had taken up residence in Caesar's office. Stark was openly enjoying the line of dancers that paraded in to speak to them.

"Damn waste of time, for all the information we's getting." Jones wanted to get rolling, slap around a few stoolies, get to the bottom line. It wasn't a dancer done this; women poison or stab. They don't shotgun off a man's face.

"Only one left, okay with you?"

"Just get to it."

Stark almost spit out his coffee when Sunshine came in. She was that good looking. He eyed his notes and motioned for her to sit, not sure he could speak without stumbling over the words. "Sunshine O'Shay, is that right?"

"Yes sir, that is my name." She focused all her charm at Stark. He was handsome, in cop kind of way, with his long sideburns and thick mustache.

"Call me John."

"Okay, John. You all have any idea who done this?"

"Not yet, but we'll find the perp, trust me. We always get our man."

"What are you, a couple of Mounties? You Dudley Do-Right?"

Stark was suddenly embarrassed. He searched his notebook like some answer was deep in there. Jones asked if she knew anybody that wanted Otis dead. Her laugh told him what he already knew. The list of folks who wanted the whoremaster dead was long and wide.

"That'll just about do it." Stark finished writing her address in his notebook. "If you think of anything else, you give me a call." He passed her his card. She leaned over the desk and with her eyes locked on his, she took the pen from his hand and wrote on his notebook.

"That's my number. You bored Saturday night, say eight, call me. I might be hungry for dinner." As she walked out, she swung her hips just enough to keep his eyes on her.

"What the hell was that?""That, Detective Jones, was the famous Stark charm."

"Don't smell right."

"Jealous?"

"Not in this life, white boy."

Driving back to the LAPD Homicide office, both detectives were thinking about Sunshine, for very different reasons.

King Charles and Ray-Ray sat in King's office behind the Watts Head Cutter's barbershop. Guns, drugs, women, King ran the black side of the ghetto. No one so much as got their hair conked without his knowing about it.

"Jimmy G's dead. Took a gauge to the head."

"No real loss there, King, right?"

"Took out Caesar, same way. The Italian mother-rapers didn't sanction any hits. I didn't. So who the hell did it?"

"Could be Jimmy G pissed off some husband? Caesar, that spick been just begging to die for a time now."

"Ray-Ray?"

"Yeah, King?"

"Find out who the hell is killing folks without my say-so."

"It is done."

"Good." After Ray-Ray was gone, King sat back, put his feet up on his desk. He struck a kitchen match and fired up a robusto. Jimmy G, Caesar and he had all come up together. They were the young lions of crime. Hell, they brought about the treaty between the Mexicans, blacks and Italians. They carved up the city and got rich in the process. They all played high school football at Franklin. Senior prom, they all were there. It was when they came together. In many ways, that was the beginning of their triumphant rule.

1955, Compton. Kendra looked in the mirror and liked what she saw. The pink taffeta prom dress was filled out in all the right places. Sure, she wished she had some more breasts, but what she had looked good. She heard the knock at the door. She knew it was Otis, but she hung back. She'd let him sit with her father for a few minutes, let the old man scare him. As long as Otis behaved and didn't get Pop's Irish up, he'd fare okay.

"You look more beautiful than Dorothy Dandridge." Otis was driving his Ford.

"I don't, and keep your eyes on the road."

Dressed in his father's suit, he was so handsome, it was as if she had never seen him before. He wasn't big, or strong, he didn't play ball, but something about his glasses and shy smile on this night was making her feel different in a very good way.

1973, Los Angeles, Homicide Department. Jones hefted a stack of files. "Somewhere in all this mess is an answer."

"Why can't it be a coincidence?" Stark pulled up his tie.

"I don't believe in coincidences. Two dirtbags get their heads cleaned with a gauge, two days apart? No, they connected, just can't see how yet."

"You need me to stick around?"

"Nah, you gots a date with a dancer. Go on. I'm waiting for a call from Smitty in the gang unit."

"Alright, I'll get with her twice, once just for you Jones."

"Just check her ID first, hate to have to haul you in for staggi."

"She's over eighteen."

"Maybe just."

"She dances at Pussycats."

"Oh yeah, that's right, they never ever had an underage stripper."

"Screw you. You're just bustin' balls because she went for me." Stark was sure Jones was wrong. Damn, she had to be eighteen. He took his '67 Firebird, six years old, but still badass. If this didn't get her panties wet, she was frigid.

Across town Sunshine was slipping into a white go-go dress. She had showered and put on a wig, long and straight, just the way white men liked. She finished her make-up and did a twirl in front of her mother's bed.

"Baby girl, you look amazing. Your daddy be so proud of you."

"You sure about that, Momma?" Sunshine held a water glass with a straw to her mother's lips. Her mother was quadriplegic, she had been for Sunshine's entire life.

"Look at you, darlin', you are amazing. Yes, he would be proud."

"Do you think he's watching us?"

"Every moment."

Sunshine kissed her mother and went to wait in the living room. She watched the phone. Begging it to ring. Finally, at a quarter to eight it rang. She had it her hands on the second ring. On a pad she wrote down an address on West Century Blvd. near Inglewood. She, hung up, and hoped her father looked away sometimes.

Stark glided the Firebird to a stop. He splashed on liberal amounts of English Leather. Lifting his lip, he checked his teeth, smoothed his mustache, and was ready. The house was a GI home built for returning soldiers after WWII. The lawn was longer than the neighbors. For a flash Stark saw himself pushing a mower and Sunshine handing him an icy tea. Shook his head and cleared the thought. Love them, leave them, move on. Sunshine opened the door and his resolve was gone. When she took his hand, she could have led him anywhere.

"Momma, this is Detective Stark."

"Um, call me John, Mrs. O'Shay."

"We'll save first names until we know each other better."

"Fine," he didn't like her firm, cold eyes. Eyes that looked like they could see through any snow job he wanted to run.

"Detective Stark?"

"Yes ma'am?"

"You take care of my baby girl. You keep her safe out there."

"Don't worry, I'm packing, I'll keep her safe."

"There is a bad man wants to—"

"Momma, no." Sunshine silenced her. "Sorry John, she is a worrier. Now good night, Momma, I love you."

Stark waited until they were in the Firebird before he spoke. "Where would you like me to take you? I know a steak joint up on Sunset."

"Older white cop with a younger Black girl? We better stay down here."

"I'm not that much older."

"Relax. I like it."

"You are eighteen, aren't you?" He tried to sound casual.

"Are you planning to sleep with me? Bit forward, Detective." She stared at him, her face flat of emotion. He stammered and started to blush. She left him hanging then finally let out a laugh. "I'm eighteen, turned a few months back. So if, IF, you get lucky you won't wind up in the pokey. Now why don't you take me to Bertha's Soul Food on West Century. Feed me and we'll see where the night takes us."

"Sounds good." Stark was glad to have it all out. His face cooled. From the corner of his eye, he saw that she was scanning for a tail. She was subtle, but it was clear she was afraid someone might be following them.

"Sunshine, you know you can trust me, if you're into some kind of trouble."

"I like you, John, no, really. But I have a past. If you knew..."

"Girl, I, well we all have secrets. I've done some stuff I wish I hadn't."

"My mother can't work." Sunshine looked out the window. "I was fifteen when she had the accident. We needed money. He said he was a good man and he'd never make me do anything I didn't want to."

"Who, who hurt you?"

"King Charles. He is a...he will...he gets girls for, you know."

"He's a pimp."

"Yes. Two months ago I turned eighteen and went legit. I started dancing at Pussycats. I don't work the cribs, just dance, you have to believe me." Stark passed her a starched white handkerchief. She dabbed at the tears running down her face. She slowed her breathing. She leaned her head on his shoulder.

"I'm sorry, John, really I am. He's still looking for me. If he finds me, who knows what he might do. I know he's killed more than one girl. Had one of them drink Drano, another he ODed on smack and pushed her off the San Pedro Bridge. If you want to take me home and forget we never met, I'll understand."

"Never happen. I got a feeling you are going to change my life. Now let's get to the eating; I am starving."

Bertha's was a small house converted into a restaurant in the '60s, the name spelled out on the roof in ruby neon. With yellow and purple paint, it was anything but subtle. Sunshine ordered chitlins, oxtails and gravy, mac and cheese. Stark teased her about how skinny she was. He ordered the fried chicken, greens, rice and beans. Bertha's didn't have a liquor license, but there was a bucket of ice stuffed with bottles of beer under the counter, not for sale. You took them and tipped accordingly.

In between bites Sunshine gave Stark an idyllic picture of her growing up. Her mother and father had been the perfect couple. Dad worked helping to build airplanes in Santa Monica. Her mother had been a nurse. Sunshine wanted to go to college, be a teacher. "That dream died when I took my first trick. And all that destruction because a drunk driver missed a corner. Killed my dad, crippled my mother...Shoot, here I am crying again. Sorry." She dabbed her eyes, looking down at the handkerchief. "I covered it in eye make-up. Sorry, I'll wash it."

"Don't worry about it."

"But I do." Reflected in the glass covering a print on the wall, she saw King Charles enter. He was resplendent in his purple crushed-velvet trench coat and matching slacks. Alligator shoes. A fur-lined fedora. He even carried a gold-handled walking stick. Ray-Ray held the door for him, he was in a simple pinstriped suit and a bowler.

Sunshine waited for them to sit. Then with a clumsy elbow, she dumped a bowl of red beans and rice onto Stark's lap. "Oh, I'm so sorry!" Jenny May came out from behind the counter with a large white towel and a bottle of club soda.

Sunshine watched the detective disappear into the rest room. Then she was up and moving fast. Straight up to King's table, she moved the waiter out of the way. "They won't be staying."

"Who the hell are you?"

"Me? I'm the one knows why your partners got smoked. Now you still want this man standing here while we talk?"

King waved the waiter away angrily, "Get the fuck out of here. When I want food, I'll come see you."

"Certainly, Mr King." The waiter disappeared, probably checking his underwear.

"Outside." Sunshine stood and walked out. King had to move to keep up.

"Not him." Sunshine pointed at Ray-Ray. "He stays in the restaurant."

"Nope. He goes or I go home."

"Boss, I'll be a hundred feet away, max." Ray-Ray said, turning away.

"Okay. Keep your damn eyes open and off the waitresses." King watched Sunshine walking toward his Cadillac Brougham. He knew her from some place but couldn't place her.

Detective Jones was running full lights and sirens. Last he heard, Stark was going to a soul food joint. Somewhere on West Century Blvd. He was with Sunshine and had no idea what he was into. It had taken the guys from the gang unit to piece it all together, but they had. Sunshine was anything but a civilian. She was a combatant. Blowing across Hawthorn he traded paint with a UPS truck. The driver called him a "stupid nigger." Would have upset him, might even have used his .38 to knock out a few of the cracker's teeth, but his partner was on the line so he kept blasting.

In the Caddy, King looked her over like he was deciding whether or not to eat her. "You a brave, little girl. You know who I am?"

"Yes, I do, Chucky, I do."

"Chucky? No one...not since school...oh mother fu—you are."

"Yes, I am."

King's mind raced. This girl could have been Kendra nineteen years ago. But Kendra was in a chair, no way she could have...

"Do you know why I'm here?"

"I—we didn't mean to hurt her. We were just messing around and she stumbled...Really it was an accident. Ask..."

"Who? Jimmy G? He didn't have any good answers. Caesar begged, told me it was all your idea. He did say my mother was asking for it. Well, he almost said it. Couldn't finish with his face all over the pier."

King closed his eyes. The night flooded in, drowning out the present.

It was on a deserted road up behind the Griffith observatory. After the prom, they had failed to hook up with any bitches. So King, Jimmy G, and Caesar, they headed up to the overlook, to drink some beer and fuck with some kids.

Kendra had decided on the dance floor that tonight was the night she would give herself to Otis. He was a good man. She loved him like no other. He made her feel shy when he came around.

Otis had been gentle when he unbuttoned her gown. He touched her body like it was precious. She arched her back, pressing her near naked body against his. Their lips met. The kiss wasn't gentle; it was hungry. He pulled her legs apart. She guided him into her. She screamed his name, told him how much she loved him. He held her close, echoing her words of love. He'd thought she was the one for him since the fourth grade, but now he knew. He really knew. When the release finally came, he let out a howling scream.

That was the sound that attracted the three football players. They ripped the Ford's door open. The naked couple tumbled out onto the dirt. They circled around them. "Well, well, Otis Four Eyes. How the hell did you get this fine woman into your car?"

"You get her drunk? That it, ese?" Caesar asked.

"Nah, bet he hit her with a shovel."

"Jimmy right about that? He hurt you?" King moved in closer.

Otis stood, facing the bigger man. "Let her go."

"Four Eyes, you giving orders?" King drove his fist into Otis's gut, doubling him over. On the way down, Caesar hit his face, spraying blood into the dust.

Kendra threw her body over him.

"Kendra, time you was with some real men." She spat up at King. A good glob hung off his chin.

Caesar laughed. "Hey, King you gots some on your chin."

"I know what the hell I have and where. Get that bitch."

Otis whispered, "Now, don't look back."

And he was up, his fists were full of loose dirt. He threw it in the two nearest faces. He threw wild unfocused punches. One caught Jimmy G off guard; he stumbled back, his nose bleeding. Caesar nailed Otis in the back of the skull with a baseball bat he used as a walking stick. Otis crumpled. King laid his boots into Otis.

Kendra was running around the car to get in the driver's side. She tripped on a tree root. For a brief moment she thought she was flying. Then she landed hard and tumbled. When she stopped moving, she had lost all feeling below her neck.

King looked at Sunshine sadly. "You killed Caesar and Jimmy G over a mistake? We never meant to hurt your mother."

"But you did mean to kill my father. Nobody beats a man to death by accident." Before he could speak again, she raked his face with her long nails, drawing blood. He yowled and slapped her. Blood came from her lips. She scratched the other side of his face. This time he punched her nose. It flattened in to a bloody pulp. Her blood splattered the windshield.

Sunshine kicked the car door open just as Stark cleared the diner's door. She fell back screaming, "No, King, don't shoot me... No, please. Stark, help."

Stark's .44 Magnum exploded into the night. He punched two fist-sized holes into the windshield. The first shot took King's neck out, the second shattered his chest.

The siren filled the air as Jones bounced into the lot. He jumped out shotgun in hand. He searched for a threat, saw none. He leaned into King's car. "He's still breathing."

"Get his gun before he plugs you."

"He ain't got no gun, Stark. Way you hit him he couldn't move far. No gun. Did you see a gun?"

"Hell yes, I saw a gun. He was trying to kill Sunshine."

Jones moved around the Caddy and helped Sunshine up. "He didn't have no gun, did he?"

"I'm sure I saw one. Detective Stark wouldn't have shot him if he didn't, would he?"

"And that's how it will have to play. I read the file on your mother's accident. And what happened to her date. Odd that all three dead men went to that same prom."

"Quite a coincidence, isn't it?" She gave him a subtle wink.

Jones dropped an untraceable throw-down pistol into the Caddy. Stark would get a commendation for bravery for saving the young woman's life. Their being on a date would never be mentioned.

Ray-Ray called on Sunshine late one night. He brought her a briefcase. They stood on the front porch like two old friends chatting. "I have to know, Sunshine, what made you believe you could trust me."

"Well Ray-Ray, greed and fear. You wanted King's empire. And you know if you screwed me, I would find you."

"And what if the cop hadn't shot King?"

"I would have used the .32 in my jacket pocket. Same one I got pointed at you."

Ray-Ray looked at her hand. It was in her jacket pocket, aiming at him. He started to laugh. "Nothing gets past you."

"Not much."

It wasn't until she was in her mother's room that she counted the money in the briefcase: $30,000. Her mother smiled at her. It was done. She closed her eyes and drifted off to sleep, the sleep of the righteous. Sunshine watched her mother sleeping for a time, then slipped from the room.

Thinking it all over, Sunshine finally felt relief. Killing one man is hard. Killing two is near impossible. But after three, it just started to come naturally.

THE END

Walter Himes spent most of his all-too-brief life in San Quentin for shooting a white man seven times in the face. Besides the seventeen Stripper Assassin tales he put out from behind bars, he also wrote Black Is Black, *a manifesto that provoked the prison riots of 1979. That same year, he was found dead in his cell. The official coroner's report states this was death by suicide, but many still believe a guard killed him over a $30 gambling debt. JOSH STALLINGS discovered this story from 1974 while cleaning out his grandfather's gun safe.*

APACHE BLOOD
in
A GOOD DAY TO DIE
by Edward T. Johnson
(discovered by Brad Mengel)

THE QUIET OF THE DESERT was broken by the roar of dune buggy and trail bike engines. The two Apache warriors looked down from their vantage point on the mesa. The older of the men watched through binoculars, observing the progress of the Mafia button men.

The older Apache motioned to his grandson. "I think today is a good day to die, Dalton."

The younger man pulled the trigger of his rifle. The left tyre of the lead dune buggy exploded, causing it to flip, disgorging the hit men. Two of the four men were crushed as the buggy landed on them.

The shooter looked away from the scope on his rifle. "It will be, for them," he said with grim determination. There was a flash of pain in his eyes as he remembered what brought him to this point.

Three months earlier, Trooper Dalton Hollick had been called in to the office of Captain Vern O'Sala of the Special Branch of the Arizona State Troopers, known as The Rangers. Dalton's whipcord frame, perched on the edge of the seat, reminded the captain of the grace and fluidity of a puma.

O'Sala resisted the urge to order the young officer to get a haircut. As an undercover officer, Dalton was subject to modified grooming standards. O'Sala gave Dalton his assignment. "The organised crime team have evidence to suggest that the Scambini crime family have expanded. They've asked for our assistance. I want you to shake some sources and see what intel we can gather."

For the next three days, Dalton worked the streets. Some thought he was a dealer working to finance an Indian uprising; others figured him as just a low-level career criminal. On the fourth day, the undercover Ranger struck gold as a goombah made him an offer he couldn't refuse—an audience with Don Louis Scambini.

The Mafia don sat beside the pool of his mansion, sipping espresso. The gold chain glinted off his bare chest as he watched the new girls from his club dive into the water. The girls frolicked. The lines of coke they had just snorted had lowered their inhibitions, and they started kissing. Don Louis considered expanding into the porno business; he'd get his consigliere to look into it once he dealt with the Indian.

Reluctantly, the don pulled his eyes away from the debauchery as one of his bodyguards informed him that Dalton had arrived. The silver-haired mafioso pulled on a robe, tied the sash over his expansive waist, and walked into the house. The bodyguard did not follow.

Another bodyguard stood watch over Dalton as the don entered the room. "How, Chief!" Don Louis greeted the undercover lawman, his arm up with the palm out. "I want to smoke the peace pipe." The bodyguard laughed at his boss' joke.

"Cut the crap, you paleface asshole," Dalton snapped at the mob boss. "That's why we will rise up against you."

The don plopped down behind his desk and pulled out a bundle of cash from the drawer. "Quit the shit, Tonto, I know why you've been sniffing around. Here's twenty-five thousand for your war chest; now back off. You're not the Lone Ranger."

Dalton noticed the insulting tone and the emphasis on the word *ranger*. Protocol dictated that he take the money to make his case, but the smug Mafia chieftain's condescending attitude angered the young law officer. His Apache blood boiled. He threw the cash into the don's face and walked out before the bodyguard could react.

Dalton reported the incident to Captain O'Sala and spent the rest of the day filling out paperwork. At the end of the shift, he returned home, drained and exhausted by the endless red tape that seemed to constantly take him off the street and hamper his effectiveness.

But as soon as he saw that the front door of his house had been kicked in, all traces of fatigue left his body. He pulled his .45 and stalked through the house. The ground floor was clear, but there were signs of a struggle in the kitchen and potato chips scattered through the TV room. Dalton felt fear course through his body. Naomi would never have left the room in that state.

A muffled scream came from above. Dalton resisted the urge to race upstairs. He reacted as the Apache warrior he had been trained to be by his grandfather. The lessons from his childhood came instinctively as he moved silently up the stairs.

The first thing he saw was the door to his son's room and the pool of blood seeping under it. Another cry came from the master bedroom. Dalton moved down the hallway like the wind. The open door exposed the sight of a tall, swarthy man leaning over his wife with a scalpel.

An Apache rage overtook Dalton's reason as he let loose with a war whoop. The swarthy man turned to find the barrel of Dalton's gun whipped across his face, knocking him unconscious.

Dalton looked at the blood-soaked bed and the brutalised body of his wife. He'd heard rumours of the "turkey doctors," but this was the first time he'd seen their handiwork. The ruined body of his wife showed him the extent of their sadistic depravity. Her lidless eyes stared at him, as her split and busted lips struggled to form words before she gave a loud sigh and died in his arms.

There would be time to mourn later. There was a chance Brendan might still be alive. Dalton moved to his son's room. Horror clenched at his gut as he opened the door.

Brendan's body lay on the floor. The intruder had stabbed the boy and slit his throat. The young boy had fought and died hard. Dalton felt his heart torn from his chest as the child he loved, his legacy, lay still.

With a savage fury, Dalton returned to the unconscious turkey doctor and woke the man. The scalpel, still slick with his wife's blood, now went to work on its former master. The groggy torturer awoke to feel the tip touching the edge of his lower eyelid.

"Too bad there's no ant-hill around here," Dalton said with an evil grin. "Us Apaches like using them, but I'll improvise."

The turkey doctor emptied his bladder. Dalton looked with disgust at the wet patch and started his interrogation. Before long, the turkey doctor quickly spilled everything he knew about Don Scambini's operations throughout Arizona, including the fact that it was Scambini's order to kill Dalton's family.

He pulled his pistol and pointed it at the man who had killed his wife and son. If he did this, he knew that his time as a lawman was over.

The bullet left the barrel of the 1911A Colt pistol at 825 feet per second and entered the skull of the turkey doctor. It ploughed through the brain, exited the back of the head, and buried itself in the floor of the bedroom before the sound of the gunshot stopped ringing in Dalton's ears.

There was no going back now. The turkey doctor was Dalton's first kill. All that mattered now was revenge on everyone responsible for the death of his family.

He grabbed a duffel bag. As he moved through the house he filled the bag with weapons, including the tomahawk Naomi had bought him for his birthday, and other items he would need for his war on the Scambinis. The last item he added was a family photo. The smiling faces of his wife and son would be how he hoped to remember his family and not the bloody corpses that were currently searing into his memory.

Dalton set fire to the home he'd made. The investigators would assume that the turkey doctor's body was his. If everyone thought Dalton dead, it would give him greater freedom to strike at his enemies.

Leaving the house, Dalton made sure that no one saw him as he made way to his jet-black gelding, Desperado. The horse was stabled on the outskirts of Phoenix. As the young man saddled up, he dwelt on his loss and how he would make Don Scambini pay.

Dalton's first order of business was to find his grandfather, Mark Hollick. The older Hollick was a former trooper. Since his retirement, he had returned to the reservation, immersing himself in the tribal ways. Dalton had last spoken to him a week ago when the old man called before going into the desert wild on a vision quest.

The ex-Ranger pushed his horse hard to make his grandfather's campsite before dawn. The Arizona sun was brutal at this time of year. Dalton did not want to be riding in the daylight. Several miles out of town Desperado picked up a stone and could no longer be ridden. The smart move would have been to find shelter from the sun, but Dalton needed to assure himself that his grandfather was alright.

Dalton's wiry frame wandered across the Arizona Plains, leading his horse. His black Levis were dusty after the hard ride. His raven black hair drooped over his dark face, his hat long ago blown from his head, dangling down his back held by the chinstrap.

The campsite he sought was not far, but the heat made it feel like a thousand miles. Desperado stumbled and fell. Dalton tried to get the horse to rise, but it was done. Dalton forced himself to stand, lacking even the energy to brush the alkali flakes off his shirt. He knew that he was exhausted, but he refused to give up until he found his Granpappy Mark's camp.

He staggered another three steps, stumbled, and fell. Barely conscious, he dragged himself onto his hands and knees and crawled over the next mound. The sight he saw was enough to energise him. Dalton could barely stand but he managed to stagger into the camp he'd been desperately seeking.

Mark Hollick cooked a jackrabbit for his lunch, when he looked up to see the dusty figure of his grandson collapse in front of him. The old man moved to his grandson's side.

"They're all dead," Dalton croaked through his parched throat and passed out.

Over the next few days, Mark cared for his grandson. The physical wounds and exhaustion soon left the young man, but the psychological damage was far more severe. It seemed that revenge was the only thing that mattered anymore. Mark worried that the Apache blood of his grandson was too strong and the young man was on a path to self-destruction.

The old man knew too well his grandson's pain and need for revenge. In the 1930s he'd ridden the vengeance trail, bringing terror to the White Hood cross burners as Wind Walker. Mourning the loss of his granddaughter-in-law and great-grandson, the old man once again felt the pull.

When the younger man was physically capable, the pair left the camp and made their way to a nearby mesa. They built a medicine lodge. As the older man conducted the Wind Walker ceremonies, Dalton swore vengeance on the Scambini crime family over the smoke of several burning medicine pouches. Mark then showed him the war paint of the Wind Walker. The older Apache sang the old songs of the vengeance trail as he threw several medicine bags into the flames. The contents made different-colored plumes of smoke. Dalton stood beside the fire clad in a breechclout and a pair of moccasins.

"Who seeks to ride the vengeance trail?" Mark asked in Apache.

"I am Dalton Hollick. The blood of the Apache people flows through my veins."

With the blade of his tomahawk, Dalton slashed his right palm and made a fist. After the blood dripped through his fingers, he put a bloody handprint on his chest.

"I found my family murdered. Their spirits cry on the wind for me to avenge them. I give me solemn oath to heed their cries and walk the vengeance trail."

As Dalton made his vow, Mark applied his war paint, singing songs of the Wind Walker. The blue lines on the cheek bones symbolised the wind calling for vengeance. The two red lines running down his cheeks signified the blood debt to be paid.

After the ceremony, the old man led them to his Jeep, parked south of the campsite. The pair drove in silence as they moved through the desert towards the ghost town of Suggerton. (Check out the The Range Riders adventure novel *Sugger's Folly* for why the town is deserted. Available wherever books are sold.) Dalton looked in amazement as his grandfather parked behind the saloon and pulled open the doors of a bomb shelter.

"I had this built just before you were born," the old man declared. "The shelter will be your base of operations."

Dalton looked around at the weapons and equipment that his grandfather had stockpiled in case of a nuclear assault on America. He knew that he couldn't ask for a better base.

According to the intel from the turkey doctor, there was a shipment of laundered money coming in from the Turtolini crime family over in Texas on the first Monday of the month. Scambini had a business relationship with Luca "The Turtle" Turtolini. Dalton had read as much in the Scambini file when he was still a Ranger. While the Turtle's driver would take different routes from Texas to Phoenix, the Scambinis always had the money delivered to the same safe house in Queen Creek. The strange thing was that the delivery never happened if a raid was planned by any law enforcement agency.

The Hollicks scouted the safe house, identifying all the escape routes and assessing their security. The property was owned by Salvatore Lettieri, one of the Scambini's lieutenants and top leg breakers back in the '50s. The old man was supposedly retired, but when they saw him in the garden, Lettieri looked like he could still take care of himself.

Lettieri shared the house with a woman the Apaches assumed was his wife. It was difficult to prepare for the woman's reaction to the planned attack. A respectable wife of her age might faint, but a retired moll would likely join the battle.

The day of the delivery, the Lettieris received a visitor, a young man who might have been their son visiting for dinner, except for the gun under his jacket that marked him as Mafia muscle.

An hour later a green car with Texas plates pulled up in the drive. Two hard men stepped out of the vehicle with a suitcase and walked into the house. Twenty minutes later the Texans left. Dalton and his grandfather got into position.

The muscle shook hands with Lettieri at the front door and walked out with the suitcase the Texans had carried in earlier. He opened the front door of his gray coupe and dropped the suitcase into the passenger seat. The young man turned to Lettieri, but whatever he planned to say to the older man was lost as an arrow pierced his throat and severed his vocal cords. The young man grabbed for his neck as the life seeped out of his body.

Lettieri reached for the gun under his armpit when he saw Dalton racing towards him. The handgun was barely clear of the holster when the head of the tomahawk buried itself in the old mafioso's leg, severing the femoral artery. A geyser of blood erupted from the wound. It was a only a matter of seconds before the old man lost consciousness and less than a minute before Lettieri was dead.

Dalton had been far enough away to avoid the arterial spray, but the woman standing behind Lettieri had not been so fortunate. As she screamed Salvatore's name, she stepped forward and brought up a sawed-off shotgun she'd been concealing behind the door jamb. An arrow whizzed through the air where her head had been a fraction of a second earlier and buried itself in the door.

The old woman was the threat they had feared. Dalton had to react quickly. A shotgun was deadly at that range, and his grandfather would not have enough time for another arrow. His options were to move away and hope that the pellets had spread enough to avoid serious injury or to move in under the pellets before they spread too much. Dalton chose the latter and dove under the projectiles as she fired. He curled his body in a tight roll, landed on his feet, and sprang upright right in front of the woman. He brought up his right fist and smashed her jaw. Her teeth snapped together as her head whipped backwards and she lapsed into unconsciousness.

Dalton cursed under his breath. He did not like to hit women, but more disturbing was the attention that the shotgun blast would bring. Typical response time for Phoenix PD was five minutes, give or take. They had to pull out now. Dalton gave the call of the spotted owl, the prearranged signal for retreat. Then he let out an Apache war whoop and scalped Lettieri's lifeless corpse.

The former lawman grabbed the suitcase, then rushed to remove any evidence and retrieve any weapons. As he tried to pull the arrow from the front door, the shaft snapped, leaving the head. Dalton walked down the drive and climbed into his grandfather's jeep. As the two men drove off, Dalton looked over his haul: the shotgun; two .38 Smith & Wesson revolvers; and half a million in untraceable bills.

This was the first of several raids against various Scambini criminal enterprises. In all cases Dalton let out a war cry and scalped at least one of the criminals he had killed. Not that Scambini made things easy for the vigilantes. Guards had been increased on many of the high-money targets. On their most recent run, hitting an illegal casino, the vigilantes were followed by two vehicles as they made their escape. They lost them, but the damage had been done. They had let them get too close. The Mafia now had enough information to start searching for the men.

Dalton and his grandfather knew it was only a matter of time before they were found. They set up an ambush from a mesa twenty miles away from Suggerton and waited. From the moment the Cessna buzzed over the desert and spotted the Jeep parked in the open, the two Apache warriors anticipated the roar of the dune buggy and trail bikes.

"I think today's a good day to die, Dalton," the older man intoned as his grandson pulled the trigger. The tyre of the dune buggy exploded.

"It will be for them." The younger man replied as he viewed the devastation of Mafia goons before pulling the trigger again. He watched as the dark Perspex face shield imploded under the bullet's pressure. The remaining rider spun his bike in a tight turn that flung the desert sand as he fled the scene.

That left the two survivors of the dune buggy. Dalton handed his grandfather the rifle and slid down the rope on the side of the mesa. As he moved towards the men, the handle of his tomahawk beat a reassuring tattoo on his thigh. He had his gun ready for trouble like he'd been trained at the academy. The first man he came to was a curly-haired goombah with neatly trimmed moustache and a neck that bent at an unnatural angle.

Dalton moved carefully toward the last man. He looked a bit older. Dalton hoped that this meant he was the leader. The Apache moved closer. It appeared that the Italian was unconscious. Dalton moved in to check for a pulse. A fistful of sand flew into his face as the man leapt up. The cunning mobster had been playing possum.

As the grit of the sand buried itself into his hazel eyes, Dalton dropped his gun. As soon as it hit the desert floor, the Apache avenger knew that he had made a mistake. He sensed, rather than saw, the tough mafioso dive for the weapon. Acting on some primitive instinct within his Apache blood, Dalton pulled the tomahawk and sent the blunt side of the axe smashing into his opponent's temple. The mafioso dropped like he'd been deboned.

The mobster returned to consciousness with a pounding headache, not helped by the hammering he heard. The smell of a wood fire wafted into his nostrils. The man tried to sit up, but he found that his arms and legs had been staked out. The sun beat down on his naked body. He felt a heat on his thighs that was too hot even for the desert sun. Antonio "Tough Tony" D'Allesandro was suddenly very scared as he craned his neck to see around him.

An old Indian sat between his feet. Between the hammering sounds Antonio heard chanting. The hammering stopped, and an Indian face covered in war paint appeared in his field of vision.

"Wh-what's happening?" stammered the Mafia hard man.

The Indian smiled with no warmth or humour. "Let's call it an Apache truth ceremony. There's a small fire between your legs which will get larger. Hot coals will be placed onto your body, searing through your skin."

As if on cue, a couple of sparks leapt from the fire to his hairy belly. Tough Tony squirmed. "You'll get nuttin' from me," he said unconvincingly.

"That's fine," Dalton continued, his face impassive. "The fire will roast your prick, and your balls will burst like popcorn kernels. I've bet the left one will go first."

The blood drained from Tony's face as he thought about his reputation. No woman would want a man with a fried pecker. With that, Tough Tony burst like a dam, spilling all the information about his boss's operation, including Scambini's meeting the next night at the construction site on Indian School Road.

Tough Tony wept as he felt the fire being extinguished and his bonds cut. Dalton helped him to his feet. "Phoenix is that way. Tell Scambini I'm coming to get him."

The construction site on Indian School Road was a mob operation. The concrete foundations contained the bodies of a snooping journalist, a stoolie, and a club girl who had rejected Scambini's advances. During the day it was a hive of activity. At night it became a clandestine meeting ground.

Two low-level soldiers stood guard. Sol the Shiv had brought a Thermos of hot coffee to ward off the chill night air. He shared it with Mikey the Mooch.

"I can't see nuttin'," the Mooch complained, as he downed his third cup of java.

"John Wayne said that's when you have to worry about an Injun." The Shiv's hand hovered over his pistol.

"I thought that was Clint Eastwood," said the Mooch. Regardless of who gave the advice, its accuracy was soon proven as an arrow pierced Sol's right eye. The Mooch dropped his coffee and fumbled for his revolver, but an arrow made its way into his heart.

Dalton moved swiftly and silently onto the construction site, his pistol ready for almost anything. The sound of voices wafted on the night air as he moved through the partially completed building, seeking the men responsible for the death of his family.

"Are you sure it's not that asshole from California scalping my people? I heard he likes to leave arrowheads, and he hit Vegas recently," Dalton heard the angry voice of Don Scambini growl.

"Lou, I told you it can't be. The FBI had reports of him in New Orleans, and they say he doesn't scalp people," replied a familiar voice. "I think we have a renegade Apache running around."

Captain Vern O'Sala. Dalton stopped, stunned at the revelation. The gruff older cop had never been overly friendly towards him, but to think that he would sell out his team for some extra cash was nearly impossible. Dalton felt his blood boil. His anger overtook his common sense, and he let loose an Apache war cry. He dived and rolled into the area where the two men stood. The Indian's first shot barrelled into the forehead of the Mafia chieftain, ending the life of the man who ordered the death of his family.

As the Indian lawman turned to deal immediate justice to his former boss, he found himself on the receiving end of a vicious punch. Dalton's head spun, droplets of blood spraying across the room. He lost hold of the gun. It skittered along the floor, coming to rest in a corner.

"I should have known you wouldn't be dead," the captain declared as he raised his leg to launch a brutal kick at Dalton's ribs. O'Sala had come up from the streets, and his time behind a desk had not softened the man. The steel toes of his boots struck the younger man hard.

"You should have taken the money and joined us."

It hurt Dalton just to breathe as he rolled away from another kick. His vengeance trail seemed to be at an end. He cursed mentally that his grandfather was watching for intrusions from outside.

Dalton pulled his tomahawk and used it to block the captain's next kick. The sharpened axe bit deeply into the captain's right calf. Sinews and tendons parted under the force of the blade, which only stopped with a sickening thud as it struck bone.

The strength of the blow sent the captain off balance, and he collapsed to the floor. Dalton was on the warpath, taking all his rage and grief out on the corrupt officer who sold his family's future to line his pockets with blood money. His hands wrapped around O'Sala's throat and tightened. Several minutes later, Dalton relaxed his grip and returned to his senses. He'd never know if the older man bled to death or if he had suffocated. He didn't really care. Dalton stood painfully and retrieved his tomahawk. He then undertook the grisly task of scalping both men. These would be the final two scalps he would claim in his war on crime, but not the last lives.

Mark came down from his sniper's nest. He remembered that riding the vengeance trail was a lonely path, and he would help Dalton in anyway he could. He found Dalton standing over the bodies of the two men.

"It is done," the old man intoned.

Dalton knew it was not. He could never return to conventional law enforcement as long as there were criminals willing to subvert and undermine justice, to tear apart and destroy families with their actions. He vowed on the scalps in his blood-soaked hands that he would fight on.

THE END

Edward T. Johnson was a prolific Australian author working mainly in the Western genre in the '60s and '70s. His most famous series, The Range Riders, featured hard-riding gunslingers: Christopher McGann, Matt Fortune, and the Apache Scout, Hunter Hollick. The Range Riders rode through the Old West righting wrongs and making the frontier safe. Johnson then branched out with various spin-off series and stand-alone novels.

In 1975, he attempted to break into men's adventure with a series featuring Hunter Hollick's great-grandson Dalton as a Mafia buster in the mould of Don Pendleton's The Executioner. According to his commentary in the anthology, Johnson's Jubilee, *he wanted to call the series The Wind Walker, but Flying Coyote Press changed the name to Apache Blood.*

Often cited as the hardest of Johnson's books to find, copies often sell for over $100 on eBay. BRAD MENGEL was lucky enough to find a dog-eared copy at an antiques store hidden under a pile of horror movie tie-in novels priced at 50 cents each. He haggled the owner down to 35 cents.

THE SILENCER
in
THE SILENCER STRIKES
by Mal Radcliff
(discovered by Gary Phillips)

BOOKER ESSEX, now known as the Silencer, grabbed the hood in the fedora with an arm around his neck just as the second hood let loose with a burst from his Thompson machine gun.

"You goddamn moulie," were the hood's last words before bullets from the chopper ripped a diagonal up from his stomach across his chest, his body jerking at the impact of the high-speed .45 rounds.

As those rounds tore through the crook's body, Essex was already moving. Crimson spread like ink blots on the dead man's custom-made dress shirt as his corpse collapsed onto the floor. Returning fire to drive the other two torpedoes back, Essex had shoved the body aside and dove through the swing door into the kitchen.

"Hold on," the machine gunner said to the third hood next to him, who began to advance. "Looks like this fuckin' jay-bo ain't gonna be easy pickins like we figured."

The third member of Laugher Graziano's gang nodded briefly. He carried a snub-nosed .38 revolver in a hand with a diamond pinky ring in a gold setting. The two separated some, each slowly approaching the kitchen door of the Fuzzy Feather Gentlemen's club. The metal rear door was locked and they heard no gunfire indicating their quarry was trying to exit. But they figured he wouldn't leave, as they had the bait.

"We'll deal with you after we take care of this mook," the one with the handgun whispered. He shook the barrel briefly at a woman in a short robe tied up on the stage. She was a stripper in the club, on her side, bound and gagged, a colorful silk tie around her mouth.

Her eyes were wide not with fear, but with defiance. Her blonde hair was tangled and unruly. To the side of the stage, a staircase led to the VIP section on the second floor. A steam room and curtained alcoves were available there.

Now the gunmen were on either side of the swing door, the Thompson man looking through the portal-style window. The lights were on inside, but Essex wasn't visible. There was a long counter with stainless steel pots and pans suspended above on hooks, and they assumed he was low behind that.

"You'd think it being all white in there the jungle bunny would stand out," the other hood cracked nervously.

The stripper, who did the bump and grind as Ginger Strawberry, swore at them but it came out muffled.

The machine gunner eased the swing door open with the muzzle of his magazine-fed Tommy gun, hoping the Silencer would show himself to take a shot. Nothing happened. He reared back and looking at his partner. They reached a silent decision. Together they both crashed into the kitchen. The Thompson handler laid down a barrage to keep the Silencer crouching, while the other hood's goal was to round the counter and blast him.

But a step away from the counter, the lights went out, and there was a hiss like the quick release of air from a truck's power brakes. Then cold silence. Diffused spill light came in through the portal window, illuminating little.

"Tony," the snub-nosed man ventured. Tony was the now deceased Thompson gunner. "Tony," he repeated. Again no answer, and he backtracked out of the kitchen in a hurry. He took hold of the trussed-up woman and, sliding her off the stage, got her to her bare feet. He dug the business end of the gun into her cheek.

"Okay, hotshot, better show yourself, or your girlfriend here gets got," he called out. There was no movement from the kitchen, and he repeated his threat. He undid the tie over Ginger Strawberry's mouth.

She began, "Why you lousy lowlife scum—" He struck her in the face with the pistol. This elicited a groan, as he intended.

"That's enough," Essex said from the kitchen doorway. He had one hand holding the swing door open, the other one out of sight. His voice was sibilant, shadowy, as if talking was an effort. It was not the voice he'd always had.

"Throw your piece out," the remaining hood demanded.

"Don't do it, Book," the woman advised.

He did as ordered. The gun was a modified .32 semi-auto machine pistol with a 20-round magazine and was fitted with a stubby sound suppressor on the muzzle. Twin tubes led from the suppressor back into the body of the weapon.

"That's something," the hood said admiringly of the gun. He gestured with his revolver, using the woman as his shield as Essex had done with the first hood. "Now come all the way out with your hands up."

The Silencer did as ordered again. He wore a jean jacket over a ribbed turtleneck and flared slacks that broke just so on his Nunn Bush boots. His Fu Manchu mustache glistened with sweat. Unlike the current style, he didn't sport an afro. Rather he kept his hair boot-camp short.

The gunsel wore a checkered leisure suit, his shirt open to expose his hairy chest and a heavy gold chain over the thicket. He smiled. "The boss is gonna be happy to have your magic gat," he said, referring to the specialized weapon. So-called silencers really weren't silent like in the movies. It muffled a gun's report, but you could still hear it, just quieter. Essex's weapons were truly mere whispers when they went off.

In a flash the thug took the gun from the side of the woman's face, and as he squeezed the trigger to kill Booker Essex, he was quite surprised to feel a sting at his temple. He hadn't heard a thing.

"What the fu..." he muttered then fell face first onto the plush carpeting of the Fuzzy Feather, the body dying as his brain ceased function.

Essex crossed the distance and set the wobbly Ginger Strawberry in a chair.

"How'd you do that, Book?" she asked.

"Ever see the show, the *Wild, Wild West*? How ol' Jim West had this derringer on a slide mechanism up his sleeve?" He held his arm such that she could see the end of what looked like a small rectangular box with four holes in the end of his sleeve.

"Your version of that," she said. "Always cooking up a gadget."

"Better get your stuff and let's get out of here before the fuzz come pounding through the doors."

"Good idea. I've got the cassettes too." She stood and the robe flapped open, revealing her sculpted nude torso and sequined G-string. Essex looked away, his face warm.

Strawberry, whose real name was Marcia Mathers, noted this with a wry smile. She came over to him, pressing herself against his back. The blonde put a hand on his shoulder. "I know women don't scare you, Book."

He looked sideways at her. "It's not that, Marsh. But you're Bobby's sister."

"I'm also my own woman. And we're not kids anymore."

"Ain't that the truth," he agreed.

She kissed him on the cheek and went into the dressing room to get her clothes on and retrieve her purse and items. Thereafter the two left the club by a side door for Essex's three-year-old 1972 Ford LTD. The vehicle had a pristine Landau top and mag wheels, with a big block 460 Brougham engine under the hood. There were special items Essex had also built into the car besides further souping up the motor. He brought the machine to life, and Mathers wasn't surprised she could barely hear the thing running.

"Living up to your name, huh?"

"Guess so." He turned on the heater and a police scanner hidden behind a fake grill in the dash.

Tires crunched over gravel as he drove off in the dark of post-three A.M. from the strip club. The place was a few miles out of town off the highway, mostly industrial facilities around, large structures made of metal sidings and low roofs. The trees were bare, their limbs pointing up to the wintery sky as if accusing the weather of indifference.

Paul "Laugher" Graziano, sometimes called the Laughing Man by friends and enemies, wore slacks and slippers and an athletic undershirt underneath the silk robe he'd tied around his trim waist. He was pushing sixty but maintained a regime of racquetball, swimming, and athletic sex with young women his daughter's age. His nickname was derived from a childhood incident when he was eleven.

He and a friend had been running from a copper after robbing a blind newshawker at his sidewalk stand. They ran into the street, and Graziano was struck by a street car, causing nerve damage in his face. He was caught and sent to reform school. The other kid, Benny "Bean Pole" Mathers, got away. Thereafter the left side of Graziano's face drooped, and he learned to talk out of the other side of his mouth. His melancholy appearance earned him his opposite sobriquet.

He prided himself that he pretty much weighed the same as he had when he played basketball at Theodore Roosevelt High. They were the Rough Riders. That is before he was kicked out of school for taking bets on the games—the same school that, some years later, Booker Essex, Marcia Mathers and her now-deceased brother, Robert, had attended as well. Less than a year after they had graduated, Essex was drafted and Bobby Mathers volunteered for Vietnam.

Laugher Graziano puffed on his thin cigar, looking out the window from the study to his backyard and the pool he had better cover soon. A few ducks swam about in the water, quacking happily. What did it mean to be happy, he pondered as he turned back to Loomis Kassel, his Bill Blass-dressing, Yale-educated, half-German, half-Italian consigliere.

The time was just past dawn, and both men were aware of what had gone down at the Fuzzy Feather a few hours before. Indeed, Kassel had already dispatched a crew to clean up the mess. Due to having a homicide cop named Bert Chastain on the pad, he'd gotten a call from the detective and, with his help, was keeping a lid on the matter—for the moment.

"I know," Graziano began, unprompted. "I should have listened to you and not given in to my weakness. But who the fuck checks on the background of these broads? They all use a made-up name strippin' and hookin' on the side." He shook his head. "Who could figure that chick would be undercover snatch?" He laughed sourly at his joke.

"We not only need to deal with her, but this colored gentleman."

"I need to color him red."

Kassel adjusted his Yves St. Laurent-designed frames. "I have a solution, only it's going to cost."

The Laughing Man spread his arms wide. "Doesn't it always, Loomis? Doesn't it always?"

Ever since physically recovering from the fire resulting from the bomb, the Silencer had gone underground. With Chastain, Graziano's gang, and the self-styled revolutionary Rahim Katanga and his bunch all crowding him about making deadly inventions for them, he had little choice. But before it all changed, he and Bobby Mathers had managed to make it back to the world from 'Nam and opened their auto garage. It didn't hurt that both men had earned a few medals and were welcomed back as hometown heroes.

At their Danang Drag Motor Specialists shop, they repaired everyday cars and customized those who could afford something special. Life was good then.

He looked toward the sound of water coming from what had been the boss' office and the private bathroom and shower within.

In there Marcia Mathers was finishing up and turned off the hot and cold faucets. Leave it to Booker, she noted appreciatively, to be able to bootleg electricity and running water into a place that went belly up months ago.

She pushed the pebbled glass door open and stepped out of the shower, taking off the rack one of the large towels Essex had provided. Drying off next to the portable heater, she stood in the compact office area he'd converted to a kind of bedroom with a cot, lamp sans shade and numerous technical books on a makeshift shelf. There was a photo taped to the wall of Essex and her brother as soldiers in a jungle clearing in Vietnam. Both had vacant smiles on their faces—the smiles of men who had seen and done too much over there.

There were no pictures of Charlotte Sumlin about. There was, though, a charred piece of what had been the hand-painted sign over their garage. The fragment leaned atop some of the books, and Mathers picked it up, looking at it wistfully. She vividly remembered that terrible day. She'd just gotten off the phone with her brother, and it would turn out to be the last time she'd speak to him.

Mathers learned later that afternoon about how a bomb had gone off in the garage. Her brother, the police surmised, must have been talking to Charlotte Sumlin, who'd stopped by to see Essex. Essex had been away to pick up a part and was just driving up when the blast went off. From his eyewitness report, Sumlin had been in the open bay of the garage, waving at Essex. Bobby Mathers was behind her, wiping his hands on a shop towel. Then there was the orange-red flare that filled his vision and the boom of the exploding sticks of dynamite. His windshield shattered into his face from the concussive force.

She put the fragment down, and, taking the towel from around her and unwrapping the other one from her wet hair, she got dressed. Marcia Mathers came into the kitchen area—mostly a jury-rigged stove that had been thrown out, and a coffee maker—where he was preparing breakfast for both of them. Her hair was wet from her recent shower, and she smoked an unfiltered Marlboro. She wore tennis shoes, jeans, and a sweater top.

"Hash and eggs," she said, chuckling. "Some things don't change."

"I've added paprika," he said, turning off the fire as he stirred the concoction in a skillet.

There were two plates on the one small table, and she picked them up so he could spoon out food onto them. There was toast and fresh coffee, too. Essex had turned this corner of the once-thriving refrigerant coil factory into living quarters, and more. There was a work bench nearby with parts and tools strewn on it, a blueprint tacked to the wall above it, as well. Also hanging on the wall were three different shoulder holster rigs with specialized silent handguns in each.

Sitting and eating, Essex said, "I got a wig for you and some padding to make you look less, you know."

"What?"

"Voluptuous," he got out. "Recognizable I mean."

"No, I meant what the heck are you talking about?"

"So I can get you out of town," he said.

"I'm not leaving."

"But Graziano's on to you, Marsh."

"He's on to you, too."

"I'm prepared."

"Then prepare me. We both loved him, Book. I want to get his killers, too."

He was going to argue but could see she was in no mood for the hassle. He allowed, too, that a smart, sexy woman who, on her own, did a gutsy thing like infiltrating the strip club, knowing it was owned by the Laughing Man, then making sure to insinuate herself near him to learn a few of his secrets—well, that was certainly not someone you sent packing, given the firefight that was about to light shit up.

"So what's out next move, sarge?" she said, chewing on the hash and eggs.

"You know that waiting ain't my bag, but they'll make a move. Soon. That smart boy of Graziano's, Kassel, he's like those West Point greenhorn lieutenants we had to suffer in 'Nam. He's read up on his Alexander the Great and von Clausewitz. He's going to bring in the heavy hitter and draw us out to trap us."

She regarded him. "Always thinking and always prepared."

"Let's hope so," he said dourly. "But in any battle, there's always the unexpected factor, that turn of bad luck or roll of capricious fate you didn't account for."

"Seems we're both pessimists." She got up from her seat and picked up her plate and his, even though neither had finished breakfast. She put them on the stove, as there was no sink.

She turned back to him, and her intent was clear in her eyes as she took off her shoes using her feet.

"Look, maybe this isn't such a good idea," he hedged. Because of vocal cord damage from the fire, his voice was coarse and whispery. And at the moment, he was so caught up in conflicting emotions he could barely talk at all.

"Maybe," she said, unzipping her jeans and stepping out of them. "Most times you've thought of me as a sister. And me, you're my other brother. We've known each other since junior high, Book. The two white trash kids, miserable thief for a father, and that goofy black kid who always had his nose, appropriately, in a book. We've known, too, that we've gone back and forth in our feelings for each other." She paused, a solemn look settling on her face, then added, "Charlotte isn't coming back. But don't misunderstand, I'm not pretending I'm her. I'm not trying to take her place."

"I know."

She was close on him now, and he leaned forward and gently kissed her mound encased in her lacy black panties. She caressed the top of his head. He looked up at her, his hands on her thighs.

"This might be our one and only time. We might not come out of this whole or alive," she said, her voice as hoarse as his. She touched a tear at the corner of his eye, the scars from the fire on his face. She undid his zipper and straddled him. They made love as the Laughing Man and Kassel planned their executions.

"How is it you call yourself a cop, Chastain?" former petty street thug Ronnie Brownlee, who now went by Rahim Katanga, growled. As leader of the Ministers of Praxis, names were everything.

The beefy cop spread his arms wide. "Hey, I'm doing my job here, Ronnie boy."

There was bristling from the other members of the Ministers of Praxis, MPs for short. The two uniformed officers with Chastain, one black the other white, reacted too. Their hands went toward the hilts of their tethered nightsticks.

The plainclothesman continued. "It's a known fact your little troop here has had run-ins with them Reds." He gestured with his hand as if conjuring up the name. "The Luxumberg League," he finally said, snapping his fingers. "Them."

"They wouldn't kidnap our youth, Chastain," a woman with a bubble afro said.

Chastain gave her an up-and-down, like sizing up a double cheeseburger slathered with bacon and onions. "Y'all say four kids went missing after they attended your propaganda class."

"After school program, policeman," a tall MP emphasized. "We help them with their math and reading skills."

Chastain pursed his lips, biting back a sarcastic comment. "So anyway, these four don't make it home afterward." He consulted his notepad. "But these are teenagers, between 13 and 16, you said." He looked up, a sincere expression on his face. "They could be off smoking reefer or grabbing a car to go joyriding, doing who knows what they get into at that age."

"Jesus," the woman exploded. "We're calling your boss, Chastain."

He laughed hollowly. "You call on us oinkers only when this kind of shit allegedly happens and you expect the department to be at your beck and call. But any other time, you're spitting on us and cursing us out."

"How about you just do your job, man?" Katanga said.

"We're on this," the black officer answered.

Chastain shot him a withering look. "This matter will be dutifully investigated. Starting with me grilling their parents, a couple of whom, single mothers and all, have records." He and Katanga glared at one another. Then Chastain exited the storefront office. He was followed by the two uniforms, who looked embarrassed.

"I'm calling Councilman Ricks," the woman with the large afro said, stalking toward a dial phone.

Katanga had a different idea.

As a youngster, Graveheart, not a family name, was fascinated by TV western shows like *Have Gun Will Travel* and *The Rifleman*. This was not unusual for a red-blooded American male of that generation, as kids were given cap guns modeled on their favorite lawman's six-shooter, or on bounty hunter Josh Randall's tricked-out sawed-off rifle from *Wanted Dead or Alive*. It wasn't the delivery of frontier justice that fascinated him, but the power those masters of the gun wielded on such shows. Seemed whatever bit of folksy wisdom they dispensed had more import given their handling of shootin' irons.

Of course the fact that these actors were the leads and therefore the script was tailored to show them as infallible and stalwart seemed lost on Graveheart. Or more likely he'd long ago learned to ignore such realities. Ever since he was big enough to hold a gun, he had. Not only learned to hold one, but use it quite well.

The limestone quarry was at the opposite outskirts of town from where the Fuzzy Feather strip club was located, though both were off the same highway. The facility was owned by a middle-aged, country-club-going, married church deacon who, in cliché fashion, had tumbled hard for one of the big-breasted strippers at the Fuzzy Feather. Laugher Graziano had some compromising photos, and thus he had no choice but to let his facility be used for the nefarious undertaking underway there this weekend.

The trap was simple. The kidnapped teens were in a van wired with dynamite in the quarry pit. The instructions were relayed by several dope fiends and other such riff-raff along the underworld grapevine. The Silencer was to appear at dawn, or the youngsters would be sent to Kingdom Come.

His LTD drove up on schedule, and he exited the vehicle. It was cold, and he was wearing a full-length Super Fly-style patterned coat and a broad, flat-brimmed hat with a buckle headband. He had on shades, too.

"How do you know you won't be cut down as soon as you step out of your car?" Mathers had asked. "Somebody with a rifle and a scope. What do you call 'em, a sniper?"

He was cleaning one of his guns and looked over at her. "You've read Ralph Ellison's *Invisible Man*?"

She had a hand on her hip. "At your urging, yes," she answered sharply.

"There's a few soul brothers and sisters, skycaps at the airport, housekeepers at a couple of the swank hotels, and what have you that I make sure to put a few extra twenties in their Christmas funds each month."

Essex derived income from several patents he owned or had sold for goodly amounts. One of his innovations had been a prototype for a miniaturized walkie-talkie, a kind of phone the size of a cigarette case you could put in your jacket pocket—inspired by those episodes of *Star Trek* he watched as a kid. He started to reassemble his weapon. Essex had invested his monies in such enterprises as a childhood buddy's black hair care products line and an auto parts chain.

"Yeah?" she said, interested.

"So white folks see them as part of the furniture. They're there, but not there, dig?"

"What're you getting at, Book?"

He smiled. "Figuring some newcomers might be coming to town, I spread extra green around and got the lowdown."

"Yeah?" she said.

"Yeah," he answered.

"You know what they say, Silencer." Graveheart was talking. "I thought you'd be taller." He stepped out from the girders of the elevated office shed made of corrugated metal. Several massive dirt haulers and crane trucks were parked about as well.

"Ain't no stress." The other man was unbuttoning his coat. A slight breeze came up, exposing the shoulder holster underneath, strapped over his black turtleneck. Sweat dappled below the edges of his sunglasses.

The two were about 25 feet apart. They stood down each other on the edge of the main pit, the van with the captured teens at the bottom. The wind ceased. Graveheart—all in black including his Stetson, a six-shooter strapped around his waist gunslinger fashion—spread his boots a bit further apart. He was in his shooting stance.

"This is how it works, hombre," he said. "You live, the kids go free. You die, they die."

"Let's get to it...honky."

The Silencer took a step to the right, and time slowed as the two readied themselves for the showdown. It was only seconds that went by, but each worked to keep his heart from thudding too loudly in his ears. Each took the measure of the other, each with eyes on the opponent's hands—and then, in the time it took a dog to flick its tail, the guns came out. Both men fired, the Silencer's round zinging past Graveheart's torso.

Conversely, the Silencer dropped his modified gun, clutching his chest as he went over onto his back. Graveheart had grouped two dead center mass.

The out-of-town hitter had assumed he'd feel more elated, but it was what it was—killing was becoming as blasé to him as going to the corner store for a carton of milk. How sad. He raised his hand to signal for the toggle switch to be flipped, transmitting a radio signal to the dynamiter to blow up the teens. But nothing happened. He looked over to where two of Laugher Graziano's men were supposed to be crouched down beside the huge tires of one of the big haulers.

He couldn't see them from where he was, but why hadn't they stood up once the Silencer was put down? Smith & Wesson in hand, he advanced. Both hoods were proned out, dead. The remote control device was gone. The Silencer had struck.

"Holster your piece and let's settle this for real, Graveheart," Booker Essex called out. He wore no fancy coat or hat but was in sans-a-belt slacks and a black turtleneck similar to that Rahim Katanga, as his stand-in, wore. His gun in its shoulder holster.

Graveheart knew better than to try and spin around, firing. He was fast but not inhumanly so. He'd be dropped in a blink. From above he heard a sound and, glancing up, saw a female head with a puffy afro atop the raised office. In the clean light of morning, he could easily see the glint off her rifle. She'd slept up there through the night.

"I'll be more fair than you," Essex continued as the gunman stepped away from the truck. "You win, you walk away."

Graveheart didn't waste energy or risk distraction with a response or gesture. His hand trembled slightly from excitement. Every sense was breathlessly on edge in him. It was as if each millimeter of his skin was a receptor for all the atoms swirling about him. He'd never felt this alive before. This was a challenge.

Nothing happened, then simultaneously both men drew their guns and each fired a single bullet. The bang of Graveheart's pistol was the only one audible. They gaped at one another and Graveheart worked up a crooked smile as he wheeled about and fell over, exhaling one last time.

The teenagers were freed, and Katanga and his Ministers of Praxis started to leave. The militant paused and looked back at the Silencer. "You did good, brother."

Essex nodded and they went their separate ways. He still didn't know which of the three had been responsible for the bomb. He wouldn't rest until he found out.

Bert Chastain had a big grin on his mustachioed face as the foxy blonde lead him by his erect penis to one of the happy alcoves after his steam. After the deaths here at the Fuzzy Feather and the subsequent newspaper investigation, Laugher Graziano had been forced to sell the establishment. Not much was known about the buyer, but he'd retained a number of the girls who'd worked their under the old management—and he'd re-opened the upstairs VIP section as well. One of those chicks was this knock-out, called Ginger Strawberry, who had his stiff johnson in hand, leading him.

"Baby, I can't wait to get down with you."

"Me either," she grinned, looking back at him.

In the alcove the blonde sat him down on a built-in bench. He now sat on the towel he'd had around his waist. She kneeled before him, Chastain's erect member quivering. That feeling and his hard-on faded fast as an arm went around his neck and the cold muzzle of a modified .32 pressed against his temple.

"Essex," he wheezed.

"Listen to me, asshole," the Silencer said to the suddenly uncomfortable and vulnerable nude man. "I knew sooner or later you'd come around for your usual taste," he began.

"I'm a cop, Essex, if you kill me they'll hang your black ass for sure."

The Silencer squeezed harder, choking his captive. "Don't kid yourself, Chastain. As shitty as you are, won't too many of your fellow blue on blues get too worked up about your demise."

"Look, I already told you," Chastain said, his voice cracking some. "I had nothing to do with planting that bomb."

"Shut up. For now you're of value to me. Make sure you let the other scumbags like you, the vice cops on the make, the robbery-homicide boys getting their cut, that the Fuzzy Feather is open for business. Let the word go out to the crooked city council members, judges, all of them—got me, Chastain? Tell 'em they get a discount."

"What the fuck are you up to?"

"What my loot in-country would have called reconnoitering."

Chastain understood. "You want dirt on them. You got this joint bugged."

Essex released his hold and tapped the bent cop twice, hard, on the cheek. "Now you're getting smart. And just in case that rat brain you call a mind is thinking of crossing me, you should know I'm just taking over what the Laughing Man started."

If it was possible, Chastain's eyes got wider. He'd done all sorts of activities and had certain conversations over the years at the Fuzzy Feather—activities that could get him fired and conversations that would get him federally indicted.

"Looks like I got no choice. I'll be your Huckleberry...for now."

"Good boy," Essex said, disappearing into the passage behind the trick panel in the wall he'd come out of to surprise the cop.

Marcia Mathers had stood before the two in her short robe and heels, though she'd tied the robe shut. "I'm the manager here now, so you'll report to me. We clear?"

An uppity, devious colored and a broad had him by the short and curlies. What had he done to deserve this? "We're clear."

She walked out, and after getting dressed and back outside in the wintery evening, Chastain pulled his coat close. Despite being a stone killer, the idea of not knowing when the Silencer would strike next made him uneasy—very uneasy.

THE END

No one could have shown more enthusiasm than GARY PHILLIPS did when we brought up the idea of Blood & Tacos. In his words, "I got a Mal Radcliff story no one's ever read, baby! The Silencer, baby!"

We know we don't have to tell you who Mal Radcliff is. We tried to contact Mr. Radcliff, but due to gambling and other debts he has not maintained any one address for too long since his heyday. Anyway, we hope you've enjoyed this 1975 masterstroke by a true legend.

TIGER TEAM BRAVO
in
BONDS OF BLOOD
by Lance Matrix
(discovered by Matthew C. Funk)

THE TIGER LEAPT the ramp, caught air snarling, all four tires smoking, soared over the jeeps of the Colombians. Met the highway still gunning it. Stacked shocks ate the impact, and the car shot for the big rig ahead.

Banzai Billy Takamura smoothed a hand over his pomade hair. Relaxed into the waft of Marlboro and fuming rubber. Gave Colonel Professor a nod of his mirror shades.

"Ramp was just where you said it'd be."

Colonel Professor didn't look up, eyes fused to his homemade transponder. "Kill point's in five minutes."

Banzai ground snakeskin boot into the accelerator. Highway vanished. The cartel big rig loomed—a white chip in the shimmering blank of Texan desert.

Gunfire from the jeeps behind. 9mm slugs tapping on the 2-inch steel plating Banzai had welded to the Tiger. A sound that echoed the heavy pour of Khe Sanh rain to both men.

Colonel Professor tilted out the window with his MP-40 and let the machine pistol yell at the Colombian gunmen.

Banzai launched on. The Tiger closed to 200 yards on the big rig. Two more jeeps pulled alongside the truck from the front. Slowed by its flanks to cut off the Tiger.

The Tiger's rear-glass spiderwebbed with dozens of bullet prints. Ricochets kicked the tires. Banzai caught a whiff of sweat through the leather of Professor's bomber jacket.

He stuck the Marlboro in his lips; stuck out the empty hand to Professor. Colonel Professor filled it with the MP-40.

Banzai ripped the wheel left. The Tiger spun. Professor worked the brake.

Banzai stuck the MP-40 out the window.

Tires shrieked over V-12 engine roar. The MP-40 firing was a bright white line of noise. Banzai's aim honed to pure fate behind mirror shades.

Professor cancelled the brake. The Tiger spun on. The two jeeps spiraled off the road, loaded with two dead drivers and two dead gunmen.

Banzai wrenched the wheel in line with the big rig. Gunned the Tiger deep into the red line. Professor watched the dying jeeps flip behind.

"Couldn't have just shot them aiming with the rear-view, Banzai?"

"Don't be ridiculous."

"Four minutes until kill point."

Kill point—the moment when the mission failed. The instant both men had been outrunning since Tiger Team Bravo had been abandoned in the Cambodian jungle to march their way out of a war that had canceled their existence.

Neither man frowned to think of it. They hadn't frowned since they'd been orphaned to that long march from enemy lines with Captain Teague and their other teammates left for dead behind them.

Outrunning that moment was what they did. It was who Tiger Team Bravo was.

Banzai kept it in the red and Professor kept the blank expression on his slate black face. He'd worn it since he smelled the pre-historic flowers and burning fuel of Vietnam a decade ago.

"Three minutes, thirty."

Banzai had his own clock: seven seconds before the jeeps alongside the truck trailer would reach its rear.

He punched nitro. The Tiger's roar sliced into a scream. Asphalt disappeared.

Five seconds. 100 yards between the Tiger and the cartel trailer's rear.

Three seconds. Banzai lifted the MP-40 again. Sneered to ash the Marlboro.

One second. Banzai jerked the wheel right.

The Tiger's front bumper clipped the rear of the jeep to the right just as it dropped past the trailer. Slammed the smaller vehicle into a skid. The coked-up jeep driver panicked; the skid became a spin.

Banzai balanced the MP-40 on his arm, sent a cloud of 9mm Parabellum into the jeep on the left. Opened the driver's skull like a can of creamed corn. Sent the gunman sprawling.

The Tiger pulled straight. The two jeeps joined the others twisted aside the nameless desert highway.

"Three minutes." Professor lifted the M79 grenade launcher from the roof rack. Rolled down inch-thick bulletproof glass with his other hand.

The target held more than 300 kilos of Colombian flake. The cartel used it as a mobile command for its drug shipments: always moving, shifting the routes of its drug runners to dodge state cops and feds.

It had taken Tiger Team Bravo three months for their source, Baretta, an ex-Army Intel joker they knew from MACV-SOG, to worm his way into the cartel enough to cough up one of the big rig's routes.

It would be worth it.

The brain-trust of cartel trade in the south, the big rig held the records of all cartel border runs.

As Banzai brought the Tiger to within 50 yards of the 18-wheeler's rear doors, the big rig showed it held some secrets, too: the doors blew wide to show a cage of steel plate sprouting a .50 heavy machine gun.

Banzai tore the Tiger to the side as the .50 opened up, noise shaking the windshield. Slugs designed to chew up aircraft metal like rice paper chunked the road.

Professor had no choice—he leaned out the window with the grenade launcher.

The gold-toothed cartel gunman tracked them with the 600-slugs a minute coming from the red hot barrel of the .50.

Banzai nodded at the road ahead. "Looks like your calculations were a bit off this time, Professor. Tunnel's coming up in two miles."

Professor aimed the grenade launcher. Slugs bigger than his hand sang around, creased his beret with violated air.

"One minute to the tunnel." Banzai said.

Professor replied with the cough of the M79.

The grenade soared over the big rig's profile. It dipped. The shell slammed into the roof.

Smoke billowed rot-yellow from the big rig.

"It's all part of the plan." Professor ducked back into the Tiger. The sound of a descending plane rumbled through the window as he rolled it up.

Banzai glanced up as he braked the Tiger. Jasper was dive-bombing the Cessna out of the invisibility of the high, powder-blue sky toward the yellow smoke trail. Vaquero already clung to the landing gear, tassels snapping from his red-and-white calfskin jacket.

The Cessna's shriek grabbed the highway. The cartel gunner tilted the .50 up to greet it. Tracers ribboned the air.

Tilting and swinging like a gut-shot crow, the Cessna wove between the blazing slugs. Jasper pressed his arsenal of crooked teeth toward the windshield, put the prop plane into a straight dive.

The Tiger followed to watch. It was Jasper's show now.

The cartel truck shot into the tunnel. The Cessna shot after it.

Jasper tilted the wing of the plane and coasted into the opposing lane.

The tunnel was dark and tight as a snare around the plane. Nothing new to Jasper. The run through the tunnel would only take him a minute. Buzzing the triple-canopy tree lines of Indochina had lasted five years.

"Keep it steady, *hombre*," Vaquero yelled to the massive Cajun pilot.

"Steady as a coon hunter's rifle," Jasper hollered back. Spiced his words with a laugh. Saw the gold-teeth of the drop-jawed cartel gunner as the plane pulled alongside the trailer and only grinned wider.

Jasper touched the Cessna's wing with a bit more tilt. Vaquero tensed on the landing gear, an arm's length away from the trailer's roof.

A Buick station wagon's headlights stabbed for the Cessna from the oncoming lane.

"Hold onto your linens, Vaquero!" Jasper yanked the stick. The Cessna soared over the Buick. Left wheel caught some camping gear and sent skis skittering on the tunnel floor.

Jasper dipped back.

"Intensity Level Bravo!" Jasper matched smirks with Vaquero.

"All the way!"

Vaquero jumped.

His fingertips met the edge of the trailer roof, clamped instantly, destroyed friction. Landing and hauling himself up was a single motion. Flung his spidery body onto the roof with hands still Mojave dry.

Jasper whirled a wave goodbye that went unseen. Vaquero dashed doubled-over for the trailer's rear. Tunnel ceiling scythed a foot above his head. It did not slow him. Such fear did not exist for this man who had spent half a decade charging Vietcong in lightless passages below the surface of the earth.

He reached the trailer doors as the gunman was pulling them closed. A twist of his body and Vaquero went through the closing gates like a lance. His two snakeskins cracked the gunman's jaw in four places.

The trailer's interior glowed blue phantasmal in fluorescents. Vaquero spared no moment to take in the shock of the four cartel men and their *jefe*. He dove into them with fingers hooked and lips drawn as a garrote.

One drew his .44 Magnum fast. Vaquero splintered his wrist with a one-hand twist. Flung him into the next fastest. Wet snaps as his human missile landed.

A third cocked the action on an AK-47. Vaquero slid forward, took his legs out with a spin kick. The same kick widened, clutched the falling man's neck perfectly tooled to snap bone, broke him.

The fourth man spun his rifle on Vaquero. An instant of hesitation was all Vaquero needed. A wrist-throw tore the gun from his grip, an arm bar blasted his shoulder from its joint, a palm to the throat slammed it shut to any air.

Now Vaquero looked around. The *jefe* was a man with a trimmed beard and a false beauty mark on one fat cheek. He was diving for cover under a bank of computers.

Vaquero dove on top of him. He snatched the drive of the computer and tucked its suitcase-sized bulk under one arm. A last glance around confirmed there were no other records—only cheap furniture and a fortune in cocaine.

Vaquero spun and ran for the trailer doors.

The *jefe* lifted a Colt .45 in a trembling, four-ringed hand.

Vaquero leapt from the trailer without stopping.

He landed on the hood of the Tiger, dead-center on its tiger paw logo of red-and-black stripes.

The sound of the Cessna dropping a barrel of napalm at the head of the tunnel sent the *jefe* to his knees in the trailer.

The Tiger sped to keep Vaquero balanced. He seized the curve of its hood. He held tight as Banzai slowed to avoid the inferno opening ahead.

The truck could not slow in time. Hydraulic scream muffled by the explosion of napalm. The trailer jack-knifed into the cab.

The cab sheared into the flames that choked the tunnel.

The Tiger spun. The glow of the exploding big rig cloaked it. Banzai gunned it.

Jasper cackled on the Tiger's radio. "Feeling that Bravo mojo?"

It was time to head home.

Home was many different things for these men.
The war had bound their fates.
First in the silent pines and starvation of Green Beret survival training at Fort Benning.
Then the five years "in country," suffering and dealing suffering in a jade-and-clay land, so vastly strange and horrible it often seemed only the stitching of the red-black tiger stripe patch of the 5th Special Forces Group they shared held them together.
Then the message, received in Cambodia over their stained and fading radio from Da Nang, disavowing them and condemning them to fight their way back to a civilization they no longer understood.
Tiger Team Bravo was bound together as orphans of war.
They belonged somewhere, though. They had families.

Vaquero's home was a duplex in Scottsdale. He pulled up outside in his Ford Bronco, bought with cash and rebuilt with his wife's help.
He took notice that the building's paint was already fading under the stiff Arizona sun. Another chore to see to. He liked that.
He grabbed his duffel from the truck bed. A new tool set clicked inside—a Christmas present for Alexandra, his wife. It held other things he carried at all times:
The yin-yang symbol from his sensei that Alexandra had made into a keychain. The survival knife from Benning. The pair of taxidermy rattlesnake heads, dried into a fanged snarl, for luck.
Vaquero smiled at that luck as he took the stairs to his apartment two at a time. He was fortunate enough to have a simple life. Work and love were easy when unquestioned.
He never questioned, never suspected, what he found when he opened the door.

Jasper's home was not a building, but a land. He knew every copse of pine and ball cypress he drove by on that last stretch into Bayou Lafitte.

He thought of all the places that this one place contained: The flatboat docks with their twelve-foot poles, where he could wile away a pair of days just drinking and trawling. The floating bars strung with Christmas lights and the hoot of zydeco music.

Today it would be a visit to his old man, though—to the stilt house cradled in the roots of the banyans he'd climbed as a kid. It was a special occasion.

That it was the holidays was incidental. Today was special because the cartel job had won him enough money to buy his pa his own shrimping boat. No more seasons having to put up with Buford Clemens as a sloppy, stuck-up skipper.

Jasper left the cartel cash out in the Dodge. He took into the stilt house what he always had on him: Pair of dice. Deck of Tarot cards from New Orleans. Black Leatherman tool.

He had a six-pack of Abita in hand, too. He damn near dropped it at what he found inside the stilt house.

Banzai felt as at home at Long Beach, California as he did anywhere else. He stepped off the bus and walked to where he could see the waves. The waves understood him, and he them.

Life and home to Banzai was like a tide: surface and motion ever-changing, substance always the same.

Childhood had been one place after another—Sacramento, where his mother's grave was while his father was busy dying in the 442nd during World War II. Then Omaha, Kansas City, Pittsburgh, as his grandparents fled the memories of internment in California. Then back to California, to here in Long Beach, as they returned to make peace with those memories.

He glanced around the edge of his mirror shades at the dormered houses packed close along Ocean Boulevard. His grandparents were in one—they were his constant.

Banzai carried little up the flagstone path, flanked by Zen rock gardens, to their house. No identification. No cash. Only his shades and a set of needlenose pliers, useful for hot-wiring, lock picking, stabbing.

This, he thought, was a useful life: constantly ready for motion, with love of family as core.

After seeing what their house held, Banzai wasted no time rushing to a payphone to call Colonel Professor.

Colonel Professor had made Compton into his home. It had taken work.

He piloted the Tiger down Imperial, one eye on green lights popping on and off along the dashboard. Each green light meant the security measures he'd installed every one-hundred yards around his house were still alive and unviolated.

It gave him calm. Knowing his girls were safe meant the world to him.

When he had returned from Vietnam, they had become his world. Their mother had abandoned them to him. She claimed it was out of disgust over what he had done overseas. He doubted that. Why abandon the girls if that was the case?

But things were what they were. Life went according to plan.

Colonel Professor did the best he could to make it go according to his plan.

He had to. Above all, for the sake of his girls—Marsha was on her way to nursing school. Angelica hated a lot about ninth grade, but gymnastics and flute were passions that saw her through the lack.

There was too much lack, too much loss in this life, for him to fail them.

He clicked a button on the Tiger's ceiling to open the iron gate of his driveway. Another button on the dash disabled the traps in the yard. A final button opened his garage.

Motion sensors along the rose-circled house's perimeter sent data by radio to the Tiger's homemade screen.

The pale-green read-out told him what he would find inside.

Colonel Professor gave himself fifteen seconds to hunch over the wheel, face split in grief, sobbing.

Then he cut himself off. He checked inside to confirm what his machines had told him. After he had seen, he picked up his phone and dialed to send out a code to his team: Threat Level Bravo.

Colonel Professor knew, even before they called back to confirm the meeting site, that his team had something else in common now.

All their families were gone.

Tiger Team Bravo assembled in the parking lot of Johnie's Coffee Shop. Even Jasper looked as grim as Colonel Professor always did.

"So cough it up, egghead." Jasper spat a brown string of dip. "Who stole our people?"

"I have some leads."

"Thought we were dead on paper, hombre," Vaquero said, shaking his head, boneless with sorrow. "Who would know enough about us to come after our families?"

"Our list of enemies is long," Professor said. "Private mercenaries operating on US soil tends to draw attention. In the two years since we escaped the war zone together, we've brought down crooked cops, Mexican gangs, industrial tycoons."

"Baretta knew," Banzai said. "He's about the only one who does. Maybe cartel surveillance could pick up Vaquero's wife..."

"Her name's Alexandra, *hombre*. Use it."

"But my grandparents?" Banzai went on. "I've only visited them twice since we got back."

"Same with my pa," Jasper said. "He don't even have a phone or power."

"Like you say, Billy," Professor said, "Only Baretta knew enough about our families to put an enemy on them. Especially so quickly after the big rig went down. It makes sense that kidnapping our loved ones is retaliation for stealing the cartel records."

"Well, there you go," Jasper said, nodding eagerly. "Plain as the Ace of Spades. Baretta."

Professor scowled up at the coffee shop's sign, its curving letters blinking against the brown-and-orange blaze of the Los Angeles sky.

"It's when things make sense that you've got to worry," Professor said.

They found Baretta in his French Quarter loft, his high tech ransacked into a glittering mess around him, holes through his head. The bullet had punched from one temple through the other. They left his eyes intact to bulge like the note stuffed in his mouth.

Jasper pulled it out, spread the wadded paper. He read it as Professor examined the bullet holes.

"It's in Mexican," Jasper said. He handed it to Vaquero. "You read it."

"I'm Brazilian." Vaquero frowned. "We speak Portuguese."

"Well *pardonnez-moi*. Do you read Mexican or not, cowboy?"

Vaquero shrugged as he scanned the note. Banzai paid no heed, lost in the sepia of a photograph—one taken of his grandparents when they were in the Internment Camp in California.

"Outlaw thugs, it says," Vaquero read, "I guess that means us. Return what you have stolen and we will return your families."

Professor traced the angle of the bullet hole to the wall: a nest of splinters held a gold wad. He plucked it free, weighed it in his palm.

"Then it gives a time and place for the drop." Vaquero finished. They all looked to Professor. He displayed the slug on his hand.

"A solid gold bullet."

"Manuel Segura," Vaquero said.

"The one that got away, huh?" Jasper said, swatting Banzai on the shoulder. Banzai kept his mirrors fixed on the photo. Jasper turned from being ignored, spat on the floor. "Knew we should have smoked that greaser when we had the chance, 'stead of just freeing all them *chicas* he had locked up in his plantation."

"At least we know where to find him," Vaquero said.

"That's what bothers me," Professor said.

All of them watched him. He led them out the rainbow screen of beads curtaining the loft's exit.

"How you figure?" Confusion crushed Jasper's expression. "Who else uses gold bullets for his executions? Got to be Segura."

"Think about the angle of the bullet," Professor said, voice a rasp below the hollers of the French Quarter crowd as he led Tiger Team Bravo into the swelter of New Orleans' streets. "Where have we seen that before?"

"Only in 'Nam." Vaquero was quick to answer. "In one temple, out the other. That's how the ARVN used to do in the captured Cong."

"Well, other than that little hitch in our giddy-up," Jasper said, "Makes sense that it'd be Segura. He deals with the cartel and has a grudge."

Professor answered only with the deepening of the worry lines in his dusky face.

Manuel Segura's antebellum mansion sat on a sprawl of Louisiana land abandoned by the census to the teeming of the bayou. But even before its moss-draped ivory columns were raised, pirate maps had been drafted in Indian ink by smugglers shuttling slaves and tobacco into the colonial territories.

Those maps were ash now. Their embers still glowed only on the tongues of the Cajuns, passed down through generations.

Government forgot those weedy canals, but to Jasper Babineaux they were vivid as the lines in his palm.

Tiger Team Bravo glided up their mystery in a flatboat, skin shadow-torn with black camo, night vision crisp as jungle cats.

The channel ended in the green gum of undergrowth, fifty yards from a grove of spruce by the Segura plantation's slave quarters. Vaquero took point, slipping them through roots gemmed with blue lichen, past wire snares laid by Segura's hired trappers, into the heart of the plantation.

They clipped through the chain link gate bordering the mown lawn.

They fanned out around the house, adrenaline prickling at the absence of guards.

They encircled the manor, its wedding-cake height lit sparingly on all floors, a ghostly orange watched by Banzai as he waited at the tree line to deliver covering fire at an instant's demand.

Doors were forced at the same moment. Vaquero led Professor up the back porch. Jasper stormed the kitchen's side door with sawn-off shotgun goring ahead.

No gunshots came to Banzai's pitch-perfect hearing. Only the grumble of bull frogs and the rippling of gar in the bayou. He dashed to join the others.

Their room-to-room took five minutes. Colonel Professor spent half of that watching out the windows. He didn't need to say what was written in his scowl:

This was a trap.

When the shapes of men with rifles drifted like smudges of cinders from the plantation's borders, Professor keyed his radio.

Jasper was already on it, calling in from the third-floor bedroom.

"Found Segura. He's got and in-and-out hole through his head."

"Incoming Tangos," Professor whispered back. "Move to the upper floors to lay down fire."

"Eighty-six that idea, chief," Jasper answered. His boots thumping down the stairs were the only sound. "Head to the basement."

"We'll be blockaded in there," Professor answered.

Jasper bounced down the last step, slapped his commander on the shoulder, and flashed a crooked grin. "Just trust me."

They dashed for the cellar as machine gun fire shredded the silence. Glass popped. Wood clattered with a hundred dashes of lead.

Tiger Team Bravo fled into the cellar door with puffs of butchered furniture behind them.

Banzai slammed the cellar door. He shot the iron bolt home. A leap brought him onto the soil of the basement floor with his comrades.

He found Professor staring at the central support beam.

"I don't hear them comin' in," Jasper yelled above the snarls of gunfire overhead. "No boots or nothing."

Professor clicked on the flashlight affixed to his combat webbing vest. The light shone on a bulk taped to the beam, amidst the clutter of Segura's pinball machine collection.

Atop a column of compound explosive, a clock's third hand sped away the final thirty seconds. Professor's jaw went tight as his haircut.

"Time bomb."

"Well, don't that beat all," Jasper said with a smirk. "Should have figured something like that."

"You figure how we get out of this?" Vaquero said.

The clock spun past twenty seconds. The gunfire above faded as the hostiles withdrew. Professor sized up the bomb: four pounds. Enough to atomize the house.

"Better figure it fast," Professor said. "Fifteen seconds."

Jasper angled a thumb at a colossal wooden armoire against the wall. "Then we better duck behind that, pronto."

They ran for it, with ten seconds ticking away faster than even Professor could keep up.

After Manuel Segura's mansion vaporized in a bright-red ball, the squad that had surrounded it spread back into the bayou.

The plan was to disperse, check in with Commander Delta to confirm the mission's success, then lay low for a few days.

Sergeant Bear Collins hunkered in the brown-green stew of an inlet, listening to his teammates call in on the radio. Bear was last to key his transmitter.

"All clear here," he said. "Hell of a job, Tiger Team Delta."

Unlike the times in the past he'd said it, Bear didn't smile. This mission felt even more sour than his first. He'd thought nothing could be worse than the slash-and-burn jobs he'd done outside of Hue City. Knowing otherwise made him sick in his gut, and Bear hardly ever lost his appetite.

That gut dropped as he heard a branch shift behind him.

Bear swung around his M-16. His aim found only darkness. He kept his sights on it a second longer to be sure.

A second too long. A bayonet pressed to his throat from behind.

"Y'all look like you got plenty of dumb ideas in that hairy head of yours," Jasper said, pressing the blade closer. "Don't pay 'em no heed. Just drop the gun."

Bear weighed his options. Jasper cut them down to one by sinking the knife enough to draw blood.

Bear's rifle splashed to the ground.

Vaquero stepped out from behind the tree that had stolen Bear's attention. Colonel Professor followed. Banzai circled to Bear's side with a pistol to his head.

"How the fuck did you manage it?" Bear blurted.

"Just some local know-how," Jasper said.

"Local know-how ain't enough to survive being blown to smithereens."

"It is when it tells you that these old plantations have secret tunnels out to the slave quarters, so that the masters could have their nightly fun."

"Well fuck me sideways."

"We'll get around to that," Colonel Professor said, shark-dead stare fixed on Bear as Vaquero watched the perimeter of the grove. "Tell us who's behind this."

"You tell me this," Bear said. "Would you give each other up if you were in my position?"

Professor just stared.

"That's what I thought," Bear said. "Same rules apply."

"I figured that," Professor said. "So why's he doing this?"

Tiger Team Bravo showed Professor the same puzzled look. Bear smiled.

"Same reason as got us all into this mess in the first place," Bear said. "He's following orders."

At a snap of Professor's fingers, Jasper brought a pistol butt down on Bear's skull. Bulk splashed into the bayou. Professor turned the knocked-out soldier over to keep him from drowning.

"You want to explain all of that to us?" Jasper said.

Professor looked to Vaquero. He got a nod.

"I know what you're thinking, *jefe*," Vaquero said. "That the Ozark shipping address in the cartel's records is making a lot of sense now."

"Ozarks?" Jasper said. "You mean..."

"It means," Professor said, "we have a call to pay on an old comrade. Captain Teague has some explaining to do."

"This is a real end run, *amigos*." Vaquero said, giving a sour look to the map Jasper spread.

"Not like we don't know the field." Jasper flashed a smile.

It was true. The Ozark forest they hunkered in, a spot on the edge of the map they gathered around, even smelled as they remembered. The decade of time since they trained here had changed so much in their lives, but the rhythm of the scissoring wind, the pine and soil aroma thick as gravy, even the rustle of animals in the mist, remained.

"Shocked to my spurs you didn't recognize the address on the cartel list at the first glance, Professor." Vaquero glanced at Professor Colonel, crouched nearby keying a long-range radio. "Getting old?"

"Been old since I was young." Professor lifted the transmitter to the rim of his beret. "No, I didn't suspect the address until we found out Teague's Tiger Team was involved. It's not like I'm an authority on secret Special Forces training grounds' street addresses."

That sobered Vaquero. He tugged a jacket tassel. "Think Teague's behind this? Some kind of revenge thing against us?"

Jasper didn't look up from his study of the map's clouds of green and tributaries of yellow, the rises and vales of the secret training ground. "Maybe he crawled out of Indochina with some Golden Triangle heroin connections."

"We'll know soon enough, cowboy." Professor said to Vaquero.

They held each other's stare, Vaquero's demanding certainty, Professor giving only confidence in reply. Vaquero dropped his head first, shook it. "A real damn end run."

"Nobody knows these woods better than us." Jasper tapped the map's right border. "Now look here, y'all."

"I'm looking, I'm looking," Vaquero said. "You looking, Banzai?"

"I'm always looking. You just can't see it."

Jasper grinned big enough for Banzai and him both, then traced their infiltration route. The wind gusted and ebbed, shuttling eddies of mist through the rearing pine. As the radio clicked in answer to Professor, he spoke.

"Hello. Been awhile."

Jasper walked his fingers along a narrow yellow slash—a dead-end valley—on the map. "Right here's the draw where we set up that ambush, back in the day. Wiped out them weekend warriors on our war game finals, you remember?"

"Hard to forget," Vaquero said, smirked, rubbing his sun-ripened neck. "Though I don't remember much about the week celebrating that came after."

Jasper whistled. "All's I got to remember from that's the tattoos, myself. Anyhows, that there draw's got a defilade up on its south ridge we can slip through, right into the heart of the training ground forest."

"Okay, but how do we get to the draw?"

Professor squinted at the dusk bruising the spine of the mountains, spoke evenly into the radio. "Understood. I don't owe you anything either. It never was about owing. You know that."

Jasper skittered his fingers along the yellow of the map, then skipped them into a green patch in its center. "Well, we just march right up this private road until we can see this here elevation, about 800 yards shy of it, and cut into the woods bearin' north-northeast from there."

Vaquero frowned. "What if Teague's people have advance snipers covering the road?"

"They don't," Jasper said."

"What if they do? What if they shoot us?"

"They won't."

Vaquero sighed. Wind and birds held their breath, and the only sound was the rumble of a monotone voice on Professor's radio.

It paused, and Professor was quick to answer. "That's right. This is about honor. That you can trust in."

His Tiger Team exchanged dismayed looks at his answer. Jasper was first to shrug it off and started circling his finger around the green patch, the target, on the map.

"Once we make it through the draw," Jasper said, "they'll have pickets around the main site."

"And, we can guess," Vaquero said, rocking on his snakeskin boot heels, "a house where they're holding Alexandra and your families."

"Right." Jasper couldn't smile at that. "We just slip in through the pickets, then make contact at the back of the house."

"Easy as that." Vaquero's tone was flat as a folded flag.

"Easy as that." Jasper said.

"I know we're putting our lives in your hands. Like I said, it's how it's always been. We'll see you soon." Professor keyed off the radio and turned to the stares of his men.

"Got the uniforms?" Professor Colonel asked Jasper, sending him rummaging in his Confederate-colored rucksack.

"How'd you get those anyway, Jasper?" Vaquero slipped off his jacket.

"I'm a person who knows people." Jasper snapped on a grin. "Besides, since the war, this stuff's just been collecting mold down in Mississippi. Easiest thing in the world to pinch a few for the price of a case of beer."

"Let's suit up and hit it," Professor said.

Jasper was first to put his fist out. His voice had a heavy sobriety to it for once. It didn't weigh down his smile. "Intensity Level Bravo."

Professor nodded and held his knuckles to Jasper's. "All the way."

The others joined, completing the circle of fists. "All the way."

As countless times before, they broke ranks, suited up and marched into the woods as though they belonged to them.

Captain Teague turned from watching General Parkinson burn the ledgers in the trashcan. He stared at the mellow spill of Ozark forest out the bay window of his three-story lodge. Past the reflection of his glower, one eye slashed by a long-scar from Hanoi shrapnel, the sight of mist-ringed trees rolling down the mountain soothed the disgust rising in him.

These dense and gauzy forests were a familiar sight. Teague chose this place as his hideaway after the war because of that familiarity. Their resemblance to the Central Highlands of Vietnam made living in America feel less like being on an alien planet.

"Rotten cocksuckers," General Parkinson said, inspiring a nervous glance from the three MPs clutching M-16s by the study's doorways. "Can't even clean up a simple mess."

The sight of burning records brought a different familiar feeling to Teague. He kept it to himself. Telling Parkinson of how he'd watched Dial Soapers—rear echelon officers—burn records of the Tiger Teams at 5th Special Forces Command before Saigon fell would be wasted on the general.

"I told you they'd be a hard target," Teague said, still standing sentinel at the window.

"Your team was supposed to be harder still," Parkinson snarled at him, dumping more files stuffed with cartel payments and cocaine distributors' names into the trashcan blaze. "Fight fire with fire, right? You were supposed to be America's best."

"We are," Teague said. His shoulders couldn't get any straighter. "But so are Tiger Team Bravo."

Parkinson scraped ash from his hands onto his dress greens. Gave Teague his worst Fort Bragg scowl. "I'd hoped the millions of dollars your Tiger Team Delta is tasked to protect were incentive enough to prevail."

"Millions in drug money."

"Don't play the innocent." Parkinson wadded his swollen features into red contempt. "Whether it was heroin from the Golden Triangle in Laos or coke from Colombia, black ops cash has to come from somewhere. Nothing changes."

"No," Teague said, turning from the window. "Nothing does."

Teague's radio buzzed. He answered it.

He listened, Parkinson staring fixedly at him. "That was Tomahawk," he told Parkinson. "They caught Tiger Team Bravo just outside the rear perimeter, trying to slip through disguised as Guardsmen. He's bringing them in"

"That's more like it." Parkinson shoved the grill of medals on his chest out to match his grin. "We'll get them to tell us where the cartel records are. Then we'll liquidate them and the hostages and move out."

Parkinson looked around for a way to extinguish the burning files. He picked up a decanter of Glenfiddich '37, considered it, and then put it down. "Find me a way to put out this fire."

The study doors parted and Tiger Team Bravo were marched in at gunpoint. Flanked by four MPs, carrying their M-16 carbines, the team looked shaken and weary in shabby Guardsmen uniforms. Teague neither smiled or frowned to see them.

Parkinson stood astride Teague's Buddhist prayer mat, beaming.

"Well, you dumb son of a bitch," Parkinson said to Colonel Professor, who glowered back from below his skewed beret. "Got anything to say for yourself?"

Professor didn't reply. Parkinson's smile went fish-bone thin.

"You can start by telling me where those cartel records are."

"I have only one thing to tell you," Colonel Professor said.

The smile didn't shift, but Parkinson's eyes readied some venom. It slipped into his tone. "What's that, Colonel?"

"It's time for some Bravo mojo."

Parkinson only had time to wrinkle his nose. The MPs that brought in Tiger Team were already tossing the carbines to them. In a single smooth motion, as if both teams were one, Tiger Team Bravo caught up their rifles and set them on Parkinson while their MPs drew sidearms and aimed them at Parkinson's men.

Parkinson's MPs dropped their hands from their holsters. Parkinson dropped his jaw.

"What the fuck is this?" Parkinson said.

"Fine work, Tiger Team Delta," Teague said to the MPs allied with Bravo.

From behind Banzai's left shoulder, Bear tipped the MP helmet he wore at his commander. "Our pleasure, boss. Good to be back on the right side."

"Get the greenhorns out of here," Colonel Professor ordered. At Teague's nod of agreement, the counterfeit MPs led Parkinson's men away with their white gloves raised high.

"What are you doing, you traitorous cocksucker?" General Parkinson roared at Teague, tone sour as the cigar scent staining his liver-hued lips. "Kill them all!"

He spun to find Teague holding Parkinson's own ivory-handled Colt on him. His gaze floated between his lost pistol and Teague's scowl as if deciding which was deadlier.

As Banzai shut the study doors, Tiger Team Bravo clustered around Parkison. Colonel Professor nodded at Teague.

"Captain," he said.

"Colonel," Teague replied in his coffin-groan of a voice. "I would say it was good to see you, but given the circumstances..."

"Understood. Seems it's always that way, Captain."

"Yes it does, sir."

"Traitor," was all Parkinson could spit.

"This the fucker who stole my pa?" Jasper poked the chill of his rifle barrel into Parkinson's neck.

"As if his kind hadn't already done enough to my grandparents," Banzai added, the burn of his glare showing even through the mirror shades.

"Traitors!" Parkinson bellowed. "All of you. Betraying your country."

"By surviving?" Colonel Professor held out his hand to Teague.

"By not betraying each other?" Teague filled Professor's grip with the General's Colt.

Parkinson's laugh had a disease in its cough. Stare stuck to Tiger Team Bravo like Agent Orange. "No, you fucking grunts. By not letting the war end when we told you to. By not doing as you were fucking told."

Colonel Professor put the Colt's sight on Parkinson's temple. His stare in reply, cool and heavy caliber. The Ozark wilderness outside a perfection of silence packaged in mist and memory.

"If there's one good thing we took from your war, General," Professor said, "it's each other."

Parkinson's lips split to speak. Professor saved the silence with a bullet through the general's skull.

The shot sped through both temples and out for the forest to keep. Parkinson's body shook the ash of the burning files as it fell. It sprawled stiff on the prayer mat, frozen to be forgotten on the floor above where Team Tiger Bravo's families waited to be joined.

THE END

MATTHEW C. FUNK has been a lifelong fan of Lance Matrix's Tiger Team Bravo stories, one of the great mercenary team series. If they ever decide to revive it, no one knows the canon like Funk. A quick warning: if you ever get the chance to see Funk's mint-condition complete TTB paperback collection, don't touch. That is, if you prefer your ass unkicked. Thanks to Mr. Funk for choosing this gem from 1976.

FATHER DUKES
in
DOPEHOUSE INFERNO (abridged)
by Milt Walsh
(discovered by Bart Lessard)

WEST 44TH STREET, Delaware City. On a map, a simple line. On the ground, the brink of hell. Once it had marked the edge of the meatpacking district. But the cattle trains had stopped coming in, the A & P began to stock wheat germ, and the breed had changed along with the times. Gangs, pushers, junkies, hookers, pimps, longhairs, immigrants, radicals, catamites, welfare cheats—these were the new flesh. With something like pride they had kept the old nickname for their new haunts: the Killing Floor.

The border was clear even without a map to mark it. On the far lane of West 44th, long cars cruised by slow—candy-colored cars with furs inside, cars with gleaming hubcaps, cars with chandeliers, cars that bounced. The stoops held a crowd, colored men in suedes and furs and pegged pants and purple fedoras. A purring crew of whores and punks met their every whim. Men in stained raincoats roamed the concrete in between, eyes cast down, seeking a chance, a fix, a woman, a pretty boy, an exit. Every car stereo and pocket hi-fi blared the savage thrum of disco.

But none of this netherworld dared cross the fading paint that marked the middle of West 44th. Not one pimp sedan ever made a left across the other lane. Something held them all back. Kept them in check. Told them, here, and no farther.

Nowhere was the gutter stench stronger than in the loom of the burnt-out tenement. It stood in the center of the block, and it had no right to stand at all. Like the furnace of hell had in the time before time, it had caught fire. And like hell promised to, it had people in it yet: shadows glimpsed through the broken windowpanes, mysterious comings and goings. At any hour day or night the walks around it teemed with the lowlife, peddling dope and lust, preying on the weak. The building should have been condemned, scrubbed clean with a wrecking ball, but building inspectors never came—scared, bribed, both.

Inside the blackened tower, near the entry, was a ground-floor apartment. Here a short swart man strutted in, followed by a mouse of a woman painted up like a billboard. The man was Big Baby—a quarter Puerto Rican, a quarter Turk, two-fifths Negro, the rest miscellaneous. For a look he kept a pacifier in his mouth and curlers in his hair. He set his takeout chicken and jelly donuts beside a bare mattress. He lit a Sterno can for ambiance. A puddle of light spread from the wick.

"Please, Baby," said the harlot. She ran her shaky press-on nails over her arms. "I'm hurting real bad."

Wet gold flashed as Big Baby smiled. He drew a fat knife and stabbed a wall. The handle took his cheetah coat. At the window he parted the Hefty bag curtains and threw open the broken sash. In came a draft of filth. A garbage strike was on. To Big Baby it smelled like payday.

Big Baby turned back around, his gold teeth tight on the sucker. He reached down. A zipper spoke. The harlot's eyes went wide.

"Feast those eyeses, child," he said. He held his asset out to the Sterno light: a paper twisted at both ends, the load within no fatter than the snout of a rat. Also, he had taken out his dick. "The fo-real deal. Aca-ma-pulco Gold. Straight froms the Promised Land." He meant Mexico. "Ninety-nine and foaty-fo one hunnerts percent pure, know what I'm saying?"

This was all a mumble through the sucker, and a speech impediment, but the whore was all eyes and few ears. And two knees, which she now went to. It showed initiative, Big Baby thought. "Oh yes, please, it's just what I need," she said.

In a fit of giggles, Big Baby missed the uproar right outside. Dopers and dope dealers breaking into a run, shouting, screaming. A honking horn, the swoop of a trash can in flight, a shatter of glass, a gush of malt liquor. It was the sound of a coming storm. A storm that walked on two feet like a man. A man with a right like a wrecking ball. A wrecking ball long overdue for the demolition.

Big Baby said, "Let's us opens the flo to a bit of...negotiation."

"So a blowjob?"

The window burst. Big Baby spun around and the whore fled, scuttling into the dark. What the dim light first made a wet sack of garbage was actually Sir Weasel in his bespoke velvets. A member of Big Baby's own street gang, the Ladykillers. He had been left outside to keep watch while Big Baby got his checkup—him, Man Sam, and Poppin Snake. A shard had cut Sir Weasel's throat. The lifeblood shot out onto the boards in farting pulses. *Phbbt! Phbbt! Phbbt!* His hand went limp. A .38 tumbled free.

Big Baby tucked himself away, but his sudden soft-on had done most of the work for him. He took up the gun and ran into the hall. He thought twice, came back in, threw on his furs, pulled the knife, primped his curlers, and ran out again.

Too late. There in the unlit and blackened entry stood a shape. A figure cast tall and broad by the flickering street lamp in the background.

Big Baby ignored the animal fear and brought up the weapons. He spoke through the pacifier. "Just got yoself a discount. Don't you know where you at? This Pipe's house. This where the Pipe play. And now you gonna pay too. Pay to play."

Without a pause to ask for clarification but slow enough that Big Baby could finish his thought, the figure stepped in. A patch of light from a lamp in the stairwell crossed the beefy chest. The clothes were pitch black except at the very front of the collar. A single square of white. A white now flecked with red, a windowpane where the blood of atonement showed in the dark.

Big Baby thought, *A priest? Couldn't be—*

But the man came on, the patch of light moved up past the collar, the iron jaw, the copper mustache. To the eyes, where it held.

Father Dukes!

The rubber nipple fell from Big Baby's mouth. The .38 shook in one hand, and the knife in the other. His knees had turned to warm water. Actually he had pissed himself. His polyester socks squished as he took a step back. That fierce blue, that fire. *This mother be crazy!*

And that was Big Baby's last thought before a fist knocked the curlers from his hair.

Atta boy, Mick! a raspy voice said. *You showed dat schwartze what's what!*

Lefty Sofer had been his cutman back in the prizefighting days. The crusty yid had gone to glory not long after, or to a cozy nook of hell. But death hadn't stopped old Lefty from chiming in.

And watch the footwoik!

The Reverend Michael Muldoon, better known as Father Dukes, stared down at his limp and bleeding handiwork. He plucked a tooth from the callus on a knuckle and threw it over a shoulder.

The priest was in a fury—a rage as red as the hair atop his head and fanned out upon his lip. He hadn't felt an anger so deep since his final bout as "Dukes" Muldoon. His famed "sucker hook" had given the challenger brain damage. Wally "Twos" Phelan had been a gentle giant and a swell guy—not bad for Black Irish anyway. And though he had never been too sharp—he took "Twos" because he could count no higher—he hadn't deserved a diaper and a padded ward.

The champ had thrown down his gloves in disgrace. He had sworn to his dying mother that he would enter the seminary to make amends. She hadn't asked him to—had met the suggestion with a silent roll of her stroked-out eyes—but it had seemed the right thing to do. He couldn't remember a seminary, but he was punchy himself and that was beside the point. He had the collar, the book, and a flock to tend, there in the seamy streets of Delaware City.

Father Dukes had served as an ambassador of sorts for the neighborhood families. The gang lords of the Killing Floor knew his name, his past, and better than to cross the paint at West 44th.

And the priest had let himself feel content—to let the scum bubble as long as it kept to its toilet, a toilet being optimal placement for bubbling scum. But somehow Jenny Stupek, five years old, the cutest Polack you ever saw, had gotten her hands on the "product" and taken it for makowiec. Now she lay in a hospital bed, a tube up her nose, while bags dripped into her and a heart monitor peeped like a sickly bird.

Rage. Rage!

The priest reached down. With a single hand he hauled Big Baby upright and floppy, a leisure suit full of chewing gum. He held him against a charred wall and slapped him awake.

"Where is the Piper?" Father Dukes roared. The Piper, the mystery man, Delaware City's "King of Boo."

Big Baby had reached up to his hair. "My treatment!"

"The Piper! Where?"

"O.K., O.K., holy rolla. Pipe be upstairs, alls the way ups top. But you never make it."

"And why not now?"

"The flos, they guarded. Each one mo thans the last. Mo guns, mo weapons." Big Baby smiled short of teeth, working up the nerve. "Mo pain."

A swoop to the chin put Big Baby through the cindered wall. His lifts dangled from the hole, shivered, went still in the sift of ashes.

You gotta step it up now, boychik! Lefty said from eternity. *Timin' is everything!*

Twelve floors. Like the Stations of the Cross. And at the last came the nails, right? His mustache took a curl and his eyes a feral glow. He could hardly wait.

[On the next three floors, Father Dukes faces the last of Big Baby's gang, a zombie-like horde of junkies, and an evil rock and roll band, in that order. —Ed.]

but the fire hose held. A last lunge got Father Dukes up and over. He crashed through the upper story window in a burst of glass, rolled, halted in a crouch.

As his head cleared he stood, coughing, patting out the flames on his clergy shirt. Absently he yanked the drumstick from the wound in his thigh. When the bloody shaft fell from his grip there was no clatter, no ring of wood on bare wood. It was then that he noted the carpet at his feet. Brand new. An undyed and slubby wool pile. Tasteful, some might say. That much was lost on the street-smart priest, who slept on under-washed rebar with a cinderblock for a pillow, but the pattern in the brocade was not: cocks and cherubs in a frolic. There seemed to be some kind of subtle message in it.

I gotta bad feeling about dis, said Lefty, and he wasn't alone.

The priest took a jolt from his hip flask as he looked about. There was no sign of old smoke, no char, only fresh paint and a minimally furnished open floor plan. A sea of low shag, sprawling marble countertops at an island wet bar, recessed ceiling lights, a pit with a circular sofa. Conversation pieces, floral arrangements, very important works of art. Someone had not just rebuilt, but... redecorated. At the perimeters were window treatments—a lace of sorts—one of which he had knocked loose with his crashing entry. It lay on the carpet like a spurned bride.

Father Dukes thought it looked like an airport lounge, where fancy jets flew fancy people to parts unknown. So at first he took the three slinky figures lounging in the pit for stewardesses. They were sprawled about a glass table loaded with wine spritzers and plates of crab rémoulade with rocket and endive. Father Dukes saw only low tide on rabbit food with a side of sissy. But then the three stood, and even for all the vamping fuss of their movements, the priest saw that they were no ladies.

The three formed a delta, fists set high to hips, elbows out. The one in front wore a double-breasted silk frock and took pursing sips of smoke from a cigarette holder, theater-length. His glossy black hair bore a bolt of witchy white, curlicued at the end. The two behind him wore tight striped jersey shirts, capri pants, no socks, and side-gusseted dress loafers.

He in front took up a quizzing glass on the end of a waist chain and gave Father Dukes the once-over, pinkie akimbo. "Black, before Labor Day?"

Nancies! Lefty said.

One in back said, "He's made a dickens of the drapes."

"I'll fetch the club soda," said the other, looking at the carpet behind the priest.

"Hold off for now, Beauregard," said the leader. "We'll be needing more than just a spot treatment." The three had fanned out.

"Mama told me not to pick on girls," said the priest. "So why don't you show me the stairs and swish yourselves on down to confession at St. Mary's?"

"Where do you think we started?" said the leader.

"I'm here for the Piper," Father Dukes said. "Stand clear."

The priest made to walk between the leader and the man to his left. He found himself flat on his back, the print of a loafer in the side of his face. Father Dukes sat up, shaking light back into his head. The three tittered.

"You're no garden-variety finook, are you?" the priest asked.

"I see what you did there," said the leader. On the priest's blank stare he sighed. "This is a dojo," he said, rolling the j like a grape in his mouth. "I am Master Anton, and these are my disciples. Scott, Beauregard, bring me the mustache."

"Yes, sensei," the prettyboys said as one, and the sound was like a calliope leak.

"I've fought kickers before," Father Dukes said, jumping upright.

"How about twirlers?"

As Master Anton said this, his disciples brought out weapons from behind their backs. Like the batons of majorettes but broken in half and rejoined with fine chain. And lacquered vivid pink. These they spun fast, changing hands, eyes and smirks locked on the priest through the flesh-toned blur.

Take care, pisher! Lefty said. *Dese faygeles, dey got a talent!*

Father Dukes could take a punch as well as he could dish one out. So he simply raised his forearms, covered up, and let the beating begin.

The queers swooped in, a wind ruffling the cuffs of their capris. The pink nunchucks caught the momentum and struck all the harder. The blows stung to the core. And again. And again. If the priest hadn't kept so thick a brace of muscle through clean living and steak dinners, bones would have shattered, organs burst. But he tensed up and took it all, a human fist. And in his clench he let his uncanny pugilist's sense study up as the assailants leapt and swung, yelping like minks in a pique. Each blow, each angle of attack went into the primal machine of the fighter's mind. He listened through the drum of their weapons on his own body to where their feet landed, to the speed of their leaps and swings, the rhythm of it all.

Father Dukes stood up, straighter and straighter, dropping his guard, inviting the killing blow to his head, proud, red, and unprotected.

They took the chance both at once. At the height of their arcs his hands shot out. In an instant he had clamped the he-minxes by the throats.

Their bodies below the neck flailed like crash dummies, and the nunchucks shot from their grips. The table broke and drenched the carpet with rémoulade and spritzer. The fatales barely had time to choke on the crushed pulp of their voiceboxes before the priest clapped their heads together like strangely ripe bowling balls.

"Oh pickles," said Master Anton. "And just when I'd got them both trained."

"That chop-socky wasn't so hot for the d."

"I wasn't referring to martial arts." Master Anton threw aside his cigarette holder and brought up his hands. The fingernails were long and sharpened to points. "I'll scratch your eyes out."

And just like that Master Anton came on like a whirling dervish. Father Dukes barely brought up a forearm before a gash opened through the sleeve of his clergy shirt. The assailant leapt past in a garish grand jeté.

Father Dukes turned and hunched low, waiting for the cartwheel to double back. When it did in a blur he tried an uppercut. But the master flowed through the strike like a saucy eel, leapt, sashayed, and landed square on the priest's shoulders.

The ankles were crossed at Father Dukes's chest. Supple thighs clamped down on his airway. The thick muscles of his all-Irish-American neck fought back like tackles in a scrimmage. He clenched his eyes shut as he heard the nails swoop in. They raked against his lids. Even there the priest had steel, and the claws did little more than mark the map of his prizefighter's scar tissue.

It was not fear of blindness that made the priest move but embarrassment: at his nape and through the silk pants he could feel the rage erection, probing, seeking a way.

"Gah!" Father Dukes threw Master Anton through an urn of daffodils. But the sleek homo landed in a handstand among the shards and petals, legs wide, pup tent pitched. Father Dukes rubbed the back of his neck, wishing for a grill brush and lye.

Nimble little shaygetz, ain't he? Lefty said. *You gotta use the overhand right!*

"You told me never to do that," Father Dukes said.

Master Anton came to a halt. "What's that? I told you what?"

Don't klatsch with the creep, just use the overhand right!

Getting no answer, Master Anton huffed and resumed his dance. And with a shriek like a banshee in a cathouse on dollar day he shot toward the padre.

Now!

Father Dukes felt the power flow into his shoulder and the opposite foot. Time slowed as the punch reeled out. Pie-eyes and man-talons filled his vision, an intersex harpy on the kill. And then he saw his fist connect in a flare of white adrenal light.

The priest came to from his pugilist's trance, still standing, breathing deep. He looked down. The kung-fu master had fallen face up. The jaw had not only broken and dislocated but come half off in a ragged tear. The tongue lolled through the raw split aside the head. Master Anton sputtered, shook, went still in a mist of blood.

Father Dukes made the sign of the cross and went to find the stairs.

[*Floors six through ten: starved rats, Senegalese mercenaries, "The Australian," a brainwashed heiress with a machine gun, plus minions, and a Universal Life Church minister and his "love congregation." On the eleventh floor, Father Dukes beats a knife-throwing witch doctor and comes up to a mysterious door. —Ed.*]

bare steel in a steel frame, no handle, no rivet, no weld. Behind him Father Dukes heard the death rattle as Dr. Tsetse went limp upon the sewage pipe that had skewered him to the wall.

The priest was about to punch the door when he heard a metallic buzz and the pop of an automatic bolt.

The door stood ajar.

An invitation? No: a trap, an obvious trap. A wad of cheese on a wire that a rat would blush to sniff. But Father Dukes saw no other way. He was dog tired. His hip flask had been drained dry. Little of his clergy shirt remained except the scrap of black around the collar. And his bared and rippling torso told the story of battle. Cuts, burns, purpling bruises, bites (junkie and rat), boomerang welts, a cauterized bullet hole, a hickey. His suffering had a touch of Bartholomew and a bit of Matthew thrown in with a dash of Pete. All he had to do now to stand by his word—to get himself in good with the Almighty Referee and atone for his poor sportsmanship— was throw himself onto a crucifix and be a goddam man about it.

"Thy will and all that," he croaked, and pushed though the doorway.

Nothing showed at first, the light too dim, but the musk in the air was dank and heady, jungle/vaginal. Some kind of herb or spice. Father Dukes didn't know what sort—his "pantry" (the top of a stove) held salt, rock salt, and whiskey salt (a cooking experiment). Maybe it was sage. His mama had put sage in the corned beef one

Thanksgiving, that and a Pall Mall butt. "Call it a toy surprise, you foakin' gobshite," she had said, falling boozily asleep at the table.

He had been shuffling forward one foot at a time to seek a path in the here and now, and flood lights switched on mid-step.

Once he blinked away the sear of white he saw where he was: a warehouse of sorts. A clear lane lay ahead. To either side of it the floorboards were heaped high with pure, drab "maree chhhuana" (as the Puerto Ricans said). Stacked the way the city priest imagined hay might be, and were it hay and this a farm, enough to feed every steak-beast for miles.

He walked down an aisle between the mounds, eyeing it all. So much! The source of the Killing Floor's plague, this, the devil weed. A sweat came to the priest's freckled brow. He stepped lightly.

A chuckle echoed through the grass. Father Dukes stopped and crouched, ready to punch the very air.

"Behold...my empire," said a tinny voice. Father Dukes looked up and saw a P.A. speaker. And a video camera that turned to track his every move.

"Straight ahead, you'll find a stair," said the P.A., "and up the stair you'll find me. I've been expecting you, Reverend Muldoon. It's time we met. I made macaroons."

The priest did not recognize the voice, but he knew whose it had to be. He felt a thrill. One way or another, soon the hunt would end. The Piper unmasked. And punched in the head.

The stair came up a trapdoor in the middle of the floor. The space above was a simple one. An expanse of floorboards; a spotlight in the middle; a desk in the light; a man at the desk. All else was darkness.

Father Dukes could scarcely make out a face behind the glare. And there were stacks atop the desk to block the view—stacks of bundled money, heaping, overflowing, piled like sandbags for a flood.

"Let me introduce you to the family," said the voice, still amplified by a P.A. "Andrew, Ulysses, Benjamin. And Grover, sweet Grover. You can have the Abrahams."

Father Dukes heard a click. Behind him the trapdoor sealed. Another click brought on the house lights. The priest looked about himself, puzzled. All around were ropes in four parallel rows, tied at four corners in turnbuckles. He turned back to the desk. "It ain't regulation," he said.

The figure stood from his switchboard and microphone. "Nor am I, Reverend."

Father Dukes took a step back. "You!"

Him! Sheldy Pipowitz, Esquire. The shyster. The public defender who got the worst scum off on any technicality and sometimes (rumor had it) with a bribe. Delaware City's "Voice of the People," as his bus bench ads said. The oily, hook-nosed, thick-fingered—

What are you gettin' at? Lefty asked.

"If I and my money might enjoy your...full attention, Reverend Muldoon," Pipowitz said.

"What for? Pretty soon you won't have a take to count. You're gonna be counting to zero, like this: Zero. The end. Forever. And what you never counted on was me making it through your goons, one floor at a time."

A grin, a chuckle. "It is precisely what I was counting. On."

Father Dukes stared.

"You've been a thorn in my side for far too long, Reverend," said the Piper. "And now the stages of battle have worn you out. With you gone—"

"So I should just, what, stand here while you wrap that up?" Father Dukes said. He cracked his knuckles and then his neck. He could go another round or ten.

"Oh." The Piper pushed aside a stack of money. There on the desktop was a button and a bell—a ringside bell. The button he pushed straight away. Then he took up a carpenter's hammer.

Somewhere past the ropes a panel opened up. Father Dukes heard a heavy trudge. Someone, or something, growing near.

"The short of it was, I gave the shiksa the dope, that made you mad, and your anger brought you here," said the Piper. "All a part of my plan. All below, that was just an appetizer for—"

"There's really no reason to yank on my rosary and let you talk," said the priest, "when I can just ease on over and dot that 'I.'"

"Well, I do have a gun." He opened his wide-lapel coat. In a holster was a sizable revolver.

"And you didn't just shoot me because why?"

"I don't follow you."

Gun, shmun, thought the priest. He had already taken a bullet that evening, and he had found it kind of fun. Of course that had been from the hot chamber of a busty heiress. He was curious, he had to admit. The clandestine dope overlord had gone to a lot of trouble. It seemed kind of rude not to wait it out. See what happened.

What happened was this: a shadow loomed on the other side of the ropes, at a corner. As it stooped and climbed through with a leaden energy, it came into the light and took a stool.

Father Dukes gasped. "Twos!"

Wally "Twos" Phelan. He had more than a foot on the priest and had lost none of his hulking power. His shoulders rippled with the ready force of a testy elephant. But he had no life in his eyes, his hair had fallen out, his skin had paled to ghostly white, and a scar stood out on his forehead and scalp where the doctors had worked to save the brain. Seated in his corner, he looked like a Frankenstein in a diaper.

"Say hello to my champion," said the Piper. "I fetched him out of the V.A. a year ago and began his training. More like a circus bear than a ballerina. But memory did most of the work. Or what memory was left after you made applesauce."

The Piper brought up the hammer and swung. The bell rung, and the old familiar peal went up Father Dukes's backbone.

And not just his, it seemed. Twos came up from his corner, fists ready. Suddenly the brain-damaged heavyweight's eyes had more light to them—almost a focus. And what they were looking at was Father Dukes.

"Wally," said the priest, "listen up. It's Mick. Mickey Muldoon. You don't—"

On he came. A great arm swung. Father Dukes scarcely had time to feint and bob. The wind from the miss blew his hair back. It was as if a city bus had leapt past his head.

The Piper rang the bell again. Phelan went blank, turned around, and returned to his stool. Father Dukes stood his ground, catching his breath.

"Take a moment to reflect," the Piper said, "on everything that led you here. On every gear and mainspring I had to put in place in order to make this timepiece run."

Timepiece? That reminded the priest.

"Do you have the time, Mr. Pipowitz?"

The Piper sneered, rolled up a sleeve. "A grown man in need of a wristwatch. Look at this one, right here. Note the gleam—the refulgent splendor of precious gold. Twenty-four karat, encrusted with diamonds. A masterpiece of horology, it costs more than your entire parish—"

"But does it tell the time?"

The Piper was about to answer, or gloat some more, when the whole building shuddered. Stacks of money fell from the desk. The Piper grabbed the corner and looked around in bewilderment. Phelan yawned on his seat and let out a string of drool.

"Never mind," said the priest. "It's straight-up midnight."

"What have you done?"

"I left my poor-man's watch downstairs, you see, on the ground floor. To time a bomb—a firebomb. Jellied gasoline and white phosphorus. Got a little help from my republican uncle. Also I scraped off a lot of match heads. By now the flames are to the third floor. What the devil started here, God will finish." The priest winked. "God or his palooka."

The Piper reeled back in horror.

"But please, do tell me more about that fine gold watch."

In a panic the Piper swung the hammer. The bell rang. The colossus rose.

Father Dukes's attention went to his own defense. One well-landed blow from the retarded juggernaut would kill him outright.

The Piper had taken a walkie-talkie from the desk. He was screaming into it: "Send the helicopter! The chopper! Now!"

A ham fist shot for the priest's head, then another. He weaved and ducked, stepping back.

He's got a reach on him! Lefty said. *You gotta swarm in and use it!*

"Use what?" The priest pedaled back from an uppercut.

You knows what!

"No. No! Not that, Lefty! Never again!"

Dis time it's different! It's for the best, boychik! Look! The Piper, he's gettin' away to the rooftop!

The priest spared an eye. Pipowitz was nowhere to be seen.

The glance cost him. Phelan half-connected on a jab, and it sent Father Dukes hard into the ropes. They twanged like bowstrings and threw the priest back toward the shambling behemoth. One arm shot forward like a battering ram. A quick slip got Father Dukes under it but put him off-balance. He rolled on the floor and came upright. Smoke was already leaking up between the boards, he saw.

No time! said Lefty. *Think of the goil. The goil!*

The image came. Sweet Jenny Stupek. One time a lightbulb had burnt out in a lamp at the church. Without being asked, the little girl had dragged out a foot ladder and climbed it, trying to put in a new bulb for her manly priest. She had met her inevitable failure with a cute stamp of her foot and a squeaky *humph!* If only she'd brought two more little Polacks to turn the ladder for her and the bulb in her hand. Those golden ringlets, now spilled onto a hospital gown. A tube up her nose. The foam on her rosebud lips. The whites of her eyes shot with red. Her little body convulsing from the overdose. The reefer. The Piper's venom.

Father Dukes screamed in fury. Phelan had come up close, a mighty fist cocked.

Time slowed as the maneuver began: the dreaded "sucker's hook." Father Dukes twirled his left fist to draw attention, and then sent it out at arm's length to one side. The dopey giant's eyes tracked it all the way out, and he turned his head, opening the sweet spot. Then came the right, a searing blur like a meteor strike, so hard that the fighting priest himself blacked out on impact.

He came out of the battle trance. The force of his own blow had knocked Father Dukes flat onto his back. The right arm lay useless, the wrist broken, the fingers curled up like the legs of a dying roach.

Above him the colossus towered. In the side of his head the fist print showed: the shape of knuckles in flesh and bone.

But the eyes were more lively now. Sleepy but there. Phelan glanced about. Something knocked loose had been jolted back into place.

Phelan glanced down, saw the priest. "Mickey?" he whispered.

But then the damage had its way, and Wally "Twos" Phelan fell once more, face forward. He struck the boards as hard as a timber. Blood trickled from both his ears.

Even in his grief the priest saw that the smoke was really spurting now. He felt the heat through the wood. The fire had reached the cache of devil weed just below him. The smoke changed color and density, pouring up through the floorboards a rich and milky white.

Before the priest could rise, block his nose and mouth, he had drawn a lungful. The toxin entered his bloodstream and flowed into his brain.

And...wait. What was he doing here, hurt like this, and hurting others? Hate and anger were only pain, after all. He looked around him at the wreckage, the smoke, the prone body. He frowned. What did he accomplish by inflicting more pain except bring it back on himself under another mask? He would have to rethink his life.

Easy, kid! Lefty said. *That's the boo talkin'!*

And what was that voice? So much was just illusion, a phantom of his own device. He, the sovereign being presently known as

Michael Muldoon, was the seat of his own torment. But he could become a lotus.

No, kid, noooo! the voice screamed. But it was already fading, already gone.

He wasn't even sure what a lotus was, but he knew he could be one. A voice from a far minaret was telling him so. By forsaking desire he could reach wisdom. The inner light. Perhaps he'd open a wellness center—

A clout, square on his head.

"Ow!" He rubbed at the welt, a pain all too familiar but unfelt for many years. He looked up.

There stood a vision of his mother in her Irish tam and shabby housecoat. Her hair the same red as his own, her face pinched, a rigor mortis of disapproval she had worn all her life. The clothes were charred and stank of sulfur. She waved the rolling pin and spoke in a brogue as thick as champ despite five generations in the New World. "Look at you, pinin' like a foakin' Loyalist twat! Find the man in you and get on that Haybrew cuntiballs!"

"Mama! Did the angels send you from heaven?"

She brushed a giant maggot from her housecoat. "Er, they did! They did at that! Now let's see us some wab, you chape lousy faggot! Up and after him, boy!"

She had already become a smoke—plenty of which had filled the room, he now saw, along with the orange firelight fanning up between the floorboards.

"Love you, Mama!" he shouted.

Sheldy Pipowitz, Esquire, alias The Piper, stood at the edge of the roof. Looking down he saw only flames, and out in the night below, crowds that had gathered to watch. The heat blew back his curls and the brightness lit up his beady eyes. He backed away.

He turned around, looked to the nighttime sky. He could hear but not see the helicopter. All around him the roof tar steamed. Soon it would bubble.

His shirt, checkered slacks, and game-show blazer were stuffed fat, as much of the gelt as he could save. The Grovers had gone in first, secured in the front elastic and Y-fly of his underpants. He imagined the tickle of the presidential whiskers. Sweet Grover, second only to gentle Ben, who was stuffed down the back and reaching for the front. "Not now, you tease, we're making our getaway!" Ulysses shifted under his shirt, a bit of nipple play. Too bad about poor Andrew, left down below. But Old Hickory had been through worse.

Pipowitz checked his gold Rado. It could tell the time in Monte Carlo, Beverly Hills, London, Paris, Rome, and Gstaad, but now all he cared about was the tick of the second hand. The chopper would only be another minute or two. His mysterious superior had sworn a five-minute exit. And his mysterious superior was never wrong, never late.

The lawyer's eyes shot to the roof access. The stairwell. Orange light flickered within and smoke billowed up. He smiled and wrung his hands together. The priest could never make it through that. Even if he survived the final bout.

And yet the Killing Floor mastermind had a moment of doubt. The priest had shown some mettle. A bullheaded tenacity. And yes, the luck of the Irish.

A noise came from the stairwell even as the chopper blades became a clear beat and underlying whoosh. Pipowitz took a step back. The roofing tar stretched between his sole and his footprint like a strand of taffy.

Oh, right: he had a firearm. Pipowitz drew it from the holster and kept a bead on the stairs. "So much for your sweet science, you shillelagh-humping paddy sheep rapist."

Behind him the smoking rooftop burst. He spun in time to see his doom: Father Dukes, sooty black, grinning wide-eyed like a one-man minstrel show of death. [*The similes of Milt Walsh do not necessarily reflect the views of Bart Lessard or the editor and publisher of* Blood and Tacos. *—Ed.*] His red hair had been singed down to a stubble and roof debris stuck to his shoulders. Sparks shot up from the exit he had just made, then the very tongues of the flames.

"Never could find the goddam stairs," said the smoldering priest.

The Piper's hand shook. The revolver tumbled free.

"Have you ever once shot that thing?" Father Dukes asked. "Set up a line of cans, maybe?"

The shyster's eyes went to the priest's deadly right. He saw that the arm was broken, hanging useless. "You're out of the match," he said, getting back his nerve. "A technical knockout."

But the left came up, and it wasn't empty. Gripped firm was the hammer the Piper had left below, the hammer used to strike the ringside bell.

"Wrong," said the priest. "Round three." He swung.

The whole oily wig seemed to dent, tucked into the cranium. The eyes popped from their sockets, bloody and agog. At first the priest thought the lawyer had stuck out his tongue. But the pinkish-beige and squiggly surface protruding from that open mouth could only be human brain.

Dead on his feet, the shyster fell aside, the hammer lodged in place. Wads of money fell from his collar and waist, flitting away on the heat-gust of the inferno.

"Now how about those macaroons?" said the fighting priest.

Cookies or no cookies he smiled, contented, ready for his victory pyre and a little family reunion. He was reaching for his hip flask—there might be a happy dribble in it yet, just a taste to tide him over before the pearly gates—when he saw the helicopter.

It came through the thickening smoke, hovering only ten yards off. The rotor wash cleared the view. The machine was not what he expected. Sleek, sinister black, with blacked-out glass. Not the sort of thing a sinful sheeny tightwad like the dead Pipowitz would choose for a rental. Instead it looked...bank-y. And fine watch or none, the Piper couldn't afford bank-y.

The priest watched the machine. He knew he was being watched in turn through that inscrutable glass—he and the cash-stuffed corpse at his feet.

And just like that, the black helicopter pitched and sped off. Father Dukes watched its flight. A corridor that led straight to the high-rises on the far side of Delaware City. Looming like hell's own fortresses. Well-defended fortresses that had to be, what, sixty floors each?

So it went farther up. Lower down. Whatever. Goddam it, he would have to live.

Dat's the spirit, pisher! Take it all the way!

"Lefty! I thought you were gone!"

A shudder interrupted the reunion. The whole building groaned and leaned. A fireball roared up the sides. The roofing tar went ablaze.

The tenement's boined through, Mick! She's comin' down! You gotta jump to the next roof!

"That's crazy!"

Just like you, boychik! It's one story shorter. If you rolls, maybe you won't break your neck!

Father Dukes made the sign of the cross. Then he crossed his fingers. With a furious sprint, he shot toward the curtain of flames at the edge

[*He makes it. THE END —Ed.*]

The street-tough priest and heavyweight boxer Father Dukes graced several softback originals stuffed into ferry terminal twirly-racks of the 1970s. But owing to the publisher's noncommittal efforts with glue binding and a soda-pulp paper stock that might best be described as "twiggy," only one fragmentary copy of this particular outing is known to have survived. BART LESSARD found it tucked into the dirty insulation behind his broken water heater. He painstakingly reassembled the gist of the missing parts by posting a question thread to the "pefo" forum on Craig's List, then trying again under "libtards" and "over 50."

BLOOD AND SWEETGRASS

in

THIS REZ IS MINE

by C.W. "Pops" McEwen

(discovered by Chris La Tray)

A LIGHT BREEZE gathered the thick cloud of marijuana smoke and floated it directly into the path of a mother and her three children. The woman wrinkled her nose and cast a dark glance up the rising slope that ended in the shade of an immense cottonwood. Her expression paled at the sight of the men sprawled there, and she put her hands on the backs of her two smaller children to hustle them forward. She hissed several words to her teen daughter, who loitered several paces behind with a smile threatening her lips. The girl rolled her eyes then quickened her pace in her mother's wake.

The gang of Gravemakers, seven men and two women, who rested in the shade passing joints and sharing a fifth of Jack Daniels, laughed and jeered. They were a rowdy bunch, aware and reveling in the discomfort their presence evoked in the more wholesome people forced to pass by them on their way to cool off in Frenchtown Pond. It was a community place, on the edge of a small town, just off I-90. Like the locals, these scruffy motorcycle outlaws were here to escape the heat of summer-come-early in western Montana. But unlike the folk splashing at the shores of the small pond in shorts and swimsuits, the bikers made few concessions to the heat when it came to their attire. All wore boots and jeans, men and women alike; some even covered their denim with leather chaps. A couple were shirtless, though most wore T-shirts or stained muscle shirts. They all wore leather vests emblazoned with the red, gold, and black colors of the Gravemakers MC, with their almost comical pistol- and machete-wielding skeleton mascot in an oversized sombrero at the center.

No one dared laugh in passing, however. Only the ignorant or the young even glanced.

If not for the marijuana, it's likely the stench of their sunburned and unwashed bodies, soured by sweat, oil, and gasoline, would have been the primary assault against the summer air. Still, the reek was not unnoticed.

"Do you never wash," a quiet voice said, "or did the back alley whores who squeezed you out into the gutter not teach you such things?"

As one, the bikers turned their heads to face the speaker. He was tall, dressed not unlike them in cowboy boots and jeans, and shirtless beneath a vest. His vest was of deer hide, however, with fringe around the bottom seam. Where Gravemaker skin was sunburned and lined, bristling with hair, his was copper and smooth. His long hair, so black as to shimmer blue in the sunlight, floated like a halo in the kiss of wind around him. He crossed his arms over the single bear claw that hung from a cord around his neck, the movement sending ripples of muscles up and down his biceps.

A large silver belt buckle at the front of his jeans was etched in swirling script: Native Pride.

The Gravemakers' faces froze, incredulous; joints half drawn upon, whiskey in mid-guzzle, laughter dying before it could pass gapped teeth.

The speaker laughed. "Do not look so surprised," he said. He glanced to the left of the bikers, where their hogs, menacing even at rest, were parked, to a young Indian woman cowering under the watchful eye of another woman in Gravemaker colors. "After all, you cannot expect to take one that belongs with the People and not expect retribution."

The gang staggered to their feet. One of the Gravemakers took two slow paces forward. He was not tall, but powerfully built; almost rectangular in shape. His hair, streaked with gray, was pulled into a single braid that trailed down his back. Pale, illegible tattoos in greenish-blue etched his chest and arms like a highway map. He spit, only half of the output making it through the patch of beard and mustache that ringed his mouth.

"And just who the fuck are you?" the biker said. "You look like Tonto, but I don't see no fuckin' Lone Ranger."

The Indian smiled, waiting for the laughter from the biker gang to subside. "My name is Blood."

"Blood? Is that supposed to scare me? 'Cuz it don't."

"It is nothing more than my name."

"Maybe I'll call you Buck instead." More laughter from his companions.

Blood shrugged, his gaze narrowing.

The Gravemaker produced a switchblade from his pocket and flicked it open, the blade glittering in the sunlight. "Well, Buck, you should know, we Gravemakers take what we want, when we want." A murmur of assent echoed his statement as the bikers produced a clatter of weapons: an assortment from blades to blackjacks to chains.

Blood didn't waver. "Not from the reservation you do not," he said.

"You ain't on the rez no more, Chief."

The Indian uncrossed his arms and squeezed his hands into fists. Veins bulged, sinews popped. "North America is my reservation."

With a yell the leader of the Gravemakers hurled his body knife-first at Blood.

Dancing aside as if his Tony Lamas were bare feet, Blood avoided the clumsy charge and with a "Hiiii-YAH!" struck a thunderous blow with his elbow against the back of the biker's neck. The man skidded face first across the weed-choked ground, the toes of his boots leaving twin trails in the dirt.

With whoops and screams the remaining bikers engaged the Indian; a stomped-up cloud of dust soon obscured the action.

Blood was a cyclone of fury, a dust devil of destruction beyond the abilities of the gang of simple brawlers. He exceeded anything they had faced or even seen before. Their lack of organization worked against them in their first rush to attack, and Blood took full advantage of it. His fists and elbows struck like hammers, his knees and feet like cinderblocks. He eschewed picking up any of the more lethal weapons being wielded against him, even though he had ample opportunity to do so. In fact, a large knife was sheathed at his back, though his grip never strayed to its carved-antler hilt.

In moments it was over. The bikers littered the ground surrounding the tree, men and women alike, moaning in pain or unconscious. Streams of gory red seeped from noses, lips and foreheads, and several limbs were bent at unnatural angles.

The Indian called Blood stood a moment, his hair streaming behind him, chest heaving, sweat glistening, surveying the battleground. Satisfied, he turned and strode to the young Indian woman who now stood near the motorcycles. She watched him approach with wide eyes and quickening breath. Her face spoke of youth while her body, in hip-hugging bell-bottom jeans and a denim halter top, declared her woman.

Blood gently took her chin between his fingers. He turned her face—angular, beautiful—from side to side to check for damage. "Are you hurt?" he asked.

"I am not injured," she said.

"Did they...?"

"They did not," she said. "They said something about a party tonight, though. That...that I should be ready."

Blood nodded, rested his hand on her shoulder, and then pointed toward the parking lot thirty yards distant. "You'll see my truck there. Wait for me."

At each motorcycle Blood gripped any wires he could and yanked them free, immobilizing the gang's means of transportation. He then moved through the fallen bikers and searched their bodies, throwing small handfuls of marijuana and pills into piles all around them and tossing aside weapons. He faced the growing crowd of people who had left the shores of the pond to bear witness to the mayhem. One boy began to clap, then a girl, and finally the adults joined in. Cheers followed.

Blood held up his hand but did not smile. "These bikers are criminals!" he said as the applause died away. "And they will not be down long. Whoever has the fastest car, or lives nearest, should go and call the police. There are enough drugs here to have them all in jail."

"I'll do it!" a man said. With a serious look on his face he ran toward the parking lot.

Blood turned and saw that the woman he had saved had not followed his instructions. Instead she stood over the biker leader, staring down with an angry look in her eyes. The man sputtered at Blood through gritted teeth. "You're dead, Buck. You're one dead fuckin' Injun!"

For the first time Blood drew his knife, then kneeled beside the biker. He held its point just before the man's eye, dangerously close to piercing the orb. "Remember my face, white man," he said. "And make sure you describe it well to your friends. Because if I see any of you again, there will be war. See me first and run. You may live." He grabbed the man's ponytail and then with a jerk of the hair and a sweep of the blade cut it free. Finally Blood reversed the angle of the blade and struck a heavy blow with the hilt against the biker's temple, knocking him back to unconsciousness.

Blood stood. The girl looked at him with wonder. "I have heard about you, Blood," she said. "I would have thought you'd kill him. I would have thought you'd kill all of them."

Blood looked away. He looked at the victims of his wrath, then at the faces of the crowd still watching him with admiration and fear. He turned his dark eyes back to the young woman. "On another day, yes, they would pay with their lives. But not today." Sirens kicked up in the distance.

"I would kill them," she said.

"Not here," Blood said. "This is a place for families."

Blood pulled his battered red '64 Ford pickup off at the truck stop at the intersection of I-90 and Highway 93. From there it was only a short drive to the southern border of the reservation. The girl went to the restroom to wash her face and hands. Blood bought a foam cooler, a bag of ice, a 12-pack of RC Cola, and two Snickers bars. He stood outside waiting for her, leaning against the bed of his truck, sucking down an RC and munching one of the candy bars.

He turned the can in his hand. It was some special edition. MLB All Stars. Rod Carew, Minnesota Twins.

Blood knew there were still many proud, brave Indians in Minnesota.

The sun was angled slightly to the west. The rays beat against the asphalt until it softened, the heat reflecting off its surface. Blood closed his eyes, feeling the heat of the truck's metal against his back, then the trickle of sweat that traced the length of his spine until it gathered at his belt line.

Traffic on the highway was a steady rush and rumble. A trucker rode his jake brake as he slowed, then turned into the lot, sputtering toward the diesel pumps, the noise more like a train than anything else.

When Blood opened his eyes the girl was approaching. She'd pulled her hair back and tied it in a loose braid. Her face was clean and fresh, her eyes large and dark. The girl was more young than woman, but Blood could appreciate the curve of her hips, the budding fullness of her chest. She came close and stopped in front of him. Blood offered her a Snickers. She peeled the wrapper halfway off, her eyes never leaving his face, then slowly eased the bar into her mouth and bit off a chunk. More sweat burst from the pores all over Blood's body as she licked a smear of chocolate that had caught on her lip. He turned to hide the flush of his face and dug into the cooler for another soda. He glanced at it, then handed it to her.

"It is a George Brett." He looked away, embarrassed. "I got a Rod Carew."

"Thank you," she said.

"We should get going," Blood said. "I have a safe place I can take you."

The two climbed back into the truck. Blood ground the gears pulling back onto 93, then turned north up the long climb that topped out at the reservation boundary.

"How did you even know about me?" the girl said, her arm out the window, her hand held into the wind so that the speed of their passage forced it up and down, up and down. "That those bikers had taken me, I mean."

"I have eyes all over the reservation," Blood said.

"More like mouths."

"Mouths?" Blood said, glancing in her direction.

"Yes, my big-mouthed aunt. She works for The Colonel."

"You should not talk about her like that," he said. "If not for her, you would likely be dead." He stared directly at her. "Or worse."

Minutes passed in silence but for the wind blowing through the open windows, the big tires whining over the highway. "They are planning something," she said. "Something big. Something to do with the powwow."

"That starts in two days. How do you know this?" Blood said.

"I heard the bikers talking about it. They made some kind of deal with The Colonel."

Blood frowned. His face flushed dark. "I knew it would come to this. It is time I had a smoke with The Colonel."

"I will help you."

Blood shook his head. "You are brave, Daniela, but such is not for you."

The girl laughed.

"Did I say something funny?" Blood said.

"No one calls me that."

"Calls you what?"

"Daniela."

"What do they call you?"

She moved closer and leaned into Blood's ear, her lips barely touching the lobe as she said, "Sweetgrass."

Night settled over the hulking log building with the large sign that read *The Colonel's Trading Post*. Night lights came on. The occasional car pulled off the highway and coasted onto the concrete pad between twin sets of gas pumps. Others pulled up in front of the building to shop at the small store for snacks and sodas.

In the lot across the highway, more lights glowed, creating pools of shadows among the dozen small shacks that advertised *Fireworks*. Days away from July 4th, the Bicentennial, a steady stream of cars pulled into the lot, even as others pulled out and headed back toward the city, away from the reservation, their illegal booty stashed in trunks and backseats.

A dark van eased into the parking lot of the trading post, away from the booming fireworks business, and disappeared behind the building. Minutes later a short, fat Indian woman exited the front of the store, lit a cigarette, then immediately threw it into the lot before going back inside.

"There is the signal," Blood said, putting aside a pair of binoculars. He waited in his truck off to the side of the makeshift fireworks lot. "Are you almost finished back there?"

"Almost," Sweetgrass said. Her fingers worked at his hair, weaving it into a tight braid. At intervals she removed something from the dash board, something that glittered briefly in her fingers, something she weaved into his braid.

"Finished," she said.

When Blood opened his door, Sweetgrass put her hand on his arm. "Let me go with you," she said.

He shook his head. "If those people leave, and I do not come back, you must warn the reservation. If I cannot stop them, it will be up to you."

"Someone needs to watch your back."

"You will be."

Colonel Judge Officer did not like to be threatened. And he was being threatened.

The Colonel was a large man, even seated behind his desk. He wore a white cowboy hat with twin braids hanging over each shoulder. A stylish tan western blazer covered his ample frame. His features were strong, if gone to fat. Two massive Indians stood behind him on either side, arms crossed, looking fierce.

The Colonel dragged on a cigarette, and then tapped the ash into a tray overflowing with butts.

Across the desk a man in a wheelchair continued to speak. "After all, Colonel, you said you could take care of things. This shit doesn't feel like 'taking care of' to me."

"A bump in the road," The Colonel said. "Nothing more than an inconvenience. There are plenty of women on this reservation; plenty of young, beautiful, and eager women."

"But my men—"

"Your men acted foolishly. You should be punishing them instead of bringing your complaints to me!" The Colonel roared, half-rising from behind his desk. "They were hardly fifty miles from here and never should have stopped. If they had done as I suggested, we wouldn't be having this fucking conversation!"

Anger gurgled beneath the surface of the man in the wheelchair's gaze. Like The Colonel, he was an old warrior, gone to fat. He had a heavy beard, though his head was shaved. He wore the colors of the Gravemakers, and the knuckles of his hands turned white as he squeezed the arms of his chair. Two Gravemaker bikers stood behind him, poised to act with the slightest signal, staring bullets at The Colonel's statue-like bodyguards.

A tense moment stretched, then the man chuckled, relaxing into his chair. "Officer, you're right. Goddamn if you are, Judge! We shouldn't let the actions of a few stupid shitheads derail a perfect fuckin' deal, now, should we?"

The Colonel smiled, though without warmth. Only his wife called him Officer, and then it was Colonel Officer, and even then only when he demanded it during sex. No one called him Judge. Not to his face, and never within earshot of anyone who may report it. "No," he said. "We certainly shouldn't."

"And the product?"

"On the grounds. Under guard in my trailer as we speak," The Colonel said.

"Then let's fucking drink!" The man in the wheelchair reached into his vest pocket and pulled out a flask, chuckling at the flashes of alarm that passed over both Indian bodyguards' faces as he did so. "To drugs and money and pussy!" he said.

The Colonel produced a flask from his own jacket and unscrewed the cap. "To business."

They drank.

"And this 'Blood' motherfucker," the man in the wheelchair said. "We don't have to worry about him fucking with us any more, right?"

"Blood will be...taken care of," The Colonel said.

The man in the wheelchair nodded. "Who is he, anyway?"

The door at the back of the room burst open in a shower of splinters and wood paneling. The corpses of the two Gravemakers who had been guarding the black van outside flopped on the floor, their throats gruesome, open gashes. A lean, dark form followed them into the room, eyes blazing.

"I am Blood," he said.

The man spun his wheelchair around to face the newcomer. "What the fu—?"

"Kill him!" roared The Colonel.

All four bodyguards leapt into action. The first came at Blood with brass knuckles; the Indian ducked under the biker's roundhouse swing and drove his knife up under the man's ribcage. The force of his blow, and the man's own momentum, buried the blade so deeply that it emerged from his back; Blood was forced to let go of the hilt or risk having the weight of the man pull him down as well.

The hesitation nearly cost him. The other biker swung a heavy sap. Blood turned away, but still took the blow on the left side of his back. The man was strong, and knew how to wield the weapon; Blood was driven to one knee.

The man raised the sap to strike again; Blood twisted his head in a half-circle, snapping his braid like a whip. The biker cried out and staggered back, dropping the sap and grasping at a spray of blood from his face. Blood came to his feet, wiping away a dripping cut on his own cheek, then smiled wickedly. He lunged at the biker, whipping his head back and forth, swinging his braid so sharply it nearly cracked. The man dropped to a knee, clutching his throat.

Blood didn't watch him die. He turned in time to see both Indian bodyguards facing him with raised revolvers. The guns boomed in the close confines of the room.

Blood dropped onto his right shoulder and rolled forward, bullets whistling just above him. One struck the side of the gashed biker's face, ending his death throes with the finality of oblivion.

Blood's booted foot kicked at the two-handed grip one of the Indian bodyguards had on his pistol, pushing the next shot into the ceiling, while Blood's other leg swept the gunman's feet out from under him. The man went down with a crash. Blood let his momentum carry him in a half-circle toward the other gunman. He came up in a crouch, swinging his braid at the assailant.

This man had seen Blood's hair in action, and sought to defend himself by catching it in midair. He screamed at the folly of his actions when four of his fingers were sheared off just above his knuckles. His thumb hung by a thread of skin and muscle, a razor blade pulled from Blood's lethal braid still embedded in the meat of his hand.

The revolver the man dropped barely hit the floor before Blood had it in his fist. He fired a single shot into the man's face, then turned and delivered two more rounds into the prone form of the other bodyguard.

Less than ten seconds had passed since Blood burst on the scene.

The man in the wheelchair looked to The Colonel in time to see a panel sliding closed in the wall, with The Colonel on the other side. Turning back around, the biker saw that Blood had witnessed the same disappearing act.

The man screamed and hit a button on his wheelchair. It leaped forward with a squeal of tires, catching Blood by surprise. The Indian was knocked sprawling to the side. He rolled to his feet in time to see the wheelchair, and its raging occupant, disappear out the shattered door he'd arrived through.

Blood wanted The Colonel, but a quick inspection revealed it would take some time to figure out the mechanism to open the sliding door. Meanwhile, the Gravemaker leader was getting away. Deciding a quick course of action, Blood went after the wheelchair.

Outside Blood could only guess which direction the man had gone. He guessed left, the shortest route around the building, and sprinted in that direction, glancing inside the black van as he passed. Blood came around front of *The Colonel's Trading Post* and skidded to a stop: there was no sign of the wheelchair or its occupant. Then the whine of a racing motor grabbed his attention.

The man in the wheelchair had gone the opposite direction from Blood and circled around. Now he was racing across the parking lot toward him. Panels in both arms of the chair dropped open, and the splatter and flare of small arms fire erupted from within.

Blood leapt behind a row of metal garbage cans at the corner of the building. A sharp pain ripped at his lower leg, telling him he'd been kissed by at least one bullet.

The turbocharged wheelchair raced by him, bounced across the field bordering the lot, and headed for the open highway.

The man in the wheelchair did not hear the howling engine of the battered red '64 Ford pickup. It roared across the highway, barely missed an oncoming motorist, and scored a direct ramming hit.

The wheelchair flew through the air as if it were a football punted by a giant. In midair the man fell from it and bounced on the ground; the Ford's momentum carried it forward, but even though she stood on the brakes, Sweetgrass could not stop it from grinding the man beneath its wheels. The lurch as the truck plowed over the sudden corpse was enough to make Sweetgrass bash the top of her head against the roof and nearly throw her out the open window.

In seconds it was over. Sweetgrass sat panting at the wheel; the door was pulled open and Blood was there. "Are you all right?" he said.

She nodded. And smiled through the lip she'd bit bloody without even noticing.

An hour later and ten miles away, Colonel Judge Officer watched from a distance as a trailer parked in the vendor area of the powwow grounds burned a bright flame against the night sky. Thousands of dollars, with the promise of thousands more, were going up in smoke, but his expression was passive. He licked his lips, then rolled up the window of his brand new 1976 Cadillac Eldorado and sighed. There would be other deals. And other opportunities to even the score with the man called Blood. The car pulled away, headed north.

Blood watched the same burning trailer, from a vantage much closer. A quick call from a pay phone to a trailer a half mile from the powwow grounds put phase two of the plan in action. A squad of young Indians had swept into the night, quickly overcome The Colonel's guards—who weren't expecting any trouble and were half drunk—and seized the contents of The Colonel's trailer, ostensibly there to sell trinkets to powwow visitors. Instead it was full of narcotics, meant to be disbursed to the crowd, in hopes of converting a whole new batch of thrill seekers into addicts. The Gravemakers would supply the product and The Colonel would share in the proceeds.

A solid plan, but for one thing. They didn't take into account a man named Blood.

"What are you going to do about The Colonel?" Sweetgrass asked. She stood beside Blood, half supporting him and his wounded leg.

"His day will come," Blood said. "We will smoke together yet, you'll see."

"I intend to be there," Sweetgrass said. "Just try and stop me."

Blood laughed. "I have already tried once, and failed. I will not try again."

He looked at her face, into her eyes, then leaned forward and kissed her. It was a deep kiss, and lingered long.

"You seem eager to try other things," Sweetgrass said when they came up for air.

"That I am," he said, his voice husky.

"I would invite you to my house, but my aunt and her big mouth will be there."

"Then I guess it is time you saw my trailer," he said.

The pair turned and walked back to the truck. They got in, and Blood pulled away from the powwow grounds. As they pulled onto the dark road that led east, away from the highway and toward the Jocko Hills, Blood said, "At least The Colonel learned one important lesson tonight."

"What's that, Blood?"

"He learned," Blood said, "this rez is mine."

THE END

C.W. "Pops" McEwen is the pseudonym for the authors Rory and Roisin McGarrity, a married couple. While squatting as members of the Cherish Wind Commune on the Northern Cheyenne Indian Reservation, they became fascinated with Native American culture, though fearful of the Cheyenne people. So rather than talk and interact with any of the natives, they chose to write about them safely from afar.

For the sake of authenticity and to establish the existence of "Pops," the couple used a photo of Andy Devine taken on his deathbed.

This first installment in the Blood & Sweetgrass series from 1976 began a franchise that would last for over twenty adventures. CHRIS LA TRAY stole this book from his uncle's bookshelf, replacing it with a library sale copy of Journey to Ixtlan *with the spine turned inward.*

BROWN SUGAR BROOKDALE
in
TITTY TITTY BANG BANG
by Chester Olden Earnest
(discovered by Thomas Pluck)

BROWN SUGAR BROOKDALE motored his chopper into the sleepy town of Titwillow and plunked his behind at the luncheonette wanting nothing more than a cup of joe and a bite to eat. From the glowers of the hardhats behind him, the blue plate special came with a free ass-whupping on the side.

The waitress, a dimpled cornsilk blonde, poured his coffee with a smile. The rest of the crowd looked none too happy to see a six-foot negro in a fringed vest and cowboy boots interrupting their meals. A signed photo of Nixon grinned at Brookdale's situation from above the kitchen window, and the floor creaked as the five burly men blocked Brookdale in.

The tallest man had a mouth tighter than a chicken's ass, but he managed to squeeze out the usual: "What you doing here, boy?"

"Having my lunch," Brookdale said. "This *is* a lunch counter."

"Just 'cause there's no Whites Only sign out front don't mean you can dirty up the seats." The big man slipped a Crescent wrench from his back pocket.

"We don't want no trouble, Burl," the waitress said.

"I hope you're not here looking for the Pussywillow Palace," Burl said. "We don't serve your filthy, uncouth kind."

Cups rattled and chairs creaked as the customers leaned to watch.

"Burl, is it?" Brookdale smiled. "Let me show you something." He tipped the pitcher of cream into his cup. "Watch what happens to this milk here."

The men stared as the cream swirled into Brookdale's cup of strong, black coffee.

Burl narrowed his eyes. "If you're talking about mixing the cream and the coffee, we call that miscellany, and it's a hanging crime." He pushed Brookdale's shoulder, but the big brother didn't budge or spill a drop.

"No. The sweet white milk messed with something strong and black, and now it's gone," Brookdale said, then sipped his coffee and smiled. "Besides, it's called miscegenation, you ignorant redneck."

"Why, you dirty—"

Burl swung his wrench, and Brookdale blocked the blow with a fierce cry. He spun from his stool and sent the thug tumbling into his friends with a mighty backhand.

Burl's hard hat clattered down the counter, and his friends caught his limp body. Brookdale calmly removed his cowboy boots.

Hammers, beater sticks, and Buck knives came out as the hardhats surrounded him.

They had weapons.

They had anger.

They had the dirty laws of Jim Crow on their side.

None of that mattered to Brown Sugar Brookdale. He had the soul of a warrior.

Forged on the Detroit streets. Fired in the white man's war in the jungles of Vietnam. Tempered into razor sharp steel in the ancient temples of Shaolin.

He beckoned them over with a curl of his hand.

They charged. Brookdale snapped a flying spin kick into the faces of the first two, sending them tumbling like bowling pins. The next man set upon him with a scarred beater stick. The kind that rolls under the driver's seat of an ignorant redneck's pickup truck; the one he calls his "negro-be-good stick."

Brookdale ducked and weaved, and the weapon shattered the spinning dessert case. He palm-struck the man in the solar plexus then twice in the face, and the stick fell harmlessly to the floor, followed by its owner.

The last man's face twisted in fear, and he jabbed wildly with his Buck knife. An old woman screamed.

Brookdale tugged his *nunchaku* from his back pocket: two pieces of a policeman's nightstick, broken in half and connected with six links of iron slave chain.

The sticks blurred as Brookdale spun and swung them, and the crowd stared at the display. The knifer swung wild. Brookdale cracked the man's wrist and sent the knife flying, then upswung into his groin.

The knife stuck in the photo of Nixon behind the counter. The crowd gasped.

As the man fell clutching his pummeled manhood, Brookdale scooped some lemon meringue pie with his finger and tasted it. "Ooh, I do like a good slice of pie."

The old woman fainted into her husband's arms.

The cook popped his big bald head out the kitchen window. "What the Sam Hill's going on here?"

"Burl and the boys started a fight, Earl," the waitress said.

Brown Sugar Brookdale peeled off bills from his thick bankroll and set them under his broken coffee cup. "For the coffee," he said. "And your trouble."

"Leave my place of business!" Earl hollered. "And you too, Alice. I told you we don't serve coloreds."

A fat man complained, "Aw, don't fire Alice! She's the last pretty girl we got round here!"

Alice threw down her apron. Brookdale picked up his boots and stepped over the moaning bodies of his foes.

Brown Sugar Brookdale had found the sleepy hamlet of Titwillow in his quest to stay after dark in every "sundown town" in America and kick some redneck ass.

Sundown towns had once been easy to spot, with signs warning black folks not to be caught in them after sunset. Only in more direct and ignorant language. The signs were gone, but not the message. Some brothers in Chicago said Titwillow had the best go-go club in the country, but any black man who dared linger would disappear.

Brookdale straddled the long-forked chopper he'd fought a chapter of Hell's Angels to acquire and fired her up. Alice the waitress slammed the door as she stepped outside.

"Sorry about your job," he said.

"I should've known better." She stomped up the road.

Brookdale kicked his bike along and followed. "I appreciate you behaving like a human being. I know that takes guts, around here."

"That and a hundred bucks will pay my rent."

Brookdale reached for his bankroll.

"I don't need your charity," she said. "You sure are free with your money."

"When I get low, I bust up a Klan meeting and steal their wallets. This part of the country's a gold mine."

"I bet it is," Alice said. "Sometimes I wonder what they make their beds with, since all their sheets are sewn up into pointy hoods."

Brookdale chuckled. "You need a ride someplace?"

"On that heap? You've got leaky valves," Alice said. "I'm surprised it's still running."

"Sounds fine to me. Maybe you should stick to waitressing."

Alice snorted. "That's just to make ends meet. I'm a mechanical engineer, and if that engine makes it another ten miles, I'll turn in my slide rule."

Brookdale frowned and revved the engine. He didn't know machines. "So what are you doing in this backwater, Lady Einstein?"

"My father's the Einstein," she said. "He was hired by Willem Cain to help with the corn crops. He disappeared, and I'm stuck here. But if I leave, I'll never find out what happened to him."

"Is that when that big go-go club opened up?"

"A few months after," she said. "You're not going there, are you? It's whites-only, and Mr. Cain's got dozens of trained guards running the place. They all know karate. They train in the cornfields, in those white pajamas."

"This Mr. Cain sounds like quite the character," Brookdale said, "but I'd rather listen on a full stomach. Where can a black man get some chow around here without getting stabbed?"

Alice pointed a finger, but it didn't direct him anyplace but up.

Brookdale followed the main road out of town. He rode until he came upon some tarpaper shacks huddled along the river, where the folks had faces like his own.

Women and children relaxed as the summer heat faded into dusk, but no men joined them. As his motorcycle approached, mothers herded their children inside and slammed the doors.

Brookdale held them no enmity. They'd been driven all the way to the waterline, and any stranger playing hero would rain hell down on them long after he left town.

As the sun dipped low, Brookdale circled back through the village and saw a man's silhouette hunched under a bridge. He parked his chopper in the weeds and shuffled to the river, where an old man sat on an upended bucket and fished with a cane pole.

"Evening, old timer."

"Hush, son," the man whispered. "Gonna scare the fish. Or worse, bring the night riders."

Brookdale hunkered down on a stone. "Bring 'em," he whispered.

"You're so tough and smart," the fisherman said. "That's what my boy Cecil thought. They took him."

"If the Klan's coming, I'll break a burning cross off in their ass."

"Didn't say Ku Klux," the old man said. "They call themselves the Sons of Cain. They live beneath us, and at night they steal our men away."

"They don't look under bridges?"

The old man gave a toothless smile. "I'm too old for what they need," he laughed. "They take white women, too."

"What do they take white women for?"

"For that club of sin," he said. "Any white girl walking alone gets grabbed up like a fish on a hook." The old man tugged the pole, and it bent double. "Just like this here," he cackled.

Brookdale hopped on his bike and roared back into town, his eyes peeled for a waitress's uniform.

The main road was empty, the windows shuttered. Not a soul dared walk the streets. Neon flickered in the distance. Brookdale headed that way.

The Pussy Willow Palace glowed crimson at the edge of town. A busty neon dancer straddled the doorway and shook her goods in a manner that would give a real woman two black eyes and a concussion.

A pickup truck with the headlights dark patrolled the club's perimeter. Men in *karategi*—karate uniforms—stood in the back. The truck stopped and the *karateka* filed out, searching alleys and buildings.

Brookdale puttered his chopper to a stop and kicked off his cowboy boots. He took his *nunchaku* and stalked his prey. As he neared the truck, Alice ran barefoot from an alleyway and screamed. Brookdale caught her and covered her mouth.

"Ready for that ride? Get on my chopper, while I take out these fools."

A dozen men in white robes boiled out of the alley and surrounded them. Brookdale uttered a harsh cry and spun through a nunchuck *kata* to keep them at bay.

Two men stepped from the alley and racked their shotguns. Burl, with his cheek swollen like half a grapefruit, and Earl, the cook from the diner. They leveled the shotguns at Brookdale's chest. "Strip him down," Earl said.

Alice rolled in on the chopper, the engine wheezing. It backfired, and the Sons of Cain pulled her from it and let the bike crash onto the pavement.

"Told you it was dying," she said, before a man's brick-breaking karate hand covered her mouth.

The Sons of Cain took Brookdale's chucks and tugged off his vest, leaving his rippled mahogany chest bare.

"Told you not to stay after sundown," Burl smiled.

Brookdale did not struggle against his bonds. A Zen man knows to reserve his strength. The truck rolled into a corn maze, and Alice bounced against him. He steadied her with his shoulder.

The trucks parked in a flattened crop circle. Burl whistled. The circle of cornfield shook, then lowered into an underground silo.

"We built all this," Alice said. "Willem Cain said he was creating a new Manhattan project, for the future of mankind. We built state-of-the-art labs, and he paid us well."

"But why's it all secret?" Brookdale asked. "If he's helping humanity, something don't jive."

"Silence," a beefy karate man said. He raised his hand, the edge horned and callused.

"I'll speak if I damn please," Brookdale said.

When he brought his hand down Brookdale twisted to take the blow, and then shouldered him above the knee. The karate man tumbled over the tailgate into darkness, his scream sharp and brief.

Two karate men knelt and chopped Brookdale. He took the blows in silence.

Light broke from below as the elevator entered a bright room. A row of white men in whiter lab coats stood waiting. A goat-like little man sporting an even whiter suit and a monocle stood in the center, tapping a jeweled, white gold cane.

The henchmen dragged Brookdale and Alice off the truck at shotgun point and threw them at the suited man's feet.

"This is the one you wanted," Burl said and bowed.

The karate men saluted. "Hail Cain!"

"Hello, Negro," Willem Cain said in a nasally clipped voice. "I hear you are talented in the ways of brutal combat."

"My name's Brown Sugar Brookdale," Brookdale said. "And I assure you, you're messing with one brutal combat negro."

"Perfect for our experiments," Cain said without lowering his gaze. He twirled his scepter and lifted Alice's chin with its spangled bulb. "You've done fallen down the rabbit hole this time, missy," he said, baring white little teeth. "Your father will be glad to see you."

"What is all this?" Brookdale asked.

Burl jabbed Brookdale with his twelve-gauge. Cain strode down the line of scientists. "I don't expect you to understand, but you are witnessing the rebirth of the world's greatest civilization. The antebellum South. When men were gentlemen and women proper."

"No one likes a sore loser," Brookdale said.

Burl cracked his cheek with the shotgun barrel. "Quiet, boy."

"You're gonna wish you filed the sights off," Brookdale said.

"And why's that?"

"It's gonna hurt more when I shove it up your ass."

Cain shook his head. "See? Gentility is a thing of the past. Lust has destroyed the Southern ideal. But I have discovered a way to harness it. Thus, I have built the biggest and greatest monument to debauchery in the nation. I have made a science of sin, to turn it back against the most powerful generator of lust on the planet." Cain whipped his scepter toward Brown Sugar Brookdale's rippling muscles. "The male negro."

Brookdale chuckled. "Well, despite the correctness of your theory, you sound about as crazy as a shi—"

Cain thumbed a jewel on his scepter. It fired a red-feathered dart into Brookdale's chest. Brown Sugar took a shallow breath and slowed his heartbeat, but the tranquilizer worked fast.

Cain frowned at him as if scolding an impertinent child. "Give him a double dose," he said. "And send sweet Alice to the Slutting Chamber."

Alice cried, "What have you done with my father?"

"You will meet him soon enough," Cain said and smiled. "He built the Jezebel machines."

For Brookdale, everything went black. And not in a good way.

Brookdale woke to the ruby glow of napalm and the lung-shaking thump of artillery in the jungle night.

"Gimme tracer fire on that berm, soldier!" Sgt. Kowalski hollered.

Brookdale leaned in to the hungry M60 and fed it a belt of ammo. Green phosphorus lasered to the target. Chief Zero, their short Pima Indian, hurled his grenade true. Three black-clad Charlies flew into the air, silhouetted briefly by shell bursts.

They cut through the VC line and mowed them down like chaff, but their glory-hound Lt. Calloway overextended again. The Cong closed the pincer behind them and cut the platoon to shreds. Alone and with nothing but Zero's tomahawk, Brookdale hacked his way through swarms of hard-fighting little men until the jungle came alive and shook and slapped him awake.

"Get up," a hushed voice said. "The fun's about to start."

Brookdale jumped to his feet and gripped the man by the chin and back of his neck, ready to snap his spine. Brown Sugar opened his eyes on a slim brother wearing nothing but a loincloth. The man froze. Behind him stood two dozen other brothers in similar attire.

"Easy! There's plenty of karate crackers if you want to kill someone."

Brookdale released the man and surveyed the room. Steel walls painted red. Windows up high, with one glass wall opening on a stage. Above, lab-coat men studied them. Spotlights strobed the stage, and saxophones blared.

"Sorry, brother."

"I'm Cecil," the tall man said. "I was the doctor in Skunk Hollow, before Cain kidnapped us." He extended a strong, smooth hand.

"I met your father," Brookdale said and shook his hand. "I'm Brown Sugar Brookdale, general ass-kicker."

Cecil chuckled. "You look like you could kick your way through half the Klan, but Cain's about to start his show. It's best if we play along, you dig? At least until you get your strength."

The men lined up by the glass, and Brookdale joined them.

On the stage, scantily clad women sashayed and bowed, facing away from the one-way mirror. Their audience lay beyond, cheering and clapping at the parade of fine white flesh.

Cecil and the brothers whistled and rolled their eyes. All shuck and jive.

Brookdale looked up at the scientists and played along. The women took turns writhing on poles and flicking their tongues. They were fine enough, but their eyes were heavy-lidded, their motions mechanical. For a connoisseur of feisty womanhood like Brown Sugar, they were as bland as Angel Food Cake.

"He's giving us a drug he thinks will cause a deadly priapism," Cecil whispered.

"A what?"

"A killer hard-on," Cecil said. He fought a snicker. The men around him winced in imaginary pain. "Come on, make it look like you're dying."

"Why should I do that?"

"He's injected us with some crazy serum that's supposed to kill us for looking at white women," Cecil said. "So grab your junk and play along. The last formula hurt bad, but this one has no effect that I can tell. Let's make 'em think it nearly kills us dead."

Brookdale shrugged and writhed on the floor with the rest of them, trying not to laugh.

After the first girl finished, a strong freckled redhead crawled onto the stage, naked as the day she was born. The crowd roared. Brookdale peeked through his mock grimace.

He winced at the expression in Alice's eyes. Her limbs moved against her will as her body played out a scene of lustful worship against the marble statue of a Greek god. Brookdale tore his face away from her humiliation and glared up at the lab coats watching.

Cain's smile flashed from above, and the bulletproof glass ate his laughter.

When the show was over, Burl and Earl emerged from the room's only door. Earl stood guard while Burl let loose with a fire hose, soaking the men and driving them to a tunnel exit.

Karate men with strange pistols herded them down the tunnels to a grimy underground cell. The water hoses reminded Brookdale of a lesson of Shaolin: It takes many years, but water can wear through a stone. He didn't have years, but he would bide his time.

And then he'd shove that scepter down Willem Cain's throat.

"Any of you know how to fight?" Brookdale asked after they received their meal pills. They tasted like chalk but filled the belly.

"We've been trapped here for months," Cecil said. "There's no way out of here, Brookdale."

"We'll see about that," Brookdale said. He stretched his neck, popping the vertebrae.

"Anyone who fights, or even rebels by not watching the sleaze show, is used for weapons testing. Pulling the trigger, or playing target."

"They make us shoot each other?"

"The guns were blowing up in the rednecks' faces," Cecil said. "Until they made us do the shooting, with another gun to our head. Then the ray guns started working."

"Ray guns? Like in *Flash Gordon*?"

"No joke," Cecil said. "They aren't perfected yet, but they'll knock you on your behind and singe off that mustache of yours."

Brookdale frowned and listened.

"From what I can tell, Professor Rutnik is the only real brains of the operation."

"Would the professor be a carrot top?"

"Why, yes he is. How'd you know?"

"That redheaded girl on stage, she's his daughter."

"We thought she escaped." Cecil looked at the floor. "Rutnik wasn't cooperating, but he'll have to now."

"If he can get me my nunchucks, I'll blow this place wide open. Ray guns or not."

Cecil chuckled. "I admire your gumption, brother. The professor supervises the injections, but we'll be under armed guard. And maybe you haven't noticed, but we've got nothing but loincloths."

Brookdale cracked his knuckles. "A warrior of Shaolin is always armed."

The shotgun twins and a half-dozen karate men led them to the science lab. The warehouse room gleamed white, cluttered with beakers, levers, and wire.

Burl prodded him ahead with the twelve-gauge. "How's your pecker feel, boy? That jungle juice making it shrivel and fall off?"

Brookdale ignored him and studied the lab. Chalkboards scrawled with scientific chicken scratch. A jet pack strapped to a crash-test dummy. A Buick convertible atop four huge electric fans. Up the line, a doctor examined each prisoner in turn and then passed him on for injection by a lanky man in a lab coat and glasses. He sported a spray of orange hair and beard and the same fierce eyes as his daughter.

Brookdale's reflexes sensed the inspection line's natural weak point. Burl had his back and Earl covered the professor, but the henchmen were scattered between the science projects. Brookdale scanned for a weapon. He froze when he saw his *nunchaku* on display in a bell jar, wrapped in copper wire. The Sons of Cain had it surrounded.

Brookdale knew how to make use of his environment, and his nearest weapon was a racist cracker with a bad attitude.

"You should get some of that serum, Burl. Might make your johnson visible without a microscope."

Burl raised the twelve-gauge to crack him on the skull. Brookdale spun and delivered a power punch to the ribs. The shotgun blast shredded ceiling tiles, and the dust fell like snow. Burl bent double and Brookdale twisted the shotgun from his hands, cracking his chin with the stock and sending him tumbling through a candy-colored collection of flasks.

The prisoners panicked, and the Sons of Cain leapt into battle. Earl aimed his twelve-gauge, and Professor Rutnik stuck him through the hand with a syringe. Earl cried out, and the shotgun barrel hit the floor.

Brookdale took two steps and leapt with a flying kick. His foot sank into Earl's belly and sent the man sprawling.

"Shoot them!" Cecil hollered, before a karate man chain punched his chest.

"No," Brookdale said. "It's not the Shaolin way." He spun the shotgun like a three-foot staff and cracked one karate man across the face, then pushed two more over a table of devices.

The air sizzled with electricity. Half a dozen karate men flew to the floor, their *gi* smoking. Professor Rutnik scowled and aimed a bulbous weapon shaped like a power drill. "Freeze," he said. "Or be prepared to eat science."

The henchmen raised their hands.

Brookdale offered the professor his hand. "Brown Sugar Brookdale."

The prof shook it. "Doctor Ernesto Rutnik. Alice told me about you. They have her in the Jezebel chambers."

Brookdale helped Cecil off the floor. "Let's lock these brainwashed bozos up and go kick some Cain ass." The brothers cheered as Rutnik handed out futuristic weapons.

"I took the liberty of supercharging your *nunchaku*," the prof said. He handed them to Brookdale. The chain sizzled with power. "Hold it by the rubber insulators and strike with the copper catalysts."

Brookdale smiled and tucked them into his loincloth.

"We'll need the guards to open doors. Cain made me install fingerprint scanners."

Burl and Earl groaned from the floor. Brookdale grinned and leveled the shotgun at their faces.

"Wait—you said that ain't the way of Chow Mein!" Burl cried.

"Shaolin, you ignorant fool. I took a vow against firearms when I joined the temple," Brookdale said. "Shooting people is not the way of the Buddha. But that big-bellied brother didn't say nothing about sticking shotguns up an evil cracker's ass."

Burl and Earl hobbled and whimpered at the front of the battle line. Brookdale followed with a twelve-gauge in each hand.

"Cain began as a philanthropist," the prof said. "Alice and I streamlined corn production, and soon it fed the poor of the entire region. He gave me free rein to develop new technologies, so I worked on my dream: the flying car. To unshackle humanity from the earth!"

"How much gas does it use?"

"That's the beauty of it—it runs on corn! When Cain saw it, he flipped his lid. Locked me up and built the Pussy Willow Palace. Here's the door."

"Open sesame, crackers," Brookdale said. He jabbed the shotguns in deeper. The two men fought to slap their hands on the palm reader. The door shushed open, and they tumbled face first on floor, the shotguns wagging like dog tails.

The Jezebel chambers were lined with silk pillows and naked, drugged women. Two bulbous white electrodes hummed from the ceiling, and the enslaved ladies fanned dozens of bare-chested karate men and tittering scientists in smoking jackets. Cain himself sat enthroned on a velvet divan atop a purple dais. Alice and three similarly overabundant stunners hung on his knees.

Brookdale spun up his electric *nunchaku* with a fearsome cry. "Party's over, peckerwoods!"

"Seize him!" Cain shrieked.

The karate men leapt from their pleasures and attacked. The nunchucks crackled like an exploding lightbulb. The first henchman flew across the room, hair puffed up like a French poodle.

"Damn, Professor!"

The chucks whined like jet turbines as Brown Sugar mowed through his foes. Brothers in loincloths fired ray guns and sent henchmen sprawling. Professor Rutnik fired at the white electrodes, which slumped and fell like deflated serpents. Women shrieked and covered themselves with pillows, free from the Jezebel machine's spell.

Cain strutted from his throne and twisted his scepter. The end sprayed open with a bouquet of spiked leather, a sizzling cat o'nine tails. He whipped his way through friend and foe, his strikes sending men to the ground clutching their limbs in pain.

"The final battle has come," he shouted. "Just as Father predicted."

Professor Rutnik fired. The ray blast ricocheted off Cain's whip.

Cain cackled. "When our housekeeper sneered that one day a man like Reverend King might be president, Father laughed and said we'd have jetpacks and rocket cars first!" He cracked the whip and struck Professor Rutnik down. "And you, you brought that terrible future to pass!"

"You madman," Rutnik said. He clutched his singed hands. "We could have fed the world!"

"I had to return humanity to its glorious past," Cain said. He raised his whip in a finishing blow. "You left me no choice!"

"Wake up and taste the future!" Brookdale sailed over the fracas and took the blow. The cat o' nine tails striped his back. He landed at Cain's white-loafered feet.

"Never! Your kind were not meant to rule!"

The air crackled as Brookdale snapped through a lightning *kata*. The sparks reflected in Cain's monocle, mirroring the fear in his eyes.

Cain raised his whip to strike. Brookdale pounded him with a sizzling tattoo of blows, driving him toward the wall. Alice, clad in the bloody *gi* of a fallen warrior, took up a ray pistol and blasted the wall behind him. Cain tumbled through the gaping hole onto the stage of the Pussy Willow Palace.

Brookdale leapt onstage with a fearsome howl and brought his foot down on Cain's chest. Men scattered and women screamed as they beheld the terrible fury of Brown Sugar Brookdale and his ear-splitting war cry. Cain collapsed in a heap, his scepter-whip rolling slowly off the stage.

Sweaty men dropped their dollars and stampeded for the doors. Brookdale snapped his chucks at the stage curtains, unleashing a lightning bolt which set them ablaze.

He turned his blood-streaked back on the shrieking mob of Southern elite and helped his brethren herd the enslaved women through Cain's conquered lair to their freedom.

The shrine to Babylon collapsed in flames. Cecil led the freed men home to Skunk Hollow, keeping the professor's weapons for the next time evil came to town.

Alice blotted Brookdale's wounds with a wet cloth as her father showed off the flying Buick Electra 225.

"You turn the stereo to FM and pop the cigarette lighter, and it turns back into a normal Buick," he said.

"I'll take it," Brookdale said.

"Daddy, let him rest," Alice said. She wore a pair of horn-rimmed glasses, her red locks thrown back wild. "What will you do now, Brown Sugar?"

"I should return to Shaolin Temple and pay my respects," Brookdale said, climbing into the driver's seat. "But Cain got me to thinking. If we've got flying cars, maybe it's time this country had a bad-ass black president, someone who'll show those oil sheiks who's boss and get us out of this endless war in Asia."

Professor Rutnik rubbed his chin. "I'm not sure the world is ready."

Alice slid over Brown Sugar's lap to the passenger side. "Let's blow this crazy corn town."

Brookdale arched an eyebrow. "I offered you a ride this morning, and you flipped me the bird."

"I like 'em big, strong, and not as smart as me," Alice said. She squeezed his arm. "Besides, you'll need me to fix this thing."

The professor held up a pistol. "You sure you don't want a couple of these?"

"The last thing we need is a ray gun in the White House." Brookdale laughed and gave the Buick some gas. The fans lifted it off the ground with a whine of chopper blades. "Besides, I don't need a gun to break my foot off in Tricky Dick's ass!"

Alice clutched his arm as he raced the Buick into the warm black night.

THE END

"Brown Sugar" Brookdale, the black Vietnam Vet kung fu master who "broke his bare foot off in the ass of The Man," was the creation of Chester Olden Earnest. Brookdale went through many incarnations. He was originally created when Earnest, a Harlem protege of Richard Wright, saw the success of, but did not read, the plantation pulp novel Mandingo. *Earnest assumed the title referred to an Australian aborigine who could transform into a were-dog to fight injustice.*

The first Brookdale novel, Brother Coyote, *reflects this. Brookdale was cured of lycanthropy in the second volume, where he encounters the eponymous Witch Queen of New Orleans. Our selection came late in the series and shows how Earnest successfully merged social consciousness with the martial arts novel.*

THE ALBINO WINO
in
LONGHAIR DEATH FARM
by Clifton Wetzel-Bulinger
(discovered by Cameron Ashley)
"This time...they've hunted the wrong albino!"

BRONTE FOX slid a pale couple of fingers through the fencing that divided them and stroked the Albino Wino's head. "They hurt you," she said.

The Wino sat up, pulled away from her touch. He inspected his swollen face with his own large, rough hands, and, noting his split lips, he spat out a viscous glob of blood and mucous-flecked saliva upon the straw that lined his cage.

How long had it been since his arrival here at this death farm? Weeks, easily. His hands shook. He needed a drink. Outside of a homemade merlot that Theseus Jones, the leader of the longhair cult that kept him prisoner, shared with him right before his thrashing, he had gone pretty much sober.

There was a small minibar bottle of cheap rum he kept against his genitals in times of true emergency. And as true emergency was undeniably now, he pulled it free from its hiding place and drained half of it. It was nowhere near enough, but the rum's warmth spread down his throat and into his belly. He lay down in the fetal position (as close as he could get to a full stretch in this welded-together coop) and thought back to how it had all began.

He remembered being sick and tired of the city: Vietnam protestors, music gone to shit, the vestiges of Flower Power clinging more tendril than blossom to the culture at large. Concrete so hot it seemed to sweat. Being rousted from shady spots by cops who had more booze on their breath than he did, traces of whores' smeared pink lipstick on their crotches, bad intentions in their baton swings.

He remembered a brawl with the Silver Dragons, an Oriental street gang from Chinatown who picked on the homeless both for fun and to practice their roundhouses. The ensuing fight, ten-on-one with the one handily winning, was broken up by a big side of beef of a cop who saw the chance to vent some aggression on a stone drunk albino man just trying to get by.

The back-alley brawl was already won, silver satin-jacketed youths sprawled everywhere, their mean streaks punched out of them, at least for now. The cop saw the Wino standing at alley's end, blood dripping from his skinned knuckles, a butterfly knife stuck clean through a segment of thigh. A filthy circus freak, grubby as a pit fighter, pale as the Angel of Death. The cop went straight for him, nightstick swinging like a rotor blade. Little did he know that the Silver Dragons weren't the only cats in town who knew some kung fu. The Wino had learned much in his years on the road.

The Albino Wino blocked the first attempt at a braining, grabbing the cop's wrist, snapping it, and peppering his body with palm strikes and chops. The cop staggered back, snarled, and scooped up the fallen nightstick with his good hand. The Wino grabbed it as it swung towards him. He snatched it from the cop's grasp at the very same moment he pushed the big cop back with a front kick.

The Wino snapped the nightstick over his knee in a hopeful display of don't-mess-with-this-super-whitey and said, "Stop."

The cop shouted, "Screw you, pinky!" and pulled his gun. The Wino hurled a sharp shard of nightstick—he aimed for the gun barrel, but his aim was off, brain fuzzy from some strikes taken in the brawl with the Dragons.

The shard of nightstick buried itself in the cop's jugular. The cop cried out and dropped the gun. He pulled the stake-like piece of wood from his throat. Arterial spray graffitied the alley walls, and he fell dead.

The Albino Wino knew he had to split. When the establishment and the anti-establishment were as bad as each other, all a man had was himself, his American know-how, his fists, and his will to survive. The world was going to hell. It was no place for one as distinctively snowy-haired and as alien-eyed as he.

The Wino pulled the knife from his thigh. Just a flesh wound. He bound it tight with two tied-together bandanas and looked around for Chalky.

Chalky sat on a trashcan, the bloodied-up corpse of an alley rat in his mouth. As usual, when the Wino found action, Chalky had to have some, too. The Wino scooped up the albino cat, who purred at his touch and closed his eyes, one sky blue, the other emerald green, contentedly as the Wino wrapped him up in his bindle.

The Wino pulled a bottle of something cheap from his mid-size knapsack and took a healthy pull. He came up for air then went in again and drained the bottle.

It was time to hit the road.

It was whimpering that woke him. At first he thought it was Bronte Fox, but even in the half-light he could tell that the beautiful albiness was not the source.

It was the man in the third cage.

Bronte crawled to the cage wall that separated her from the Wino. "You passed out. It's Johnny. They took another piece."

In truth, all the Wino wanted to do was stare at Bronte, luminous in the moonlight that filtered through the cracks and gaps in the barn. She was unearthly and elven in her beauty, full-lipped and armed with eyes a hypnotising streak of light blue. Her hair seemed spun of stars, cascading over her slender shoulders.

Johnny cried again, and the Wino wrenched his eyes off Bronte and focused on the whimpering mess on the floor of the third cage. The Wino knew little about Johnny. He was the first captured of the three; that much he knew, and he knew it only because Bronte had said as much. He didn't care for Johnny, who was a bearded longhair himself—belonging more to the obsolete tribe of hippies refusing to give up their naive dreams of transcendental trips and free love than to the clan of the outcast albino. The Wino knew that there was no place but the here-and-now and that absolutely nothing was free. Johnny hadn't done himself any favors either, for when the cult members came for him, he begged off, pleading with the shotgun-wielding longhairs to take the Wino first, or Bronte, if only they would spare him. He returned hours later, unconscious and minus an arm.

The other arm had been taken this time. And a foot. Soon there would be nothing left.

As Johnny tried to push himself up off his piss-stained straw with nothing but stumps, the Wino cracked a smile.

Bronte looked at him. "Why are you smiling?"

The Wino playfully put an index finger to Bronte's nose. "Honey, we need something to toast with. Champagne would be perfect, but I'll quaff the fumiest, most blindness-inducing hooch from the filthiest inbred-owned still if that's all we could get."

Bronte's brow furrowed. "Why?"

"They're savin' us, honey. They're savin' us for later. We got time to make a plan. Maybe not a lotta time, but we can get outta here."

Now it was Bronte's time to smile. "We?"

The Wino touched her hand. "Yeah, *we*. You may be just some rich albino girl gone off the rails, but I ain't letting something as beautiful as you end up in some crazy hippie's stew."

Bronte placed her forehead to the cage bars, her lips poked succulently through the metal lattice. The Wino rinsed his mouth out with a swig of rum from the minibar bottle, thought about spitting it out, but swallowed instead. As his lips met hers, the chanting started from outside. The longhairs were feeding.

"You're special, man, don't ever forget that. What you got, what you are, man, the universe has blessed you, man." That was what the male longhair said to the Wino shortly after he and his girlfriend picked him up.

The Wino was averse to hitchhiking, but he needed to split the city and split it quick. The car picked him up ten miles outside the city limits, passing him at first, then stopping and eventually reversing back to where the Wino walked along the roadside.

It was the girl who convinced him to take the ride, strawberry blonde and braless. If longhairs did one thing right, it was that their women didn't mind showing what they had and sharing it around. The girl could've filled out a sweater two times larger than the one she wore. She smiled and beckoned to him and told him they were going more than halfway towards where he wanted to be. Still, the Wino was suspicious. It was the cop car that tore past, sirens blaring, heading right back from where he'd come from that convinced him, finally, to accept the ride.

It was the biggest mistake of his life.

They gave him beers and called him "man" and asked about his life.

They mocked the war, they mocked the establishment, they mocked the president, they mocked all but the place where they were headed.

The Wino, beer-buzzed, felt his lips loosen, felt a rant coming, felt the urge to tell them that their side, their bullshit "counterculture," was just as bad as the Man was, and that the only way out was to be alone—was for a man to forge his own path, seize control of the universe by the throat, and punch destiny in the face until it yielded.

But he made not a peep, which was strange because he wanted to.

And then things blurred and went spacy and for a moment he thought that maybe they were right, these hippies, maybe, just maybe, there *was* something more, something other, something beyond. But no. It was just the Mickey Finn the dirty, cheating longhairs spiked his beer with.

And then he woke up caged. A beautiful woman next to him on one side, a whimpering, spineless geek on the other. Each of them "special." Each of them caged. Each of them afflicted with albinism.

And then he met Theseus Jones.

Theseus Jones was tall and thin and had a pock-marked face indicative of childhood chicken pox or acne so bad it would make the world itself blush for you.

The Wino was brought before him by two longhairs so put together that they clearly were on a diet of more than just lentils—an observation that proved apt once the Albino Wino learned what it was, exactly, that went down here.

He didn't see much of the compound's property on the trip up to the main house—thrown into the back of a pickup truck, one Longhair Charles Atlas driving, the other in the back with him, pointing a sawed-off in his face—just that it was as large and unkempt as the armpits on a longhair dude's old lady.

The main house was just a large, open space. Naked couples lay on cushion-covered floors, intertwined, locked at the genitals. The Wino's albino eyes struggled to adjust as he was dragged past the armed guards at the door, through the squirming masses, to Theseus Jones himself, who sat on an oversized wicker chair that looked like some abominable longhair throne.

The big longhairs dropped him at Theseus' feet. The Wino looked around, waiting for his eyes to focus, waiting for what seemed to be one huge, moaning, soft-skinned, writhing organism to cease its amorphousness and bleed out into separate shapes. Once it did, he looked up at Theseus who wore a crooked-toothed grin. A woman was on her knees before the cult leader, fellating him. She groaned as though hypnotised by the swollen organ between her jaws.

Theseus introduced himself and then said, "I like you. What's your name?"

The Wino replied, "They call me the Albino Wino."

Theseus chuckled. "Kooky handle, man."

The Wino shrugged. "It fits."

Theseus leaned across the arm of the wicker throne and produced a wine bottle. He uncorked it and handed it to the Wino. "Try it. Homegrown."

The Wino shook his head even though the urge was strong. "Had enough of your booze in the car. I'm all napped out, thanks very much."

"It's not drugged, I assure you, man." Theseus himself drank heartily. He held the bottle out for the Wino, who took it on this second offering.

Drinking deeply, the Wino said, "You gonna tell me why I'm here, or we just gonna sit around and get drunk? That's cool with me, but if you're looking for me to participate in...this"—he gestured at the longhairs humping like animals on the ground in more positions than he knew existed—"you gotta know I ain't no swinger."

Theseus went to speak but stopped himself. "One moment," he said right before he ejaculated furiously.

The Wino went to avert his eyes, but there wasn't many a place to avert them to.

The woman in front of Theseus got up off her knees, wiped her mouth, and winked at the Wino as she passed. It was the longhair chick from the car, the one who spiked his beers and bewitched him with her breasts, now on full display, slapping together meatily with each footstep.

"You're next," she said, winking and running her fingers through the curling flaxen thatch between her legs. She disappeared through the copulating masses, a naked, golden-haired apparition treading lightly amidst a vibrating minefield of flesh.

The Wino drank deeply from the bottle. Good hooch. Not that he'd admit it to Theseus. "Okay, what the hell is going on here?"

Theseus laughed some more and tucked his member back into his linen trousers. "All in good time, man. First I need some medication..." He snapped his fingers, and a young girl appeared, fourteen at most. Timid and flushed, she was dressed in a sheer white dress. She held a large tray, lines of powder expertly placed upon it. Alongside the lines was a small, hollow tube, carved from wood and stained near black. Theseus patted the girl on the head, picked up the tube, put it to his nose, and snorted up the lines.

The Wino shook his head. "Coke? That shit'll rot your brain."

Theseus wiped his nose, beckoned the girl to leave. He said, "That's not coke, man. That's *bone*. Grade-A albino bone."

The Wino almost dropped the wine. "What?"

"That's right," Theseus pointed at The Wino. "Your kind, you got the magic in you, brother..."

The Wino lunged for Theseus, managing, just, to get a hand to the cult leader's throat before the big guys came back. The Wino went to fight, but the drugs were still residually with him and his reflexes were off. It didn't take long before things went black again, this time far more unpleasantly.

Time passed and became something slippery. Counting the minutes was like grabbing fistfuls of running water. His minibar rum bottle emptied, here came the delirium tremens—nausea, trembling, fever. Unable to hold down the plates of gruel and boiled vegetables.

The tale unfolded in a fever-dream, at times narrated by Bronte, at other times narrated by Theseus himself, who may or may not have actually come to visit. Theseus as African Missionary, sent to save, finding only superstition and black magic. The myth of the albino as something magical, possessed with healing powers.

The Wino saw African albinos brutally slaughtered, their flesh consumed, their bones ground to powder and ingested. A lifelong migraine sufferer, Theseus was offered the services of an albino girl. He took her and was healed. He still wore the girl's powdered thumb bone in a vial around his neck.

A powerful speaker, a charismatic man, Theseus founded this longhair death cult, hopped up on the bones of American albinos, hunted and captured by roving teams, prepared by jaded ex-hippies burned by Vietnam, by Manson, by Altamont, their dreams soured, fighting the awfulness of the new America with a greater awfulness. All of them warped through indoctrination and cannibalism. There was no denying their health, however—this, Bronte could attest to, as every second night, she was sent to "cure" some ailing cultist of his "affliction" through sex magic she had no idea she possessed.

One day, Johnny, little more than a bobbing torso by this point, did not return. The Wino knew that he and Bronte would have to make good on their escape plans.

He looked deep into Bronte's eyes and said, "This here horrible shit can no longer stand."

The weapons at the Wino's disposal:

The empty minibar bottle he still kept nestled against his genitals so that he could inhale the dwindling fumes and transport himself to seedy big city bars.

And:

The uncanny, almost alien sexuality of Bronte and, apparently, his own uniquely musky brand of rugged albinism.

It was the couple who had picked him up and drugged and captured him that showed the most interest. She had made her own curiosity and arousal known at the Wino's first meeting with Theseus. Her boyfriend, or whatever you would like to label him, was clearly enraptured with Bronte. He had had his share of her, Bronte told the Wino, but so taken was he that he spent more time stroking her ivory skin, her alabaster hair, than he did penetrating her.

The Wino couldn't blame him. Bronte was a mesmerist, unaware of the extent of her own loveliness. Should they escape this death farm, the Wino fully intended to probe whatever magic lay beneath the colorless cloud of her ghostly pubic hair.

The couple came essentially unarmed. She with a kitchen knife, he with a pitchfork. They stood nervously in front of the cages, lit by twilight cascading in through the open barn door—a young, stoned, sensual, hippie version of the couple in Grant Wood's *American Gothic*.

The Wino pleaded with them for booze. So drained was he from withdrawal that the only way he could sexually perform was with a spiritual fortification that had less to do with Jesus or Buddha and more to do with Jack Daniels and Johnny Walker.

And so eager were the couple for extended healing sessions that they complied, smuggling in cups of some feral moonshine that tasted of potatoes, oranges, and bakery goods. Whatever it was, it did the trick. The Albino Wino was shortly restored.

The initial escape was easily done, after three nights of not at all unpleasant copulation, the four of them loosed upon the barnyard dirt. Freed from their cages by the longhair male—who, it turned out, was some sort of trustee, possessed with a set of keys to everything on the farm, and bewitched into rule-breaking sexual sessions through Bronte's longing, lingering gazes. On the third night of these clandestine moonlight rendezvous, the girl let their fate slip.

"Thank you," she said, "for spiritually fulfilling me and healing my debilitating hepatitis with your seed."

The Albino Wino fumbled for his pants while the girl played with the fine gossamer of his chest hair. "What are you talking about?" he asked.

The girl rolled off of him and turned to her side, her back to the Wino. "Tomorrow," she said sadly, "Theseus will take your arms for the ritual..."

The Wino rubbed his face. "Tomorrow..."

Bronte, feigning sleep, visibly stiffened in the moon glow. She and the Wino exchanged a glance, a nod. The Albino Wino rolled, uncovered from a clump of hay the smashed top half of the minibar rum bottle, and grabbed it by its stubby neck. Springing to his feet, he leapt upon the longhair male and raked the jagged edge of the bottle across his throat. Bronte gave a short shriek as the blood spray painted her bosom and face, streaking her hair pink.

The longhair girl fell agog at the sight. Bronte Fox, bloodlust and, yes, possibly envy building up inside of her, called for the girl's blood. Bronte fell atop her like a snowy blizzard. The girls, both naked still, writhed upon the ground until Bronte plucked an old horseshoe from the hay and bludgeoned the girl to death with it.

Covered in gore, but semi-clothed at least, the duo snuck out of the barn. The night was cool but clear, and under the moonlight the

Wino and Bronte seemed as though one with the stars, beautifully iridescent, a constellation of two—the Vengeance Seekers, perhaps, one day to rise above this mortal coil to sit beside Orion the Hunter.

The Wino clutched the longhair male's pitchfork, Bronte the girl's kitchen knife. The lights in the compound's main house glowed in the distance. Theseus would be in there, fornicating and snorting the bones of their pale brothers and sisters.

They met little resistance on the way to the main house, and what resistance they did meet, they dispatched like spear-hurling primitives, pitchforks rocketing javelin-like into jugulars and sternums. Their opposition, conditioned by spiritual nonsense to believe that these beings in all their albinistic glory were something other than human, were defeated at the mere sight of them as they creeped like pale spectres through the scrub.

The most troublesome were the two large longhairs who had given the Wino his beatings. But by the time the Wino and Bronte encountered them, they had firearms. The Wino shot out their kneecaps and left them writhing on the ground, giving them something to think about. With each cult-sentry dispatched, so did their arsenal increase, inevitably to the point where so burdened were they with weapons that many they left with the dead.

Cultists, roused by the fighting, fled through any available exit. The Wino and Bronte shot as many as they could. Vengeance is a black and murky beast that clouds judgment and dampens all sense of kindred humanity at the best of times, but the Wino felt no kinship with these cannibals; the world would be better off without them. The chaos, the storm of people fleeing, helped protect them from the gunfire of those remaining. The Wino lost his right earlobe, torn free by a lucky shot. With blood trickling down his pulsing neck, the Wino unloaded with return fire, blowing the shooter's brains out the back of his head.

By the time they discovered Theseus Jones, sleeping still in some drugged stupor, a trio of buxom beauties by his side, the Wino and

Bronte were surely fixed to fight an army of trained killers, never mind this lot of beardy, tripping rabble.

The women fled screaming but were gut-shot by a grim-faced Bronte, the red mist far from settled in her eyes.

"I can make you a God," Theseus said upon awakening to find the Wino poking the barrel of an AK-47 in his face.

The Wino shook his head. "I don't want control over no man, no institution, or no cause," he said. And with that, the great Theseus Jones closed his eyes, clasped the vial around his neck and was turned into a bloody, chopped-up cadaver in a hail of righteous gunfire.

They found the still, and the Wino drank deep. Having had their fill of killing, they let the remaining cultists run free. The little girl who served Theseus his bone powder caught the Wino's eye. She mouthed the words *thank you* and was gone before the Wino could respond.

Bronte shared a drink with him, coughing the moment the shine hit her lips. The Wino laughed and drank some more. With breath like gasoline, the couple headed off into the night.

Some ways down the trail that led to the highway, a mewling was heard.

"What was that?" Bronte said.

The Wino shushed her with a pasty index finger to her lips. A blinding flash erupted from the scrub, leaping into the Albino Wino's arms.

"Chalky!" the Wino exclaimed. "Drawn by the scent of the poisonous hooch on my breath, no doubt. Thanks for waiting around for me, buddy."

Chalky, apparently none the worse for wear from waiting weeks for his master, purred and nuzzled the Wino's snowy beard. The Wino turned to Bronte. "You ain't got no allergy to cats, I hope? This little guy's been with me through hell and back, and I ain't about to throw him over for some piece of sweetmeat."

Bronte Fox answered by scratching Chalky under the chin and passionately kissing the Wino on the mouth. Tongues doing the Watusi together under the full moon, the Wino finally pulled free. He said, "I swiped us some cash from some dead longhair fool. Let's you, me, and Chalky find us a place we can get us something good to drink."

With that, the trio headed for the highway, on to bigger adventures and deadlier foes.

THE END

Keep an eye out for the magnificent return of the Albino Wino in his next white-knuckle adventure:
A PALER SHADE OF WHITE!

Special thanks to CAMERON ASHLEY for contacting Clifton Wetzel-Bulinger directly. A lot has changed since this story was published in 1978, and we appreciate Mr. Wetzel-Bulinger's bravery in agreeing to reprint the story, considering that he is now the Poet Laureate of the Isle of Man (best known for his villanelle "Alabaster Rainbows"). Look for the subtle social commentary that marks all his work, as well as his trademark albinocentric underpinnings.

DEAD EYE
in
END OF THE RENAISSANCE
by Guy Rivera
(discovered by Ray Banks)

THEY WERE HEADED for Yuma, six of them in the back of an open truck, another two squeezed into the cab. They'd been travelling for a couple of hours when they saw the young Mexican kicking dirt by the side of the road. The Mexican wore a dark suit, and a pristine white shirt. On his feet were black cowboy boots with silver spurs that jangled every time he dug his toe into the dirt. He carried a white stick in both hands. Behind his sunglasses, his sightless eyes were open and dead in their sockets. He said his name was Victor Cruz, and he was grateful for the ride.

Eduardo, a talkative man with a farmer's accent, was the one who told Cruz where they were going. There was work in Yuma, he said. They were trying to rebuild, start again. Cruz nodded like he was listening, but all he really heard was an old story badly told. There was no hope in Yuma. There was no hope anywhere.

After a while on the road, Cruz closed his eyes, a force of habit, and felt himself drift, the gentle rocking of the back of the truck like a hand on a cradle.

The workers smelled of stale sweat, even staler mescal and nickel cigars. They chattered about television, the US Army rerun favorites that had the main character's name in the title—Lucille Ball, Mary Tyler Moore, Dick Van Dyke and Carol Burnett—and then they talked about drinking and gambling and their families. They complained about money, and there was a brief spate of filthy joke one-upmanship, culminating in a long story about a vaquero's daughter with a snatch like a bucket. The man sitting across from him had too much phlegm in his throat and he breathed heavily.

He told a joke about Eduardo's mother. Eduardo exploded in mock rage. There was laughter, a chorus of jeers and some horseplay—slapping and play-fighting—before Eduardo's voice cut short and a warm spray hit the side of Cruz's face.

He opened his eyes, but saw nothing. He felt the air buffet at his right, Eduardo toppling forward into the middle of the truck. The other men panicked. Shouting, moving around, a lot of noise.

They were so loud that Cruz barely heard the second shot.

One of the front tires blew. The truck fishtailed. Cruz hung on. He turned his face upwards. The sun was gone, so they were in the mountains. Which meant there was a sniper up there somewhere and his aim was good. Cruz yelled at the men to jump. He felt hands on him, guiding him to the back of the truck as it careened off the road. Then he leapt, airborne for split-second before he dropped to the ground, kneeled into a roll which he broke by digging his stick into the dirt and hoisting himself upright. He heard the men scatter around him, looking for shelter. He heard them yelling at each other.

Then he heard the other men. They shouted in bad Spanish and better English. They were broad-voiced, professional bullies, the kind of men whose confidence came from the large guns they pointed at small people.

Cruz spat the foul taste out of his mouth and turned. The men continued to yell in a monotone. "Get on the ground, face down, palms flat, mouth to mud, mouth to goddamn mud." He heard the workers do as they were told. He tapped one of them with his white stick as he walked past. They were all on the ground. That was good. It meant they wouldn't get in the way.

Another shout, rising in pitch. The man shouting at him was keyed up and obviously armed, and there was already too much blood in the air for him to take it easy.

"Get your ass in the dirt, Pedro. Mouth to mud."

Cruz stopped. His left hand moved to the top of his white stick, his thumb pointed up. One man in front of him, over six foot in height, the smell of fresh sweat on him and something else, unnatural, coming in small bursts, punctuated by a wet clicking sound that came from his mouth.

Juicy Fruit.

The gum, accent and psychosis added up to an American, and not a soldier, but Army trained. A merc, then, and a cocky one at that.

He felt a punch in the middle of his back. "You deaf? Down on the ground."

Similar height to Juicy Fruit. He'd shoved with his right hand, which put the gun in his left and made him a southpaw. He heard the scuff of a boot about thirty feet away behind him to his left, at about eight o'clock. A cleared throat belonged to another merc about ten feet behind the Pusher. That was four. Probably at least another two in the pickup that rumbled at one o'clock, no doubt blocking the Mexican truck's path. This new pickup was a customized Dodge, the chassis hanging low and most likely armored. It was tooled under the hood, a high-horse police interceptor engine with a nitro feed. That kind of customization was a white man's folly, and one that required money, just like this small private army that surrounded him.

Six of them, maybe more, armed with machine guns and God only knew what else.

Cruz liked those odds. They were interesting.

"Goddamn it," said the Pusher. He scuffed his boot, telegraphed his move to shove another square hand against Cruz's back.

Cruz dropped, twisted, let the white stick show itself as a shikomizue, separated now into blade and cane, and then he lifted the sword high, hard and tight. He jammed the sword up under Pusher's ribs and swung him round as he heard the thump of rifle butt to Juicy Fruit's shoulder. Juicy Fruit unleashed a bark of bullets that tore the scream from Pusher just as quickly as they tore through his back. Cruz leaned in, found Pusher's sidearm with his free right hand, pulled it upside down and squeezed the trigger with his little finger until he heard Juicy Fruit hit the dirt. He straightened, tossed the sidearm, kicked Pusher from the blade and then dropped to where Pusher's rifle lay. A rattle of machine gun fire tore up the ground by his knee. Cruz span, pointing the rifle at the source, let rip in a tight arc, round after round punching through flesh, metal and rock before the clip snapped empty. He tossed the rifle, picked up his sword and rose through a blanket of smoke.

Someone behind him, approaching slowly. Cruz waited, played dumb until the sneak was within range, and then swiped a high boot across his face. Spur caught cheek, there was a brief sound of skin flapping like a pennant in a strong wind, and then Cruz lunged with the sword. The sneak grabbed Cruz's shoulders. Cruz pushed him off and heard him drop.

Breathing hard. Throat dry. Again, waiting.

If there were any alive and well, they'd try to kill him. They always did.

But there was something else. A slow clap that sounded as if it came from the Dodge. Cruz raised his head.

"Very good, Mr. Cruz."

Cruz smelled ozone, heard a crackle off to his right, growing louder.

And then something grabbed him by the heart and the world shattered into nothing.

He awoke to the smell of a woman, the touch of a woman and the voice of a woman telling him to be still. He ignored her, tried to sit up, but someone had replaced his spine with an iron rod and his head with a cement block. He grunted in pain and felt himself weaken. The woman hushed him back to the pillow. She spoke Spanish, she was young and she smelled like the air after it rained. She had a voice that spoke to him from the past, reminded him of girls who were too pretty to talk to, and for a second he felt like drifting off again.

"Where am I?" he said.

"Fort Johnson." She moved a cloth over his forehead. "You are a guest of Captain Glenister."

"Guest?"

"Yes, señor. He looks forward to meeting with you."

Cruz moved away from her. The simper of the "señor", the lightness of her touch and her cowed manner told him she was a whore. She stayed away as he shifted himself upright and gritted the pain away long enough to swing his legs over the edge of the bed. His boots found a stone floor. He tapped the floor with one foot. They'd taken his spurs. He felt the girl move to the end of the bed, heard her dip the cloth in water. He stood slowly and stamped his boots a couple of times, just to hear the echo. He was in a small room, open to a corridor to his left. He went over to the open space and his hands found bars. He breathed out. No spurs, no stick, and a whore to keep him company.

"What's your name?" he said.

"Rita."

"What is this place, Rita?"

"This is Fort Johnson. This is Captain Glenister's new settlement."

"A building?"

"A town. Built by us for them."

"Them?"

"The Renaissance Men, señor."

The Renaissance Men. Of course. Back before the Wall, there had been a border, and that border had been patrolled by a group called the Civil Defense Corps. These men and women good and true used to pack high-caliber hunting rifles into their armored trucks and go looking for wetbacks to cap.

Good clean American fun.

When the Wall went up, the corps members lucky enough to have made it to Mexico or the Upper States became Minutemen, Wall walkers. They were cowardly scum to a man, smug and fat and safe behind the scope of their sniper rifles, and Cruz had already burned a few on his travels, but they were saints compared to The Renaissance Men. The Minutemen went home at night; The Renaissance Men continued fighting their good fight and broadcasting their white power propaganda to what was left of the nation. Captain Glenister must have been this chapter's leader. It wasn't a name he knew, but he would soon enough. Because Glenister had known his name, and that spelled trouble of a different sort.

"How many of us are there?"

"I do not know, señor. Hundreds, maybe a thousand. The men they keep in barns down by the river, the women in dormitories by the big house. The men work until they fall."

"And the women?"

"We are for play."

He returned to the bed and took Rita's hand in his own. He touched something rough and raised on the back of her hand. "What's this?"

"They mark us, señor, they—"

He put a finger to her lips. She breathed warmly against his touch. He leaned in to her. "Tell me everything you know about this place, Rita. And tell me as quickly as you can."

He counted the steps from the cells to what Rita had called the big house. Two armed guards flanked him. They were both taller than him and they didn't speak much. They smelled of good sleep, old sex and chewing gum.

Rita had spelled it out for him, every last inch of it, so he could almost picture the journey he was on. He'd been in a cell down in an annex to the whores' dormitory. The cells were rarely used. "The men have cattle prods," she'd said, and if the rebellion was any more serious than that, the offending party would be shot in the head as an example to the others.

Workers, and their lives, were cheap.

The stone corridors led to somewhere warmer and softer, and then outside, where Cruz felt the wind on his face. The wind carried the sound of the workers from down in the valley. It was all mechanical noise. No voices other than the odd shout from one of the guard, who tagged their pep talks with racial slurs.

It was a short walk across open ground to the big house. This was where Glenister and his men stayed. Cruz was taken up four steep wooden steps that led to a porch and the front doors of the big house. The way Rita described it, the place must have resembled something like a plantation house, a huge white palace on a big brown hill. Inside, it was supposed to be decorated with scavenged luxury. The floor under Cruz's feet was marble and his steps echoed through the large entrance hall as he was led to Glenister's office.

Captain Troy Glenister was a man who wore his influences on his sleeve. Rita had talked of a room draped with the stars and stripes and hung with paintings of stern men in old-fashioned clothes. Glenister's chair was leather, large and heavy. It had to be, because Glenister himself was large and heavy. His breathing was labored, but Cruz didn't take that as a sign the man was weak, just that he was overweight. The clicking sound that came from somewhere near his lap meant that Glenister was playing with Cruz's shikomizue, sliding the sword from the cane and replacing it.

When he spoke, his voice was thick with butter and low like a Baptist preacher. "I must say, Mr. Cruz, this toothpick of yours is quite the weapon. Doesn't look like much at first glance, and yet you used it to carve up my boys like they were wet-eared grunts. Even more impressive considering your obvious handicap. You are actually blind, aren't you?"

Cruz nodded.

"Not so impressive that you couldn't see a shocker coming, of course." He chuckled. It was a throaty sound. "You're not the only one around here with a talent for customization."

"It won't happen again," said Cruz.

"I'm sure it won't." Another click, louder, Glenister shutting the shikomizue unnecessarily hard. "Perhaps I should have shot you. But the thing is, Mr. Cruz, I'm not a bad man, despite what that little whore may have told you. If I was a bad man, I'd have my boys pop a head every time someone looked weary. I wouldn't

have gone to the trouble of providing them with the cattle prods."
He cleared his throat. "A chain boss don't blow holes in his own
damn gang just because they set it down without permission. Hell,
you'd never achieve anything that way. Have one guy dragging six
corpses, and besides, I'm well-versed in psychology, Mr. Cruz. I
know the beaner mind. If I had my boys use deadly force every
time your Pedro pals out there acted uppity, we'd have rivers of
blood. A beaner would rather die than work hard, am I right?"

Cruz smiled but said nothing.

"But you buzz the son of a bitch with a thousand volts, he'll
know who holds his balls. And he'll sure as hell think twice about
resisting the yoke again."

"Or he'll learn to avoid the buzz," said Cruz.

"Nah, your average beaner don't think like that."

"I do."

"I said average beaner." There was a smile in his voice. "You're
Victor Cruz, boy. You're the Dead Eye. Ain't nothing average
about you."

"The price," said Cruz.

"You're goddamn right, the price." There was a wet sound as
Glenister rolled his tongue around the inside of his mouth. It was
the noise of a hedonist. He ate too much, smoked too much, drank
too much, and if Cruz didn't kill him, a venereal disease would.

"How much is it?"

"Six million."

"Old or new?"

"Old."

Getting up there. Add a couple of thousand for every uniform
slashed to ribbons, every milk-fed American mouth that bit the
dust. It would be a lot more soon enough.

"I don't see how you're worth it," said Glenister. "But then I
didn't see the beauty in this here sword stick, either."

"You want me to show you?"

Another throaty laugh. "You're unarmed and blind, and you
don't know what I have pointed at you."

He did. It was a Colt Anaconda, stainless steel finish and a walnut grip. Rita had remembered the name of the gun because it was the same nickname Glenister gave his dick. The Anaconda held six and because Glenister was lazy, it would be held at hip height as he lounged in his chair. Unless he was a crack shot or incredibly lucky, a sudden movement from Cruz would mean three or four wild panic shots and a throbbing wrist that would make him pause long enough for Cruz to grab his meaty hand, shove the barrel up against his chins and press on his trigger finger until the gun clicked empty.

But that wouldn't do. That wasn't the plan.

"You're calling in the bounty," said Cruz.

"Already done it. They'll be here Sunday morning."

"I see. In that case, I have a few requests."

"Requests? You don't get to request nothing, Cruz."

"For six million, they'll want me pristine. They won't pay full price for damaged goods. You look after me, you'll look after your money."

"Six million's a lot of money, Cruz. I could stand to lose a little bit of it."

"But you don't want to. You're a grasping asshole. You'd never forgive yourself if you lost a single dime of that bounty. If I'm the six million dollar man, I refuse to live like a pig."

He didn't say anything. Cruz guessed he was thinking it over.

Finally Glenister said, "What do you want?"

"I want a room here."

"Very well."

"I want the same meals as you and the guards. Otherwise, I want to be left alone."

"Why?"

"Because I want the whore you sent me. When I'm finished with her, she can go back, but otherwise she's mine."

"Okay. That's fine. Was there anything else?"

"No. I'd like to be shown to my room now."

The room was only fit for a blind man. It was comfortable, but according to Rita, every stick of furniture in here was old, dirty and ugly. It didn't matter. The only thing that mattered was that he and Rita had privacy to practice. The girl was trustworthy and had already proven herself a quick learner with a good memory. Cruz only hoped that she was as good a teacher as she was a student.

The first night she spent with him, they practiced disarm and destroy techniques designed to bring down the bigger assailant. He concentrated on a few quick and dirty moves—the girls didn't have time to learn much more than that, and they had to do it right. Everything else would be easy just as long as that first strike hit home. Because tomorrow was Saturday, and that night would be the only clean opportunity they'd have. Saturday night was when the house guards laid down their arms and commenced to drinking and screwing their brains out. Only Glenister and Cruz were allowed to have whores in their own rooms, and so the guards had to stagger across to the dormitory, where, of course, the girls would be waiting for them. Only this time their smiles would be genuine.

Cruz ate his afternoon meal, but refused his dinner. He preferred to stay hungry. It would give him an edge. At eight o'clock, the guard outside his door knocked off for the night. Cruz lit a cigarette. By the time the ash reached the filter, he heard the guards carousing downstairs. According to Rita, they would continue like that for a few hours before they left the big house.

He waited. He heard the guards moving downstairs. Heard footsteps on the marble floor of the hall. Heard the front doors open and close. He saw them in his mind's eye, moving out across the moon-drenched countryside in a slow zig-zag towards the dormitory. He moved his head, stretched his neck. He saw them bursting through, drunken grins, shoving each other as they picked their favorites and dragged them off to their respective rooms.

Midnight was the agreed time. It was the only time Cruz could hear. On the stroke of midnight, the church clock in the middle of Fort Johnson would chime twelve times. On the first chime, the girls disarmed their johns with a chop to the Adam's apple, a well-placed fist to the balls, or a pointed hand in the eye. By the third, they had the guards' sidearms. By the sixth, the guards were dead or incapacitated, and those puritan assholes who had stayed away from temptation would be next as the crackle of gunfire that had originated in the dormitory moved towards the big house.

Cruz stood and opened the door. Rita had gummed the lock so it wouldn't secure, but until now it would have been suicide to attempt an escape. He moved quickly and silently into the hall. Counted his steps once again, skimming a wall with one hand. He walked with his head down, listening. The rooms were empty on this floor, but there was the sound of laughter and music downstairs. A door opened and the laughter grew louder. Cruz counted three or four. He touched the wall until he found a door and pushed inside as the laughing merc climbed the stairs. Cruz left the door open, disappeared into the shadows. The merc stopped on the landing and then crossed in front of the open door, a breeze and whiff of cheap bourbon like an olfactory tracer. The merc opened a door, closed it. Then Cruz heard the sound of water on water, hitting it from a height.

The merc was taking a leak.

Cruz kicked open the bathroom door. He felt the air shift in front of him and planted the heel of his hand in the merc's throat. He grabbed a fistful of ear and hair and slammed the merc's head into the nearest solid object. Something crashed off its fixtures. Cruz grabbed at the merc's belt, found the cattle prod, and forced it past the merc's teeth before he flicked the switch. The merc went rigid, there was the smell of burnt hair, and he tumbled backwards into what sounded like a tub where he kicked the sides in an off-beat jig before he passed out.

Cruz returned to the landing just as the front doors opened and the girls rushed into the hall, shouting and screaming. The music jumped in volume as one of the mercs came out to investigate and caught six bullets from four different guns. Cruz moved to the next flight of stairs. He heard Rita's light step as she raced up to meet him. She was breathing heavily. "It worked, señor! They didn't stand a chance!"

"There's another in the bathroom," said Cruz. "I'll be back. I need to deal with Glenister."

"I'll take you."

"No. It's okay."

"You don't know the way."

He put a hand on her shoulder. It was bare. "Secure the downstairs, Rita."

She opened her mouth to say something, the spit clicking against her tongue, but he turned away before she could speak. He took the stairs that led to the top floor and Captain Troy Glenister's suite. He followed the smell of sex and the sound of a television tuned to static and opened double doors.

There was movement, but only slight. The sound of silk sheets and a water bed. The hedonist at rest.

"Cruz?" He sounded groggy.

"Fort Johnson, named for Andrew?"

That throaty laugh again. "This is a country for white men and by God, as long as I am President, it shall be a government for white men..."

"Where are my things, Glenister?"

The water bed made a sickening noise as Glenister moved on it. "He was an idealist who never went to school, and he became the leader of the free world."

"It wasn't free then."

"And it isn't now. Who the hell do you think you are, Cruz? You know I could call for a guard—"

"Your men are dead. The whores are in charge. And you have a choice. You can try to squeeze your ass through the bedroom window, pray you don't break anything when you hit the ground and then run for your life, or you can die right here and now."

Glenister laughed again. It was strained. He moved quickly, or tried to, and Cruz knew the Colt was within reach. He lunged forward, felt the air crack with the first bullet, ring with the second, but the third stayed exactly where it was as Cruz kicked the gun from Glenister's grip and sent it bouncing across the floor. He grabbed Glenister by what felt like a robe and hauled him across the room. He swung the fat man into the hissing television set, smashing it and raining hot sparks against his skin. Glenister dropped to the carpet and Cruz lost him for a moment.

He straightened up and stood stock still. Listened. Heard the fat man scrabbling on the floor. He was making a noise like a truffle pig. Then Cruz heard him stand and then the squeak of a cabinet door. He pictured another gun, but didn't move. Glenister was breathing heavily, but he was doing it through a smile.

Cruz heard the click of his shikomizue. Of course he'd kept it. And of course he meant to kill him with his own sword. It was the kind of cheap irony that appealed to men with dull minds. Glenister tried to creep to one side, but his breathing made locating him easy. "You're a dead man, Cruz. You might have the whores on your side, but I have the whole US Army. I spoke to General Jackson himself, did you know that? Stonewall himself. We're old friends. Anything happens to me, you're a marked man. So now you have a choice. You can take those whores and get a few hours' head start on the United States Bounty Service, or I can kill you now."

Cruz made his choice. Glenister panicked as he lunged. The fat man's feet shuffled for purchase. Cruz threw a jabbing kick under the fat man's arms and caught him in the gut. It didn't move him, but it made him belch air and swing wildly with the sword. Cruz stepped to the side of the swing and the gust of wind it produced, then dipped into its arc and grabbed Glenister's sweaty forearm with one hand, his bicep with the other and pulled the arm down sharply across his knee. There was a terrific snap and the smell of urine filled the air as Glenister became liquid in Cruz's grip. Glenister screeched and rolled away, the sword thumping onto the carpet. Cruz dropped to a squat and picked up the sword, following the sound of Glenister as he whimpered and crawled back to the water bed.

"You haven't...you haven't won," he said, but his voice was too high-pitched to be confident.

Cruz touched the blade of the shikomizue. It needed sharpening, but it would do for what he had in mind. He heard Glenister scrabble on the carpet.

"You're still a dead man. Jackson won't stop. He'll send more men after you. They'll find you."

"And they'll die, just like the last man he sent after me, just like every opportunistic scumbag who thinks he can make his fortune on the backs of the poor. Just like you, Captain Troy Glenister, and all your men. We didn't draw first blood, but we'll definitely draw last."

"Yes, you will," said Glenister.

Glenister let out a cackle and rolled to one side. And Cruz realised why the fat man had crawled for the bed rather than the door. He heard the metallic click in Glenister's hand and prepared to bring the sword down just as the Colt Anaconda roared its resistance.

There was a sudden rush of air, and then it was all over.

Rita was waiting on the landing when Cruz emerged from Glenister's room. He kicked the sheet-wrapped bundle on the floor in front of her. It made a wet sound. He pointed in its general direction with his stick. In his other hand he held his silver spurs.

"A present," he said. "Something to help get the new regime started."

Her voice remained at the same height, so she must have opened the bundle with her toe. "His head."

He'd expected her to be shocked, to act like a woman, but she hadn't. He was impressed. "You'll need it to assert power."

"I didn't do it."

He smiled. "Yes, you did."

"What about you?"

The smile faded. "There will be men from Mexico City arriving here in a few hours. You need to be ready for them. Tell them what happened, mention my name if they ask, but make it clear that you're in charge now and that you and the rest of the people here will defend this town with your lives. You have an arsenal, you have resources, and you have a reason. They won't have the guts to push you. They'll be outnumbered and outgunned."

"I don't know."

"You can do it, Rita. You're the strongest person in this whole town."

She kissed him on the cheek, and he turned into a second kiss that caught him on the mouth. She pressed herself against him. He allowed her for a moment. The warmth and smell were comforting.

"Victor..." she whispered.

"No." He broke the embrace and gestured to the head again. "Take it to your people."

"Thank you."

He nodded. She picked up the head. He listened to her light footsteps on the stairs as she descended and something stumbled in his chest.

He heard a cheer from the women downstairs, then the sound of them running out the front doors and a rising commotion from the valley. Cruz attached his spurs and then tapped down the stairs.

Outside, he heard a mixture of male and female voices, the male outnumbering the female, but the female clearly the ones in control. Above them all was Rita's voice, confident and charismatic, telling everyone what had happened, and how they didn't have long to get organized. Cruz listened to her for a few seconds, then pushed his way out through the back of the big house.

Perhaps people really were capable of rebuilding what they had, given the right kind of head start. And perhaps Yuma wouldn't have been such a dead loss after all, but Cruz doubted that it would be better than what Rita and her people could manage. They'd have to change the name of the town, though. Fort Johnson, the man Glenister had named it for, Glenister himself and the ideas he stood for, they were all dead. They were relics to be buried and forgotten.

That was the message the boys from the Bounty Service would get when they arrived. And if they needed it repeated, well, Victor Cruz—the Dead Eye—planned to do so until that whole damn Wall came down. Until then, he would carry on walking and enjoy the first warmth of dawn on his face.

THE END

As RAY BANKS is the definitive authority on the life and work of Guy Rivera, I will defer to him for insight. From the introduction to his monograph, The Writer, the Man, the 'Guy': A Critical Deconstruction of Guillermo Rivera:

"Guillermo 'Guy' Rivera (1935–1989) is primarily known as the creator of the Dead Eye series, which started with Dead Eye *(1979) and ended with the posthumous* Lay Down Your Arms *(1990). The series was, as Rivera himself put it, "the sum total of my passions*," and was a sometimes schizophrenic attempt to mix the legends of Zatoichi and Zorro with spaghetti westerns, Italian Mad Max rip-offs and leftist political ideals. A heavy smoker and drinker, Rivera died of congestive heart failure in 1989 in his home town of Agua Prieta, Mexico.*

* *"In the Zone," interview with Bob Leland in* Dangerous Horizons *magazine, July 1988.*

CHINGÓN: THE WORLD'S DEADLIEST MEXICAN

in

BLOOD AND TACOS

by Brace Godfrey

(discovered by Johnny Shaw)

CHINGÓN STOOD in the shadeless, dusty road in front of Mesa Verde's only cantina. He squinted up at the blazing sun without blinking, practically daring the fiery orb to blind him. Chingón had lived in the heat of the Mexican desert all his life. If it thought it could best Chingón, it had another think coming. The sun had done its damnedest in its effort to burn him but had only managed to tan his skin to the texture of fine Corinthian leather.

Looking toward the eight motorcycles parked in front of the cantina, Chingón thought back to his meeting with La Boca and the rest of the Brown Panthers. Their reputation was solid, and word was that nothing got past their network of gardeners, Mexican restaurant mariachi musicians, and border informants.

According to La Boca, The Red Devils were heavy into the white slavery market, usually transporting and selling unlucky Mexican and South American *chicas* to sweatshops and underground sado-brothels. But according to the *vid de uva*, at that moment, they were holding a white girl. One that wasn't for sale.

The information that La Boca had given him had better have been righteous. The last thing Chingón needed was to charge into the building and fail at getting the girl back. There was no reward money for a dead U.S. Senator's daughter, and he was running out of time.

If Chingón failed his mission, Senator Gray, one of the staunchest anti-crime lawmakers around, was going to make a statement announcing that he was dropping out of the Presidential race. The man didn't want to—he was the frontrunner—but that was the kidnap demand. Drop out of the race, or your daughter dies.

Chingón and Senator Gray agreed that the most likely person behind this dirty trick was his opponent, the lily-livered, anti-gun Governor Deutsch. But there was no way to prove it. And Senator Gray wasn't willing to risk his daughter's life over his political career.

Senator Gray couldn't go to the authorities. He couldn't go to the Secret Service. He couldn't go through regular channels. So he had found Chingón.

The man was scheduled to give his abdication speech on Wednesday at noon. It was Tuesday, and Chingón needed to get lucky.

He lit the stub of a cigar and walked toward the cantina. One minute of thinking was too much for a man like Chingón. He was a man of action. A man of violence. A man.

Chingón kicked open the saloon doors, splintering wood and shattering the door from its hinges. Sneaking in back doors was for weak men and Canadians.

The eight drunk and leather-clad men squinted as they lazily turned. A motley band of bearded and leathered *pendejos*, thought Chingón. No sense of style. No hygiene. No knowledge of mustache wax. No class.

"You must be the one they call Chingón," Branigan, the leader of the Red Devils, said. He was the biggest of the bunch with a face that sported a cobweb of scars and arms blue with tattoos. "They say you're the World's Deadliest Mexican. Is that true?"

They had known he was coming. That was not good.

"Many have been curious about Chingón's deadliness, *gringo*," Chingón said. "Most of them are *muerto*. Dead and buried. Because I killed them. Killed them until they were dead. Dead and buried."

"If you want a drink, I can't help you. This bar has gotten some standards. It's become civilized. It no longer serves mud people, particularly Mexican'ts," Branigan said, scratching the Swastika tattooed on his neck.

"Chingón just wants the white girl. She's here. Do not try to bullshit Chingón," Chingón said.

"What is it with you Mexicans and blondes? Can't you stick to your own kind?" Branigan laughed.

"Chingón did not say that she was blonde," Chingón countered.

"Either way. There ain't no white girl here." Branigan glanced at a side door for just a moment, but it was enough for Chingón. He knew where she was.

"She is here. And she better be unhurt and unraped," said Chingón.

"She's unhurt, but I can't make any promises on the other. My men have been known to have their fun," Branigan said, his smile revealing half a mouthful of black teeth.

"Chingón will settle for alive. From the photos I know that *chica* is *un tamale caliente*. Some temptations are difficult to resist." Chingón smiled.

"The girl is not for sale. Not until tomorrow. However, we have a limited selection of darker meat." Branigan's voice started to show some irritation.

"Let's not continue this game. You know who she is and why Chingón is here." Chingón mirrored the biker's irritation.

"Maybe." Branigan glanced around the room at his men.

"Her family hired Chingón to get her back. And once Chingón has been paid, Chingón never backs down. Chingón never surrenders. And Chingón never compromises," Chingón said about Chingón.

"Twenty thousand dollars. Double what we were paid. That's what it will cost. Pay the money and you can walk out of here with her," Branigan said.

"Why should Chingón pay one *centavo* when you are going to release her for nothing?" Chingón confidently stated.

A voice from the back of the cantina cut the silence. "Let's throw the beaner out already. That is, unless he would like to clean our toilets before he goes. I know how much Mexes like to get on their knees and scrub white men's shit."

The voice came from the shadows beyond the pool table. Chingón recognized the camouflage-clad man that walked out of those shadows as Walker. Unlike the others, he was not a biker, nor a member of the Red Devils motorcycle gang. Walker was a mercenary, a gun-for-hire, and the second-best knife fighter in the world.

This wasn't Chingón and Walker's first encounter. They went way back. (*Editor's note: You can read about their epic knife fight in Highline Publication's earlier Chingón: The World's Deadliest Mexican adventure:* OAXACALYPSE.)

"The only toilet in here that needs cleaning is your mouth, Walker," Chingón said. "And Chingón would clean that for free, *pendejo*. With his fists."

"I'll get the plunger," Walker hissed, whipping a butterfly knife from his sleeve and putting on a show of steel and speed. He made the deadly blade dance in the space just in front of his body. The sound of the metal slicing the air cut the silence of the still bar.

After the show was over, Chingón slowly clapped his callused hands. "Impressive. But does it cut as well as it dances?"

"It's about time you and I answered that question once and for all." Walker took two steps forward, blade at the ready.

"That's enough," Branigan barked. "You sound like women. I'll make it easy for everyone. We'll all kill the Mex bastard. Lazarus! Wolfe! Red Devils!"

Branigan swept his eyes around the bar. As he made eye contact with each man, they stood and turned to Chingón, revealing weapons that ranged from heavy chains and pipes to very powerful firearms. One of them had a trident.

Chingón smiled through gritted teeth. "Be careful, Branigan. There are only eight of you. You're outnumbered, *cabron*," Chingón said. He threw his poncho over his shoulder, revealing his infamous bullwhip on one hip and a bandolier of grenades across his chest.

Chingón was known by many names: The *Matador* of Mayhem. The *Caballero* of Catastrophe. The *Hermano* of Hurt. The *Patrón* of Pain. And the admittedly less-inspired *Jefe* of Internal Injuries.

There was no doubt that he truly was the World's Deadliest Mexican.

Feared for his prowess with his bullwhip, Marta, and his deadly accuracy with grenades, like a snake charmer or a lion tamer, Chingón had learned to tame man's most dangerous weapon into something he could massage and control. His reputation was spread by the few that had seen him in action. Very few. Most of the others had exploded. And the explosions had killed them.

Branigan reached for the pistol in his waistband, but Chingón beat him to the draw, throwing a grenade in the big biker's lap. With his knowledge of angles and precise placement, he was able to focus the blast. Branigan exploded in a burst of blood and gore, staining the ceiling and the mirror behind the bar. Only his blood-filled boots remained.

Without hesitation, Chingón had Marta out and cracked the whip loudly, pulling the trident from the hands of an advancing biker. He grabbed the biker by his vest and dropped the bearded man with one well-placed haymaker to the temple.

The large biker crashed to the ground with a loud crash.

"Now it's a *fiesta*," Chingón screamed like a madman.

The six remaining men opened fire, the shots just missing Chingón as he dove over the top of the bar. Ricocheting bullets pinged from wall to wall, creating a violent orchestra of death, a symphony played in lead major.

"*Caramba*," Chingón said to himself, plucking two fresh grenades from the bandolier. He waited for a lull in the maelstrom and then lobbed the two grenades in the direction of the charging men. He grabbed a bottle of tequila as he ducked back behind the bar.

The explosions shook the cantina. Chingón almost spilled his tequila. He looked up at the bar for a lime but found none. He would have to settle for the Mexican firewater neat. And as uncivilized as it felt, the burn of the alcohol steeled him for the second half of the battle.

By his count, there would only be three men left alive, but one of those men was Walker, the only real threat to Chingón.

The silence that followed the explosions was deceptive. They were waiting for Chingón. He knew there was more fight to come. It was quiet. Too quiet. He waited as patiently as one can.

But Chingón wasn't the kind of man that was going to wait all day. Two minutes was long enough. It was time to act. Mexican standoffs were for a different breed of Mexican.

Chingón stood up from the bar, grenade and whip at the ready. The roar of a machine gun belched fire and lead. Blood erupted from Chingón's shoulder, knocking him down.

"Aaaaaaahhh!" Chingón screamed, holding the wound and falling back behind the bar.

It hurt, but Chingón had lost count of the number of times that he'd been shot. The bullet hadn't hit anything vital—most likely ricocheting off another bullet still lodged in his body—but there was a lot of blood.

His heart said attack, but the smart thing to do was retreat. Chingón hadn't survived a thousand battles by being stupid. He had survived them by exploding people.

He remembered the door that Branigan had glanced at. The one where the girls were stowed. If he could get to it, he could wrap his wound and return to the melee.

He made a run for the door, pulling its latch as bullets dimpled the plaster near his head. He tossed a grenade at the gunfire without his usual deadly accuracy and dove into the room, closing the door quickly behind him. The explosion shook the door, but it held.

When he turned, he was in a dimly lit space with no furnishings or windows. On the floor in front of him were four naked women with their arms and legs bound. Three of the women were Mexican nationals, and the other was Amanda Gray, the youngest daughter of Presidential candidate, Senator James Gray.

Looking up with her soft doe eyes and a surprising strong voice, Amanda Gray said, "Who are you?"

"I am Chingón. Your father sent me," Chingón said, already cutting through the ropes that bound the women.

Chingón draped his poncho over Amanda Gray's nude body, admiring her alabaster skin. "Do not worry. It's not the first time four nude women have needed Chingón, *mamacita*. Although the circumstances the last time were quite different. Do you know how to use a gun?"

"I was the captain of the Carrie Chapman Catt Academy for Girls' skeet and target shooting team," Amanda Gray said proudly.

Chingón tossed Amanda Gray an automatic pistol and handed the three Mexican women the throwing knives that he kept in his boot. They appeared to be comfortable with their nudity. And with the throwing knives. Chingón liked that.

"Shooting men is a lot different than clay pigeons or paper targets, *chica*," Chingón said.

"They are not men. They are animals," Amanda Gray said. "And it's animal season."

Amanda Gray loudly racked a bullet into the chamber. The last time Chingón had seen a woman with that look in her eye, he had almost lost a testicle to the business end of a pitchfork. This girl was fight-ready and blood-lusty.

"Now you sound like Chingón," Chingón said, sounding even more like Chingón than Amanda Gray did.

"What's the plan?" Amanda Gray asked.

You don't need a plan when you have angry Mexican women on your side.

The two remaining bikers didn't stand a chance against the naked fury of the naked furies. Nobody stabs quite like an angry *señorita*. Let alone three of them. Chingón and Amanda Gray were relegated to the sidelines while the three women went *carnicería* on their former captors.

Chingón's only disappointment was that Walker had already split. Running away with his tail between his legs to report back to his master like the dog that he was.

No matter to Chingón. He had the girl, and now it was just a question of returning to Los Angeles to deliver her. And receive his money.

When the carnage ceased, the Mexican women—now wearing the leathers of the dead bikers—offered their bodies to Chingón. As tempted as he was, Chingón was on a schedule. And when he was with three ladies, he preferred to take his time.

Chingón and Amanda Gray walked across the road to Chingón's lavender 1964 Chevy Impala. Riding Astro Supremes with 5.20 whitewalls, Chingón's ride was barrio beautiful, the crown jewel being an airbrushed image on the hood of a topless woman wearing a sombrero, riding a comet, and pulling the pin out of a grenade with her teeth.

"That was anticlimactic," Amanda Gray said. "I didn't even get to shoot anyone."

"Be careful of what you wish for, *mamacita*," Chingón said. "This day isn't over."

While Chingón preferred to drive the Impala low and slow, now was not the time for cruising. Grabbing the scorpion-in-polyester-resin knob of the shifter, he slammed the Impala into gear. They hit the highway in a cloud of dust and gravel spray.

"I never thanked you for saving me back there," Amanda Gray said, watching the desert blur past her. "Thank you."

Chingón grunted his response. He glanced at the girl. Maybe sixteen. Old enough. He liked the way the tattered leather vest she had found looked against her pale skin. And the way she was sitting, he could see one of her perky breasts underneath. Chingón liked that, too.

Seeing that young flesh brought his thoughts back to his own youth and his life before he became the World's Deadliest Mexican.

It seemed so long ago that his wife Juanita was murdered by those drug-runners. How he had gotten his revenge. Bathed in blood and mad from grief. How he had found each link in the chain until he destroyed all the men responsible. No matter that they were villains or *vaqueros*, politicians or policemen, they had scheduled their execution when they had killed the only person that Chingón had ever loved. And would ever love. It was impossible for Chingón to remember the humble *campesino* (farmer) that he once was.

The shattering of the back window jolted Chingón from his memories.

"*Coño!*" Chingón shouted. "My Chevy."

Looking in the rearview mirror, he eyed the two Jeeps on his tail. One driver and one shotgunner in each vehicle, the smoke from one of the shotguns still exiting its barrel. Walker sat in the backseat of one of the vehicles, picking his teeth with his knife and grinning like a bastard.

"Get down," Chingón said, but Amanda Gray wasn't going to miss her second chance for a scrap. She turned in her seat and aimed the pistol out the window, firing three quick rounds at the Jeeps.

Three holes in the Jeep's windshield later, and in the most undramatic of fashions, it slowed to a stop with the horn blowing full volume and two dead men looking asleep save for the holes in their foreheads.

The other Jeep kept on, gaining ground and returning fire. Chingón hit a switch on his dash, setting the hydraulics in motion. The back end of the Impala lifted, taking away the angle on the back window.

Chingón eyed the road ahead. And the curves into the mountains. This was going to get *loco*.

"Grab the wheel," Chingón said.

Amanda Gray grabbed the small chain steering wheel as Chingón pulled four grenades from his bandolier, two in each hand.

The gunman in the Jeep had swapped out his shotgun for some kind of machine gun. He opened fire, lacing a row of puckered holes in the side of the Impala.

"*Pinche pendejos,*" Chingón proclaimed. And like the image of his dead wife on the hood of his car, he put the pins of all four grenades in his mouth and pulled.

"Let's dance, bitches," Chingón laughed as he dropped the grenades one by one out the window.

The Jeep darted out of the way of the first grenade, the explosion just missing. Weaving to miss the next grenade, it overcompensated and spun out. Ultimately, the error saved their lives as the other two grenades exploded in front of them.

While Chingón had meant to end the battle there and then, he would take the delay as a victory and put some distance between the Impala and the Jeep.

Taking back the wheel from Amanda Gray and driving like a madman through the windy mountain roads, he just missed a semi on a blind corner. The tiny wheels just held onto the tarmacadam.

"Do you see them?" Chingón said, eyes focused straight ahead.

"They're about three turns back. What are we going to do?" Amanda Gray said.

"Chingón is tired of running," Chingón said.

He slammed the brakes and expertly slid the car behind a gigantic boulder. He jumped out, pulling at two more grenades.

Standing just behind the boulder at the side of the road, he pulled the pins on the grenades, closed his eyes, and waited. He listened to birds' wings miles away, the wind brushing the mesquite, and the approaching tires of the Jeep.

Chingón threw the two grenades in a high arc almost straight up in the air, and then walked into the middle of the road to face the oncoming Jeep. As it rounded the turn, the murder in Walker's eyes was revealed for only a moment.

"*Adios, cabróns*," Chingón said.

The arcing grenades made their descent and with perfect timing landed in Walker's lap.

"Motherfu—" Walker said.

The Jeep exploded.

The burning metal carcass flew over Chingón's head and off the steep cliff behind him. He lit his cigar on the burning hulk as it passed and walked back to his Impala.

Running his finger along the line of bullet holes in the side panel, Chingón said, "*Puta madre*, I wish I could kill them again."

He got in the car and turned to Amanda Gray. Chingón said, "I think that's enough adventure for one day. Let's get you home."

On seeing his daughter alive, Senator Gray was overjoyed. So much so that he paid Chingón double the asking price. That was on top of the bonus that Amanda Gray had given him on the ride back. Not money, but mouth sex.

Chingón shook the man's hand and said, "And while I did this for the money, I also did this for what is right. No woman should be stolen by any man. Men cannot make their own rules. They must follow the rules made for them by other men. And as long as people do not abide by those rules, Chingón will be there to punish them with the lash of his whip and the explosion power of his grenades. Because there are no rules for Chingón. Chingón follows no man, but enforces their rules, for money. And men best follow those rules. Because they are the rules. And rules must be obeyed. Rules."

"I agree," Senator Gray said. "Now I must go. I have an election to win."

And with that, Chingón turned and walked to his Chevy Impala. He usually left politics for men with bow ties in their dresser drawers, but he was going to make an exception for Governor Deutsch. He thought he'd pay him a visit and see where he stood on the death penalty.

THE END

This is the story that started it all. JOHNNY SHAW found this 1979 exemplar while cleaning a recently deceased uncle's attic. Amid a shocking amount of strangely specific pornography was a box of Brace Godfrey books. Godfrey, known as "The King of the Three Shots," wrote over 200 novels and penned numerous series, but none of them ever got past the third book. Some of his best remembered series include Codename: Black Belt, The Expunger, W.E.R.E.W.O.L.F. Squadron, *and of course,* Chingón.

VIPER
in
SHADOW SISTERS OF SHINJUKU
by Tony Amtrak
(discovered by Garnett Elliott)

FORTY STORIES UP, the Big Ginza discotheque cast a glitzy eye over smog-laden Shinjuku skyline. Getting there required a short trip on a private elevator. It also required the doorman's approval.

He was a former sumotori, squeezed into a white dinner jacket. Thick arms folded, face impassive as an executioner's, he pronounced judgment on every gaudily dressed, would-be clubber who approached the elevator's mirrored interior. Those who got the nod stepped inside. Those he declined slunk away, to seek the district's easier pleasures.

Viper Ogata watched from the lobby as a trio of burly Australians tried their luck. He in the lead had at least six inches on the doorman. Grinning, he attempted to brush past like no one was there. A hand the span of a dinner plate shot out and pressed against his chest.

"Hey now," the Aussie said in passable Japanese, "that's not—"

The doorman grunted. Viper stepped aside as two hundred pounds of blond gaijin went hurtling past, to strike a chrome table face first. The foreigner's buddies hurried to help him up. They shot backward looks at the doorman, who waited with arms crossed like before. Calm as stone.

"Let's go," one of the Aussies said. "I know a brothel where they *want* our business."

It was Viper's turn.

He sauntered to the elevator, fishing in his blazer's pocket for a cigarette. The sumotori shifted a little to the left and blocked him.

"No yakuza."

"What?" Viper put extra incredulity into his voice. "Who do you think runs this place?"

"The Okajima family, under Boss Tsutomo. And you're not with them."

Viper popped the cigarette in his mouth but didn't light it. "Look, I'm in a hurry. My friend called and said she needs my help. She works up there." He pointed at the ceiling.

The doorman blinked at him.

"Big trees hate the wind, you know," Viper said.

"What the hell does that mean?"

He answered with a punch, hands moving so fast the Rolex on his wrist made a golden blur. Two knuckles seemed to brush the fabric just above the doorman's gut. The big man let out a breath. A look crossed his face like he was pondering some formidable problem. After several seconds of not breathing, his cheeks began to purple.

Viper leaned close. "The Gichin Fist," he whispered, "first of the Seven Techniques of Ancient Ryukyuan." He patted the doorman's shoulder. His hand flashed out to stab the elevator button, and he stepped inside.

The doors shut with a chime. Viper paused to admire the multiple reflections of himself. Slender as a bamboo shoot, but tough like steel wire. He smoothed his tie. Music vibrated from somewhere above; it became deafening when the doors slid open and Donna Summer hit him with a wave of syncopated noise.

Bodies jerked atop the flashing red and yellow squares of Ginza's dance floor. A spinning mirror-ball cast a thousand diamond fragments. People moved aside for Viper as he headed towards the bar, his eyes wary behind mirrored sunglasses. He refused to take them off, even at night. A young salaryman hurried by holding two beers in tall paper cups. Viper snatched one without resistance. He drained half the contents in a single swallow, nose wrinkling at the malty taste.

"Viper! Over here!"

Mikki waved to him from behind the crowded bar. He threaded his way over. The fat executive on the stool Viper wanted suddenly remembered an urgent appointment. Mikki leaned across the counter to light his cigarette, her western-sized breasts straining against a red sequined top.

"Sachiko's looking for you," she said.

"Uh-huh. Where's she at?"

Mikki gestured towards a far booth, almost lost in the shadows. The angle afforded a nice view of her cleavage. "She's worried about something."

"So I gathered."

"What's so great about her, anyway? How does she rate a personal visit from Viper Ogata?"

"Sachiko's an old friend."

Mikki's eyelashes lowered. "You making any new friends?"

"Perhaps. Be patient."

He left his beer on the bar. Sachiko had been working the Shinjuku district for three years, a hardened pro at twenty-two. It took a lot to rattle her. But something had. She sat hunched in the dark booth, hands gripped around a tumbler of amber fluid. The sweep of her long bangs concealed her face.

"Relax," Viper said, sliding into the cushions across from her. "I'm here. What's all this nonsense about someone trying to kill you?"

Sachiko didn't look up. Didn't speak.

Viper watched the dancers making fools of themselves. "C'mon, Satch. My time's valuable. What's going on?"

No reply.

"Satch—" He reached over to brush her hair back. Sachiko grinned out at him in an empty-eyed rictus. A feathered dart, about three inches long, jutted from her neck. Her hair had been covering it.

Viper glanced sidelong at the dance floor. Could her assassin still be here? All he saw were drunken, gyrating idiots. A professional would do the job and leave.

Stray flashes of light from the disco-ball wandered across the table. One passed over Sachiko's hands, where something gleamed. He lowered his sunglasses. Yes, she was holding a piece of plastic, pressed against the tumbler. He pried her index finger away and removed a white rectangle, the size of a domino. A stylized egret was stamped in gold paint on one side. The number '102' on the other.

Frowning, he slipped the plastic into his blazer pocket.

"Back so soon?" Mikki's smile drained away when she saw the look on his face.

"Wait twenty minutes and call the cops," he said. "I was never here."

Boss Gomyo sat with his gut wedged up against the pachinko machine. One hand worked the lever, sending tiny steel balls through the lighted pins at a steady pace. The other shoved rice crackers into his mouth. Every now and then his new flunky, Shigeda, held a cigarette to Gomyo's lips for a quick puff.

He played, snacked, and smoked this way for a solid fifteen minutes before making a slight nod in Viper's direction, indicating he was ready to listen.

Viper cleared his throat. "Boss, I was wondering if you could tell me what this was." He slid the rectangle from his pocket and presented one side, then the other.

Gomyo's eyes flicked away from the machine exactly twice. "'Resplendent Egret Joyous Massage.' It's a parlor run by the Okajima clan. That's a guest pass."

Viper put the plastic away. "Thanks."

"You gonna tell me where you got it?"

"Off a dead prostitute in Shinjuku. She was a friend of mine."

Gomyo pushed himself back from the machine with a grunt. "Observe," he told Shigeda, and turned to slap Viper so hard his sunglasses flew off and struck an old woman playing three machines down. The woman pretended not to notice. A school of bright stars swam across Viper's vision.

"That," Gomyo said, "is what happens to people who trifle with my time. And I *like* brother Viper, here. He's my number one enforcer."

Shigeda sneered. He looked all of eighteen years, wearing an open-collared dress shirt and gold chains. "I don't see what's so special about him."

"Viper spent some time in Okinawa, on the lam. He met an old man there. Didn't you, Viper?"

"Yes, boss."

"The old man taught him a few tricks."

"I was a poor student, boss."

"Ah. Modesty." Gomyo returned to his game. "Shigeda, pick up the man's sunglasses. He gets anxious without them on."

Shigeda scurried to obey, though his face burned red. Viper grabbed the mirrored shades from his hands.

"Go find your whore's killer, you soft-hearted moron." Gomyo's attention stayed fixed on the cascade of shiny beads. "If you start a war with the Okajima people, I'll want a whole pinky. Not just the tip."

Viper bowed and got the hell out of there.

The Resplendent Egret parlor was sandwiched between a ramen shop and a record store the size of a bedroom closet. Viper stepped into a shabby, yet clean front room. Gilt-framed prints of birds hung on the walls.

"Good afternoon, sir."

The old Korean woman behind the desk nodded when he showed her his pass. She led him down a hallway to a room marked 102.

"An attendant will be with you shortly, sir."

The room smelled of disinfectant. There was a bench with a slim beige mattress on top, a folding table, and a paper robe hanging off the door. Traditional biwa music strained from overhead speakers.

A depressing place. Viper sat on the edge of the mattress and closed his eyes. He tried to imagine Sachiko working this very room, but the vision wouldn't come. He recalled instead the first time they screwed, standing up in an alley behind the Amada Club. The alley had smelled like piss, and a family of stray cats kept brushing against his ankles during the act.

The door creaked. His eyes snapped open. A young woman in a cheap pink kimono entered. Her long hair was hennaed brown in the current fashion.

"Please remove your clothing."

He shrugged off his blazer. "Easy money for you," he said, pulling a roll of yen from his pocket.

She slipped the front of her robe open without hesitation. A pale nipple peeked out.

"No, no," he said. "I just want to ask you about someone."

"You are...police?"

"The furthest thing. Sit down." He patted a spot next to him on the mattress.

She sat. Her hands, he noticed, glistened with massage oil. "There was a girl working here not long ago. Sachiko. Part Chinese. You remember her?"

The woman shook her head. "I'm very new."

"What about the other girls? You think they might know?"

"I can ask. You're the only customer for the moment. The rest of the girls are out back, having a smoke."

He peeled off several thousand-yen notes. "Show them that."

She took the money, bowed, and left.

He waited less than three minutes. The door slammed back open and a pair of broad-shouldered, dead-eyed men wearing loud Polynesian shirts burst in. Viper, half-expecting such a welcome, shot off the mattress and kicked the first one in the throat. He bent double, and his partner threw a reverse punch Viper could've seen coming through miles of fog. He sidestepped, looped a hand under the man's armpit. Twisted at the waist. The heavy flew six feet and crashed into the folding table.

Viper ducked out into the hallway. A slender man barreled towards him, tugging an automatic from his linen suit. The sight of the gun caused time to slow. Between heartbeats, Viper flicked the six-inch tanto from his belt and hurled it overhand. The blade seemed to tumble lazily, taking an eternity to bury itself deep in the gunman's wrist. A jet of bright red sprayed from his ulnar artery and doused the prints along the walls.

"Stop!"

Now a second man was coming down the hallway; tall, with a shaved head and a golden earring dragging at one lobe. Behind him, the old Korean woman and Viper's would-be masseuse watched with terrified eyes.

"Viper Ogata," the man said, "I'm Kanbei Kana. Do you recognize me?"

Viper nodded. "Underboss to the Okajima clan."

Kanbei drew a handkerchief from his pocket and clamped it around the gunman's spurting wrist. "I suggest we call a truce."

"Agreed." Viper glanced into room 102. The thug he had hip-thrown swayed to his feet. Beside him, the first heavy clutched at his neck and breathed with gurgling noises.

"I see you live up to your reputation," Kanbei said, a note of approval slipping into his voice. "You went through these three like they were bean cakes."

Viper shrugged. "I doubt if you would've been so easy."

"Who can say? But I'm assuming you didn't come here to start a brawl."

"Someone killed my friend. A working girl named Sachiko."

"Sachiko. Yes." Kanbei yanked the knife from his underling's wrist. The man groaned, and pressed the blood-soaked handkerchief tighter. "She was a top earner here at the Egret. A good girl. You and I should speak in private."

Ignoring the scowls of Kanbei's men, Viper followed the underboss into a back room. Several chairs were arranged around a battered table, with a teapot in the center. Kanbei poured two cups of pale emerald liquid. He sipped and watched Viper for several moments before speaking.

"Sachiko's is only one of several recent deaths here in Shinjuku," he said, his broad face hardening. "All prostitutes. Three of them were with the Okajima clan, but there have been independents killed as well. It's affecting the girls' morale."

Viper tasted his tea. Gyokuro, the finest quality. "Some kind of sex-killer?"

"I understand that's the usual motive in these cases. But I was able to examine two of the bodies myself, before police arrived. Let me show you what I found."

He excused himself and returned to the room moments later holding a square of folded cloth. Inside, the wicked shapes of shuriken gleamed.

"Lodged in the girls' throats," he said. "Both had been smeared with poison."

Viper recalled the dart jutting from Sachiko's neck. "A professional assassin."

Kanbei nodded. "I thought maybe another yakuza family had been behind the killings, to disrupt business. But your presence here seems to contradict that."

"Boss Gomyo has no interest in prostitution. He sticks to gambling and loans."

"Gomyo." Kanbei made a face. "That fat old carp. Listen, Viper, why don't you ditch him and work for me? Boss Tsutomo values skilled fighters. Gomyo's old-fashioned and treats his men like dirt."

"That may be true, but he's still my boss."

"Screw that 'jingi' crap. I'll pay double what he's giving you."

Viper set his cup down, hard. "I shared sake with him. What kind of man would I be, if I went back on my oath?"

Kanbei's eyes narrowed, like he was sizing Viper for a punch. He ran his finger along the bridge of his crooked nose. Gradually, some of the tension left his jaw. "You're right. Honor has its place. But perhaps in this case we can still work together. Avenge Sachiko's death and put a stop to these killings."

"Go on."

"There's one establishment in Shinjuku seemingly unscathed by the murders. The Red Pagoda, a love hotel run by a madam named Pinku Serizawa. She's quite the mystery woman. None of her in-house girls have been touched."

Pinku Serizawa. The name struck Viper as familiar, but he couldn't recall details. "What are you proposing?"

"An investigation. You could enter the Pagoda the same way you entered here, posing as a client. Mari could go with you."

"Mari?"

"The girl you were questioning."

Viper mused over the idea. "What about the cops? You've got a couple on your payroll, surely."

"They claim to be following all leads. But you know the police. We yakuza are not bound by crippling restrictions."

"True."

"I could have several cars full of men surrounding the hotel. At a signal from you, they would come swarming inside."

Viper drained his tea. "A mixture of deception and overwhelming force. I like this plan. I like your spirit, Kanbei Kana. My only stipulation is this: we act at once."

They took a taxi from the Resplendent Egret parlor. Mari had changed into a tight-fitting denim skirt, white satin blouse, and knee-high black leather boots. She crouched in the cab's cramped space next to Viper. The driver had given him a knowing leer when he named his destination.

Traffic slid by, swimming through a haze of rain and smog. Mari leaned her head against the passenger window. "You must've really loved this girl," she said.

"Love?" Viper frowned. "We screwed a lot, in the beginning."

"But you're risking your life to avenge her."

"I considered her a friend."

"Just a friend?"

He had to think about it. "When we met, we were young and had a sense the world was using us. As time went by there was less physical contact but more...intimacy. It was a strange relationship."

"You're a strange man, Viper Ogata."

"Yes. And now you risk your life for Sachiko's death, too."

"I'm not afraid." She wedged herself tight beside him, nuzzling her soft lips against his neck. "I feel like the safest woman in the world."

Twenty minutes later they pulled up to the Red Pagoda. Four stories of curving eaves, each smaller than the one below it. Fuchsia neon blurred the raindrops clinging to the cab window. Viper paid the driver and helped Mari out. The rain had stopped, but the air still felt slick, like warm grease. There were several discrete entrances along the ground floor. No windows, he noticed, except at the top. That could make signaling someone outside a problem. He scanned the street, wondering when Kanbei's backup would arrive.

"Not sure I like the looks of this," he said.

"C'mon." Mari tugged his wrist towards an entrance, her expression mischievous.

A wall of colorful lit panels dominated the lobby. Each one depicted a room, decorated in a particular fetishistic theme. There were rooms made up like Osaka bars, rooms done in blue with polyurethane waves crashing above the bed, rooms crammed with pinball machines...

"I want this one. It's got a horse." Mari stabbed a button beneath a panel. The panel went dark.

A frosted glass window lit in the adjacent wall. It slid up several inches and a pair of elderly hands reached out, to gesture at a placard hanging alongside. The placard gave hourly and overnight rates.

Viper counted out enough yen for a night's stay. The hands whisked the money away, to return moments later with a key. Their room was on the second floor.

"Do you have anything with a view?" Viper asked.

The window clicked shut.

Mari hummed a pop song as she nudged him to the elevator. The doors opened before she could hit the button, spilling out a balding executive-type with a slim black woman on either side. The girls were doing their best to hold him upright. He grinned at Viper through a sake haze. "You've got to try the Savannah Room," he said. "Real grass. It sways in the breeze and everything."

He wobbled off.

The second floor had thick carpeting, lit by ankle-high strips of purple neon. Viper found their room easy enough.

The first thing he noticed was the horse, impaled on a candy cane-striped pole jutting from a round bed with fuzzy pink sheets. Mari clapped her hands together. The horse looked like it had been salvaged from a children's carousel. A black leather saddle covered with chrome studs hugged its back.

He turned to lock the door. When he turned around again, Mari had shucked out of her blouse, denim skirt, and panties. She still wore the boots, though. She'd found a riding crop from somewhere and smacked the weighted end against her palm.

"What're you doing?"

"We're in a love hotel, aren't we? Don't tell me we're just going to watch TV."

"This is an investigation."

"Sure it is. Come over here and investigate, already."

"What the hell." Viper took off his blazer and unbuttoned the silk shirt underneath. Mari cooed when she saw the rainbow of irezumi tattoos circling his shoulders. He slid the tanto out of his pants. "Can I get a drink, first?"

"You're going to need it."

Midway during the performance, she reached up and tried to tug the sunglasses off his face. He pushed her hand back down against the sheets. Gently.

"I've never known pleasure on such a scale before." Perspiration beaded Mari's pale skin and soaked the bed.

"It was...creative."

"Where did you acquire such stamina?"

"Martial arts training." He propped himself up on one elbow to check the time. Two hours had passed. "Tell me what you know about Pinku Serizawa."

She pouted. "Back to business?"

"I'm afraid so."

"I've only heard a couple things. She's strict with her girls, but they're very loyal. And she wears a veil. Some client cut her face when she was first starting out. That's the rumor, anyway."

"Do you think she could be the killer?"

"Can't say."

Viper massaged his lower back. "I'm not sure how to go about this. Sneak around the building? See if I can get one of Pinku's girls sent up here?"

Feminine laughter echoed through the room. Startled, Viper whipped his head around. The laughter hadn't come from Mari.

"Let me save you the trouble, Viper Ogata," said a woman's voice. It sounded tinny. "Interesting pillow talk. Good thing I decided to listen in."

The door to the room made a thudding sound, just before ear-splitting psychedelic rock came crashing in from hidden speakers. Viper felt the bed moving underneath him. It was revolving, and the carousel horse started to bob up and down on its striped pole.

Mari screamed.

He caught a glimpse of movement in his peripheral vision. A bamboo shaft poked from between the vents of an air duct, set near the ceiling. The shaft angled down towards Mari.

He snatched up his tanto and threw it. The blade traveled straight, like an arrow, slipping between the vents. The bamboo sagged, convulsed. A purple-feathered dart struck the horse's rump and stuck there.

Viper ripped the cover from the air duct, reached up and pulled. A woman's limp form tumbled out and hit the carpet. She wore dark clothes and a partial face mask. The tanto's hilt protruded from her left eye socket.

"Kunoichi," he said, his words lost in the rock music's din. Mari screamed some more. He cast the blowgun aside and searched the body for further weapons. The shadow warrior had a wakizashi thrust through her sash. Instead of shark hide, the hilt had been wrapped with pink suede. He grimaced, but took the sword anyway.

Mari shouted questions. He motioned her for silence as he pulled on his slacks. The door wouldn't open; the thudding sound must've been magnetic bolts being thrown. He stepped back, spun, and kicked with all his strength. The door flew off its splintered hinges.

He checked the hallway. Empty, for now. He ducked back inside, grabbed Mari's naked form, and dragged her from the wailing guitars.

"We've got to get out of here," she said, eyes wide.

"Follow me."

He padded down the hall to the elevator. Trying to escape by the ground floor was too obvious. Likely, there'd be an ambush waiting. Going up seemed the best option. If he could reach the topmost tier, he could try to signal Kanbei's men through the windows. Provided they were actually outside.

Mari reached for the elevator buttons. He slapped her hand away. "Too easily trapped." He led her to the stairs. A glance through the fire window showed the stairwell empty. He shouldered the door. His brain whispered an urgent warning and he looked up, in time to see a second kunoichi braced spider-like near the ceiling. She hurled an egg-shaped object at his feet.

He shut his eyes. A searing flash burned red through his lids, and he smelled acrid smoke. Eyes still closed, he activated technique five of the ancient Ryukyuan school: the Ghost and Body Spirit Emulsion. Like a bat navigating darkness, his mind reached out and pinpointed the woman's ki energy as she leapt down. He thrust up with the wakizashi. There was the sensation of wet resistance, and then a groan. A weight slumped to the floor.

"Come on," he said, snatching for Mari's hand. He pulled her through the cloud of yellow smoke and bounded up the steps, two at a time.

They reached the last flight. Viper threw the door open and rolled out into a high-ceilinged chamber with wooden flooring and tatami mats. Plate glass windows let in the last of the evening's graying light. He sensed subtle shifts in the air before him and whipped his sword up. A shuriken clanged off the blade. He parried three more, swatting them aside with lightning-quick swipes.

"Come out and face me," he shouted, while motioning with his left hand for Mari to stay put in the stairwell.

A half dozen shapes melted out of the shadows, like phantoms made real. All women. All wearing the same dark clothing and head masks of their assassin caste. As one, they drew blades and closed on Viper from every direction.

His mind drifted back to his training in Okinawa. How the old man would spar with him while they were both knee deep in the freezing ocean. Viper used only his hands, while the master wielded a bo staff of ancient oak. For hours they would weave and feint and block, until Viper's lips turned a chattering blue and his forearms ached with bruises.

He recalled that training now, his body moving on impulse to the rhythms of a lethal dance, sword flicking out like an extension of his warrior's soul.

Seconds passed. When it was over, six dead kunoichi lay sprawled at his feet. The wakizashi's blade felt heavy with gore.

"Impressive."

A woman floated down from the ceiling. She wore a skin-tight pink bodysuit and pink satin veil. Rhinestones glimmered in a butterfly pattern across her chest. Viper knew this seemingly magical descent was another ninja trick; a coil of fine wire looped over a crossbeam, let out slowly. Still, the effect was uncanny.

Her small feet touched the floor. "I suppose it was only a matter of time before the yakuza showed up." The veil muffled her voice, but Viper recognized it as the same one that had spoken to him and Mari.

"Pinku Serizawa." He raised the wakizashi like an accusing finger. "You're the one behind all the killings."

She bowed. "Fine deductive work, Viper-san."

"But why? And why have you trained these women in the Way of the Shadow?"

"Not well enough, it seems." She glanced at the corpses strewn around Viper. "The murders are strictly business. I want to establish a monopoly on prostitution in Shinjuku, draw all the working girls away from their stupid pimps. The training is for their protection. And mine. I knew filthy men like you would eventually invade my temple, looking for their cut. That is why you're here, isn't it?"

Viper shook his head. "You owe me a debt. Of vengeance."

Pinku's bitter laughter rang through the chamber. "How ironic. It was my disfigurement, at the hands of yakuza scum, that led me on my personal path of vengeance. I suppose things have turned full circle."

"For the death of my friend, Sachiko, I claim your life."

She beckoned. "Come and take it."

He rushed towards her, blade held low. She met him halfway, turning cartwheels gracefully as a pinwheel. He slashed. She vaulted without effort, up over the sword, her body tucking into a somersault. Viper felt a sudden pressure on the back of his neck. He sprawled forward, dropping the wakizashi but managing to keep his balance. She'd kicked him in mid-air.

"Slippery bitch," he said. "I'll—"

But she was on the offensive, her limbs blurring towards him in a series of palm and wrist strikes. He blocked two frenzied blows, only to have a third find his groin. Reeling, he tried the Gichin Fist. She dodged aside. Her fingers raked across his chest, tearing skin.

"You've met your match, Viper Ogata." He sensed she was smiling beneath the veil. Steel climbing-claws jutted from the fingertips of her right hand. "I'm fast as you. Faster."

As if to prove it, she feinted with her claws. Viper's hands tracked upwards to block, and her left came out of nowhere trailing something shiny. There was a metallic click. Two chrome, fur-lined handcuffs encircled his wrists.

Pinku chuckled. "Who knew bondage gear made such good weapons? I doubt if you'll be able to fight as well without your hands."

"Try me."

"Oh, I will." Still chuckling, she drew a huge purple dildo from behind her back. Her fingers closed around the shaft, twisted. Out slid an eight-inch blade of gleaming steel.

A war-whoop echoed from the stairwell.

Mari came bolting past, shrieking, one of the downed kunoichi's daggers in her clumsy grip. She aimed a blow at Pinku, but before it could connect the ninja master ran her through with the dildo-sword. Mari drooped to her knees, muttering Viper's name.

He took two running steps forward. His legs leapt in the intricate movements of ancient Ryukyuan technique number three: the Yoko Tobi Geri, or Flying Side Kick. Distracted by Mari, Pinku had no time to dodge. Viper's heel made a satisfying *crack* as it connected with her chin. She shot backwards. Her lithe form struck a window and sailed through in a shower of broken glass.

Viper landed close enough to see her slide down the eaves, shattering neon tubes as she went. She dropped out of sight. There were two distinct thuds moments apart, then the sickening wet sound of flesh striking concrete.

That should be enough to signal Kanbei.

"Viper."

Mari crawled to him, trailing slick blood across the varnished floor. He knelt and grasped her hand. Pinku's thrust had opened her gut from hip to sternum.

"You did it," she whispered. "You avenged Sachiko's death."

"*We* did it."

"Viper, I've only known you a short time, but I..."

Her chest heaved. The rest of her words were lost in the death rattle.

Outside, through the shattered pane, he heard multiple clunks of car doors opening and slamming shut. Soon, gunfire would echo through the building as Kanbei's men battled the remaining kunoichi. Pinku Serizawa's reign was over. But what did that leave him with, exactly?

He contemplated the price of vengeance as the sky darkened, and Shinjuku skyline glowed in the distance.

THE END

Very little is known about the elusive Tony Amtrak—mostly rumors and conjecture and rumored conjecture. Some say he was a former Italian mafioso, now in witness protection. Others claim he was yakuza, now in witness protection. The only detail the rumors share is that he was a criminal of some kind, which may account for the lags between publishing dates for his most famous series, featuring Viper. Luckily he got time off for good behavior. Or he escaped. Or witness protection.

GARNETT ELLIOTT found this 1980 martial arts adventure under the passenger seat of a rental Toyota Corolla in Yuma, Arizona. He also found three .38 shell casings, a catcher's mask, a Ping-Pong ball, and a woman's pump, size 6.

A.R.V.N. WAR CHRONICLES
presents
NEVER SAY GOOD NIGHT IN SAIGON
by Greg Peppard, Jr., 1st Sgt., US Army (Ret.)
(discovered by Jimmy Callaway)

IT WAS 3 A.M. and the VAA Nightclub was enjoying another quiet evening. The rain pattered its soft staccato on the tin roof, accompanied by the dribble-drop of the leaky patches in the ceiling into old gourds. Mama Tu had gotten the children to sleep around midnight and allowed herself to doze in her chair.

But just as she was nodding off, Yen awoke, fussing in her crib. Mama Tu gripped the worn bamboo arms of her chair and hoisted her tiny, wrinkled form up and over to the infant. It wasn't just that Yen was the fussiest baby she had seen in all her years, it was that she was the saddest. As if the oddly rounded eyes had glimpsed her future and that of her homeland. It pulled at a place deep inside Mama Tu every time the baby girl looked at her.

Wrapping the child in her blankets, Mama Tu picked her up. As she walked the baby around the room, she sang softly:
Vì dầu cầu ván đóng đinh,
Cầu tre lắc lẻo. gập gềnh khó đi.
But in Saigon, peace never lasted for long. Just as the lines in the baby's tiny forehead softened into slumber, a big man wearing a burlap sack for a mask kicked in the front door and aimed an AK-47 at Mama Tu. Two others followed, hurriedly closing the door behind them. They were also armed and masked—one an even bigger man, and the other a skinny young woman.

Yen did not rouse from her sleep.

Xuan Loc was forty miles north of MACV, but it took Corporal Mathes nearly an hour to get there. He'd learned to drive on the freeways of Los Angeles, but that was nothing compared to Saigon during rainy season. The greasy rain slid down in lazy sheets. Motor scooters and Renaults slalomed through the traffic, horns bleating and braying. It was a little easier going once outside city limits, and Mathes finally arrived at III Corps and met with Major Le.

"Bonjour, Corporal," said the little major as he returned Mathes' salute. "And how may I be of service to the United States Army today?"

Mathes frowned. "I'm sorry, sir, didn't Major Taylor call your office?"

Major Le cleared his throat. "And how may I be of service to the United States Army today?"

Mathes' frowned deepened, and then it hit him. He retrieved the transfer papers Major Taylor had given him: yesterday's copy of *Le Courrier du Vietnam* wrapped around five American twenty-dollar bills.

Major Le took the papers and smiled. "Please follow me, Corporal."

Mathes had been in-country for a year, and he still couldn't get used to these ARVN officers, their accents more French than Vietnamese. But he saluted properly and followed Le to a group of Quonset huts. Two ARVN privates came to attention on their arrival. They held their M-16s to the side, order arms position. Le barked at them in Vietnamese, and one of the privates opened the padlock on the door.

"Sergeant Tinh!" Le shouted in English. "Front and center!"

In the shadows of the hut, through the drizzly rain in his face, Mathes could see several figures stirring from various positions of confinement. And then through the door came the meanest-looking gook Mathes had ever seen.

Like a lot of Vietnamese, he was a little guy, but he stood as though he were Atlas, as though he held up the world without breaking a sweat. His face looked carved from stone—hooded almond eyes and a scar across his brow gave him a permanent scowl. His wide shoulders strained at the dingy tigerstripe cammies. His biceps bulged at the sleeves. His hands were as cracked and dirty as his combat boots. He blinked at the gray light of day, and his eyes landed on Mathes.

"Got a cigarette, Joe?" he said.

"Sergeant Tinh," Major Le said, "I am temporarily releasing you into the custody of Corporal Mathes. Our American allies have a situation they feel you are well suited to handle. Upon completion of this mission, you are to return at once to serve the remainder of your sentence. Is that clear?"

Tinh grunted. "Mm. Yes, sir."

Le smiled at Mathes. "He is, as you say, all yours, Corporal. Please extend my regards to Major Taylor."

Mathes saluted again, doing his best not to show his dislike for this little ratfuck officer. Tinh caught his eye and winked.

In the jeep, Mathes handed Tinh a pack of Luckies and matches, both wrapped in cellophane. Tinh carefully unwrapped them, poked a nail into the corner of his mouth, and lit it, striking the match with his thumbnail, his hand protecting the flame from the wet.

"Mm," he said, "makes a fine tobacco. Thanks, Joe."

"Mathes."

"Thanks, Mathes."

"Had you in the stockade, huh?"

Tinh raised his eyebrows. "Yep."

"What for?"

Tinh shrugged. "Don't know. Could be anything. I was drunk."

Mathes grinned as he fought to keep the Jeep in the flooded ruts of the dirt road. When Tinh tried to hand back the smokes, Mathes waved him off.

Major Taylor had gotten bored with lobbing darts at the picture of Henry Cabot Lodge. So now Sergeant Kitchen stood in front of the dartboard, doing his best to stand completely at attention.

"Uh, sir?" he said.

Major Taylor closed one eye, aimed. "Hold it right there." Taylor released the dart and reformed the part in Kitchen's hair. "Excellent. Yes, Sergeant, what is it?"

"Sir, I don't mean to, you know...I just don't understand why this Tinh, sir? Why bring a gook in on American business?"

"Tell me, Sergeant. You're gunning for the OCS, are you not?"

Kitchen stiffened a bit, allowed a small smile. "Yes, sir."

"Well, one thing I can tell you," Taylor said, flinging another dart. It hit the wall just past Kitchen's ear. "Explaining yourself to non-coms is not a habit you want to get into."

"Yes, sir."

"On the other hand," Taylor said, "I am bored out of my mind right now. Sergeant, whatever your feelings about this mission, it's simply not something we can ignore and hope will go away. It calls for action, not advice."

"All due respect, sir, but we're all pretty bored around here."

"Today, yes, but that will change any minute, if it hasn't already. That fucking idiot Diem had to go get himself assassinated. And now I hear the reds have made the Gulf of Tonkin into a practice range. If the White House has its way, this war will get hot overnight."

"That's great news, sir!"

"Yes, well, officially, I applaud your enthusiasm, Sergeant."

"Thank you, sir!"

"Unofficially, I think you are a braying jackass. I may be bored keeping MACV fully stocked with paper clips, but I didn't join this man's army to fight phantom commies in canopy jungle. If we go to war, fine, but I see no reason to hurry it along."

"Can't we get SOG to take care of this, sir? Isn't this their specialty?"

"Indeed it is, but without a handwritten invitation from LBJ, the only thing the Studies and Observations Group will be studying and observing is as much pussy as they can handle. Which is quite a bit, to hear them tell it." Major Taylor leaned back in his chair and hurled a dart into the drop-tile ceiling. It took its place with four or five others, along with a few sharpened pencils.

"So we go to ARVN," Kitchen said.

"And so we go to ARVN. Let them get what action they can before our Marines come over and hog all the enemy rounds."

"But this Tinh, sir, he's—he's not even an officer."

"Don't be a complete idiot, Sergeant. ARVN's officers run their army like Sergeant Bilko ran his motor pool. They'll rob you blind, and then steal your smoked spectacles. The enlisted men are the only ones worth a shit, and Sergeant Son Tinh is better equipped for this sort of thing than even an American officer, present company very much included. Any more questions?"

"No, sir."

"Good. Now, hold perfectly still..."

Mathes burst into the room, and Taylor's dart landed point-first in Kitchen's knee. Kitchen bit the inside of his cheek to keep from screaming. Mathes had to clench his own fists to keep from laughing.

"Major Taylor, sir!" Mathes said in loud, shaky voice. Kitchen stared daggers at him. "Reporting with Sergeant Tinh as ordered, sir!"

"Very good. Sergeant Tinh," Taylor said, returning their salute, "I trust all is well in the 18th?"

"Yes, sir."

"Lovely. At ease. Sergeant Tinh, as I'm sure you're aware, we have quite a situation on our hands."

Mathes glanced at Kitchen, the dart in his knee, sweat beading on his forehead. When Taylor wasn't looking, Kitchen plucked the dart from his flesh, visibly blanching at the sight of blood on the tip. A strangled giggle escaped from Mathes.

Taylor turned quickly. "Is there something funny, Corporal Mathes?"

"Sir, no, sir!" He kept his eyes on a corner of the ceiling.

"As I was saying, Sergeant Tinh," Taylor said, "we have a situation here and I feel you're the only man I can turn to."

"Mm. Thank you, sir."

"Yes, well, don't thank me yet. Tell me, Sergeant, have you ever heard of the Vietnam AmerAsian Nightclub?"

Thuy was trying to think. He allowed his fists to unclench and focused inward, on the formations therein. Once again, he felt serenity and tranquility in his grasp, if only those bastard mongrels would shut the fuck up.

Fists clenched again, Thuy rose from his mat and stomped over to the bastard pen, where the mongrels mewled and whimpered. Father had always told him that he was the most impatient, irresponsible boy he'd ever seen—could never wait for anything, but always late for everything. But even as a young whelp, he could not possibly have made this much noise!"Quiet!" he shouted, his long mustache trembling past his chin. "You have been fed! There will be no more!"

My poked her head up through the trap door in the far corner. A smudge of dust lay above one thin eyebrow. "Thuy!" she said. "Why do you shout at them? They cannot understand you."

"They will learn!" Thuy said. "Yes, they will learn their true purpose if I have to beat it into them!"

My climbed into the room and shook her dirty slippers off, revealing her delicate feet. As she approached the pen, a troubled look disturbed her features. "Oh," she said, sniffing at the air, "no wonder they're upset. Don't you smell that?"

"All I smell is the Yankee blood in these...mutants."

"They need to be changed," My said, retrieving clean diapers from the bureau, some old safety pins from the glass jar atop it. "Go back to your meditations, Thuy. I will change them myself."

"Sergeant Tinh," Taylor said, "as you know, the American military has had a presence in your country for some time, back when your people were fighting the French. Though our government has been careful to stress that we are not here as combat troops, that does not preclude some engagement with the natives. Do you understand?"

"No, sir."

"Right. Well, Sergeant, when men—soldiers—are overseas, it does not take long before they miss the comforts of home."

"Mm. Boom-boom."

Mathes dug his nails into his palms. In nine weeks of Basic, he never cracked once, and here he was going to lose it in front of a Major, a First Sergeant, and an ARVN Sergeant on a top-secret mission. Fuck this country.

"Yes," Taylor said, clearing his throat, "boom-boom. And boom-boom, as history has shown us, leads to children." The Major actually began to redden a bit. "Now, Sergeant, a man cannot simply bring home a child at the end of his tour. The wife and kids might not take well to a new baby brother or sister."

"*Bụi đời*," Tinh said.

"Yes, I believe that's the native phrase. Not as harsh as the English—"

"Bastards," snarled Sergeant Kitchen.

"Thank you, Sergeant. Now, lest you think all Americans heartless, Sergeant Tinh, there has been a sort of enterprise enacted to look after these children, to try to keep them off the streets."

"Mm. This nightclub."

"Yes. Vietnam AmerAsians is the quaint label our government gave these little bundles of joy. Despite whatever monetary support their fathers see fit to part with, their mothers often must continue to work, as waitresses, bar mistresses—"

"Whores," said Kitchen.

"Sergeant Kitchen, do you want to take over this briefing?"

"Uh, no, sir, I—"

"The VAA Nightclub," Taylor went on, "is the home of an old mama-san who watches over these infants. A Mrs...what's the name again, Sergeant Bigmouth?"

Mathes actually whimpered a bit in the back of his throat.

"Tu, sir," Kitchen said. "Mama Tu, the men call her. Sir."

"Yes, and unfortunately, Sergeant Tinh, these children have just last night been kidnapped from under Mama Tu's watchful eyes."

"How many?" said Tinh.

"Three boys and a girl. We received word that they are being held for ransom at $10,000 apiece. Even if we had the money, which we don't, there is little doubt these children would not be returned alive."

"Yes, sir. You want me to find these *bụi đời* and bring them back alive."

"Can you do it, Sergeant? We need it done quietly and very, very quickly."

"Yes, sir."

Taylor smiled down at him. "Very well. We have picked the right man for this job. Dismissed."

"Sir?"

"Yes, Sergeant Kitchen."

Mathes dared to take his eyes from the ceiling and saw Kitchen glaring at him as he spoke. Glaring and grinning. "Sir, as grateful as I'm sure we all are for Sergeant Tinh's help, perhaps it would be wise to send one of our men along with him." He paused, and Mathes could have sworn he was about to lick his lips. "In a purely advisory capacity, of course."

My hummed as she tended the cookfire, boiling some milk. A loose strand of hair hung in her face and she brushed it back behind her ear. Thuy felt the foolish yearning for her he'd felt when they were but children. He hurriedly pushed it away. "Woman!" he said. "Where is my supper? Must I wait until these brats are seen to?"

"They'll be awake soon, Thuy," she said softly. "Even sooner if you don't keep your voice down."

"This is my home! I'll speak as I please."

"It was your idea to bring these children here," My said. "Your glorious five-day plan."

"I will not be mocked, woman," Thuy said as he strode towards her. "Not even by you."

Hai ran into the hut. "Sir! The Americans have enlisted Son Tinh, sir! Just as you said they would, sir!" Hai's broad grin and lazy right eye made him look more like a stupid kid than usual.

Thuy allowed himself a smile. "Excellent news, comrade. Assure Le he will be justly recompensed."

Hai frowned. "Sir...?"

Thuy fetched a weary sigh. "Tell Le he will get boo-koo reward. The weapons have all been cleaned and inspected?"

"Yes, sir!" Hai said, "I inspected them myself."

"Well, I suppose we'll have to hope for the best anyway."

Hai smiled, but My scowled at Thuy. "Thuy! Hai has done nothing but serve you loyally. Must you be so...so unpleasant?"Thuy grunted. "Good work, Hai. Go below and tell the men to prepare. We should expect Sergeant Tinh in the next 36 hours. 48 at most."

Hai saluted and hurried down through the trap door.

My smiled after him. "You see—"

Thuy gripped her by the arm and whirled her around. "You will not chide me in front of my troops, woman! Understand?"

"Thuy, you're hurting me—"

"Do you understand? Answer me!"

My's eyes flashed, but then she lowered her head. "Yes."

"What?"

My's lower lip trembled. "Yes, sir."

Thuy released her arm.

The milk began to burn, and the smell of rancid almonds floated on the air. In their pen, the mongrels awoke and began crying.

The Nightclub was a few blocks away, but Tinh insisted they go up to the marketplace, procure themselves some cigarettes and some *bac si de*. Mathes glared at him. "Hardly the time for a drink, Sarge."

"Always time for a drink, Joe."

"Man, goddammit—my name is Mathes. Corporal Mathes!"

"What's your first name, Mathes?"

Mathes' face got redder. "All right, it is Joseph, as a matter of fact. But you didn't fuckin' know that!"

"Mm," Tinh said, the corner of his mouth tugging up a fraction. "You don't like this mission, do you, Mathes?"

"Following some crazy Arvin Christ-knows-where to save a handful of half-gook bastards? The fuck do you think? That sound like a good mission to you, Sarge?"

"No, it don't," Tinh said. "But it does sound like you need a drink."

Even in the rain, the marketplace was packed, water dripping from the colorful overhangs at each stall. Mathes had never ventured down here, preferring to take his chances on whatever C-rations they had back at MACV. And with good reason, he now saw. Everybody in the marketplace chattered loudly, bickering back and forth. Mathes saw bottles of wine with scorpions in them, fertilized duck eggs eaten with a spoon, and in one lone stall was something called *thit cho*. Mathes asked Tinh what that was.

"Mm. Dog meat."

Mathes almost puked right there. "Jesus Christ, man!"

"Mm. Big in Hanoi," said Tinh.

Mathes followed in Tinh's steps. No one seemed to give the big Yankee a second glance, but Mathes couldn't shake the feeling they were all staring. They arrived at a stall, and Mathes stationed himself in the corner where no one could sneak up on him.

The stall's owner greeted Tinh with a hearty smile, and Mathes was surprised to see Tinh smile back. They took the next minute to scream at each other in Vietnamese and French.

"Hey, Tinh," Mathes said, "calm down. What's the problem?"

"We're haggling. How much money you got, Mathes?"

Mathes shrugged. "I dunno. Fifty bucks."

"Mm. Lemme borrow it, huh?"

"What?"

"You want this mission over with ASAP, right?"

"Well, yeah—"

"Then borrow me fifty bucks."

Mathes reached for his wallet. His eyes popped. "My fuckin' wallet's gone! Goddammit, I—"

Tinh held up his wallet. "Gotta watch that, Mathes. Lotsa pickpockets."

Mathes snatched at it, but Tinh removed the cash first before handing it back. Tinh looked at the owner, held up the money.

The owner turned and hollered at the back of the stall. A moment later, a small boy appeared carrying a case of Lucky Strikes. Tinh handed it to Mathes. "Makes a fine tobacco."

Mathes grunted.

Tinh and the owner spoke some more, their raucous Vietnamese giving Mathes a headache. The owner reached under the table and produced an unlabeled bottle. Tinh took it and they yelled at each other some more until the owner handed him another bottle. Tinh handed over Mathes' cash.

"Let's go," he said.

In the jeep, Tinh pulled the cork from one of the bottles and took a pull, then another. He handed it to Mathes.

"I'm driving here, man."

"Mm. I know." Tinh pushed the bottle at him.

Mathes took it and glanced down at the milky stuff inside. Looked harmless. How much bite could there be in whiskey made of rice? He put the bottle to his lips and knocked back a quick slug.

Fire immediately spread over his tongue. Mathes jerked the wheel to the left, almost plowing into a scooter. As Mathes corrected the jeep, a cottony feel dripped down his throat, coated his guts. It felt like a thin layer of Fluffernutter in his esophagus.

"Mm," Tinh said. "Good?"

Mathes smiled and nodded.

"Mm. Good."

They found Mama Tu on the porch of the VAA Nightclub, bundled up in her chair, watching the drizzle and smoking a cigarette. She didn't look any worse for the wear to Mathes, except he'd never seen her scowl quite like that. Could just be that he'd never seen her in the light of day.

Tinh bowed deeply to her and nudged Mathes to do the same. Tinh elbowed Mathes again, and Mathes handed her one of the whiskey bottles.

She leaned forward to take it. "Thankee, Joe."

"Yes, ma'am."

Tinh handed her the other bottle. She said in Vietnamese, "They stuck you with this round-eye?"

"He's here in an advisory capacity."

Mama Tu laughed. "And who's going to advise him?" she said, smiling warmly at Mathes. Mathes smiled back. The rain came down harder, but she did not invite them onto the porch.

"Mama Tu," Tinh said, "please tell me what happened."

She pulled on her cigarette. "I was watching the babies. The boys were sleeping, but Yen began crying. She had a nightmare."

"What time?"

"About three. Then this big asshole came stomping in and shoved a gun in my face, said they were taking the babies."

"They?"

"Him and two others. Wearing masks."

"What did they look like? Apart from the masks?"

Mama Tu got up from her chair and went into the house. Mathes looked at Tinh. Tinh watched the door patiently. Mama Tu returned with three glasses and handed them to Tinh. He poured as she lowered herself back into the chair.

Mama Tu said, "*Mot hai ba, yo*," and they all clinked glasses. Mathes took a sip but saw that they were draining theirs. He held his breath and guzzled his. When he brought the glass down, the rain blurred his eyes. He wiped at them, but they were still blurry.

Mama Tu said, "The leader was big. A scar down his right forearm. The other man was bigger, moved like he didn't know how his body worked. An idiot. They both had country accents. Farm boys."

"And the third?"

Mama Tu looked at her glass. "A woman. Small, skinny. Very young."

Tinh's glass shattered in his hand.

Mathes said, "Jesus! What is it?"

Tinh said to Mama Tu, "You knew who they were."

She looked at him. "I know who I wish they weren't."

Mathes had no idea what to make of Tinh's expression. Confusion? Fear? Any emotion looked out of place on Tinh, and Mathes wasn't sure it wasn't the booze talking. Jesus, these gooks could brew some whiskey.

After a second, Tinh's normal blank look returned. "Mm. Thank you, Mama Tu."

Mama Tu gestured with her glass. "Thank you, Son Tinh."

Tinh bowed again. Mathes did the same. He followed Tinh to the jeep, pulled his poncho out from under the driver's seat, and put it on. "Where to?" he said.

"Hell," Sergeant Tinh said. "But we gotta make a stop first."

The rain poured down, but the compound was largely dry. Deep in the jungle thicket, the four huts sat under protection of the green canopy. The creek that ran alongside swelled, but was far from reaching the high banks. My knew this would not last if the rain kept up like this.

She carefully walked across the rickety bridge, her yellow *ao dai* plastered to her lithe form. She stopped and looked up at the gray sky. She thought she heard a plane, her toes involuntarily curling in her slippers. But it was just her imagination.

At the far end of the bridge, Thuy unpacked the case of MON-50 claymores and handed them to My. He was in unusually high spirits, humming as he worked.

"Darling," she said, "this bridge would collapse under the weight of a large sneeze. Is all this ordinance really necessary?"

Thuy clucked his tongue. "My dear girl, once this war gets properly underway, it's only the drama anyone will remember. We have to give the fucking Americans a show or we'll never get rid of them. That's all they give a shit about: fireworks."

"The Americans? I thought Son Tinh—I thought he was expected?" My frowned up at the sky, as though the gods were listening.

"Same fucking thing, as far as I'm concerned."

"But the tunnels will be manned, there will be ground patrols inside the perimeter. Anyone with even half a brain would never use this old thing in a frontal assault." She batted at the bridge to emphasize her point. It groaned in agreement.

"If this goes like I think it will, no one will cross this bridge until it's all over. If it's me, I'll blow the damn thing myself. If it's our adversary," he said, pulling the tripwire tight across the mouth of the bridge, "then he'll do the honors for me."

And then Thuy actually smiled.

"Who the fuck're these guys again?" Mathes said. He had a terrible itch on his nose, but he didn't dare scratch.

"Old friends," Tinh said. His hands, like Mathes', were held high in the air.

The docks on this part of the Saigon River were rotting. Any boats moored were peeling apart at the seams, clinging to buoyancy. As they had approached, they'd seen no signs of life, except for some stray dogs Mathes later realized were rats. The little shipyard looked abandoned apart from the chain link gate, which looked brand new. Mathes had been admiring the action on it, how easily it rolled, when he looked up and there was a pistol in his face.

If the five men holding guns on them were bothered by the rain, they didn't show it. They stood silent, the rain hammering the hulking wrecks of pontoons and various other boats in the yard. The five gooks were dressed in ratty uniforms pieced together from other armies: a French shirt, a Russian jacket, Chinese hats. The United Nations of Fuck You, Yankee.

"Now what?" Mathes said to Tinh from the corner of his mouth.

A raucous laugh rose from behind the shack in the center of the yard. "What are these vermin we've caught?" A voice in Vietnamese. "Too skinny for wharf rats!"

"It's Son Tinh, you toothless fuck. Call off your dogs."

A tiny man came around the shack, his rusty M-16 as big as he. When he laughed again, Mathes saw his mouth, as black as the ace of clubs. "Gimme one good reason I should help you, Son Tinh!"

"Because if you don't, Gummy Ba, I'll rape that toothless hole in your head right here in front of your men."

None of Gummy Ba's men blinked, but they all racked the slides on their pistols.

"Jesus Christ!" Mathes said. "The fuck you say to them?"

"Ha ha!" Gummy Ba said. "Your ladyfriend is jealous, Son Tinh! Better send her back to Hollywood!"

"You like?" Son Tinh said. "I was going to trade you something else for help, but..."

"What're you talking about?"

"We need your help to fight Thuy. Now's your chance to get back at him for making you look like a faggot back in '55."

Ba pointed the M-16 at Tinh's face. "Help you? Gimme one goddamn reason!"

"The case of American cigarettes we got in the jeep."

"Yeah, that's a good one." Gummy Ba lowered his weapon. His men lowered theirs. "Hey, Joe," Ba said to Mathes in English, "you got smokee? Why the fuck you no say?"

An hour before, these gooks held guns on him. Now they were getting him absolutely polluted on rice whiskey and *Mu'o'i Bu*, the shittiest beer Mathes had ever eagerly guzzled in his life. As the sun went down, they cooked chickens on a spit over an oil drum, a leaky tarp keeping most of the rain off them. The wind whipped rain in at them occasionally, but it wasn't long before they were too drunk to care.

"The fuck're these guys again?" Mathes said.

"Các Binh Sĩ Cũ," Tinh replied, lighting Mathes' cigarette.

"The Old Soldiers, Joe!" Gummy Ba shouted in his face. Even past the booze and meat, Gummy Ba's breath smelled like twice-cooked shit.

"Uh-huh," Mathes said. "Like ARVN?"

"Fuck ARVN!" Gummy Ba said. "Fuck ARVN, fuck the Minh, and fuck fuckin' Uncle Ho! You like that, Joe?"

"Sure thing." Mathes smiled. Gummy Ba laughed some more and wandered off for another beer. Mathes turned to Tinh. "How do you know these nutjobs, Sarge?"

Tinh took a long pull from his bottle. "Long time ago, there was the *Binh Xuyen*. Like ARVN, but not as shitty. We were an independent army inside the VNA. Part of it, but we run our own business."

"Used to be you boys' outfit, huh?"

"Yes, a good outfit. We fight the French, fuck them up good. But they drive us south anyways. *Binh Xuyen* good soldiers, but better gangsters."

"Gangsters?"

"We fucking owned Saigon, Joe!" Gummy Ba said, loping up to them with a fresh beer in each hand. "We smuggle, run protection, kidnap rich fucks. We owned this town!"

"It's true," said Tinh. "We kept the Viet Minh and the Red Chinese cocksuckers out of Saigon. But then our leader, our general, Bay Vien, he fuck up."

"He try to take out Diem, Joe! How you like that? The fucking president!"

"He fuck up bad. Have to...what you say? Exile?"

"Exile, yeah."

Gummy Ba puckered his lips and batted his eyelashes. "He go to gay Paree! Become dancing girl! Make boom-boom with boo-koo French soldiers!" And then he laughed from deep in his chest.

"Bay Vien exiled to Paris. *Binh Xuyen* all over with, far as we're concerned. I joined ARVN. Ba stayed with his crew."

"What's left of it," Ba said.

"And Thuy?" Mathes said. "He a part of all that?"

"Mm. He went with Diem. For a time, anyway."

"Fuck Diem," Gummy Ba said with a sneer and sulked off.

"The regular VNA kicked the shit out of us. Ran us out of Saigon, pushed us back into the jungle. Rung Sat. And we kept fighting anyway. Had nothing else to do. One night, middle of a firefight, Thuy was about to slit Ba's throat until I showed up. We fought, but it was a draw. It was always a draw, since we were kids."

"Kids?"

"Mm. He had a knife, gave me this." Tinh pointed at the scar on his brow. "I took it away from him, though, tried to put it through his heart, but only managed to slice his arm open. And then Ba cold-cocked him and we got the fuck out of there."

"You guys knew each other when you were kids?" Mathes said.

Sergeant Tinh sighed. "Mathes, it's late. We got a day and a half hump to talk about all that."

"Oh, okay," Mathes said and drained his bottle. Then he spit it all out. "Fuckin' day and a half?"

It was just over a day's haul down the Saigon River to the Mekong. Gummy Ba and his crew had a gunboat that had seen its best days in the Big One. There was barely enough room for the eight of them, but they were too wired on booze and impending combat to give a shit.

As they approached Vi Thanh, Ba killed the engines. They left the boat in a meander, the trees creating something like a cave. Mathes had never seen such pitch black before. He longed for the streetlights of the city, any city.

"Let's go," Sergeant Tinh said.

They humped through the jungle, Mathes weighed down with a heavy pack full of rations. They didn't plan on being in the jungle for long but, as Ba put it, "Nobody plans to starve to death, Joe. It just happen!"

Tinh, Ba, and his men each had M1 rifles. Ba was armed with his trusty, rusty M-16. And one man, Lang, had an AK.

They had not walked long when Lang, on point, held up a hand. They all stopped. Ba and Tinh whispered in Vietnamese. Ba signaled to Lang. Lang melted into the jungle.

"Now what?" Mathes said.

"Lang's going on recon," Tinh said. "Smoke 'em if you got 'em."

"Where are we? Do we even know where we're going?"

"Yep."

"Well, how? How do you know where this Thuy is holed up?"

Tinh lit himself a cigarette, the light of the flame cupped in his hands. "Because we grew up here."

Two hours later, Lang was back with the skinny: four huts formed a square in a small clearing two klicks away. Ten men patrolling the grounds. Lights on in one hut, but men in and out of two of the other three. A creek ran along the east of the clearing, spanned by a rickety wooden bridge. Half a klick north of the bridge was a tunnel entrance. There was no way to know how many men were down there, waiting for them.

"Only one way to find out," Tinh said.

As they approached the clearing, the rain tapered off and then stopped altogether.

"Good deal," Mathes whispered.

"Mm," Tinh said, "not so much. We could have used the cover."

"You want cover, Son Tinh?" Gummy Ba said. "We can do that."

And he hurled a grenade towards the clearing.

The bullets whizzed above Mathes' head as he followed Sergeant Tinh to the tunnel entrance, the yellow trails of the bullets in the air like fireflies. Thuy's men sounded the charge, but Gummy Ba's crew remained relatively quiet, their bursts of rifle-fire short and sharp. The answering fire was long and scattered, giving Ba and his men plenty of time to maneuver while the enemy fired wild into the bush.

Mathes felt his throat dry up, nearly closing. He wished for the first time since he'd landed in this soggy nightmare that it'd fucking rain again. He held his service revolver in both hands, covering the Sarge's back. As they neared the tunnel, one of Thuy's men popped out like a jack-in-the-box.

Tinh was on him with his KA-BAR in an instant, giving the gook another smile under his chin. The next man out of the tunnel got Tinh's boot in his face. Mathes heard the man's nose smash into his own skull, and his K-rations started coming back on him. Tinh stomped the man's face twice more, just to be sure. "Let's go."

The tunnel was small, the ceiling so low that even Tinh had to hunch over. Mathes' knuckles were almost to the ground. There was little light, a low red glow, but Mathes never determined the source. He just stayed on the Sarge's heels, almost bowling him over each time they came to a cross-tunnel and the Sarge stopped to listen for approaching enemy. Mathes had no idea how long they were down there, time a distant memory, like pussy or joy. The weight of the earth above, the jungle, the foreign men and their foreign war, they all pressed down on Mathes' head, until he felt like screaming his throat raw.

At the next cross-tunnel, two men approached from their left. Tinh let the first one crawl past, and then jammed his knife into the neck of the second man. He died silently, his windpipe neatly sliced in half, but as his body collapsed to the ground, his buddy turned. He drew in a breath. Mathes raised his pistol.

"No!" Tinh said, but Mathes pulled the trigger and blew the gook's brains out the back of his hat. The shot deafened them both, and for a second, Mathes wasn't sure that he hadn't just shot himself in the head.

Tinh didn't take the time to explain that Mathes had ruined whatever stealth they'd had. He just worked the strap of the AK off the nearest dead man and took point. He moved dead ahead, heedless of any cross-tunnels.

They turned right, then left, then right again. Tinh caught sight of two more men coming at him from fifty feet away. He put his shoulders up, trying to cover his ears as best he could, and opened fire. The AK tore through both men. Tinh never stopped, stepped right over the bodies in his path. His throbbing ears picked up shouts, but he had no idea where they were coming from. He kept his finger on the trigger.

"Mathes!" he shouted. "Your six!"

Mathes turned and the big gook was on top of him. How they ever fit this boy down in this tunnel was beyond him. He was shirtless, and his brown skin almost glowed. He leered at Mathes as he brought his hands up around the young corporal's throat. Mathes stared bug-eyed as the boy—he couldn't be any older than Mathes—strangled him with his massive hands. It took Mathes only a few seconds, though, before he put his Colt .45 under the boy's chin and painted the ceiling with his brains.

"Jesus," Mathes said, his whisper loud in his skull. "Jesus Christ."

"Mm," said Tinh, "let's go. And bring your buddy."

Gummy Ba had killed at least eight of Thuy's men by himself, the jungle his cloak. He almost laughed out loud as Thuy's men ran around like cocks with no hens. Thuy must have got these faggots wholesale from Hong Kong.

Lang appeared next to where Ba squatted watching the main hut, the soft light of its cookfire in the window. Lang nodded towards it, but Ba shook his head. "This is Tinh's fight."

In the hut, Thuy sat in the lotus position, his rifle oiled and cleaned at his side. My lay on the floor, her sights on the trapdoor in the corner. The mongrels howled now. Thuy had almost succeeded in shutting out the noise, the screams, the smell of smoke. But then Hai burst in. A thin trail of blood was spattered across his face.

"Sir!" he said, "they're killing us out there! I don't know what to do!"

"You can start by shutting the fuck up." Thuy rose. He walked calmly to Hai, the idiot's lazy eye spinning in uncontrollable circles in its socket. Thuy smiled and then slapped him in the face. "And then you can close the door. We're expecting our real company any moment now."

Hai did as he was told and then squatted down in the opposite corner from the trapdoor, his rifle in his shaking hands.

Thuy stood in the center of the room, his hands clasped behind his back. The rain outside started up again, a few sprinkles on the roof, and then sheets of rain. The scar on Thuy's right arm began to itch.

Slowly, so slowly, the trapdoor opened.

My's whole body tensed, then relaxed.

A hand poked up through the trapdoor. Then the door itself opened all the way.

My fired, just once. The trapdoor slammed shut, and they heard the ladder snap as whoever it was fell back to the tunnel floor. The babies screamed louder.

Hai laughed. He bounced across the room and flung the trapdoor open.

My had time to shout, "Hai!" before a .45 round tore Hai's face off.

Sergeant Son Tinh rose from out of the tunnel. He fired Mathes' revolver at My, clipping her in the shoulder. The yellow of her *ao dai* blossomed a red flower. She fell to the floor with a cry, landing on her narrow bottom.

Tinh faced his brother. "Shall we?" he said to Thuy Tinh.

"We shall."

Corporal Joseph Mathes once saw a Marine, a big black private, smash another Marine's teeth into a curb outside a bar in Fallbrook. In high school, he saw two greasers get in a knife fight over a girl, watched as one slit the other's stomach open. The kid's guts showed, just a little, through the curtain of blood. A bunch of the guys, just six months ago, dragged him to a dogfight in Cholon, and he watched two scrawny mutts fight until one tore the other's throat out with its teeth.

He'd never seen anything like this.

Tinh dropped Mathes' pistol, and then carefully removed and laid down the AK strapped to his chest. He tossed the KA-BAR away. It landed point-first in the floor with a thunk. Thuy kicked away his own AK. He lifted his shirt to show no weapons in his belt. Then they both bowed to each other.

Thuy leapt across the room with a yell. Tinh blocked his punch and then bowled him over. Thuy landed on his back, and kicked up, catching Tinh in the chest. Tinh took three steps back as Thuy leapt to his feet in one motion, landed in a crouch, and swept a kick at Tinh's legs. Tinh jumped, bending his legs at the knees, and then landed knee-first as he delivered a tremendous punch to Thuy's face. Both men rolled back into a somersault, onto their feet, and back into a crouch. Thuy smiled at his brother. Tinh did not return it.

This time they came at each other simultaneously. Mathes, crouched on top of the tunnel's ladder, could not make out their individual fists in the flurry of blows that followed. Each man would block, block, block, every third or fourth blow finding its mark. Blood exploded from Thuy's nose, Tinh's mouth. Tinh grabbed Thuy's left arm and pulled it up behind his back. Thuy stomped his instep and elbowed him in the kidney with his free arm.

Tinh whirled back and around. Thuy spun him further, whipping him into the wall. Mathes looked to the woman still staring at her bloody shoulder in disbelief, and then moved his attention to the bamboo pen where the babies were kept. They screamed and howled. But one baby had pulled herself up and was just standing there. Watching.

Thuy pinned Tinh's throat to the wall and punched him in the breadbasket. As the air rushed out his lungs, Tinh felt Thuy's hold on his throat tighten. He butted at Thuy's face, but Thuy shook the blow off and laughed.

"When you get to hell, little brother," Thuy said, "be sure to have the devil build a new wing for all your American friends." And he reached back and drew the short knife he had hidden under his belt.

The baby pointed and said, "Uh-da!"

Mathes said, "Sarge!"

My grabbed the Colt off the floor and fired.

Thuy saw the bullet strike Tinh in the shoulder, but then felt the blood running down his own back and knew it had passed through him first. He immediately released Tinh and turned, and then My fired again, shooting him in the stomach.

Thuy fell to the floor.

Tinh coughed and coughed as Mathes pulled himself out of the trapdoor, kicked the gun out of My's hand. "Don't move, lady. We're taking these kids and we're getting out of here."

Tinh looked down at his older brother, watched the blood pool on the floor. Thuy smiled. "You might as well kill them now, Son Tinh. Fucking *bụi đời*. You know as well as I do what kind of life they'll have."

"Your blood," Tinh said. "I can smell the Chinese in it."

Thuy laughed, a pathetic wheeze. "Yes, it stinks. You should be used to it by now, though, I would think."

Tinh reached down and pulled the KA-BAR out of the floor. "Say hello to Father for me."

"I will," Thuy said. *"Chúc ngủ ngon, Son Tinh."*

"Good night, Thuy Tinh." Sergeant Tinh cut Thuy's throat. "You fucking asshole."

Son Tinh focused carefully on My's shoulder as he bandaged it but could feel her eyes boring into his face. He said, "Does this mean you'll take me back, little one?"

My laughed. "Not if you were the last bastard in Vietnam, Son Tinh."

"That's what I thought."

He let that hang in the air. My waited until he'd finished bandaging her up and looked her in the eye. She said, "Once, Thuy Tinh fought with honor for his homeland. But somewhere along the way, he began fighting for himself, and with dishonor. Bringing a knife to a fistfight was the last straw."

"Mm." Son Tinh nodded. "Can I get you anything else, My?"

"Yes," she said. "You can get the fuck out of my house."

Son Tinh gave a sharp whistle. After a few minutes, Gummy Ba returned it, signaling the all-clear. Mathes and Tinh came out, each with two babies in his arms. All of them except little Yen cried and screamed in the rain.

Even with the ringing in his ears and the screaming bastards in his arms, Mathes smiled hugely at Gummy Ba and his men standing at the bridge. "Well, goddamn, boys!" he said. "Mission accomplished, huh? Let's go home." He stepped onto the bridge and Gummy Ba hauled him back.

"You fucking crazy, Joe?" he said and pointed at the MON-50 poking out from under the bridge, glistening in the rain.

"You want whole place go up?" Ba said.

"Sure he does," Tinh said. "But not tonight."

THE END

San Diego is a military town, and lifelong resident JIMMY CALLAWAY has met many retired soldiers in his time. Greg Peppard, a grizzled former Army sergeant, often frequented the convenience store where Callaway worked for a number of years. Over time, a grudging friendship grew out of a shared fondness for Lee Van Cleef movies. Turns out Peppard had more than a few stories published— stories he based on his tours in Vietnam during the final ten years of his military service, from 1963–1973. His work never cracked the big men's adventure market, appearing in such forgettable titles as Man Digest for Men, General Macho, *and* Highlights for Green Berets. *This story is one Peppard never managed to sell before he quit writing altogether and bought a small hardware store. Mr. Callaway would like to thank Matthew C. Funk and Johnny Shaw for their assistance in restoring this piece to a publishable form.*

STUDS WINSLOW
in
STUDS WINSLOW AND THE BITCHES OF THE FIFTH REICH
by Halloran Oates
(discovered by Todd Robinson)

STUDS WINSLOW focused his breathing, eyes open a sliver.

Deep in.

Hold.

Slooooow exhale.

He blocked out the cries of the Caribbean seabirds swirling above his boat, *The Goateed Mollusk IV*. He pushed away the warmth of the blistering equatorial sun. He tasted the salty ocean air on each breath he drew deeply into his belly.

Exhale.

The gentle rise and fall of the boat helped with the breathing meditations he'd been taught by Master Fang Fang in the lost city of Quangtang. Lost, that is, until Studs had found it. (Check out the exciting adventure in *Studs Winslow and the Lost City of Master Fang Fang*.)

After he'd fought off the nine dead soldiers of Emperor Hing and released the city from its thousand-year curse, the grateful Master Fang Fang had rewarded Studs with the secret practices of his temple. One of which was the meditative breathing that allowed him to make the deep dive that he'd soon be undertaking.

He drew his attention to a point of red on the horizon.

Deep in.

Hold.

Slooooow exhale.

The point of red turned a chocolate brown, then the darker hue of untainted coffee. Then that point split into two as Studs realized that he was now staring at the perfect nipples adorning the breasts of Cookie Cutter.

"Damn, Studs, you not done yet with that Chinese hoodee-doo?" Cookie shook her head, playfully expelling the water from her regal afro.

Studs wiped the water from his muscular, sunburned chest. "You'd think that a woman with your education would have a little more respect for the ancient arts," Studs said as he flipped an unfiltered Lucky between his lips.

"Damn, Winslow. You know me. You can take the girl out of Detroit..."

"Then send that girl to Oxford, then Harvard. Offer her the highest academic honors and dual doctorates in archeology and mystical artifacts..."

"...but you ain't gonna take the Detroit outta that girl." Cookie smiled at Studs as she wrapped her arms around his rippling waist, her soft pillowy breasts pressing against his ribs. She reached into the front of his bellbottom jeans, under his swim trunks.

"I hope you're not starting the fun without me," said Lily, the Swedish backpacker they'd picked up at Dirty Jack's Oyster Bar the night before.

Lily hadn't been Studs' first choice. Studs had wanted to take the local waitress with them, but Cookie had one sexual rule and one sexual rule only—only one black girl at a time on Studs' boat. She said that two Nubians at a time brought out "the Africa" in her. Studs had no idea what that meant, but he was curious to find out one day.

As Lily pulled herself out of the water, the sun glistened on her naked white skin. She arched her back, pointing at Studs and Cookie with her Swedish torpedoes.

"We ain't lighting those kind of fires just yet, baby," Cookie said, retrieving Studs' lighter from his trunks.

"Says you," Studs said.

"You got work to do first." Cookie flared the lighter, lay the flame against the tip of Studs' coffin nail. "Speaking of which, I can't get as deep as you..."

Lily chuckled. She'd learned all too well last night, late last night, and early this morning, that not all of Master Fang Fang's ancient oriental secrets were necessarily breathing-related.

Cookie rolled her eyes, but a smile curled the corner of her lush lips. "BUT, from what I could see, that didn't look like no Spanish galleon down there."

Studs undid his thick skull-and-crossbones belt buckle and dropped his jeans to the deck. "Well, we'll find out one way or the other, won't we?"

Studs flipped his cigarette into the ocean, planted a hard kiss onto Cookie's open mouth, and then dove into the sea.

As she watched Studs' shadow disappear into the depths, she muttered under her smile, "Crazy-ass cracker."

Studs pushed deeper and deeper towards the unclear object resting on the ocean floor. As he got closer with each breaststroke, the outlines of the sunken boat became clearer.

Cookie was right. That was no Spanish galleon that had been put in a watery grave by the forces of Poseidon. Meter by meter, Studs realized just what was sitting down there.

And he was none too happy about it.

Sweet Eleanor Roosevelt, thought Studs. That's a goddamn Kraut *Schnellboot*. Studs had seen plenty of S-Boats during his stint in the Navy during WWII—hell, he'd even jumped aboard one when he and the Screamin' Seamen took down Hitler's Mer-Man program—but he'd be a monkey's uncle before he ever expected to find the wreck of one in the Caribbean. (To find out how Studs defeated the Mer-Men, read *Studs Winslow's Screamin' Seamen*.)

Finding a remnant of Uncle Sam's old adversary had Studs' full attention. To the point where he didn't notice the immense shadow bearing down on him.

The rows of teeth opened inches from his face before Studs noticed the ten-foot tiger shark. Studs twisted his body away from the monster as the hellish jaws slammed shut. The leviathan passed by, then turned back to claim the meal that it had oh-so-narrowly missed.

Studs cursed himself for his rookie lapse as the beast charged him a second time. He didn't want to use the bowie knife strapped to his thigh, but he unsheathed it just in case.

The shark opened its mouth again.

Studs waited.

At the last second, he pistoned his legs and glided above the shark's snapping maw. With his free hand, Studs grabbed the shark's dorsal fin and allowed the giant fish to pull him along. The shark bucked and writhed, but to no avail. Studs drew himself down the side of the shark and locked eyes with the beast intent on tearing him to pieces.

Animal to animal, eye to eye, and man to beast, Studs passed along to the shark the predatory message from time immemorial that he was nobody's lunch.

Studs felt the murderous fish relax underneath him, cowed before the greater warrior. He released the dorsal fin. The beast circled once, laid its coal-black eyes on Studs' rippling muscular form, then swam into the depths to find a more agreeable meal.

Studs couldn't be sure, but he thought that if the shark could have reached whatever passed for its forehead, it would have saluted him.

Turning his attention back to the dive, Studs worked his way back through the briny sea towards the S-Boat. When he reached the ship, he swam to the bow and wiped away the algae that had grown over the ship's name.

Feuchter Traum.

Damn.

Studs had heard of this boat. And of all of the items that it had carried back to *der Fuehrer* during the war. Rumors whispered in the darkest alleys of Berlin of the curses that the men who piloted the ship endured after each voyage.

From the looks of the long tear along the hull, the boat's final curse had been its own when it hit the reef that Studs knew had taken many a boat on the south end of the island.

Working his way topside, Studs tried to pry open the ship's hatch, but years underneath the surface had wedged it shut beyond repair.

For anyone who wasn't Studs Winslow.

As he put his considerable strength behind the effort, Studs felt the first licks of oxygen deprivation in his lungs. The hatch began to give with a rending screech. Almost, but not wide enough to fit into.

The tussle with the shark had drained too much of his oxygen to continue any more. If not for that damned snaggle-toothed minnow, Studs might have been able to stay under another 20 minutes, maybe even gotten the hatch open on the first try.

He'd have to neuter his curiosity for the moment, return to *The Goateed Mollusk IV*, and work some more of Master Fang Fang's Oriental mojo before he could make another attempt.

As Studs kicked his legs, propelling himself towards the surface and the oxygen that his chest burned for, he saw the outline of the second boat next to *The Goateed Mollusk IV*.

Guests.

Studs didn't mind guests at all. He was famous for his parties on eight continents, if you counted Atlantis (which Studs did, after the discovery in *Studs Winslow and the Atlantean Princess of Sea-Love*). Whether the party be on his boats, at his villas, or in one of his compounds, Studs never turned away guests. As long as they were invited. (For a comprehensive list of party dos and don'ts, see *Studs Winslow's Swinging Party Guide*.)

But Studs didn't remember inviting anyone that day.

Breaking the surface of the water, Studs sucked in the sweet ocean air. He took a quick look at the new boat and felt a flicker of dread. He reached for his boat's ladder and looked straight up into the barrel of a Luger pistol.

Above the pistol was a pair of enormous breasts in a black leather bikini. Most men might not have been able to lift their eyes above the death-black chasm of the pistol's barrel, but Studs Winslow was no ordinary man. Besides, it wasn't the first pistol he'd faced that week.

After a cursory once-over, Studs tore his eyes off the leather-bound woman flesh and looked into beautiful high cheekbones haloed by golden hair and a pair of the most evil baby-blues he'd ever seen.

Above those eyes perched an SS cap.

Damn.

"Hello, Herr Winslow. It is a pleasure to finally make your acquaintance." The smile was genuine. So was the malevolence behind it.

The exhausted Studs was pulled on board by two surprisingly strong (and equally buxom) Aryan princesses in matching black leather bikinis and caps.

The first woman, obviously the leader, kept her gun aimed squarely at Studs' chiseled midsection.

Cookie was seated on the deck, still naked, arms tied behind her back.

Studs couldn't help but smirk. "You never let me do that to you."

Cookie glared at him, but her full red lips fought a smile. "You never pulled a gun on me."

"Well, not in the sack." Studs looked at Lily, still in just her stringy bikini bottom...but with an MP40 pointed at Cookie's back. "What's the deal, Lily? Why are you working with these Nazi bitches?"

Lily's eyes narrowed. "Because, Studs Winslow. I am one of them. *Heil Hitler!*" With her free hand, Lily threw a sharp Nazi salute, snapping her heels together. If Studs didn't know better, he would have sworn that the little bounce made her Teutonic ta-tas pop a little Nazi salute of their own.

"You traitorous Nazi whore," spat Cookie.

"Quiet!" Lily cracked Cookie across the mouth with the barrel of the submachine gun.

Cookie flicked her tongue to the corner of her mouth, tasted the blood there. Cookie nodded and gave a Lily a deadly look. "I'ma let you have that one, ofay."

"Enough!" commanded the Nazi bitch apparently in charge. "Do you know who I am, Herr Winslow?"

Studs rolled his neck. "No, but I've shot enough of those hats off heads to know *what* you are."

Tossing her rich blonde hair back, the Aryan bombshell laughed humorlessly. "I wouldn't expect you to recognize my father's features in me, but you will know his name. I am Commandant Helga Fuchs!"

Fuchs. Studs knew the name all too well. Many an adventure had pitted him against Hitler's greatest scientist/warlock/madman, Fritz Fuchs. When Studs and the Screamin' Seamen had detonated their explosives in the underwater Mer-Man research compound, who do you think had been conducting the experiments? When Studs was thrown naked into that Antarctic ice pit naked to fight an overly libidinous Abominable Snowman (the twisted tale of *Studs Winslow versus the Abominable Sex Snowman*), who would you guess had let the beast off its leash? When Jack the Ripper had been transported through time to 1968 London, who was at the controls of the Chrononaut's time machine? (Dig the slaughtered beatniks in *Studs Winslow Swings through Time*.)

So when Fritz Fuchs' hyper-intelligent Croco-Gorillas turned on their creator and ripped him to shreds, Studs finally thought the man and his madness had been laid to rest. Or at least been digested by Croco-Gorillas.

Studs snarled. "Yeah, I recognize the name of that lunatic."

Helga backhanded Studs across the chops. "My father was a genius!"

"Your father was a madman." Helga swung again, but Studs caught her by the wrist. "And it looks like his daughter inherited his madness."

The two silent women who had pulled Studs aboard whipped out submachine guns and aimed them at Studs' head. With her free hand, Helga pressed her Luger to Studs' temple. She slid her hand up his chiseled thigh and removed his bowie knife from the sheath. She tossed it to the deck. Lily picked up the blade and stuck it into the thin fabric of her bikini bottom.

"And you, Herr Studs, you have a remarkable physique for a man who fought in World War Two." Helga didn't sound surprised. She traced the barrel of the gun down Studs' neck, through his thick mat of chest hair, and over his flat stomach. She pressed herself against him, smelling his musk, lips brushing against his shoulder. Catching herself, Helga snapped back to attention, the business end of the Luger pointed back under Studs' chin.

Studs smirked at Helga Fuchs. He assumed that somehow she'd found out about the Fountain of Youth that Studs had stumbled upon all those years ago in Bolivia (in *Studs Winslow and Muhammad Ali in Bolivia*).

If the Nazis had that kind of regenerative power? Studs would have shuddered at the thought—

—but Studs Winslow wasn't a man who shuddered.

Studs released his grip on her wrist. "If it's the secret of my good looks you want, my answer is healthy living. If you're here to kill me, then do it."

Helga Fuchs smiled. "Oh no, Herr Winslow. We're not going to kill you. We want to hire you."

"You can't afford me."

"On the contrary, you can't afford to say no." Helga snapped her fingers. One of the mute twins went to the control panel on the *The Goateed Mollusk IV*'s winch and raised Cookie six feet overhead. With a switch of the lever, the boom turned, dangling Cookie over the water.

"What you gonna do?" Cookie catcalled. "Try to drown me? *Shee-yit*, I was Captain of the Oxford swimming team three years in a row. Don't matter my hands are tied behind my back. I could make it to shore without my arms."

"Don't think that I don't know your capabilities, Ms. Cutter." With that, Helga lowered her gun and fired the Luger.

The two small toes of Cookie's left foot popped off. Cookie howled. "Ahhh, my goddamn pinkie toe! I'ma kill you."

Helga smiled. "I'm paying you with her life, Herr Winslow. You do what we say, and we won't drop your precious Cookie Cutter. As you can see, the dip will not be refreshing."

Studs looked out onto the cruel ocean, dorsal fins already breaking the surface in the sharks' quest to find the source of the blood that was dribbling into their water.

The dinner bell had been rung.

"You're as crazy as your father, Helga."

"And you, Herr Winslow, are running out of time. You have thirty minutes to retrieve the item we have come for. In precisely thirty minutes, if you have not returned from the *Feuchter Traum* with the object I desire, I will cut the rope myself, and your precious Cookie Cutter will be torn to pieces."

"It can't be done. I need at least that much time to do the breathing exercises necessary for a dive that deep. And you expect me to make that same dive in water that you just made shark infested?"

"Twenty-eight minutes."

"I'll drown before I get down there."

"If you drown, your black beauty will not be far behind."

Cookie twirled angrily at the end of the rope. "Hey, who you callin' a...actually, both them words fit. I'ma still gonna kill you."

Helga laughed. "Such spirit! It's a shame that you are unfit to join the Fifth Reich, and that spirit will be leaving this world in... twenty-six minutes. Your move, Herr Winslow."

Studs gritted his teeth. "What is it you need me to get?"

"In 1941, the *Feuchter Traum* was on route to the Fatherland carrying a precious item...a precious item that had existed in legend amongst the Mexican people and their Mayan ancestors for centuries."

"I don't got time for a history lesson."

Undeterred, Helga Fuchs went on. "My father, knowing the powerful mysticism of the Mayan people, believed that this item would be a suitable addition to *der Fuehrer*'s already impressive collection. He sent a team deep into the jungle to an ancient pyramid, a temple many thought was on cursed land, built by a cursed people. And do you know what they found, Herr Winslow?"

"The world's greatest enchiladas?"

"They found the Amulet of Qaxteqackotittlq."

The name meant nothing to Studs.

But it meant something to Cookie. "Aw, hell no."

That couldn't be good.

"The Amulet of Qaxteqackotittlq is on that boat, Herr Winslow, and *I want it!*" Helga checked her watch. "And you have nineteen minutes to get it for me."

Without another word, Studs dove off the edge of the boat, executing a perfect jackknife.

Studs thrust his muscular body deeper and deeper into the water, moving fast not only to avoid drowning, but to get below the sharks that were quickly amassing under Cookie.

Studs took a quick look up. He saw four or five blue sharks, two good-sized bull sharks, a lemon shark, and his old friend, the tiger who'd tried to nosh on Studs only minutes earlier. Studs guessed that the blood in the water was too much to keep the old boy away, even after his encounter with Studs.

As he turned to the *Feuchter Traum*, a large shadowy motion caught Studs' eye, moving in from about a hundred yards off the boat.

A shadow that big would have sent a shiver down Studs' spine—

—but shivers didn't have a home anywhere on Studs Winslow, especially not his spine.

Instead, Studs just used it as further motivation to get a move on...before the great white got there.

When Studs reached the *Feuchter Traum*, his lungs were already aching. Studs grabbed the narrow hatch opening, planted his feet against the side, and pulled with all his strength. Forty years of rust fractured under Studs' steel will. The hatch opened.

Once inside the boat, a pulsing sensation started up behind Studs' eyes. It was a sensation he'd felt only once before, when he'd been possessed by the power of Dr. Tutu's voodoo bag in Haiti. (Dig the magic in *Studs Winslow and the Voodoo Orgy of Dr. Tutu.*)

There was something evil nearby, and Studs could feel it. He let it guide him to the Amulet of Qaxteqackotittlq.

Passing through the cabin, Studs saw a weak green light emanating from under the door of the Captain's quarters. As he swam closer, the throbbing grew stronger. The Amulet of Qaxteqackotittlq was behind that door.

Studs opened the door. The room was bathed in weak green light emanating from an ornate wooden box. A box held in the clutches of a Nazi skeleton.

As Studs pried the box from the dead Nazi bastard's hands, he noticed something...strange about the skull, particularly the mouth. But he had no time to think on the curiosities of German dentistry; he had to not drown himself. And get back to the boat before Helga Fuchs turned Cookie into fish food.

When he swam out of the cursed German *Schnellboot*, Studs immediately saw that the ocean around the *Goateed Mollusk IV* was a bloodier hue of crimson.

For a moment, he feared that he was too late, that the madwoman had tossed his Cookie to the sharks before he had a chance to return with the Amulet of Qaxteqackotittlq.

Then he saw the chunks—the remains of four or five blue sharks, two good-sized bull sharks, and a lemon shark littering the water. The great white had decided to take out the competition before meal time.

For reasons he couldn't figure out, it relieved Studs to not see any pieces of his old chum the tiger shark.

What worried Studs was that he couldn't see the great white.

Unfortunately, he didn't have the time to find him. Studs pumped his legs and worked his way to the surface before the black spots that were forming in his vision grew any larger. Studs needed oxygen, and he needed it now.

Twenty yards to the surface.

The spots grew darker.

Ten.

With an explosion of size and movement, the great white came at Studs from underneath *The Goateed Mollusk IV*. Studs broke the surface of the water and took in huge lungfuls of sweet, sweet air.

The giant dorsal fin of the great white erupted out of the water ten feet from the gasping Studs.

"My knife!" Studs yelled.

Lily took the bowie from her bikini and tossed the blade to Studs. He caught it and turned to face the leviathan.

The shark skimmed the surface, inches from Studs' chest. For the second time that day, Studs locked eyes with another of the world's deadliest predators. This one was used to being King of the Sea, however. And Studs was too tired and weak to give an effective warrior's glare.

The shark's eyes said, *You're lucky I just ate, Bub. But I'll be hungry again reeeeal soon.*

So, with a bellyful of his fellow sharks, the great white swam a respectable distance from the boats. Didn't leave, but kept its distance.

Waiting.

Studs didn't want to wait until the monster got its appetite back. He tossed the carved box onto the deck of the boat, climbed the ladder, and collapsed into an exhausted heap.

With a hunger in her eyes that wasn't too different from the shark's, Helga Fuchs picked up the wooden box and opened it. Her eyes lit with the flames of pure Nazi bitch evil. "*Mein Gott.* It's true. The Amulet of Qaxteqackotittlq!" The other women gathered behind her, their faces masked with a lust that, under different circumstances, Studs would have been more than willing and able to sate.

"I did my part," gasped Studs. "Reel in Cookie."

"Do it," said Helga, her eyes never leaving the amulet.

Lily went to the controls and dropped Cookie onto the deck next to Studs.

"What have you done, Studs?" she asked. "Don't you know what that amulet can do?"

"Guess I'll find out soon enough," he said. Behind his back, Studs handed Cookie his bowie. In all the excitement, they'd forgotten to take it from him. Cookie's cocoa forearms flexed, only the barest motion giving away the sawing at her bonds.

"It has the power to raise the dead, Studs."

"Bring him out," said Helga.

The Aryan twins re-emerged from under Stud's canopy, each struggling with one end of a coffin adorned with swastikas.

"That ain't who I think it is, is it?" asked Studs as he pulled his jeans back on over his trunks. He pulled out his smokes and lit one. Putting the pack back into the pocket, he tapped the skull's ruby eye on the belt buckle twice. The belt buckle beeped quietly.

"Prepare yourselves, Studs Winslow and Cookie Cutter—prepare yourselves for the return of Adolph Hitler himself!"

With that, the Aryan twins opened the lid of the coffin, revealing the desiccated bones within. Studs looked at the withered skull, tiny mustache intact.

"Honey, I don't think that's a good idea," said Cookie.

"Of course you wouldn't." Helga withdrew the amulet from the box, a magnificent golden medallion on a thick leather thong that wouldn't have looked out of place adorning the chest of a true disco stallion.

Tenderly, Helga lifted the head of her *Fuehrer* and placed the Amulet of Qaxteqackotittlq around his neck.

Immediately, the green glow enveloped the bones of Adolph Hitler.

"Studs?" Cookie whispered.

Pink flesh grew on the bones, oozing around itself, rebuilding.

"Yeah?" whispered back Studs.

Spots of white skin began spreading, stretching over the flesh.

"That amulet raises the dead."

Hitler's fingertips convulsed, celebrating the new life coursing through them.

"I can see that, Cookie."

Hitler's mustache twitched, became fuller.

"Yeah, but these dumb Nazi bitches don't have a doctorate in mystical artifacts."

"What's your point, Cookie?"

Hitler's eyes sprang open. Undistilled fury and hatred under the lids. And something else...

"The Amulet of Qaxteqackotittlq brings back the dead..."

Studs recognized what else was in that evil bastard's eyes, realized what was wrong with the mouth of the Nazi on the sunken ship. Fangs! Hitler's mouth was filled with fangs.

"...but as a Mayan Vampire."

Mayan Vampire Hitler leapt from the coffin with an ear-piercing screech, howling, *"Mi hambre debe ser saciado!"*

In a flash, the Nazi bitches of the Fifth Reich's expressions turned from lust to horror as Mayan Vampire Hitler tore the throat from the nearest Aryan twin, then the breast off the other. Mayan Vampire Hitler feasted on the bloody milk that poured from her chest. Her breast fell to the deck like a nippled jellyfish.

"Mein Fuehrer! What has happened to you? Stop!" screamed Helga, her gun drawn onto Mayan Vampire Hitler. She fired twice.

Mayan Vampire Hitler laughed at the smoking holes in his chest.

Lily panicked, firing the fallen twin's submachine gun wildly. Her bullets shredded the sails on *The Goateed Mollusk IV*, slammed into the engines.

Studs hit the deck.

Cookie saw her opportunity. Executing a perfect judo flip over the hail of bullets, Cookie kicked the gun out of Lily's hands.

"Didn't know I was also captain of the Harvard Kung-Fu Squad, didja bitch?"

Then with a spin kick that would have made the Atomic Samurai Women of Nagasaki proud (read the classic adventure in *Studs Winslow and the Atomic Samurai Women of Nagasaki*), Cookie cracked Lily right across her high cheekbones with a foot that was missing two toes.

Lily flipped in the air twice before plummeting into the ocean.

Cookie stood, hands on her cocked hips. "I *told* you I'd get you, ofay."

The great white was on Lily before she could respond to Cookie's funky sass. Mayan Vampire Hitler laughed and advanced on the weeping Helga Fuchs. He stopped laughing when his arms started to smoke. *"¿Qué me está pasando?"*

"Hey, Hitler!" said Studs.

Mayan Vampire Hitler turned to Studs. His eyes went wide with fear and rage as his skin began to blister. *"Espárragos Winslow? ¿Qué estás haciendo aquí?"*

"Next time one of your crazy-ass Nazi bitches wants to bring you back from the dead, make sure they don't make you a Mayan Vampire."

Small flames erupted from under the blistering skin of Mayan Vampire Hitler.

"And make *double* sure they don't do it on the deck of a boat underneath the Caribbean sun."

With a scream of unimaginable agony, flames engulfed Mayan Vampire Hitler ..

Helga Fuchs made a run for it, trying to get across the gangplank to her own boat and escape.

Mayan Vampire Hitler gave chase, covered in flames. "*Puta alemana estupido!*"

As he leapt on her, Helga fired her remaining bullets into the chest of her immolated *Fuehrer*. She screamed as his fiery fangs tore into her flesh. The two of them fell under the canopy in a flaming embrace of death.

"Daaaamn," said Cookie. "That is one overcooked Nazi Mayan Vampire Hitler jive turkey."

Studs took his bowie back from Cookie and reached down to cut loose the gangplank connecting the boats, when a charred hand slapped onto the railing of the Nazi bitches' boat and flipped the gangplank into the ocean from their side.

Laughing hoarsely, Mayan Vampire Nazi Bitch of the Fifth Reich Helga Fuchs stood under the boat canopy, safe from the deadly sunlight. "*Ahhhahahahaha!* You may have won this day, Señor Winslow, but I will return and you will face my Mayan Vampire Nazi wrath!"

As the boats slowly drifted apart, Studs sighed sadly and shook his head. "What do you think, Cookie? You ready to go shopping for *The Goateed Mollusk V*?"

"You didn't," said Cookie.

"I activated the failsafe, just in case." Studs tapped his enormous belt buckle.

"Do it," said Cookie, and dove overboard, swimming for the shore.

"What are you talking about, Señor Winslow?" Mayan Vampire Nazi Bitch of the Fifth Reich Helga Fuchs had stopped laughing, a concerned look drawn over her Mayan Vampire Nazi Bitch of the Fifth Reich face.

"Bye-bye, Helga," Studs said as he hit the ruby button on his belt buck two more times and dove over the side of the boat.

The Goateed Mollusk IV exploded as the TNT in the hold detonated. The last thing Studs saw before hitting the water was the explosion engulfing and vaporizing the Nazi boat and Mayan Vampire Nazi Bitch of the Fifth Reich Helga Fuchs along with it.

Studs smiled as he swam towards shore. His smile didn't last long.

The giant dorsal fin cut the water ahead of him, heading straight toward Cookie, her wounded foot leading a delicious trail right to her delicious body.

"Swim, Cookie!" shouted Studs. "Swim!"

Cookie turned back to see the monster shark bearing down on her. She doubled her effort, but it wasn't enough to outpace the shark.

"Nnnnooooooo!" screamed Studs as the great white swallowed Cookie whole and turned towards the greater ocean.

Studs swam for all he was worth after the great white. On another day, without the physical demands made of his body that the day had already taken, he might have caught the beast.

But not today.

Despite his effort, the great white lengthened the distance between them. The despair in Studs' chest grew over his lost Cookie.

The great dorsal fin slipped under the surface.

Studs treaded water, unwilling to give up, unwilling to face defeat even in the face of the hopelessness before him.

The great white didn't surface.

But another fin did.

The tiger shark was back and circling Studs.

Studs pulled his knife, ready to take revenge on all of sharkkind for his lost Cookie.

The shark swam by Studs. It slowed down to look him in the eye.

This time, their communication was different.

It wasn't the predatorial dance of time immemorial.

No.

The tiger shark's eyes said: *The enemy of my enemy is my friend.*

Studs nodded and grabbed onto his newfound ally's dorsal fin. In a bolt, the tiger shark was off, carrying Studs with him.

Under the surface, Studs could see the great white two hundred yards ahead, but they were gaining. The tiger shark was faster and didn't have a bellyful of Cookie slowing him down.

One hundred yards.

Fifty.

Twenty.

Then they were right beside the grey-skinned giant. Studs pushed himself off the tiger shark and plunged his bowie knife deep into the belly of the great white. The shark jerked and writhed as Studs drew his knife down the length of the monster's body. Entrails poured into the water, pieces of other sharks. Pieces of Lily.

Then a honey brown arm reached from inside, grasping for Studs. Studs grabbed Cookie's arm and wrenched her free from the belly of the beast. The two of them kicked to the surface and swam for shore as quickly as they could. The sea was red with the great white's blood as smaller sharks enacted their revenge for the giant shark's tyranny. The feeding frenzy was magnificent and terrifying.

Studs gave one last look back at the tiger shark. He gave his aquatic friend a final salute and headed for shore.

When Studs and Cookie reached the beach, a small group had gathered on the shore. Dirty Jack was one of the onlookers. He waded out and helped the exhausted Studs and Cookie onto the beach. They fell onto the soft white sand, spent.

"What the hell happened?" Dirty Jack asked.

"Mayan Nazi Vampires." Cookie said.

Dirty Jack shrugged and looked out at the fiery wrecks of the two boats. "Oh well. Who wants Rum Runners?"

Studs and Cookie each weakly raised a hand.

THE END

TODD ROBINSON has always modeled his life after the deep-sea diving adventure hero Studs Winslow. Which explains his penchant for both challenging people to see who can hold their breath the longest, and Speedos. He found this copy of Studs Winslow #94 *in a mylar bag right between #93 and #95 on his Studs Winslow shelf/ shrine at home.*

Halloran Oates (1922–1998), a WWII veteran and deep-sea salvage expert, wrote 109 novels featuring Winslow and one unfortunate nonfiction book disproving the female orgasm. He passed away in 1998 while trying to break the world record for Antarctic Nude Freediving at the age of 76. He broke the record first, though.

BATTLEGROUND U.S.S.A.:

TEXASGRAD
by Max Auger
(discovered by Christopher Blair)

THAT SIGN'S IN RUSSIAN!

At first, Capt. Mike McCreary thought the binoculars were playing tricks on him. He pressed himself further into the rich Texas soil and leaned forward into the dry grass like a crouching lion. He blinked and looked again.

It was too much to take in. Less than a mile away lay his hometown, its neat, clean buildings untouched by the Russian and Chinese death that had streaked in a year before. In fact, the town looked just the way it had when he'd left Sunny here to be safe. There it was, just west of the school: the little house they'd bought with his promotion pay. Sunny was in there. Waiting for him, but thinking he was dead.

Every fiber of his body wanted to run to her, to tell her that he'd survived. But his military training told him to stay put.

The farms and fields encircling the town of Wrangler Plains looked like a pale green quilt. He saw the workers and tractors and clouds of dust, working together to bring in the harvest, the familiar motions of bending and lifting, of wiping honest sweat from an honest man's brow. He knew that his childhood friends were down there, the ones who'd stayed home, just a few minutes' sprint from the gentle rise where he now lay.

If not for the sign, printed on a bright piece of plywood planted on the shoulder of Highway 27. In bright red letters:

Добро пожаловать на
Wrangler Равнинами, Техаса!население 1845

And printed in smaller letters:

Скоро будет переименован работника
поля, как только наши товарищи
освободиться в их умы и сердца от гнета капитала!

McCreary handed the binoculars to Spec. Charles Whitefeather, crouched beside him like one of his Comanche ancestors stalking a buffalo. Whitefeather shook his head politely. "No thank you, Captain." McCreary cursed his insensitivity: of course Whitefeather wouldn't need the binoculars. Not with his hunter's eyes.

Instead, he handed them to Private Billy LaRoy to his left. Next to LaRoy, Spec. Brad Hawker, the sniper, took it all in through his scope.

"I don't understand, Cap," LaRoy said. "Why are all them *R*s backward? I may not be no college boy, but I know when letters ain't right."

"That's Russian writing, Private," McCreary said. "It looks a little like ours, but it ain't."

Whitefeather hit the dirt next to McCreary. *"Tanks!"* he hissed.

McCreary grabbed the binoculars from LaRoy, just as Hawker muttered, "Five of 'em. No six. No, seven! To the right of the church, off the main drag."

Son of a bitch: seven tanks were rolling across Hank Steinhoff's alfalfa field. Suddenly, they stopped about fifty feet from the First Church of Christ, a row of fat iron turtles. In unison, their turrets began to swing. Even a mile away, the squad could feel the tanks' metal rumbling in their bellies.

"This doesn't make sense," McCreary muttered. "The Reds weren't supposed to this far north. Intel said we stopped 'em at San Antone."

"Those tanks are huge," Whitefeather said. "I ain't seen nothin' like that this close. Not even doing Black Ops in Europe. I feel an ill wind blowin', Captain." He paused, then added: "This is bad medicine."

They all knew the truth. Only LaRoy, as always, clung to the bright side. "Maybe they're PT-76s on a scouting run. We have to get back, tell General Pearce that the Russians are coming."

"They're not 76s," McCreary said. The dread in his voice was thicker than Texas tea. "They're not scouts. Those are T-80s. Seven T-80 main battle tanks. The Russian's aren't coming." He ran his hands through his thick black hair. *They're already here.*

McCreary looked at Whitefeather. The big Comanche had closed his eyes, smelling the breeze coming in from town. What secrets did the air hold? It was best not to ask Whitefeather when he went to...that other place.

"Hawker," McCreary said. "You speak some Russian. What does that sign say?"

"*Welcome...to Wrangler Plains...Texas,*" Hawker recited. "*Population...1,845.*" McCreary felt a stab of annoyance. He didn't need some grunt with a Russian grandmother to tell him the population of his hometown. It was 1845, same as the date Texas joined the Late Great United States.

McCreary swung his binoculars back to the tanks, parked close to the church where he'd married Sunny Summerville. There, a mere feet from the menacing T-80s, were the front steps where he'd worn his dress blues and held Sunny's hand next to Pastor Joe.

Hawker continued. "The rest of it says, *Soon to be renamed... Fertile Worker...Fertile Worker...*something...*Fields*! *Fertile Worker Fields*!"

McCreary squeezed the binoculars when he saw the distant form of Pastor Joe. The reverend sprinted down the steps and ran toward the tanks, waving his hands. The hatch on one of the turrets popped open. A gray-suited Russian tanker appeared. The Russian lifted his arm. It held a pistol.

"*...renamed...as soon as our comrades...free themselves...*"

McCreary watched Pastor Joe, unafraid, stop shy of the lead tank. He held something up in his hands. McCreary couldn't make it out, but he knew the man of God held a Bible. The same one that he and Sunny had laid their hands on to become man and wife. But as blessed as it was, no Bible could stop a bullet.

The Russian tanker fired his pistol. Whitefeather whispered something sacred and sad in his own language.

"...*free themselves...in their minds and hearts...from capitalist oppression!*"

As if on cue, the tanks fired over Pastor Joe's crumpled body. Licks of orange erupted from their barrels. The church exploded silently, slats of pure white wood spinning in godless flame.

Three seconds later, the sound arrived at Lonestar Tactical Unit 1 and shook them to their very souls.

McCreary slept the fitful sleep of a fighting man. He dreamed, as he always did, about the week before the attack. He'd known something was afoot. Troop movements in East Germany. Chinese maneuvers in the Formosa Strait. Soviet maneuvers near Turkey, practice amphibious landings in Egypt, just miles from the Israeli coast.

He hadn't talked to Sunny in three weeks. Command had canceled all leave, and McCreary hadn't been out of Silo J-47 long enough to make a single phone call. Not that he'd have been able to, anyway, with everything locked down. Hours in the terminal he shared with Lt. Jansen. As Jansen blabbed once more about the whole thing being a Communist plea for attention, the Squawker had jolted them out of their routine.

"*Juliet! Juliet-Four-Seven! Priority Message Charlie!*"

He and Jansen had sprung into action, confirming the missile codes. They'd just inserted the keys when their station, buried two hundred feet under the frozen North Dakota plains, began to rock and shimmy. The lights flickered. Surely they had seconds to live. All thoughts of conscience and doubt were swept away as he and Jansen turned their keys.

On their command, in silos buried all around them, five Minuteman IIIs breathed dragon-fire and arced into the sky, bound for glory.

"They're away!" Jansen yelled. "That's what you get for stabbing us in the back!" He turned to McCreary. "It's been an honor serving with you, Captain."

Then, the lights went out and the bunker shook. A great roaring rip in the walls and ceiling. The smell of cold and earth. Everything around them collapsed. Somewhere up there, the world exploded and North Dakota—and America herself—was bathed in an unholy nuclear fire.

The Chinese—McCreary later learned—had initiated the plan's first phase: introducing a program into the Defense Department's computers that replicated itself, like a disease. Almost like a computerized...*virus.* And like a virus, it had spread over the newly installed Inter-Network that the technocrats had insisted would keep America safe. Instead, their newfangled computers had given the Communists their gateway. Linked and spreading the contagion, every weapon that carried a nuclear tip—from bombers to missiles—was rendered inoperable. Some Asian wiseacre had added the final indignity: whenever a command was given to launch a plane, or a missile, the intercom played a tinny alien tune that only a handful of the crews recognized as the Chinese national anthem.

Then, the Chinese had launched Phase 2: sending their fifty Long March rockets high over the United States, to detonate two hundred miles up. The explosions fried every electronic circuit in the country. The Chinese hadn't tried to flatten the cities and the missile silos.

That part of the plan had been the Russians' job.

For reasons that he never figured out, only McCreary's silo—representing just five missiles out of thousands—had managed to go aloft that day. Whether they reached their targets, McCreary doubted he would ever know.

But the dreams only touched on that part of the story. Whenever he slept, his dreams always eventually led to Sunny—her long honey-colored hair, her narrow waist, her virtuous smile. Her delicate hands that could squeeze a trigger and pick off a jackrabbit at a hundred yards.

It was Sunny, the cheerleader who'd waited for him after football games. Sunny, who wore that frilly skirt, who loved him enough to let his hands roam, but who loved God and her virtues enough to make him wait. Sunny, who wore his ring as he went into Air Force Pararescue. Sunny, who talked him through it on the phone after he told her he'd washed out. Sunny, who told him to come home and marry her. Sunny, who didn't get mad after their honeymoon to Corpus Christi, when the Air Force decided that they still owned him and stuck him in the ground in North Dakota.

And of course, it had been Sunny who compelled him to claw his way out of a crooked elevator shaft and to survive everything afterward.

General Pearce studied the reports on the card table he'd been using as a desk since Omaha. Sweltering in the general's tent, McCreary stood at attention, while his men—LaRoy, Whitefeather, and Hawker—stood behind him.

"This report you filed," Pearce said. "It doesn't make sense. The First Cav and the rest of III Corps stopped the Russians and Mexicans at San Antonio."

"How do we know for sure, General?" LaRoy blurted out. "We've had spotty radio traffic from that sector since last week!"

McCreary winced. LaRoy had never learned when to shut it.

"I don't remember asking you a thing, Private!" the general barked. He shot to his feet and glared at McCreary. "Once again: an Air Force flyboy and his ragtag squad of enlistees are trying to tell me how to link up with III Corps."

"With all due respect, General," McCreary began. "This ragtag squad of enlistees and I have been the eyes and ears of this brigade since Omaha. We're telling you what we saw. An entire Russian tank battalion has taken over my town. I need to go back there."

"No," the general said. "We can't risk it."

"Can't risk it? We need intel!"

The general waved his hand over the card table. "We have intel! You've done your job. No need to put your squad—and the rest of us—at risk. So far, the Russians don't know our exact location. We've tied up their air assets over New Mexico, which is why they haven't spotted us."

"You don't know that!"

"McCreary, if these Commies catch you, they'll know we're moving south with brigade strength. At the very least, we wait for the 101st. Their radios are working. They're in Mississippi and heading this way."

"General, if I may be so bold—" McCreary began.

"No! That's my decision," Pearce said. "I'm sorry about the Russians in your town, Captain. I am." He added, with a soft tone that did nothing to assuage McCreary's worst fears, "They may be godless cowards, but I'm sure your wife is alive. You'll see her soon. Just be patient."

"General, please—"

"Dismissed!" The four men stood abruptly at attention and, in unison, turned and banged through the door into the hot Texas sun.

The four of them—McCreary, Whitefeather, Hawker, and LaRoy—entered their tent and dropped their gear on their bunks. McCreary fumed. He had made certain assumptions on returning from their scouting run: certainly after reading their report, Pearce would authorize another trip south.

But he hadn't.

Usually McCreary respected the old man's caution. It had held them at the Missouri River, just before a squad of Russian-made Mexican Hind helicopters had swooped in and wiped out the 173rd, waiting to rendezvous on the other side. The general's instincts had kept five thousand men from leaving what remained of Lincoln, Kansas—just avoiding the swarm of radioactive twisters south of Wichita Falls.

But now, the general was being *too* cautious. McCreary and his men were the whiskers of a lion that was meant to pounce. Not cower in a scrub forest west of Waco.

Behind McCreary, Hawker disassembled his rifle. "I'm sure she's all right," he said.

"You know it, Cap" LaRoy chimed in. "That Sunny of yours sounds tough as nails. Don't you worry about all the things them Russians do to womenfolk whenever they take ov—"

"That's enough, Private!" Whitefeather barked with uncharacteristic ferocity. The dreamcatcher above his head swayed from his voice.

But McCreary heard none of this. His complete focus was on his bunk. Lying on his bunk was a sheet of paper. A string of words formed a row, neatly typewritten.

In Russian.

"Hawker," McCreary said in a voice he barely heard in his own ears. "I need you to read something for me."

McCreary and his men hunkered behind the same rise where they'd spied Wrangler Plains the day before. Fall was coming, and the faint trace of their breath rose above them in the chill dawn air.

"You men don't have to be here," McCreary said. "We're defying orders. If you double-time it back to base, they might not notice you're gone."

"Too late now, Captain," Hawker said. "You know we'd follow you to hell and back."

"That's right, Cap," LaRoy said. "Ain't no Commie bastards gonna rape your town, no sir."

Whitefeather breathed a patient sigh. "Don't worry about your wife, Captain. We're on my former hunting grounds now. The earth speaks to me. The Great Spirit will keep her safe."

McCreary was moved beyond words. But it wasn't time for emotion. They had a job to do: to rescue Sunny, and, God willing, to kill some Ivans in the process.

"Captain!" Hawker hissed, squinting through his scope. "A work detail! Ten...no, twenty civvies!"

McCreary raised his binoculars. A couple dozen people walked out to Bill Dolan's wheat field. They carried scythes and hoes. Old-fashioned tools. McCreary thought he recognized a couple of them. There was Ida Grange, who'd owned the diner on Route 283. She wore a plain gray dress, the likes of which McCreary had never seen. And Bill Dolan himself, dressed as strangely in drab clothes, like something out of *Fiddler on the Roof*. He wore a wool cap. McCreary could only make out a faint red shape, front and center on the cap.

A star.

"Captain," Whitefeather said, squinting into the distance. "Company."

McCreary moved the binoculars back and forth. "Where?"

"Five guards," Hawker said, "To the right? See 'em?...Mexicans. And two Russians with 'em."

Sure enough, a squad of five Mexican soldiers, unshaven, their fatigues crumpled and disheveled, came into view. Fifty yards away stood a pair of Russian privates, distinguished by their light blue shirts, shouldering their AKs, smoking cigarettes and laughing.

"Backstabbers!" LaRoy muttered.

"Let's move into position," McCreary said. "Whitefeather, you and LaRoy circle around. You handle the Mexicans. Hawker and I will take out the Russians."

"I don't know," Hawker said. "It's not the objective. If we shoot and miss—"

"Then don't miss," Whitefeather said. "When the Mexicans start to dance, sir, that'll be your cue." The big Indian and LaRoy were already moving through the tall grass like a couple of leopards.

McCreary and Hawker had plenty of cover as they moved. A rusted combine. Three boulders. A pumphouse. Before too long, they crouched unseen only five yards from the Russians, who chattered away in their dirty, oily language. Beyond them, McCreary could see the Mexican guards, lounging next to their truck. One had his hat down over his eyes. The others leered at a group of teenage girls. The biggest soldier, with a huge, black mustache, catcalled one of the girls in Spanish. She didn't look up, only hoed the ground faster.

McCreary raised his M-16 and aimed it at the Russian on the left. Hawker had his rifle up, peering unnecessarily though the sight. At this range, Hawker would have been automatic with a blindfold. Maybe he was just being cautious.

The big soldier moved toward the girl. "*Señorita!*" McCreary heard him say. "*Eres hermosa. Venir aquí!*"

His last words. The soldier's head silently exploded. The sound arrived a half second later. The Russians jerked to attention like startled antelope.

Then everything happened fast.

The big Mexican fell to the ground like a headless sack of tamales. His men jumped to their feet. Two of them grabbed for their rifles—then began their silent, jiggling dance of death. The remaining two ran toward town.

McCreary drew a bead on the nearest Russian's chest and fired. The M-16 kicked against his shoulder with a reassuring *thump*. The Russkie was dead before he hit the ground. A millisecond later, Hawker fired at the Russian on the right—and missed.

The scrub oak tree behind the Russian split in two. Hawker's Russian looked around with big, cowardly eyes. He could see neither McCreary nor Hawker—and turned to run.

Goddammit, Hawker! McCreary thought. He raised his rifle and dropped the Russian with a single shot to the back of the head. McCreary felt the slightest tug of sadness. The Russian kid had looked all of nineteen, and now he lay dead in the dirt, with the front of his head replaced by an exit wound.

McCreary tried to quash any regret: *They invaded my home. Not just my country. The Commies are in my home town. Sorry, Ivan: you had to die.*

Across the field, Whitefeather and LaRoy chased down the remaining Mexicans. LaRoy tackled the slower one and drove his

Ranger's knife into the back of his head. He jiggled in the dirt like a beetle in some sadistic kid's bug collection. Whitefeather had caught the other one. McCreary, far out of earshot, knew what was happening: the big Comanche was drawing his knife across the Mexican's throat but whispering words of a hunter's respect into his ear as blood flowed from his body like a sacred stream.

"I'm sorry, sir," Hawker said. He looked seriously dejected. "I've never missed in my life. Too close quarters, I guess. But that's no excuse."

McCreary patted him on the shoulder. "It's all right. I never make mistakes, you know?"

"You're a good man, Capt. McCreary," Hawker said softly. "I won't let you down again."

"I know you won't," McCreary said. "Let's join the others."

Whitefeather and LaRoy were already at the girls. "It's all right," Whitefeather said to the tallest one. "We're Americans, like you!"

"That's right, miss," LaRoy said. "Head up that road. There's an American base not ten miles away. They'll take you in and keep you safe. You'll see!"

Here came Bill Dolan, running toward them, with Ida Grange on his heels, holding her skirt up from the ground. They'd dropped their tools and looked relieved to see them. Actually, that wasn't right. They didn't look relieved. They looked *scared.*

That wasn't right, either. They looked *angry.*

Dolan and Ida yelled incomprehensibly. LaRoy tried to calm them.

McCreary arrived at the group. Sure enough, that *was* a red star on Dolan's cap. And why was Dolan yelling at them...in Russian?

"*Chto vy delali?*" Dolan cried out. "*Eti soldaty byli nashi druzya! Vy uzhasno bandity!*"

"This doesn't make any sense," Whitefeather said, drying his knife on his fatigues.

Just then, fifty Russian soldiers rose from the summer wheat, surrounding them. Each soldier brandished an AK-47. The rifles' magazines curled toward McCreary's team like black fangs. A faint breeze blew, hissing through the grain menacingly. McCreary felt awash in an ocean of dread. Even the wheat had turned against them.

"Captain McCreary," an accented voice said from behind a tree. They all turned. Out stepped a tall Russian officer. He wore plain, pressed, olive-colored combat fatigues. Only the three pale stars on his shoulders betrayed his rank. "Thank you for joining us on such a fine morning as this."

"Who the hell are you?" LaRoy asked.

"I am General Yuri Azov of the Soviet Army," the general said. "And you will do well to check your tone with a superior officer, Private LaRoy, of Lewisburg, West Virginia."

"How do you know my name?" LaRoy asked.

The general ignored him. McCreary dropped his M-16 on the ground as the general and two soldiers approached. He motioned to the others to do the same. They obeyed—except for Hawker, who kept his sniper's rifle slung over his shoulder. *Good old Hawker,* McCreary thought. *A sniper to his dying day.*

"How I know is not important," the Russian general said. "Not nearly as important as the honors we will bestow upon Lieutenant Hawkerov...*of the KGB.*"

The sniper McCreary had known as Hawker clicked his heels, stood at attention, and gave the general a crisp salute.

"Lt. Hawkerov," the general said, "thank you for bringing Captain McCreary to enjoy the benefits of our worker's paradise. And thank you for delivering my note, as well! Such a brave, loyal son of Kiev!"

"Hawker!" McCreary cried softly. The sniper glanced at McCreary for the briefest of moments. What was that in his eyes? Was it shame? Were Communists even capable of such an emotion?

"I am happy to do my duty for the Motherland," Hawker said in English.

"As am I," the general said.

Azov raised his pistol. McCreary recognized it as a Nagant M1895. A seven-shot, gas-sealed revolver, issued only to the top Communist Party members. Azov was the real deal. And he demonstrated it by shooting the sniper in the chest. Hawker—*Hawkerov*—crumpled like the traitor he was.

McCreary's mind spun. "W-why?" he asked, just as a rifle butt struck the back of his head.

McCreary regained consciousness, pain glowing bright yellow in his skull. He tried to move his arms but couldn't. They were stretched behind his back. He opened his eyes to sunlight streaming through tall windows. McCreary recognized the office of Mayor Todd Houston. Same oak paneling, same fancy desk the size of a Mississippi River barge. But the walls were adorned with posters, of proud workers facing the sky under the same backward Cyrillic letters that Hawker had translated the day before—

Hawker. Goddammit, Hawker!

Whitefeather and LaRoy were similarly seated, their arms tied behind their chairs. They were awake. LaRoy had two black eyes. The scrappy little private had apparently tried to fight them off. Whitefeather didn't appear to have a scratch on him. The Russians probably knew better than to tangle with the big Indian.

Other than two Russian guards at the door, they were alone.

McCreary scanned the room. His eyes stopped on a huge oil painting, five feet high and three feet wide, hanging on the wall behind the desk.

The painting looked like something out of the 1700s. It showed a blonde woman in a blue dress, her hair tied behind her head, standing in a field of flowers. A basket of blossoms hung from her elbow. In the distance, a Russian church with three onion domes sat under yellow clouds and a red, setting sun. McCreary couldn't take his eyes off the woman.

Sunny!

The door to the office opened. General Azov wore a more ceremonial uniform, whatever it was that the Russians called their Class As. His boots shone and thumped on the old oak floor, every step a gunshot.

"I see you're awake, Capt. McCreary," the general said.

"You seem to know me quite well," McCreary intoned. His skull throbbed with every syllable.

"I've known all about you for years." Azov said, pulling an olive-colored folder off his desk and opening it. "Captain Michael McCreary, United States Air Force...born on March 2nd, Texas Independence Day...Eagle Scout...joined the Air Force's Pararescue division for training, but forced out with a knee injury obtained when rescuing a comrade from a tangled parachute line...reassigned to the 91st Missile Wing, where you performed with distinction."

"Hey, how do you know all that?" LaRoy asked.

Azov continued. "Before assuming command of this glorious invasion of your...doomed empire, I was second-in-command of the KGB. It was my job to know about every American missile officer. I know every detail, Capt. McCreary. I've followed your career. And your personal life. I was amazed at the similarities of our ambitions. Of our character. And most importantly, the fact that our wives appeared so...identical. So naturally, I studied you. And her. With great interest."

"What's that supposed to mean?" McCreary asked.

"Oh, Captain. We shall deal with that soon enough," Azov said. "We are discussing a clash of civilizations. Mighty empires, meeting on the field of battle! Our Chinese allies, tired of being a third-rate power. Mother Russia, impatient that it has taken seventy years to bring capitalism to its knees. And so we have Chinese Plan Chang Alpha 7. To erase the threat posed by the American nuclear arsenal. And it worked with 99.9999 percent accuracy."

Azov walked to Mayor Houston's liquor cabinet. McCreary remembered the cabinet from the day he'd made Eagle Scout at 17, the day Sunny had given him that chaste kiss on his cheek. That day, the mayor had toasted young Mike McCreary with a shot of whisky. The Russkie general had replaced the mayor's Kentucky gold with bottle after bottle of Stoli.

The general poured himself a glass. "Our plan was foolproof, except for you. *You*, Capt. McCreary, commander of the only

American nuclear assets that were able to leave their silos on time. *You*, who drilled your men to check and recheck their systems at all hours. *You,* whose computers were constantly resetting themselves, as per your orders. And when our blessed day arrived, it was your men who possessed the necessary reaction times." The tone of his voice darkened. "Still, of the five Minuteman III missiles that you launched, four were destroyed by our laser-based missile shield—"

"Missile shield!" McCreary muttered. "You got Washington to sign ours away in that last treaty!"

"Backstabbers!" Whitefeather said. "We Americans *always* honor our treaties!"

"Be that as it may, gentlemen," Azov continued, "the only surviving Minuteman III missile—serial No. 8534-Dash-A—was enough to destroy its target: my village of Fertile Worker Fields, fifteen kilometers east of Kiev."

"That's ludicrous," McCreary said. "Americans never target civilians. The Dash-A was aimed at a radar station—"

"Less than a kilometer away from my village"—Azov turned and gazed at the oil painting above the fireplace—"and my beloved Svetlana."

McCreary lowered his head and studied the planks between his boots.

"The day I assumed command of our hidden forces in Laredo," Azov said, "waiting for our orders to invade the United States, I learned that our motherland had escaped unscathed—except for the missile that you launched. Imagine having everything you loved wiped out by the treacherous, glowing heart of an American atom."

Azov, still holding his glass, walked slowly across the floor to where McCreary sat.

"When I heard from a minor KGB operative, Lt. Hawkerov, that you had survived the strike on your base, I was seized with anger, a thirst for revenge—and a clarity I have not known since I was a young man. I made it my duty to take from you what you took from me."

"No," McCreary whispered.

"Conquering this sector of Texas was easy," Azov said. "I was then able to locate your hometown, Capt. McCreary. To find your beautiful wife. To make her and all of the members of this... beautiful community...the beacon of Socialism that my home had been!"

"You Communist bastard!" McCreary spat.

Azov chuckled. "Do your American friends working in the fields not look happy? Do they not look fulfilled? A little hypnosis here, a little torture there...but at the heart of it all, Communism is simply a fancy word for 'sharing.' And *you* have been sharing your beautiful Sunny—or should I say, my *Svetlana*—with me for the past three months."

His voice dropped further, into an oily and sultry tone. "Her skin...so very soft on these...lonely Texas nights."

"*Nooooooo!*" McCreary screamed.

"If my Moscow command knew what I was doing in this town," Azov said, "they might strip me of command. All they know is that I have taken Wrangler Plains—I mean, Fertile Worker Fields—as my command post. A staging ground for a thrust into the breadbasket of the future United Socialist States of America. But the inspired loyalty of our new comrades, my taking of a field wife—this is my personal effort."

"And of course, you had to destroy the church," McCreary hissed.

"We are not animals, Capt. McCreary." Azov said. "We waited. And when Lt. Hawkerov let us know that you were en route, I decided that the church would be the perfect demonstration. The perfect incentive for you to visit us again."

"You've disobeyed orders," McCreary snickered. "Your own superiors can't trust you."

"As you disobeyed orders to come here," the general said. The ice in his glass clinked. "We're not that different, you and I, Capt.

McCreary. We love our countries. We love the warrior's path. But at the end of the day, we are men who live by our own rules."

Calm down, Mike old boy, McCreary thought. *There's a way out of this. Don't let him get to you.*

And in his calm, McCreary's plan gelled. He could taste its humble brilliance. It tasted like freedom.

"That's where you're wrong, General," McCreary said. "I'd never take another man's town, much less his wife. I'd never engineer a sneaky invasion of another country. That's not the American way."

Azov drained his glass and leaned forward toward McCreary. "You Americans," he said. "Always so idealistic."

"Yes," McCreary said. "Idealistic—and very good at untying knots. *Especially us Eagle Scouts.*"

Azov's eyes twitched in recognition that he'd made a grave error. Rope flew and McCreary's fist circled in from the right and smashed the good general's cheekbone. Azov crashed into the desk and crumpled to the floor. McCreary stood over Azov, fists ready.

"*Get up, you Commie sonofabitch!*"

The Russian guards at the door had already pulled their sidearms and had them leveled on McCreary. "*Ostanovit!*" one of them cried. "*Ostanovit, vas kapitalisticheskaya svin'ya!*"

McCreary turned to them. "Go ahead. Do it," he said. "Shoot me, you godless puppets! I haven't got all day."

The arrows that pierced the windows of the mayor's office hit the guards' chests so quickly it appeared to McCreary that they'd burst from their hearts. Both Russians slowly sank to their knees.

Still tied to his chair, Whitefeather let out a shrill cry. "It's my brother warriors, Captain! They heard my call on the spirit winds!"

Outside the mayor's office, three sets of dissimilar sounds rose: Russian cries of alarm, sporadic AK fire...and a hundred Comanche war whoops.

McCreary had the big Indian untied in seconds. Azov was struggling to his feet, but the general collapsed again, moaning, struggling to unholster his Nagant.

"That was some punch, Cap!" LaRoy cried. "Look at that Mongol bastard! He can't even stand!"

Whitefeather untied LaRoy. They each took one of the guard's sidearms. "You better do the same, Captain," Whitefeather said. But McCreary was way ahead of him. He grabbed Azov's pistol from the general's weakened grasp.

Outside, the battle raged. Through the windows, McCreary caught glimpses of action: scrambling Russian soldiers, flashes of gunfire, mounted Comanches in deerskin and full regalia, chasing them down. Gunfire. The twang of bowstrings and the thud of tomahawks. Screams of panic and pain.

McCreary pulled the dazed general to his feet.

"Leave him!" Whitefeather said. "The sacred battle is joined!"

"No," McCreary said. "You and LaRoy go. The general and I have someplace to be. Don't we, General?"

LaRoy was beside himself. "Let's go, Whitefeather! I always wanted to be an Indian brave! *Whoooooop!*" And out they went, leaving McCreary and the general.

"On your feet," McCreary said grimly. "Take me to my house."

McCreary's homestead lay to the north of town, away from where the battle between the Russians and the Comanches was playing out. McCreary had to resist the urge to shoot Azov, rescue Sunny on his own, and sprint out of town. But he couldn't leave his men, and bringing Azov back alive might be the only thing that would keep Gen. Pearce from court-martialing him on the spot.

As McCreary moved Azov through the abandoned streets, they saw only flashes of action through streets and windows. Tanks rumbled. Russian APCs sped along, surrounded by bands of jogging, terrified soldiers. None of them seemed to notice that McCreary had their beloved commander at gunpoint.

They neared McCreary's home. There was the mailbox, painted bright white. There was the same grass. The same picket fence. The same gate, the last thing McCreary had made before shipping off to North Dakota. The only thing that was missing was the American flag that always hung from a bracket off the porch.

"She'd better be alive," McCreary said.

The general had said nothing since leaving the mayor's office—in fact nothing since McCreary had socked him. But now the general seemed to perk up.

"Oh, she is alive, Mike," Azov said as he walked through the gate. "If things had gone as planned, she'd be baking bread like a good Russian wife. Waiting for her husband, me, to show up. To enjoy a good meal. Then enjoy her, afterward."

"Careful, General," McCreary said. Through the windows, McCreary could see that everything in the house had changed. Gone were the photos of his family, of Sunny's family, the oil painting of Jesus that Sunny had painted for the state fair. Instead, McCreary could make out mostly bare walls, adorned only with the occasional image of Marx, Lenin, and old Papa Joe himself.

Azov opened the front door. They walked inside. There was no smell of bread.

"Where is she?"

"In our bedroom."

McCreary responded by shoving the barrel of the Nagant between Azov's shoulder blades so hard that the general staggered toward the stairs. Up they went, one step, two, the steps creaking. In the distance, a tank fired. The house shook.

"My Svetlana!" Azov called out. "I have brought you a guest. He is...so...*very* eager to see you."

They reached the top of the stairs. Down at the end of the dimly lit hallway was the door to their bedroom. Where McCreary and Sunny had learned about the sacred covenant between man and wife.

"You'll be happy to know, she's been very resistant to my charms," Azov said a few feet shy of the door. "It's taken much...

persuasion to even get her to look at me, but never without distrust in her eyes. And I must admit that she has resisted even my more... *skilled* methods."

"Shut up," McCreary said. "Open the door."

The general obeyed.

The bedroom McCreary had shared with his wife had been stripped down to three things: a four-poster bed, a Soviet flag hanging from a six-foot staff in the corner, and Sunny herself. McCreary's wife was unconscious and pale, tied on the bed, clad only in the virginal white nightgown she'd worn on their wedding night. Her hair was a curly blonde halo around her sleeping head.

He couldn't restrain himself any longer. McCreary shoved the general aside and raced to Sunny's bedside. "Sunny!...Sunny, it's me! It's Mike!"

Sunny opened her eyes. They were sunken and tired—from what, McCreary didn't want to know—but they were the same bright blue. They lingered on his. He saw a flicker of recognition—and a flash of red in their reflection over his shoulder.

Instinct. McCreary turned and fired. Again, and again, and again. McCreary barely registered the sight of Azov, brandishing the Soviet flagstaff as a sharpened weapon. It was a sea of red— flapping fabric and the general's blood.

Azov staggered backward. Blood poured from his surprised mouth. But somehow, the general lurched forward again. McCreary fired twice more. And again. Then, remembering that the Nagant held seven rounds, he saved the final shot for a spot right between Azov's dark, beady eyes.

Azov's dying body lurched backward, his shiny boots clattering against the hardwood floor. Back he flew against the window, and through it, shattering the glass and tumbling to the yard below.

Sunset. McCreary carried his wife's limp form across the high school football field. He could barely take it. The unholy lines that passed on the turf at his feet. *Those aren't yard lines,* he thought. *The goddamned Reds turned this Texas high school football field into a soccer field. Soccer!*

Suddenly the sound of hoofbeats erupted. McCreary turned. Here came Whitefeather astride a brown and white paint, with streaks across his face, the color of Russian blood. Behind him was LaRoy on a gimpy palomino and no less than a hundred Comanche warriors. In prewar life, they'd been proud working men and boys on the Reservation, content to do whatever it was Indians did. But now they had revived the spirits of their ancestors.

"The battle is ours, Captain!" Whitefeather cried. "The Russians didn't quite know what to make of this outfit."

"Well, a fitter bunch I never did see!" McCreary said, happy but weary.

"Captain, look!" LaRoy held aloft a long knife. "They made me an honorary Injun!" McCreary nodded, his eyes drifting to the dark, dripping mats that hung from their saddles.

McCreary didn't want to know.

"We have to get moving," Whitefeather said. "The Russians retreated, but you know they'll be back. We have to get back to General Pearce and tell him what we know." The big Indian turned and raised an AK-47 and let loose a war whoop. The warriors behind him responded in kind.

McCreary turned and hunkered down to his wife. "Did you hear that, Sunny? We have to get going. Sunny! Sunny?"

Lying beautifully on the grass, Sunny opened her eyes.

"Sunny! Did you hear me?"

His wife smiled faintly.

"*Da*," she said.

THE END

CHRISTOPHER BLAIR found this Reagan-era classic at the Coos Bay Swap Meet on the coast of Oregon. Even among survivalist training manuals, Laser Tag accessories, and tarnished throwing stars, the embossed mushroom cloud and hammer and sickle on its cover were hard to miss. Very little is known about the author Max Auger; we do know that this is his first printed effort and a prime example of the '80s post-apocalyptic sub-genre of men's adventure.

THE CHEMISTRATOR
in
DRUG CITY, USA
by Calvin Beauclerc
(discovered by Rob Kroese)

THE SIGN SAID *Averyville, population 9,184*, but Dax Maxwell knew it by a different name: *Drug City*. And the population was about to go up by one. And then, with any luck, it would go down quite a bit—because a lot of those 9,184 people were bad, and Dax planned to kill them.

Dax hitched his pack up his shoulder and strode into town. Averyville looked pleasant enough: on Main Street, pedestrians milled busily between brightly lit stores with professionally designed signs. But Dax knew that looks could be deceiving. Just as the drugs produced in Averyville's drug factories lured their victims into a waking nightmare of unquenchable drug-thirst, the cobblestones of Main Street led inexorably to avenues paved with the cracked asphalt of broken dreams. Dax stopped in front of the plate glass window of a drugstore and lit a cigarette. He shook his head, reflecting ruefully on the series of events that led him to this moment, his mind going back, back, back...

It had all started when his uncle got him that chemistry set for his tenth birthday. After that, Dax was only interested in one thing: mixing up chemical concoctions. Dax's grades suffered from his obsession with chemistry, and he was frequently getting in trouble for his ingenious but dangerous experiments, like the time he mixed dry ice and Pop Rocks in a blender and came dangerously close to creating a cold fusion reactor.

After high school the only job he could get was working for a local gardener. Dax's job was to spray weed-killer on a vacant lot, but the lot was so big that by the time he had killed all the weeds, a whole new batch had started to grow. Determined to make a better weed-killer, Dax mixed up a concoction that was so effective it turned every plant on the lot brown in a matter of hours. The next day he got a call from a colonel in the army, who was interested in Dax's weed-killer. They drafted Dax and used his weed-killer to clear the jungle foliage that provided cover for America's enemies in a little-known country called Vietnam. They called it Agent Burnt Umber.

"There's no smoking in Averyville," said a gruff voice behind him. Dax shook himself out of his reverie and turned to see a lanky man dressed in jeans and a plaid shirt. He wore a wide-brimmed hat. A revolver hung from his belt and a silver star glittered on his chest.

"This is a free country, last time I looked," said Dax.

"City ordinance," said the sheriff. His name tag read "Parsons."

"Well, that's a real cute rule for a place known as Drug City," said Dax, dropping his cigarette on the cobblestones and grinding it out with his boot.

"No littering either," said Sheriff Parsons. "I'm gonna have to take you in."

Dax shrugged. He knew guys back in the Nam who could have dropped a knuckle-dragger like Parsons with a karate chop to the throat before the signal to pull the trigger could even get from Parson's test-tube-sized brain to his finger. But that wasn't Dax's style.

"All right, Sheriff," he said, moving toward the car. "I don't want any trouble."

"Drop the pack," growled the sheriff. "Slowly."

Dax did as he was told.

"Turn around," barked the sheriff. "Gimme your hands."

Dax turned around, holding his hands behind him. The sheriff clamped a pair of handcuffs on him and shoved him into the car. Dax smiled grimly, looking at his reflection in the police car window. What he saw was a man who had been in far worse fixes than this. Those experiences came rushing back to him, just as surely as the photons of his image bounced off the window glass and struck his retinas.

After being drafted by the army, Dax worked for Colonel Randers, the head of Special Chemical Division, on a variety of top secret projects—from formulating truth serum that could make a VC spy spill the beans on his own mother to devising nerve gas that only worked on Communists. Yet he was troubled by reports that Agent Burnt Umber was making American troops sick, and he insisted on being deployed on combat duty in the jungle to prove that the defoliant was safe. He saw a lot of men die in country, but not from poisoning—unless it was lead poisoning, from being riddled with bullets. Dax became a formidable soldier on top of being a genius with chemicals, and his squad mates called him "The Chemistrator" because of his jury-rigged explosives, smoke screens, and other chemical innovations, often concocted entirely from raw materials Dax had happened upon in the jungle. Once, he had exploded an underground VC stronghold using only bat guano and mango juice.

But that was a long time ago.

Dax stared out the window of the cop car. The pleasant boulevards making up the public façade of Averyville gave way to seedy neighborhoods populated by drug-addled crazies wearing dirty, mismatched clothing and shouting confused obscenities at invisible tormenters. In the distance, a series of factories belched black smoke into the air. Whatever household goods these factories had once produced, Dax knew that they had been retrofitted into drug factories for producing drugs.

Dax winced, knowing that these nefarious facilities were operating according to his own blueprint: the chemical recipe for synthetic synapse-incinerators that he had devised. Lost in a world of his own thoughts, he closed his eyes and reflected on how that had come about.

After the war, there was no place for men like Dax. His country wanted to forget they had ever needed a man who could kill a hundred men with only his hands and naturally occurring substances on the jungle floor. Unable to find work, Dax used his knowledge of chemistry to create a synthetic form of cocaine that was eighteen times as powerful as the real thing. And the kicker was that it was completely legal: because Dax's drug was a chemical compound that was unknown to science, there were no laws against it. The drug had many street names: Bolivian blizzard, Nicaraguan nostril nuke, Colombian corn flour.

Dax became a rich man. He got married to a model named Stephanee and they had a daughter together. They named their daughter Argonia, after Dax's favorite noble gas. The plan was to live happily ever after.

But Chico Juarez, a local drug lord, had other plans. Angry with Dax for stealing his business, Chico Juarez sent his thugs to shoot up Dax's house, killing his wife and his daughter. Dax only escaped with the help of a noxious smoke screen he concocted from Clorox and leftover packets of Arby's Sauce. That night, huddled alone on a park bench in the cold, Dax swore that he would never again use his knowledge of chemistry for evil. He found a job in another city as a high school janitor, determined to make an honest living for himself.

"Here's your cell," growled the sheriff, shaking Dax out of his reverie and shoving him into a cold concrete room that smelled like urine and hopelessness and more urine. In place of a bed was a pile of old newspapers. They reminded Dax of the time he found an old newspaper on the floor at the school, where he worked as a janitor, months earlier. The headline had read:

Synthetic "Snow" Storm Unstoppable?
"Drug City" Floods Eastern Seaboard with Cheap,
Legal Cocaine; Police Say Their Hands Are Tied
"If only someone would put a stop to this," says teary-
eyed mother whose drug-addicted son went on a drug-
fueled killing rampage to get drug money to buy drugs

That article was like a catalyst in a chemical reaction in Dax's soul, even though Dax knew that souls didn't really have chemicals in them. Thinking about them as if they did, though, made it easier for him to understand, because Dax knew more about chemicals than souls.

It was bad enough that Chico Juarez had killed his wife and daughter; now he was using Dax's own drug formula to make millions by turning decent Americans into cloud powder junkies. Dax had unfinished business in Drug City. It was payback time. Time to even the scales, like a chemist weighing out the chemicals of justice.

So here he was, stuck in a cell in Averyville, with no way out. *Or was he?*

Dax waited for the sheriff to leave, pretending to sleep. When he heard the door to the police station close, he jumped to his feet, pulling out a small plastic bag of green powder that he had hidden in his rectum. Opening the bag, he rubbed some of the powder in rings around the bottom and top of one of the bars to his cell. Before his eyes, the steel rusted away. After a few seconds, he gave the bar a powerful kick. It broke loose, flying across the police station. Dax slipped through the opening and grabbed his pack, which the sheriff had left on his desk. Where he was going, he was going to need it.

Dax paused to remember how he had first come into possession of his pack. He had been on his way home to be with his family when he had spotted the pack in the window of a store, not unlike the window of the drugstore that he would later look into and remember how he got his first chemistry set when he was ten. Looking at the mottled brown cotton bag, he knew he had to have it for his chemicals, which he always carried with him. That was a habit he had picked up in Nam, while working for Special Chemical Division. "Be prepared," he murmured to himself, recalling the Boy Scout motto. He'd never had time for the Boy Scouts, because he was so busy mixing chemicals as a kid. Maybe if he'd joined the Scouts, things would have turned out differently for him. Maybe if he hadn't stopped that day to buy the pack, he would have been home in time to save his wife and daughter from Chico Juarez's thugs. But maybes didn't put food on the table, and they sure as hell didn't bring the dead back to life.

"Hey, what are you doing?" barked a deputy who had just walked into the police station, shaking Dax out of his reverie.

Dax dropped him with an uppercut to the jaw. Sometimes the best chemical reaction for the job was the firing of neurons that caused a fist to slam into a face. Dax picked up his pack, noticing a desk calendar underneath it. Today's date was circled, and inside the circle was written:

9PM MEET CHICO JUAREZ AT MAIN DRUG FACTORY
BIG DRUG SHIPMENT GOING OUT

That was just the sort of intel that Dax had been hoping to find when he deliberately got himself tossed into jail. He checked his watch. It was 8:30 p.m. He hoisted his pack onto his back and walked out of the police station. Dax had a party to crash. A drug party.

Dax lay on a warehouse roof, surveying the arrival of six eighteen-wheelers behind a factory with a sign that read "Apex Lawn Furniture." Dax knew that the sign, like the rest of Averyville, was a lie. The Apex Lawn Furniture factory didn't make lawn furniture. It made drugs. Drugs that were made with the chemical formula that Dax had formulated. Everyone knew that Apex Lawn Furniture made drugs, of course, but new signs cost money. And drug dealers didn't have to advertise. Drugs sold themselves. How many lives had Apex Lawn Furniture ruined with his formula, wondered Dax. How had things gotten so out of control?

Dax closed his eyes and reflected on how things had gotten so out of control. There wasn't any moment he could pinpoint, however. It had been a gradual process. He probably shouldn't have started selling drugs, though. That was definitely a mistake.

Dax opened his eyes to see that Sheriff Parsons had arrived to greet the trucks. A limo pulled up next to him and a tall, brown-skinned man with dark, slicked-back hair, wearing a dark suit and mirrored sunglasses stepped out. Chico Juarez. All the players were here. Time to mix it up, like a chemist mixing chemicals in a big chemical mixing machine.

Suddenly, something whacked Dax on the back of his skull, and everything went black. Blacker than carbon, thought Dax, which was ironic because carbon's chemical symbol was C, and he couldn't.

Dax regained consciousness when someone emptied a bucket of cold water on his head. He was inside the factory, tied to a chair. Around him were dozens of pallets holding plastic bags of crazy candy. Women wearing nothing but g-strings and steel-toed boots loaded the pallets into the trucks on forklifts. Sheriff Parsons, Chico Juarez, and several of his goons stood over Dax.

"Enjoying the view?" asked the sheriff.

"I am, actually," said Dax, taking a good long look at the warehouse personnel. Either there was a correlation between bust size and forklift proficiency that Dax wasn't aware of, or these women had been hired as much for their centerfold-quality bodies as for their warehousing skill.

"Women are better workers," said the sheriff. "We keep them nude so that they don't try to steal any product. And also so that they are nude." A stunning redhead walked past with a clipboard, and the sheriff slapped her on the behind. She scowled playfully and went back to work.

"Well, three cheers for equal rights," said Dax. The sheriff grinned. But Chico Juarez wasn't in a jovial mood.

"Joo theenk joo can just walk een here and blow up my merchandise?" growled Chico Juarez, in a thick Hispanic accent. He was holding Dax's pack, which was filled with his custom-made bombs. "Who do joo theenk joo are?"

"Name's Dax Maxwell," spat Dax. "I've got a score to settle with you. Those are my drugs."

"Your drugs!" exclaimed Sheriff Parson. He and Chico Juarez laughed the hysterical laugh of evil men.

"How do you figure?" asked the sheriff.

"I came up with the formula," Dax said. "I'm the only one who has the right to sell that brain-busting bromide, and I'm closing up shop."

"I remember joo," said Chico Juarez. "Joor wife screamed like a leetle girl when I killed her. And so deed joor daughter."

"My daughter *was* a little girl," growled Dax, straining against his bonds.

Chico Juarez laughed again. "Well, chereeff, maybe we chould let Meester Maxwell sample some of *hees* drugs." Chico Juarez sneered at Dax, his eyes hidden behind the mirrored shades. Looking into the sunglasses, Dax saw his own reflection, and he reflected on the time he had seen his reflection in the front window of the drugstore earlier that same day, reflecting on his childhood and wondering where it had all gone wrong—and at that point, things hadn't gone nearly as wrong as they had in the hours since. *Or had they?*

Laughing, the sheriff grabbed a plastic bag full of fairy flakes from a nearby palette, sticking a knife into it and pulling out a knife-full of the demonic dust. He stuck the point of the knife into Dax's left nostril.

"*Dios mio!*" cried Chico Juarez. "That cloud candy is *dieciocho* times more powerful than regular cocaine. That much will keell him!"

"That's the idea," said the sheriff. They both laughed. The sheriff put his hand over Dax's mouth. "Take a deep breath!"

Dax bit down hard, his incisors puncturing the sheriff's hand. The sheriff jerked his hand away. The flesh tore, spilling blood on the factory floor. The sheriff screamed, and the goons raised their guns. Dax sucked air in through his mouth and made himself sneeze—a trick he had learned in Nam. A cloud of djinn dust exploded from his nose. As it did, Dax bit down hard on a fake molar and breathed out, blowing a red gas into the cloud. Dax clamped his eyes shut as the two chemicals reacted with a brilliant flash, blinding everyone in the room.

"Nice treeck, Meester Maxwell!" cried Chico Juarez. "But joo're going to need more than magic treecks to get out of thees one!"

What Chico didn't know was that the trick wasn't over yet. The rabbit was out of the hat, but it hadn't yet transformed into a beautiful dove. Dax had worked for months perfecting the formula for the chemical in his tooth. His eyes still closed, Dax reflected for a moment on the long hours he had spent in his lab, feverishly working on the perfect mixture. It had taken him weeks, barely sleeping, subsisting on a diet of glucose, caffeine, and his own urine. It was probably the most difficult thing he had ever had to do, except for seeing his wife and daughter killed in front of him. That was rough.

The flash disappeared, leaving behind a thick gray cloud that made it impossible to see. Chico Juarez's goons fired wildly. The cloud's corrosive properties proceeded to eat through the nylon rope binding Dax's hands, and soon he was free.

Dax put on a pair of infrared goggles he had hidden in his rectum (behind the bag of corrosive powder he had extracted earlier) and made his way through the maze of blinded goons. Topless women screamed as he ran past, but Dax kept going.

The cloud cleared. "Stop heem!" yelled Chico Juarez.

Dax dove behind a row of barrels as the goons opened fire with their AK-47s and AK-48s. Bullets ricocheted around Dax as the men converged on his position. There was no escape. He was surrounded. Dax began to wonder if he'd gotten the formula wrong. Could it be? After all the hours he had spent in his lab, checking and re-checking all of his calculations, drinking a little urine, and then re-checking them again? Having briefly opened his eyes, he closed them again, re-re-re-checking the calculations in his head. He cursed himself for not bringing any urine with him—but despite its balloon-like elasticity there simply hadn't been room in his rectum.

Just as the goons were almost upon him, it happened: the corrosive vapor ate through the plastic wrapping around the cocaine on the nearest palette and the contents spilled out. When the pernicious powder made contact with the vapor, it exploded in a flash. Then the rest of the palette exploded with a massive roar, tearing several of the women in half. The bottom half of one woman ran past Dax frantically, spurting blood from her severed abdomen. Dax shook his head. He'd seen a lot of topless babes in his day, but nothing like this.

He had to remind himself that as gorgeous as the women had been before being torn apart, they had gotten themselves into this. Chico Juarez hadn't shown Dax's wife any mercy, and Dax wasn't about to alter his plan to save a bunch of drug-pushing floozies, even if they were knockouts with boobs like giant Bunsen burners.

The blast knocked the goons near Dax off their feet, and Dax got up and ran, making his way past the trucks and into the night. Behind him, a chain reaction was occurring, one palette after another exploding with a deafening roar.

"Noooo!" he heard Chico Juarez cry. Dax turned to see the once-powerful drug lord on his knees, shaking his fists at the heavens in despair, his precious pallets of gutter glitter exploding before his eyes.

"*Adios, muchacho*," said Dax, as a stack of pallets behind Chico Juarez erupted, ripping Chico Juarez to pieces.

Dax Maxwell stood in the rain, regarding the gravestones grimly. "I did it, baby. I got 'em. For you and Argonia."

There was no answer, but Dax didn't expect one. His fingertips traced the lettering on the cold stone, and Dax thought about the acid the gravestone maker had used to etch his wife and daughter's names into granite. A simple chemical reaction, thought Dax. That's all it took to mark a piece of stone forever. That's how his heart felt, a piece of stone forever marked by his memories of Stephanee and Argonia. He had tried to live a normal life, but you couldn't live a normal life when your heart was made of stone, and it was etched with the names of the dead.

A newspaper fluttered in the wind, coming to rest against his daughter's gravestone. The headline read:

*Son of drug lord Chico Juarez elected mayor of Los
Muertos, Mexico Promises to provide employment
for thousands in new lawn furniture factory
Chiquito Juarez swears that factory is not
secretly a drug factory for making drugs*

So, thought Dax. Drug City has moved south. I guess that's where I'm headed too. He hitched his pack up his back.

The Chemistrator had work to do.

THE END

Drug City, USA *was published in 1983 and epitomizes the anti-drug hysteria of the era. It probably also holds the record for the most unsuccessful attempts to inject new slang terms for drugs (e.g., "cloud powder") into the English language. ROB KROESE picked up a copy of* Drug City, USA *at a flea market in Stockton, California, along with a poster of John Taylor from Duran Duran ("for a friend") and a complete set of Jarts.*

From the thin volume Authors Named Beauclerc: A Compendium:

Calvin Beauclerc, a bakery truck driver who lived his entire life in rural Indiana, was once detained for several hours by the local police for threatening to blow up his neighbor's collection of garden gnomes with what turned out to be a two-liter bottle filled with brown sugar and Pine-Sol. Drug City, USA *was his first novel. It was followed by* Drug City, USA 2; Drug City, USA 3: Escape from Drug City; Drug City, Canada; *and* Drug City 4: Return to Drug City 2. *Beauclerc also wrote at least six of the seventeen entries in the popular* D.R.U.G. F.O.R.C.E. *series for teens. Intended as anti-drug propaganda, it concerned a group of teenagers whose experimentation with drugs goes horribly wrong when a bad batch gives them superhuman powers. The books are still banned by most public school districts in the United States.*

BASTARD MERCENARY
in
OPERATION SCORPION STING
by Arch Saxon
(discovered by Andrew Nette)

HIS NAME WAS THONG: Thai for 'gold.' But the only thing shining in the weak sunlight that streamed through the cell's barred window was the glint on the six-inch shiv the lady-boy held in his manicured right hand.

He sliced the air in front of me, shifted his weight from foot to foot. He looked playful, but I could tell he was a professional. The way he held the makeshift blade, to cut not stab. How he kept his distance, stopped me from getting close. Thailand may be known as the "land of smiles," but the only thing the look of glee on his powdered face promised was painful death.

Lefebvre cowered behind the hired killer. Unshaven and dressed in grimy prison fatigues, the Frenchman looked like just another shit-out-of-luck inmate of the Kingdom's prison system, not the front man for an international Communist-controlled drug syndicate.

Thong made another cutting motion, testing me, gauging my reflexes. He knew he had me at a disadvantage.

I'd spent forty-eight hours in the company of two hundred men crammed into a holding cell barely big enough for fifty. Lefebvre and his bodyguard occupied one of several smaller rooms reserved for prisoners with money.

The only thing to eat had been rice porridge. I hadn't slept, constantly on guard against the rats that came out at night, not to mention much larger predators. Worst of all, I was unarmed.

"Are you ready to taste my pretty blade, *falang*?" the lady boy cooed in the local dialect favoured by Thais from the Northeast, the poorest part of the Kingdom.

Thong and I stared at each other, two gladiators about to do battle. His eyes were wide and bloodshot, a sure sign he was on the cheap speed known as *yah bah*, used by most of the inmates. As if signalling our entrance into the arena, the cacophony of human noise from the surrounding prison reached fever pitch.

"You've got one chance," I said in fluent Thai. "Put down the knife, let me have the Frenchman."

Thong put a hand over his mouth, his hot pink nail polish standing out in the drab surroundings, and stifled a high-pitched giggle.

"Don't fucking flirt, you idiot," hissed Lefebvre in Thai. "Kill him."

The Thai swung the blade savagely, missed me and followed up with a rapid criss-crossing movement. The blade bit into my shoulder, spreading a pool of dark crimson on my prison fatigues.

Emboldened by the sight of blood, Thong came in close, hoping to finish me quickly. He lunged. I careened the upper part of my body to one side as the blade cut the air where my face had been, grabbed his knife hand by the wrist and bent it backwards. It snapped with a sickening crack.

The shiv clattered to the concrete floor as the Thai fell to his knees, clasping the broken appendage to his chest. Lefebvre edged backwards across the floor until his back was pressed hard against the wall. I smiled at him, took Thong's head in my hands and twisted it sharply.

It was a thing of beauty, the look of raw fear on the Frenchman's face as I let go of the Thai's lifeless body and picked up the shiv.

"Who the hell are you?" he said in heavily accented English as I rested the blade under his chin. His breath stank of *nam pla*, the pungent fish sauce the Thais used to season all their food.

"Name's Bruce Kelly. Mates call me Boomer. You can call me your worst nightmare."

"Please, I beg you, don't kill me."

"I'm not going to kill you, Froggie. That is unless you don't tell me what I need to know."

He nodded vigorously, his pores popping sweat. "Anything."

"Start with the location of Scorpion's Bangkok headquarters."

"They'll kill me."

"Well, it looks like you're shit out of options, because I'll kill you if you don't."

"Not like Scorpion's people you won't—"

Most people think pain is the most effective interrogation technique. But in my extensive experience, one gets even better results from pain when it's combined with surprise. Before Lefebvre could finish his sentence, I drew the shiv across his cheek, paused for effect, and then repeated the action on his other cheek.

The Frenchman dabbed his fingers on the wounds, put them in front of his face. His eyes bulged as he looked at the blood.

"It'll be your ears next, then your nose. I'll keep going all the way down to your balls."

Five minutes later I had everything I needed. I threw the shiv to one side, stood, and turned to leave. A crowd of prisoners had gathered in the cell doorway: Thais, a Russian who'd beaten a prostitute to death, a couple of gigantic Africans arrested for passport theft.

They parted, wary looks on their faces.

"He's all yours," I said as I passed.

I could hear Lefebvre's screams as the guard unlocked the rusty door to the holding cell and let me out.

Three days earlier, I'd been sitting at the bar of the Sunrise Club, the joint I own on Soi Cowboy. A quiet night, monsoonal rain and rumours of another military coup keeping all but the most persistent punters off the streets and out of the bars.

Not that I minded. Hank Williams was on the turntable—there's no disco in my bar—and I nursed a cold beer. The lull also gave me an opportunity to concentrate on more important matters, like my newest waitress, Lek. She was a fresh-faced little thing from the North with an eye for making a buck in the big city and a firm arse you could bounce a five baht on.

Might have even tried my luck if it weren't for the fact that I was already exhausted after a day of lovemaking with Elise, a German Lufthansa stewardess who always paid me a visit when she was in town. She moved her body with the finesse of a panzer commander manoeuvring across the Russian steppes.

I was contemplating taking down the "Happy New Year 1981" banner in tinsel slung across the bar when a Western man walked in. He was older than me by at least a decade but still in good shape. His snow-white hair was cut military style and he wore an immaculately pressed tan safari suit. I hope he wasn't trying to be incognito because he stank of old school spook.

The man glanced around the club and walked towards me. "Bruce Kelly?" he said with a Midwestern American accent as he shook my hand. "My name's Rex Bannister, I have a proposition for you."

"That's a turn for the books. It's usually me doing the propositioning."

He didn't smile. I drained my beer, burped, and motioned across the bar to Tiger Lily, my bar manager.

"Hey baby, get me another beer. Make sure it's cold." I looked at Bannister. "Want one?"

He gave me a curt shake of his head. I peeled the tab off the can of beer and took a long drink.

"I was hoping we could talk somewhere in private."

I led Bannister to my office, a small back room that doubled as a change space for the waitresses, sat behind the desk strewn with papers, and swigged my beer.

Bannister sniffed, gave the room a slow one hundred and eighty degree sweep, as if trying to locate the source of an unpleasant odour.

"I hear you're a veteran," he said, his eyes on the centrefold of Miss April pinned to the wall just above my right shoulder.

"I've been around." I re-adjusted the patch on my right eye, the legacy of a Russian-made land mine in central Vietnam in 1969. "You?"

"Korea." He threw me a defiant look. "A real war."

I shrugged and sipped my beer. He might have been a soldier once; now he was just another desk jockey employing others to do the killing. I'd met plenty like him, uptight, church going Langley types. I'd even done some work for one or two of them in the past, which I presumed was where Bannister got my name.

"Let me make it clear, I don't like you, Kelly. I don't like your bar, your drinking, and your taste in wall decorations. But you're supposed to be good at what you do and we need your help."

"Like's got nothing to do with it, Bannister," I replied between sips. "If I only took jobs from people I liked, I'd be a poor man. Just tell me what you want, and let's see if we can do business."

Bannister swept a pair of black lacy underwear off the wooden seat in front of the desk, sat, and gave me his best man-to-man look.

"For some time now, the US government agency I work for has been tracking the activities of a highly organised drug syndicate operating in Bangkok."

I put my legs on the desk. "It's not like Uncle Sam to give a toss about a few hopheads overdosing on cheap junk."

"This outfit is different." Bannister leaned forward. "It's headed by a former Chinese Communist Red Guard, known only by the code name Scorpion. He's smart and cunning, got links with the cops, the military and Bangkok's Sino-Thai elite. Now he's expanding his operation, making connections with Communist regimes in Laos and Vietnam, opening up new trafficking routes.

"Conventional policing activities don't work against him, and he's eliminated every agent we've tried to infiltrate into his organisation. Fortunately, we have a new President in the White House, one who understands the threat posed by Communism in all its forms and is prepared to take whatever steps necessary to combat it."

Jesus, what was next, a rendition of the Stars and Stripes? I raised the beer can to my lips and gazed at Bannister.

"Let me guess: that's where I come in."

"Precisely. Find Scorpion's Bangkok headquarters and take it off the grid using whatever means necessary. We'll pay you twenty thousand US dollars, half now, half after the job is complete, plus we'll bankroll any expenses. Totally off the books, mind you. Maximum deniability."

"That's a pretty tall order, mate," I drained my beer. "Bangkok's a big city. Any idea where I would start?"

"Scorpion works through cut-outs. One of these is a Frenchman called Lefebvre. He's a veteran red, got his start organising dockworkers in Marseilles, spent time in Peking. Like all Europeans, Lefebvre has a weakness. Thai police busted him a couple of nights ago with an underage hooker in a short-time room off Sukhumvit, threw him into the main holding cell of Bangkok's Klong Prem Prison to await trial.

"Nothing that a bribe in the right place couldn't usually fix, had Lefebvre's file not come to the attention of a corrupt but observant police colonel who knew how much he was worth to the reds. And to us. While the Commies negotiate his release, we've cut a side deal with the colonel for someone to pose as an inmate and get to him first."

"And you want that someone to be me."

"Correct. Get in there, make contact with Lefebvre and find out what he knows about Scorpion's operation. Then do what you bastard mercenaries do best."

"And what exactly do you think that is, Bannister?"

"Unleash mayhem."

People like Bannister use the term mercenary as an insult. I wear it as a badge of pride.

I've been killing for so long it's like a second skin. Got my start fighting Communist insurgents in the rubber plantations of Malaya in the late fifties; then I was in the Special Forces in Vietnam. Stayed until the end of the war, didn't even bother going home to Australia. Now I sell the skills acquired in her majesty's armed forces to the highest bidder.

I don't have anything personally against the reds. Capitalist, Communist, I'll happily kill whoever if the price is right. Christ, the whole stinking world can blow itself up for all I care, as long as I have a cold beer in my hand and get paid in cash before they push the button.

Lefebvre's information put Scorpion's base in an old warehouse compound on the banks of the Chao Phraya that runs through Bangkok before emptying into the Gulf of Thailand.

The warehouse was also the headquarters of an aggressive club of body chasers. A lot of Bangkok is still made up of tiny *sois* or side streets on which most of the city's residents live their lives. But as the country's economy has grown, freeways have begun to crisscross the city, and the number of traffic accidents has risen. Without much of an ambulance service, the job of picking over the carnage is left to clubs of young men, often affiliated to Buddhist temples, who prowl the city looking for accidents. Their exploits are depicted in grisly colour photographs of mangled bodies and twisted metal prominently displayed on public notice boards. Thai friends tell me the photos are meant to reinforce the Buddhist precept that all physical matter eventually decays.

Yeah, it's strange, but no more so than a lot of the shit I've seen in Asia. I've watched a wizened old shaman possessed by a spirit so strong he could bend a steel bar. In central Vietnam, I'd seen a detachment of hardened Montagnard soldiers refuse to attack a hill they thought was inhabited by evil spirits. Hell, it's no different to the Dreamtime stories told by my father, an Aboriginal bare-knuckle boxer who'd worked a travelling circus in the Queensland outback and died broke and alcoholic years after my white mother left him and took me with her.

Besides, a gang of body chasers was the perfect cover for Scorpion's trafficking operation. What better way to move the drugs than through groups of young men who came and went at all hours of the day and night and moved across the city without arousing suspicion?

I thought all this as I stood on the deck of the sampan moored in the middle of the Chao Phraya, before turning my attention to the final weapons check being undertaken by my unit.

Getting to Lefebvre had been a solo mission. Taking down Scorpion's headquarters required more firepower.

I'd come across O'Connell hiding out in Bangkok after he had killed a high profile Republican commander in Belfast. In addition to his favourite weapon, a World War Two British commando knife, tonight he packed an Israeli-made Uzi submachine gun. Compact, able to fire up to six hundred rounds a minute. Fitted with a silencer like all our weapons, it was perfect for the kind of confined space we were about to enter.

Tiger Lily didn't just tend bar at the Sunrise, she was also a professional killer who'd learned her lethal skills from her father, one of Thailand's most renowned hit men. That's saying something in a country where having someone whacked is as acceptable a business practice as phoning a lawyer. She made the last-minute adjustments to her weapon of choice, an M21 semiautomatic sniper rifle, 20 rounds in the magazine, accurate over a remarkable distance.

I picked up my weapon from the deck, a Smith and Wesson M76 submachine gun. Yank Special Forces had used the M76 for covert ops in Vietnam, which is where I'd first come across it. The magazine held 36 soft point rounds, for maximum impact. A six-shot Colt Cobra .38 Special, also loaded with soft points, was in a leather holster strapped to my left ankle.

I had one other surprise for Scorpion. My boomerangs. Dad had taught me how to use them when I was a kid. Holstered in a leather bandolier across my chest, mine were custom-made out of lightweight carbon fibre reinforced plastic, edges inlayed with razor-sharp metal.

The game plan for tonight was simple. Tiger Lily would be stationed at the entrance to deal with unwelcome reinforcements, while O'Connell and I went in and killed everyone we could find.

Then we'd lay some Czech Semtex, acquired through O'Connell's contacts, set the timers, sit back and watch the fireworks.

I cocked the M76, looked at my team of killers. "We all set?"

"Roger, boss," said Tiger Lily.

O'Connell flashed me a mouth of bad Irish dental work. "Aye, nay worries."

The three of us stepped into an inflatable Zodiac tethered to the sampan. I waved to Tiny, the dwarf captain of the sampan, that we were ready. The red dot from the *Krong Tip* cigarette permanently hanging from his mouth bobbed up and down, indicating we were good to go.

We cut through the black, foul-smelling water, the purr of the Zodiac's outboard motor smothered by the buzz of traffic in the distance. As we approached, I could see two guards on an old wooden dry dock leading to the warehouse. Tiger Lily dispatched both of them before they even had time to unsling their weapons.

A couple of minutes later, O'Connell and I were over the brick wall surrounding the warehouse and into the compound. A row of vans used to ferry corpses was parked on one side of the main warehouse. The accordion door to the warehouse was open. We entered, our flashlights illuminating a large storeroom full of wooden coffins and other tools of the body chasers' trade.

Suddenly, the overhead lights bathed us in harsh fluoro. As I adjusted to the light, I saw at least two dozen men—Thais by the look of them, clad in pale blue body chaser uniforms that made them look like hospital orderlies—emerge from behind the neatly stacked coffins. They held an assortment of weapons: knives, machetes, crowbars, nunchakus.

The wave of blue rushed at us, faces snarling like rabid soi dogs. Instinctively, Connelly and I covered each other's backs and opened fire. Short controlled bursts mowed down the closest members of the pack, but they kept coming, clambering over their fallen comrades to get to us.

I'd been in this situation before, a trench in Vietnam, firing at wave after wave of North Vietnamese regulars, until the barrel of my machine gun had glowed red hot. But ferocity is no match for firepower, and soon O'Connell and I were surrounded by a harvest of corpses.

"Bloody eejits, that was a turkey shoot," said O'Connell as he slit the throat of a wounded body chaser.

"Something tells me that's just the start." I changed ammo clips. "Stay sharp, mate."

We moved down the only corridor, checking the rooms as we went. More coffins, a makeshift morgue, sleeping quarters. The air stank of disinfectant and we could hear the roar of the crowd from a Thai kickboxing match on a black-and-white TV that had been left on.

A set of stairs descended into a large chamber. O'Connell and I paused on a mezzanine halfway down. It was like stepping into a science fiction film: rows of large stainless steel vats, tubs of chemicals, the hum of machinery. Wires and tubes ran everywhere.

O'Connell whistled. "Now that is a shite load of fucking scrag."

I nodded. With this set up Scorpion could produce enough dope to keep every junkie in the States on cloud nine for a long time.

Two men in white lab coats emerged from behind the machinery. Lab technicians. The one closest had a pistol. His partner, a few feet behind him, raised a beaker of noxious-looking purple liquid above his head, ready to douse us.

I aimed the M70 from my hip and fired. The front of the first technician's coat exploded in a mass of red blossoms. He stumbled backwards onto his colleague, who dropped the beaker, the contents spilling over his own head and shoulders. I watched with grim fascination as the man writhed on the ground screaming, the purple liquid eating his flesh.

"Okay, enough bloody bullshit." I handed O'Connell blocks of Semtex and timers. "Let's get this over with."

We walked down the aisle, affixing Semtex to the vats. As O'Connell set his last charge, he turned to me and opened his mouth to speak. Before the Irishman could say anything, the top of his head disappeared in a crimson blur and he crumpled to the floor.

A huge, bald Oriental stepped out from between two vats, stood over O'Connell's body. He was naked from the waist up, his torso a patchwork of muscle and steel surgically grafted to his skin. His right arm was completely metal and in place of a hand was a ball covered in sharp spikes. Shreds of O'Connell's skull and tufts of his unmistakable carrot-coloured hair dangled from it.

I hesitated, transfixed by the horrific creature and the red star tattooed on his forehead. Savouring my fear, machine man's beady eyes narrowed and his face split into a malevolent grin. The hairs on the back of my neck stood on end.

I snapped out of my inaction, raised the M70, fired. The bullets ricocheted off his metal hide. I squeezed the trigger again, heard a succession of metallic clicks. The magazine was empty. Before I could reload, a swipe from machine man's metal hand twisted the barrel to one side like it was made of cheap plastic. Another swing knocked the gun from my hands.

The monster stepped toward me, raised his deadly appendage. I dodged the blow. The spiked ball missed my head by inches, tore a chunk from the nearest metal vat. Steam hissed angrily from the gash. The Oriental walked through the boiling vapour without flinching. Whatever surgical procedure he'd undergone had obviously robbed him of any sensitivity to pain.

As he walked machine man swung his metal attachment from side to side. Although I easily avoided each blow, I could feel myself tiring, while machine man, powered by an inhuman energy, showed no sign of slowing.

In an effort to lose my attacker and buy a few moments to regroup, I ducked between two steel vats, ran straight into a metal trolley loaded with glass beakers and technical equipment, tripped over it and hurtled forwards.

I don't know how long I lay stunned on the ground. I heard the crunch of glass underfoot, felt one of my legs latched into a vice-like grip. The Oriental dragged me along the floor like a carcass being delivered to the butcher's block.

He stopped in front of the damaged vat, released my leg. I waited for the spiked metal ball to reduce me to hamburger like it had O'Connell. Instead, machine man picked me up by the neck and lifted my face towards the jet of steam escaping from the jagged hole in the metal.

I tried to prise his grip off me with both hands, but it was like trying to manipulate concrete. The skin on my face burned as it neared the boiling steam.

"Halt."

The harsh female voice echoed through the laboratory. Machine man let go. I rolled, came up in a combat stance.

A tall, athletic-looking Asian woman stood on the mezzanine above me. She was clad in tight-fitting khaki *cheongsam*. Her long black hair was tied in a bun underneath a khaki Mao cap.

The Oriental giant stood still, stared at me, an attack dog awaiting his master's next command.

She threw back her head and laughed. "I can tell what you are thinking, imperialist scum." Her dark eyes narrowed as she looked at me. "You think it is not possible Scorpion is a woman."

I had to give the reds points for cunning. No wonder Bannister and his people had had so little success locating Scorpion. I stared at the creamy white skin of the leg protruding from the split in her dress, the blood red lips, the pistol in the holster nestled in the curve of her hip, as I figured out my next move.

"For decades we have spilt blood in the struggle against capitalism. Then we realised, it would be simpler if we used the West's own decadent craving for narcotics against itself. In this laboratory are the means to make that plan a reality, as your paymasters will soon realise."

Scorpion looked around the room proudly before returning her gaze to me. "Lefebvre was a fool to lead you here, but you will not live to brag of your discovery."

She barked something in Mandarin. As if a switch had been flicked, the machine man resumed his slow advance towards me. Out of the corner of my eye I saw Scorpion lick her lips in anticipation as he swung his metal fist.

I dove. The deadly wrecking ball sailed over my head, struck another vat. This time the metal fist remained lodged in the hole. The Oriental emitted a moist grunting sound as he tugged, a confused expression on his face, but he couldn't dislodge himself.

Scorpion shrieked in anger, undid the clasp on her holster to reach for her gun. With no time to go for my pistol, I grasped one of my boomerangs and threw. She raised a hand to shield her face. The boomerang struck, severing it clean off at the wrist. Her lips trembled as she stared at the blood spurting from the severed stump.

I quickly switched my gaze to machine man, still straining to free himself. I pulled out the Colt Cobra, held it in both hands, aimed, shot the creature between the eyes just as he was about to rip himself free. Machine man swayed as the hollow point round bounced around his skull. He crashed to the ground with the meat and metallic sound of a car accident.

I raised the pistol to sight the woman, but she was gone. When I reached the spot on the mezzanine where Scorpion had been, all that was left was a delicate female hand in a pool of blood.

At least I'd left her something to remember me by.

I stood on the sampan's deck, the orange glow from the burning warehouse receding in the distance.

Tiger Lily smiled, handed me a beer. Later, when I was not around to cause her loss of face, I knew she'd light incense and say a prayer for O'Connell at the rickety wooden spirit house on the pavement outside the Sunrise Club.

I pulled on the beer. The glow had almost disappeared beneath the skyline. I turned away and savoured the cool breeze of the headwind against my skin.

O'Connell knew the risks and I didn't have time to mourn.
I had the rest of my money to collect.

THE END

Arch Saxon's Bastard Mercenary series, a mainstay of the Australian men's adventure publisher Nasho Books Ltd., has had a bit of revival recently; a film version is in development.

Whether or not the books will come back in print is a different story. Huge thanks go to author and Saxon collector, ANDREW NETTE, for digging up this gem from 1984.

THE SANITIZER
in
THE POTOMAC PENETRATION
by Marion Hillberry, writing as Stack Grannett
(discovered by Nick Slosser)

THE GUARD AT THE GATE watched the WWII-vintage Army green Harley-Davidson WLA rumble to a halt before the barrier arm. For the millionth time he wondered how a janitor could afford those wheels. For the millionth time he decided the janitor, an expert with his hands, had probably restored the hog himself.

The guard didn't need ID—the man never wore a helmet—but he said, "Nice day." The janitor nodded, saying nothing as usual, and ducked beneath the arthritic motion of the barrier arm.

The guard watched him guide the chopper toward the parking structure, south of the main building, before hoisting this month's Mack Bolan adventure. He settled in for another uneventful day at the Tutelo Nuclear Power Facility.

Minutes later, a powder blue Volkswagen Bug he'd never seen before sputtered to a standstill. The woman driving squinted at the sign on the barrier, obviously unfamiliar with the facility. Peering into the vehicle, he noticed she dressed like a professional. He also noticed that several blouse buttons were undone.

He cleared his throat. "Can I help you, ma'am?"

"Gosh, I hope so," she said, pouting. "This isn't American Amalgamated Inc., is it?"

"No, I'm sorry to say." He moved his hand, which had been tickling his sidearm, so he could lean against her car. From above, her breasts looked supernaturally plump.

She dropped her eyes becomingly. "You don't by chance know where American Amalgamated is, do you?"

"No, I don't. But if you park over there and come inside, I'll try to find the spot." He pointed to the map.

"Won't that get you into trouble?"

He glanced toward the facility. "Not if they don't find out."

"Oh, thank you so much."

She parked where he'd indicated and sauntered across the road, her high heels clicking on the blacktop. This would be the last image he'd ever witness.

As he gazed, a man who resembled him in height, build, hair color, and uniform stepped behind him, put a silenced pistol to the back of his head, and pulled the trigger twice in rapid succession. The guard fell like a tipped cow.

The janitor strode toward the main building then turned toward the guard booth. He saw a woman holding what resembled a roadmap. Moments later, he saw the guard step out of the shelter, point at the map, and gesture down the road. Women, he thought. Never trust one to follow directions.

The janitor entered the main building, ready to face another day of calm predictability and Zen-like meditation, of steady, rhythmic labor through a pleasant, fume-induced buzz...which was just how he liked it.

A boy doesn't dream of growing up a janitor, let alone at a gray-on-gray nuclear plant like Tutelo. But a man on the run doesn't get much choice. So he swept and scrubbed and plunged and squeegeed and smiled while doing it. For Tutelo meant peace, a place where not even his old Agency cronies would think to seek him, because here even the lowliest mop jockey gets vetted at the highest clearance levels.

As the door slammed shut behind him, a small convoy of utility vans with darkened windows rolled through the gate—its barrier arm held high in mock salute—and cruised like Blue Angels to line up against the building. A rear door swung out and the VW woman hopped down, landing gracefully on her heels. She checked her watch—they were ahead of schedule—and positioned herself to observe the open stretch between the main building and the core containment facility.

It took twenty-five minutes for the site manager to begin his daily visual tour of the site. It took another six for the woman to pop out from behind a large pipe and sidle up next to him. Convincing him to cooperate took less than a minute and returning to the main building less than three. Including the gate, it took forty-four minutes and one dead body to penetrate Tutelo.

The woman stamped high-heeled prints like carnivore tracks straight through the recently mopped floor. Flanked by two mercenary-types—one bald, one blonde—she guided the site manager to the door that led to the heart and other organs—lungs, pancreas, and small intestines—of the Tutelo Nuclear Power Facility.

The janitor froze in place to avoid hitting her perfectly tapered legs and kept his eyes glued to the wet spot. The site manager took no notice of him, as usual.

Only the bald one hesitated, uncertainty etched upon his granite face. "Who's he?"

The site manager searched for a name then said, "Nobody. He's just the janitor."

"Leave him," the woman said. "He poses no threat."

Baldy smirked and moved on.

Peering into the reflection off the mop water, the janitor watched her deposit the mercs outside the door. He stooped for an alternate angle and observed a tight group of men stroll through the front doors and fan out to block the exits. Some carried heavy bags, others steel-gray cases. To gain a closer look he knelt as if scrubbing a stubborn spot.

The men appeared relaxed, well-dressed and fit, diverse of nationality, and conditioned for physical combat. Several men streamed past the janitor, dragging their feet through his work, not even bothering to say he'd missed a spot; he was simply a rock parting insensate waters.

He observed Baldy and Blondie calmly deflecting a pair of disgruntled lab coats away from the door. These men were disciplined and professional. Judging from the gear, they were also highly trained and well funded, which indicated only one possibility: a Communist plot.

Even if these men weren't true Reds, they would be funded by Reds. And the janitor hated Reds.

The janitor mopped his way toward the door, head down, dragging his left foot, muttering improvised lyrics to Cyndi Lauper's "She Bop." He pulled his keys, but the mercs closed ranks, blocking his path. He tilted his head, giving them a cross-eyed stare, and grunted in protest.

Baldy shoved him back. "Go she-mop over there."

The janitor pointed to the door, waving the keys and screeching. Clearly, he was retarded. The men looked at each other, worried that if he were not allowed to do his job, he'd throw a fit, screaming or banging his head against the wall. They hesitated then waved him through. He shuffled past, rolling the bucket over Blondie's foot.

Inside, the janitor tiptoed to the corner and listened. Through the open door to the site manager's office, he heard the woman:

"...no more heroes. The code please."

This was followed by the ominous *phut-phut* of a silencer.

The janitor peeked around the corner to see four men standing guard. Footsteps approached from behind.

A man addressed him: "Hey...you."

He recognized the rasp of Baldy, apparently reconsidering his decision. Planting his feet and clearing his mind of all worldly noise, the janitor gripped the mop handle as he would a Japanese *bokken*. The shaft felt good and hard in his callused hands.

"Come with me," the merc said.

The janitor shook his head, listening for the sound of shoes slapping water, marking his moment.

His moment came. With a backward jab, he drove the end of the mop handle straight into the man's spleen. Wheeling around, the janitor twirled the mop and struck the man in the genitals, the chin, and the top of his foot...in that order.

He was careful not to splinter the mop; like the Marine and his fatigues, he felt naked without it.

Tucking the handle into his armpit, he measured the distance and whipped the mop in a horizontal arc. He wrapped the wet tendrils around the man's skull, instinctively correcting for the lack of hair, calculating that to rupture a temporal artery required a mere 200 psi. Dry, the tendrils would have left welts; wet, they became the bone-dry fingers of the Grim Reaper.

The janitor keyed another door and dragged the dead man inside, discarding his soiled, useless body like a worn condom. The janitor could have searched him for a gun, but knew he wouldn't need one...no, preferred not to have one.

Down the hall, the woman's heels clacked a telegraph message. He cracked the door to watch her strut by, swinging a sawed-off shotgun, her hips pounding an inaudible bongo rhythm. Following her, the two lab coats—nerds by profession—looked smitten, ready to either drop their pants or wet them on command. At the computer control room door, the lab coats tripped over themselves trying to be the one whose keycard filled the slot.

Backing out of his makeshift morgue, the janitor slopped mop water toward the same door. Through it, he heard the woman speak:

"Okay, boys, you know what I want."

Drs. Ormond and Menefee found suavity difficult under normal circumstances, let alone staring down both barrels of a sawed-off. It didn't help that the woman aiming from her smoothly rounded hip had leapt straight out of their comic book-addled dreams.

"You've seen my authorization," she said, brandishing the shotgun with authority. "If you're good, maybe you'll see my *credentials*, as well."

This woman could read a report on the plight of Ethiopia and make it pornographic. With tinted glasses, blood red lipstick, and long, dark hair pulled back and secured with a #2 pencil, she epitomized the modern woman: the career-minded professional in sheer hose, shoulder pads, and shotgun.

By contrast, Ormond and Menefee, in clip-on ties, button-down short-sleeves, and corduroy pants, perfectly embodied the overeducated, underpaid government drones they were. Ormond the physicist studied computers; specifically, the ins and outs of meltdowns. Menefee was a policy analyst whose expertise was power plant security. Used for evil, their combined knowledge could cripple a nuclear facility like Tutelo...or worse.

"Of course, I could start pressing buttons until I caused a chain reaction," the woman said. "But then I wouldn't need you, would I?"

Panicking, Menefee said, "Well, if—if it's clear we were under duress..." Ormond nodded agreement.

"Oh, that'll be most clear," she said. "Remember, the computer will only *think* there's a meltdown."

The PhDs got to work while she watched the monitors, her face bathed in their amber glow.

"There," Ormond said. "Only one command left to type."

She licked her lips, making them glisten. "Type it," she said, "but save that final *stroke* for me."

Ormond typed.

"Good," she purred. "You know what turns me on more than thrusting one tiny atom into another, splitting it, and spewing its pent-up energy all over the other atoms until a catastrophic, earth-shaking, toe-curling meltdown?"

Ormond blinked. Menefee swallowed.

"What turns me on more are the boys who command such cosmic power."

The men were dumbfounded. They had no reference point for this.

"Don't worry, boys," she said, "let mommy drive."

Setting the shotgun across a keyboard, she dropped her skirt and stepped out of it, simultaneously unbuttoning her blouse. The combination of movements was both erotic and efficient.

She peeled her bra downward to reveal two glistening red nipples adorning two perfectly round globes, each massive enough to bend light even as she bent men to her will.

"You want?"

Was she kidding? Hastily, lest she change her mind, the two men circumvented the console.

"Ah-ah-ah," she chided. "First, show me the goodies."

At speeds conceivable only to a Fermi or an Oppenheimer, they stripped to their tighty-whities.

She crossed her legs and pulled on a pair of purple rubber gloves, snapping each one into place. She beckoned them forward, her gloved fingers running through their hair to the backs of their skulls.

"Easy now, there's enough for everyone."

Gently, she drew them toward her, their eyes wide with passion and panic, until she had each one latched on like a newborn babe.

"That's right, boys," she cooed, "knock yourselves out."

Slowly, her hands became fists gripping wads of hair, at first ardently, then sadistically. Ormond stiffened; Menefee followed suit. They gasped, muscles tensing, eyes bulging, backs arching, fingers clawing, feet kicking the climate-controlled air.

She dropped them both and watched with cool detachment as their bodies strained against the deadly tropical venom coursing through their veins and arteries. Drs. Ormond and Menefee died within seconds.

Gloves on, she peeled off the thin layer of latex that guarded her own skin from the poison. She scooted her chair toward the console and typed.

Alarms sounded: first in the computer control room, then throughout the facility. Using the backdoor provided by Ormond to a system-monitoring sub-program, she inserted a polynomial equation into a threat recognition algorithm, tricking the computer into thinking that the water level had dropped and the cooling rods were exposed, causing core damage and steadily rising core temperatures.

In short, she'd just faked catastrophic meltdown. Curling and uncurling her toes, she languorously sucked down a cigarette.

Bogus meltdown? What the hell was she up to? Push too hard and Uncle Sam might say, 'To hell with it,' and nuke the place...or worse, nuke the Russians. The janitor hated Russians, but he did so objectively. While cool logic dictated fiery hatred toward all Reds, bombing them would be madness.

The janitor needed a telephone.

Scanning the cleaners in the janitor's closet, he dumped a whole bottle of bleach into the bucket. Then he put on rubber gloves and a gas mask. Finally, he grabbed a Walkman, zeroed the volume, and hit 'play.'

Whistling "Girls Just Want to Have Fun," the janitor pulled the mop and bucket toward the site manager's office. The four men were still there, palming their weapons.

One of the men addressed him: "Hey...you."

He continued his backward shuffle.

"Hey, buddy, turn around."

The janitor slopped bleach over a wide swath. Head bent, eyes down, he covered an area about ten-feet square before looking up and acting startled. They stared at him. He pointed to his ears. Fiddling with the Walkman, he backed across his work and waited for the men to approach. They did, guns raised.

When all four had reached the centroid of the wet square, he hit 'stop.'

"You scared the shit out of me, man," he said, his voice muffled by the mask. "Who are you guys?"

"Shut up and come with us."

"Got to mop the floor. Can't lose this gig."

"Never mind the floor. Just come with us."

"Are you cops? You sound like cops." He pulled out a bottle of window cleaner and unscrewed the cap.

The man who'd been speaking cocked his weapon. "Come with us...now."

The janitor dropped the window cleaner and raised his hands. The bottle hit dead center, blue liquid splashing over the bleach.

The men stepped back, but not far enough. Death was in the air. The janitor breathed calmly behind the mask. He had only one concern: that he'd slopped enough bleach.

Mix bleach and ammonia proportionately, and the reaction produces toxic gases called chloramines. But leave a surplus of ammonia to react with the chloramines, and it produces another toxic compound called liquid hydrazine, also known as rocket fuel, which can boil, spatter hot liquid, or even explode.

The men coughed and wiped their burning eyes, while the janitor kept his hands high above his head. Before they realized he'd tricked them, they were doubled over, unable to breathe.

Panic set in. Dropping their guns, they staggered around, trying in vain to fill their lungs. One slipped and fell in the middle of the mix, dead in less than a minute. The others lurched down the hall... but it was literally a dead end.

Impassively, the janitor watched them die before keying himself into the site manager's office.

The janitor glanced at the site manager slouching in his desk chair, a half-inch diameter hole punched between his eyes. A crater in the back of his head sloshed blood and brains into a lumpy goulash on the floor. The janitor realized he was missing lunch.

"Mind if I borrow your phone?" he asked the corpse.

He found a phonebook and a flask of vodka and punched the number for the FBI switchboard in Baltimore. Vodka: the official liquor of Soviet Russia. He tilted the flask and grimaced. No wonder Soviets were so bass-ackwards, drinking rotgut like this. To win a war, even a cold one, men need something worth coming home to—a good woman, good TV, and good liquor. Fermented potatoes didn't qualify.

Baltimore answered, and he told the operator he had information on the Tutelo situation. She patched him directly into the situation room.

A man's voice answered: "To whom am I speaking?"

"Me," the janitor said, taking another swig. "Who are you?"

"The United States government."

"Which United States government?"

"Which government?—I'm SDIO."

"Never heard of it."

"It's the Strategic Defense Initiative Organization."

The janitor snorted. "We're expecting an attack from outer space, then? Where's the FBI?"

"They're here. But any breach in our nuclear program warrants SDIO attention."

The janitor chewed on that. The Agency might want him for betraying their own, subverting Operation Cyclone, and personally diverting one-hundred-and-fifty U.S. Stinger missiles away from the Afghan *mujahideen*, but the FBI and CIA were famous for not playing well together. He could talk to the FBI without fear of exposure.

But SDIO was new to the sandbox. Who did they play with? The janitor proceeded with caution.

"Still there?" the SDIO man asked.

"Uh-huh."

"Consider me deputy director of this situation."

The janitor chuckled. "Not from here, you're not."

"Yeah, well, China syndromes aren't known for their delicate beauty, so let's cut the crap. Where's the woman?"

So the woman is in charge, he thought. "Don't know. But I have killed a few of her men."

"What's a few?"

"Five down. But the situation out here is not what you think. The Tutelo Nuclear Power Facility is not—I repeat, *not*—undergoing catastrophic meltdown."

"Say what?"

"Listen, Mr. Deputy Director, if you can't keep up, give me someone who can. My schedule's packed here."

Behind him a man stepped into the doorway, crouching, his gun aimed at the back of the janitor's head.

"The whole thing's a fake. The computers were tricked into reading a bogus meltdown. The core is stable."

"How do you know?"

"I know. Now what are you going to do about it?"

The janitor drew his toilet plunger from a belt loop and twirled it like a baton. On open ground the mop offered greater reach and versatility, but for close-quarter combat the janitor preferred the plunger's maneuverability.

"Hold on," the man said. The janitor heard muffled voices. "The NRC's already begun evacuating a twenty-mile radius." The area included all of D.C.

"Evacuate the northern hemisphere for all I care. What you need to do is square it with the Pentagon. Powwow with Moscow and keep the Joint Chiefs from going on the warpath." He swung the plunger, still twirling, in a hypnotic figure-eight. "Buddy, you need to notify the President."

"Hold on." He heard more muffled voices. "No can do."

"What do you mean, 'No can do'?"

"Listen—Potomac County, Tutelo included, drains straight into the Potomac River, which runs downstream toward Washington D.C. We've got a terrorist attack and a nuclear meltdown all within spitting distance of our nation's capital. Do you understand the implications? We're talking about World War III here."

"Am I not speaking English? There is no meltdown."

The janitor stopped the plunger, mid-twirl, gripping it instinctively like a Japanese *tantō*. Before the man with the gun could react, the janitor spun in place and batted the gun away. He jabbed him hard beneath the ribs, then slammed the suction onto the man's face and pressed him against the wall. Windless, the man panicked. Instead of targeting the janitor's fingers, he clawed the thick rubber.

"Still there?"

"That makes six," the janitor said, while the gunman crumpled to the floor.

"Six what?"

"Six dead."

"Oh. Uh...who are you?"

"I'm me."

"Um...okay. To stand down, Washington—not to mention Moscow—will need more...much more."

"What the hell am I supposed to do with a phony meltdown? Fake stopping it?"

"Please hold." There was a pause. "Sir, all you need to do is fix the computer till it says we're safe. Until the computer says so, Washington won't buy it. And neither will Moscow."

"Fucking bureaucrats."

"I'm sorry, but we're out of options. Will you do it?"

"You mean clean up your mess?"

"I mean sanitize it."

The words to "Hole in My Heart (All the Way to China)" burned through his mind, but he couldn't make himself whistle the tune. The janitor downed the remaining vodka.

"Done."

Click.

He knew the Reds would never leave the computer control room vulnerable to attack; the terminals there would already be destroyed. That left only one option: the computers within the core containment facility itself.

To reach the containment facility required passing through the radiation showers—a ninety-foot-long bottleneck and potential death trap.

With a grim smile and a keycard lifted off the corpse of the Tutelo site manager, the janitor opened the chemical storage unit for supplies. He also grabbed a dozen shotgun shells and one dead Red, wheeling him down the hall in the mop bucket, arms and legs dragging.

As he'd expected, the Russians were playing it by the book—an old, dusty book. Three men—including a flamethrower—occupied the badge monitoring station at the far end of the showers. Anybody foolish enough to rush the stronghold would be rained on by bullets and baptized by fire.

The janitor dumped the Russian into a laundry cart, covered him with laundry, doused the fabric with isopropyl alcohol, and sprinkled the shells over the top. With a running start, he propelled the deadly parfait down the tunnel. It weaved and clattered over the tiles, but covered the distance in four seconds.

The Russians spurted ammunition, drilling fist-sized holes that vomited blood and brain matter as the Trojan hearse spun to a halt inside the monitoring station. Certain they had killed a potential assassin, they watched as the flamethrower unleashed hell.

At the first lick of flame, the alcohol vapors ignited. The resulting shockwave slammed the men into the equipment. Blue flames consumed the cart. Then the shotgun shells exploded like popcorn—all sound, no fury—and the men curled up, trying to protect their heads and genitals.

Like a vengeful dragon, the loose flamethrower thrashed its long neck, spitting fire. The janitor darted through the room, witnessing just enough to know the men would be charcoal before the dragon was spent.

Sharing a glass wall with the core itself, the computer room could only be accessed with the proper passcode...or a mid-sized explosion. But first, the janitor needed to get past the guards.

Using the large steam pipes and ventilation ducts crisscrossing the facility for cover, he moved ghostlike to their position and hid behind a forklift. That left sixty feet of open run, plus obstacles that offered minimal cover. He counted three Uzis and one Kalashnikov. Even for the janitor the odds were slim.

He held the plunger, reverently, as King Arthur might have held Excalibur. He doused the rubber end with blue cleaner and launched the bottle grenade style in a high arc. When it reached its zenith, the janitor howled like a wolf of the steppes to ensure his prey were alert.

"*Chto za huy?*" one cried.

"*Govno!*" another shouted.

All four whipped out their hardware and cut loose on the bottle. They stood in a circle, jerking off thousands of rounds, painting the ceiling with lead. The bottle landed at their feet, mangled and empty, but not before enveloping the men in a fine mist of blue death.

The janitor flicked a lighter, ignited the plunger, and threw the torch like he would a tomahawk. The chemical cloud became a miniature sun, engulfing the men in a yellow blaze. They scattered, screaming, their blackened bodies tumbling over rails and falling to their fiery deaths.

From the lower level, the janitor heard shouted commands and pounding feet. He didn't have much time. He leapt through shattered glass, popped a panel marked 'Danger—Do Not Open,' pulled the motherboard from its slot, reinserted it, and shut down the whole system in a matter of seconds. As the computers rebooted, the lights and alarms went out, shrouding the facility in darkness and silence.

Using the radio static, enemy footsteps, and breathing, he threaded his way back to the radiation showers by echolocation. He approached the flickering glow of the monitoring station cautiously, finding nothing but charred corpses, glistening from the spray of the emergency sprinkler system.

Halfway through the showers, he heard footsteps at the far end. It wouldn't take long before the enemy had him boxed in.

The janitor ran, turning on all the shower heads, except the center one. He pulled from his pocket two vials of cesium swiped from the chemical storage unit and clamped them between his teeth.

Soon, the thin beams of mini flashlights cut across both ends of the tunnel. Behind the flashlights, automatic weapons would be held by sweating hands and itchy trigger fingers.

The beams crossed like mythical swords, bouncing off the wet tile. The janitor spit the vials into his hand and tossed them each direction. The vials shattered mid-distance, sending up walls of sparks and flame as the cesium actually climbed the air from the force of its violent intercourse with water.

A split second later the tunnel blazed with muzzle flashes, each side squeezing their rods, squirting metal, and hailing white-hot death through the downpour.

Silence followed as flashlight beams rocked lazily to and fro, and the janitor dropped soundlessly from above. He had observed the uproar from a bird's eye view, his hands and feet pressed against the walls of the tunnel, his back flat against the ceiling. And now it was time to hole up and wait for WWIII not to show.

Clanging and buzzing told the janitor that the system was coming back online. Lights flickered. Then he heard clapping. A silhouette stepped into the far opening.

"Bravo, cleaner." It was the blonde merc.

"Custodial engineer."

"Toilet scrubber. Why do you fight us?" The merc sprung into the air, demonstrating a stunning martial arts routine. Considering the wet tile floor and tangle of dead bodies, it was impressive. Stepping over a leg, he added: "History is on our side."

"Is it?"

"It is inevitable. The USA shall fall. Or maybe you have seen too many cowboy movies—John Wayne bang-bang-bang." He performed another kick, this time a reverse roundhouse.

"You're insane."

Blondie laughed. He butterfly-kicked and stepped over another body, closing the gap. "Your capitalism's immorality makes you soft."

"Amorality. There's a difference."

"Not to the ditch digger and toilet scrubber."

"You're looking at a toilet scrubber."

"Not anymore." Blondie shifted his weight slightly, preparing for a final reverse roundhouse. To the janitor, who had been observing him closely, the move was a tell.

The janitor barely flinched. The flashlight he kicked skidded through puddles and wedged itself beneath the merc's pivot foot. Committed to his rotation, he spun out wildly, like a satellite careening out of orbit, both legs flailing comically.

The janitor drove his knee into a kidney and grabbed a fistful of hair. He smashed the man's head into the tile, twice, before his enemy kicked off the wall to free himself.

Dodging a wild elbow, the janitor bounced off the opposite wall, to execute a flying kick. He shattered the man's nose and followed with an open-hand uppercut to the voice box. Blondie hit the floor, struggling for breath, eyes rolling back.

The janitor stood over his quarry. "By the way, the meltdown was phony. There is no attack. Your bitch boss screwed you."

"*Govniuk*," Blondie sputtered.

Sensing another presence, he looked up just in time to catch her lovely, curved silhouette at the end of the tunnel shouldering what looked like a complicated stovepipe—in actuality an American-made Stinger missile launcher.

"Speak of the she-devil," she said.

The janitor ducked and covered behind the struggling merc. The rocket streaked overhead, scorching the air above him before rocking the tunnel like the proverbial hurricane.

The woman stood with her hip cocked, dangling her hardware. "Well done, *Amerikanski*, but your efforts were for nothing."

He rolled the gasping man off him, reached around, and snapped his neck.

She continued: "As we speak, my network of moles and sleepers is gathering documents—documents that will be in my hands by midnight tonight."

He blinked. "Of course! This was about evacuating Washington D.C."

She beamed. "My crowning achievement. And you have become integral to my success."

He raised his eyebrows.

"While my pawns infiltrated other targets—the White House, the Pentagon, SDIO headquarters, CIA headquarters, NASA—you were here, ensuring that America won the battle."

Now he understood. "But lost the war...in space."

She bowed her head. "Moscow cannot afford a gap in space—especially an X-ray laser gap—and by midnight tonight I will possess the information Moscow needs to plug that gap."

"To maintain equilibrium."

"If Moscow chooses to cooperate."

"Cooperate? You mean compensate."

"I'm worth every kopek."

"I'm sure you are, but what if Moscow doesn't agree?"

"There will be other bidders. Perhaps Libya or Afghanistan will go nuclear decades ahead of its time."

"You're mad," he said, even as his ears rang with the distinctive squeak of a Queens-born native singing "Money Changes Everything."

"No, the world is mad. As you Americans say, I just work here."

He stepped toward her, but she shouldered her weapon, fingering the trigger, and chided him, "Ah-ah-ah. Until we meet again."

He burrowed beneath the bodies as another rocket stabbed the air above him. By the time the smoke cleared, she was gone.

The janitor recognized the SDIO man by his voice.

"George Benjamin Kennedy. That's quite a name. Washington, Franklin, and John F."

The janitor shrugged. "I'm a patriot."

"We know who you are." The SDIO man slapped down a thick file. "Or more accurately, who you were."

"Congratulations." He glanced at the bare conference room walls, wondering if they were in Baltimore or somewhere else.

"Don't get me wrong. I understand what you did and why."

"Gee, I feel warm all over."

"Personally, I think Operation Cyclone is a bust: unclear objectives, short-term gains, and heavy long-term costs. But you left your colleagues with nothing but their dicks in their hands—a big no-no. Just imagine the fallout."

The janitor shrugged again. "Having had a couple Stingers turned on me personally, I have to say, boo-fuckin'-hoo. Can I go now?"

"Maybe later." The SDIO man slapped a much thinner file on top of the thick one. "I have a job for you."

Another shrug.

"Hey, this is your second chance, pal, but I have no budget to carry dead weight. If you're not interested, I know people who'd kill to see this file...literally." He brushed his hands to illustrate. "Or drop a major-league marker in my back pocket."

"Fucking bureaucrats," the janitor sneered. "You're all the same, sitting in your soft chairs behind your big desks, trading little favors, and trying not to expose your lily-white asses. You've forgotten what this country stands for. Well, let me tell you. It stands for the Constitution and the Bill of Rights, like the right to bear arms and refuse service to anyone. It stands for private property and free enterprise. For owning a piece of land—land God-given and taken from nobody—and using it for something like oil or cattle or building something on it like a casino. But above all, it stands for the underdog: the man outgunned, outweighed, and outclassed. He might get beat down, but he don't go down. Not for any man. Not willingly. Because Americans hate a punk. You know who said that? Patton. But I bet you forgot. So yeah, I'll take your job, but not because you threatened me. Because I didn't forget."

The janitor started humming "True Colors."

The SDIO man smirked and opened the thinner file: "Your first assignment: Code name: Scarlet Flower. Though her true identity remains unknown—even to her former employer, the KGB—she has many nicknames: the Siberian Siren, the Georgian Gorgon, Black Widow of the Baltic States, and most notoriously, the Steppenbitch. Apparently, she went rogue with a small detachment of men completely submissive to her, willing even to be castrated for her. You killed some of them."

The janitor whistled, intrigued.

"Scarlet Flower currently possesses documents critical to our national security."

"You mean Star Wars."

"The Strategic Defense Initiative, yes. We believe she'll sell the documents to Moscow for a premium, but we also believe she'll threaten to assassinate the President to fast-forward the timetable and drive up the price."

The janitor's eyes narrowed.

"You're scheduled to receive a medal at the White House in three days for your bravery in handling the Tutelo incident. We think that's when she'll strike. It doesn't give us much time."

"And this'll get me my file back."

"Well...we'll see about that. I may have more work for you."

"Fucking bureaucrats," the janitor said, even as he thought: Three days to pluck the Scarlet Flower...I can hardly wait.

THE END

Be sure to check out the Sanitizer #2: *The Iranian Insertion*

Not much is known about the reclusive Marion Hillberry, who penned the popular and patriotic Sanitizer series under the pseudonym Stack Grannett, except for the controversy surrounding his death...or rather his burial. Despite being denied enrollment in four of the five military branches due to a rare condition that caused his heart to grow upside down, Hillberry had Special Forces tattoos inked to his body anyway.

Two months after he received a military burial with all the trimmings, the mistake was exposed and his body exhumed. It now resides in a nearby cemetery under a headstone that reads:

Marion Hillberry
aka Stack Grannett
1951–1998

Though avidly read at the front,
This scribe Uncle Sam did not want.
His twenty-one gun salute,
The subject of much dispute,
Now Stack is a wandering haunt.

  NICK SLOSSER found a paperback copy of The Sanitizer #1
being used as a shim to level out a bookcase full of cozy mysteries
at Murder by the Book in Portland, Oregon.

THEY CALL HIM CRUEL
in
BURN IN
by Moses Starkweather
(discovered by Frank Larnerd)

GIVE ME YOUR MONEY."

The kid was probably twelve or thirteen, skinny with light brown skin, Puerto Rican or Cuban maybe. He wore a green Dan Marino jersey that was at least two sizes too big and hung nearly halfway down his thighs. Under the kid's right eye were the remnants of a purple bruise.

He made a stabbing motion with the gun and repeated, "Give me your money."

I had seen the kid earlier that day. He had been in the back of the arcade, hanging out with three older kids I recognized: teenage trash from Staten Island who took the bus across the Verrazano Bridge to sling herb and harass the girls from Fontbonne Academy.

They wore matching black bandannas tied around their legs. In Park Hills they might have been big shit, but to me they just looked like angry assholes hungry to shit on the world.

I had kicked out the oldest kid twice before. Once for dealing dime-bags and the second time for kicking the coin door of a Defender machine. I'd heard someone call him "Sello" once.

I pushed my way through his two friends to where Sello was playing Ghost'n Goblins. They were teenage vultures dressed in red vinyl jackets and leaking zits. Both of them were in their late teens. One looked like Charlie Brown, bald with giant jug ears; the other was bucktoothed and wearing 3-D glasses.

Sello was hunched over, his fingers bouncing from button to button on the game's control panel. He was an ugly fucker, fat-lipped and greasy looking. A Marlboro dangled from his lips as he cursed at the monitor.

"Goddamn bunch of bullshit! Did you guys see that? I swear this game is fuckin' broken."

I got close and bumped him with my chest. The game gave out a mournful tone as Sello lost a life.

He flew up, snapping. "Watch it, bitch!"

I leaned in closer and let his eyes take in my 255 pounds. I'm six two, but a foot taller with my mohawk. I flexed my arms and leaned into his face.

"I told you to stay away."

Sello took a step back, giving me a yellow grin.

"It's fresh. Ask the man."

He nodded behind the counter where my Uncle Milo counted out tokens to two kids in day-glo shirts.

I stepped in closer, so that Sello's chest touched mine.

"Get the fuck out, before I tear off your face and use it to wipe my ass."

"It's cool, man." said Sello's friend with the 3-D glasses.

"It's not cool," Sello snarled. "The Threats run with Mr. Bread now. Just 'cause you're built like Hulk Hogan doesn't mean you're bulletproof. Remember that."

I had heard about Mr. Bread. He was supposed to be a heavy, making a name for himself dealing junk and breaking arms down in Park Hills.

I showed Sello my crazy face.

"Let's get out of here," Sello said. "This place smells like shit anyway."

When they left, the kid in the Dan Marino jersey hung his head and followed.

Five minutes 'til closing, the kid came back by himself. Not playing anything, just standing off to the side, watching the demo on Bega's Battle loop over and over.

At eight, I flipped the switch behind the counter, shutting down the games. I let the last few kids duck under the retractable security gate and when I turned, the kid in the Dan Marino jersey had a gun on me.

It was a .38 revolver with a dark metal finish. In the kid's hand, it looked big and heavy. Good thing my uncle had already gone upstairs. If the kid had pulled a gun on him, Milo might have killed him.

"Here," I said and tugged on the chain attached to my wallet. "I've got twenty bucks."

I opened my wallet to show him. When the kid looked, I kicked him in the chest with my combat boot.

The kid flew backward and bounced off a Dig Dug machine, slamming into the floor. Pained sucking sounds came from his throat as he tried to draw in breath. I grabbed the gun off the speckled carpet and jammed it in the studded leather belt I was wearing.

With one arm, I grabbed the kid by his collar and jerked him off the ground so we were eye to eye. His face was panicked as silent tears floated down his cheeks.

"You still want to rob me?"

He shook his head and I set him down. I let him cough and wheeze for a minute until he got his breath back.

"Do you know who I am?"

The kid nodded, "Sello said they call you Cruel."

"He tell you why?"

"He said you pulled off a Russian guy's toes. Tony T said it was 'cause you broke Jimmy Future's legs with a shopping cart full of cinderblocks."

I couldn't help smiling.

"Sello, Tony T? Those your friends? They put you up to this?"

"The Threats," the kid said. "They said it was my initiation."

"Why would you want to join those assholes?"

The kid shrugged, "Protection, I guess."

"They hassle you?"

"Not really. But they'll kill me when they find out you got their gun."

"What's your name?"

"Hector."

"Come up stairs for a sec."

I showed Hector to the stairwell that leads to the apartment above the arcade. Inside, Milo was asleep in his La-Z-Boy, a half-eaten TV dinner and several beer cans sat beside him. I tossed a brightly colored afghan over him and switched off the television. I put a finger to my lips and Hector followed me down the hall, past dozens of Milo's Vietnam photos, to my room.

The kid stood in the door, while I pulled out my earrings and laid them on the desk. I took a moment to fluff up my mohawk and pulled the gun from my belt.

"What's wrong with it?" Hector asked, nodding at the game cabinet I had in the corner next to my weights.

"Burn in."

"What's that?"

"Sometimes, if the brightness is set to high, a monitor gets discolored so that you can still see the game even after it's turned off. Take a look."

Hector approached the arcade machine and gently traced the ghostly maze with a finger.

"How do you fix it?"

"You don't."

I opened the desk's top drawer and shook out the bullets into it. Then, I pulled some hollow points from a rectangular box I had hidden behind some socks. One at a time, I squeezed the bullets in the gun's cylinders. After that, I grabbed my jean jacket and slipped the gun into the inside pocket.

"What are you gonna do?" Hector asked.

I snatched my nunchucks off the bedpost and put them in my back pocket. "I'm gonna give Sello his gun back."

Hector followed me across 99th Street and up two blocks to the bus stop.

While we waited, the kid asked, "What time is it?"

"Eight thirty," I said. "Why? You got some place you need to be?"

Hector shrugged. "It's my dad. He gets super pissed when I'm late."

"You should have thought about that before you decided to rob me. You can go home. After I talk to Sello."

Ten minutes later we were rolling over the Staten Island Expressway. Hector sat beside me, his refection shimmering in the bus window as he looked out to Gravesend Bay. His image looked ghostly and grim.

I slipped my headphones under my jaw and popped a Misfits cassette into my Walkman. Closing my eyes, I let the music wash over me.

Before Milo came back from 'Nam and took me in, I lived with the Junkman. It wasn't a real house, it was a foster house, two double-wides welded together next to a maze of ruined cars. The whole place was surrounded by tall chain-link fences topped with razor wire. It kept people out, and us in.

The Junkman had rules for everything: how to eat, when to use the bathroom, when to sleep. He didn't allow us to look at him, or speak without being spoken to. If you broke the rules, you sat in the chair.

Stevie was one of the kids I shared a bunk with. He was quiet with hound dog eyes, but really tough. Of all the kids the Junkman kept, Stevie was the only one who never cried. He was the one who taught me how to turn off the pain. On the night I ran away, it was Stevie who called me "Cruel."

Hector and I switched buses on New York Avenue, catching the last bus to Clifton.

"What time is it?" Hector asked as the bus barreled through the evening traffic.

"Maybe nine thirty."

"Man, I got to get home."

We got off the bus at Hylan and walked past the darkened store fronts. The kid didn't talk. After a few blocks, Hector pointed at a brown six-story apartment complex.

"221. Right up the stairs."

"Wait here."

"I can't," Hector said. "I got to get home."

I moved the revolver out of the jacket and into my belt. "Alright. But if you're lying, I'll come find you."

"I promise. I ain't lying."

I nodded and watched him disappear down an alley.

Cutting through the parking lot, I noticed a Corvette with a custom New York plate.

It read: BREAD.

Inside the building, the floor was littered with trash. Wrappers, dirty diapers, and spoiled take-out covered every inch. Graffiti marred the walls with wisdom like: "Jamaykan queens can't tame me" and "If you can't fuck a 10, fuck five 2's."

I followed the narrow stairwell to the second floor and listened outside of apartment 221. Living with the Junkman had taught me how to walk without making a sound.

Inside, I could hear Pat Benatar howling over laughing voices. I reached up for the bare light bulb that lit the hallway. My fingertips sizzled, but I ignored the pain and unscrewed it. Without the light, it was dark except for the dim glow of street lights beyond the frosted windows. I put the light bulb in my jacket pocket.

I knocked on the door. I didn't worry about a peep-hole; there wasn't one.

The apartment door opened a crack. Behind the chain, I could see Charlie Brown's ugly bald head. The darkened hallway had the same effect as a police lineup; in the dark, I could see him, but he couldn't see me.

"Who's there?"

I kicked the door as hard as I could.

The door chain splintered off the wall and the edge of the door flung back, striking Charlie Brown between the eyes. He flopped backward and crumpled on the floor, unconscious.

Sello and the kid with the 3-D glasses sat on a ratty couch. On the coffee table in front of them were bags of white rocks and tall stacks of ones and fives. On my right, the TV showed Pat Benatar shaking around like a hobo with a case of the DTs. I didn't see Mr. Bread anywhere.

I stepped over Charlie Brown and put a boot on the coffee table.

"I brought your gun back, Sello."

The greasy fuck grinned. "Why don't you hand it here?"

I kicked over the coffee table, spilling their shit everywhere.

"Why don't you come and take it?"

Sello brushed himself off and said, "I'm gonna let my man take care of that."

Something smashed into the side of my face. I staggered back, bumping against the TV, making the picture jump. I saw another white blur and pain exploded through my skull. I dropped to my knees. Blood poured down my face and over my eye, but I could still make out who hit me.

He was big, tan and adorned with flashy gold chains. The seams of his expensive track suit strained against his massive shoulders. He was 6'4" and a solid 300 pounds. To me he looked like a Rottweiler with a pompadour.

In his hands was a toilet tank lid.

I said, "It's nice to see you Stevie," as he hit me again.

When I came to, I was on my knees. My head pounded like a low-rider's blown speakers. I tried to move but found that my hands had been tied to my ankles behind me. 3-D and Charlie Brown's hightops were missing their laces, so I figured that's what they used.

In front of me was the toilet lid, a dark splash of blood smeared one end.

On the couch, Sello and his boys finished stowing their shit in green duffel bags. Stevie sat on the couch's arm, dabbing at drops of blood on his sleeve with a wet rag. My nunchucks hung around his massive neck; the revolver was stuck in his waistband. Once he noticed I was awake, he threw the rag down.

"I knew we'd meet up someday," Stevie said. "I almost didn't recognize you. Your hair looks fuckin' stupid."

I spit a tooth onto the carpet. "Fuck you, Stevie."

"People call me Mr. Bread now."

"Why?" I said. "You fucking the Pillsbury Doughboy?"

Stevie kicked me with his giant Air Jordan and dark spots swam through my vision. I fell on my side and felt the light bulb in my pocket pop.

"They call me Mr. Bread 'cause I make money. This town is mine. See these little pussies? They're mine, too! That shit you spilled, that was mine. I was gonna turn that rock into six grand. Now I'm gonna take it out of you."

Charlie Brown laughed as Stevie grabbed my Mohawk and pulled me upright. Smiling, he held out his hand to Sello.

"Give me your blade."

Sello passed him the switchblade without a word. Stevie held it up so I could watch it snap open.

"You still like to play?"

He dug the blade's point into my skin and carved a long line diagonally across my chest. He watched my eyes for any sign of pain. I didn't show him any; he had taught me too well.

"Damn, Mr. Bread!" 3-D said.

Stevie sliced me again, peeling a large, bloody X on my chest. I didn't try to move away. I didn't even blink. I just took the pain and pushed it inside.

When we lived with the Junkman, Stevie was the tattletale. When we were punished, he'd stand to the side and watch us cry. Once he was big enough, he started helping. At first, the Junkman had him do little things: holding down kicking feet or snapping Polaroids.

After a while, the Junkman had Stevie doing all the punishments. That way, the Junkman could sit back and watch.

One day, Stevie showed the Junkman where I hid the sock of loose change I found in the junkers from the yard.

The Junkman said, "You stealing from me?"

I looked at the floor. "No, sir."

"Everything here belongs to me. It might look like trash, but it's mine."

The Junkman grabbed my face and held it so I was forced to look at him.

"People think you're trash, but you're my trash."

He sat on the edge of the bed and took a long drink from his bottle. Stevie sat next to him, smiling. I tried not to look at the barber chair, or the ashtray and its mound of blackened matchsticks.

The Junkman said, "Take down your pants and get in the chair."

I did as he told me. The barber chair's seat felt cool and sticky against my bare legs. The bed creaked as Stevie got up and stood beside me.

Using the Velcro straps, he tied down my hands and feet. I didn't fight back. If you fought back, it was always worse.

With the palms of his hands, the Junkman began rubbing his thighs over and over. Stevie lit a match and held it to the wire hanger.

"I'm a kid just like you," I whispered.

Stevie smiled and said, "You're nothing like me. You're weak."

I didn't cry and I didn't scream. It was like I floated outside myself, taking all my hurt and pain and shoving it down where it couldn't hurt me anymore.

Still, it was a long time before it was over.

That night, once everyone was asleep, I snuck out into the junkyard. I limped past the towers of flattened cars until I stood by the yard's rear fence. Beyond it, I could see the trees of Otsego Park sway in the midnight breeze. I sat for a long time, just trying to think. When I decided to go back inside, something hissed at me from the darkness.

Five feet away, half hidden in shadow was a steel run-through trap. Inside were two large brown rats, half-starved with their tiny rib cages showing beneath their fur.

All that pain I had pushed down began to bubble up.

In an hour, I found three more traps around the yard. One was empty but the other two had one rat a piece. It was pretty easy to get them all in the same trap.

I salvaged a box cutter and an empty twelve-gallon bucket from behind the office. A Ford provided its seatbelts. A piece of upholstery from a Chevy's interior, some rusty nails, and I was ready.

The moon was high in the sky as I set the bucket and rat trap outside the trailer door. I sat on the cinderblock steps and took off my filthy Chuck Taylors. Then, I eased the door open and crept inside.

I was careful not to make a sound.

Once in the bedroom, I carefully tied the Junkman's feet to the bed's legs with long strips of seatbelt. I moved to the head of the bed and got his left arm tied down. Circling to the other side, I heard the Junkman cough.

He turned his head and called out into the darkness, "Stevie? Is that you?"

I walked to the side of the bed and the Junkman touched my arm.

"Do you want to sleep with Daddy?"

I grabbed the Junkman's hand and slipped it into the final loop of seatbelt.

"Hey! Hey!" he shouted.

The bed lurched and creaked as the Junkman struggled. I double-checked my knots, and then took his keys off the dresser. He cursed me as I shut the bedroom door and went into the trailer's living room.

The rest of the kids were awake and gathered there. Their faces sleepy, their bare legs scarred with angry burns.

"There's a fire," I said. "We have to get out."

They were scared, but they followed me to the front gate. I took the Junkman's keys and sprung the lock free.

I said, "Run!" and slung open the gate.

They all ran, except Stevie.

"Where's Daddy?"

I ignored him and walked back to the trailer. Outside the door, I collected my things and followed the Junkman's shouts to the bedroom.

He struggled, but I sat on his chest and squeezed the bucket over his head. I had cut a hole in the bottom and nailed the upholstery over it. An X-shaped cut ensured a tight fit; the nails kept it in place.

The Junkman's voice echoed from inside the bucket. "You little shit! I'll fucking kill you!"

I ignored him, opened the trap, and dumped the scrambling rats into the bucket. Before any could escape, I slipped on the lid.

After that, I climbed in the barber chair, watched and listened.

Once the Junkman had quit moving, I grabbed the box of matches from the nightstand. I pulled one across the strike strip and watched it flare to life.

I could still hear the rat's claws scrape against the inside of the plastic bucket, along with their hungry gnawing.

I threw the match on the bed. It burned faster than I thought it would.

When I left the trailer, Stevie was on the steps. He was rubbing the palms of his hands over his thighs. I sat next to him and slipped on my shoes.

He looked up at me, his eyes wet and angry.

"He was my best friend."

I stood up. Flames licked at the trailer's windows as smoke drifted up into the starless night.

"Fuck him," I said.

As I walked to the gate, Stevie called out me.

"You're cruel!"

I didn't look back.

Stevie hadn't changed. Sure, now he was built like a tank and had seven hundred dollars in gold chains, but behind his eyes, I could still see that little boy.

He leaned down and grabbed my ear.

"I'm gonna make you scream."

I strained against the shoelaces, but it only made the knots pull tighter.

As Stevie scraped the blade through my flesh, my fingers brushed against something smooth on the floor.

I cupped the shard of broken light bulb between my fingers and sawed at the shoe laces. I didn't scream, not even when Stevie stopped cutting and tore the top of my ear free.

He held it up, admiring it.

I felt the blood as it streamed down my neck and over my chest. The piece of light bulb cut into my fingers, but I kept sawing.

Stevie said, "Doesn't that hurt, bitch?"

I felt the shoelaces pop loose and said, "What's that? I didn't hear you."

He leaned closer and grabbed my other ear.

I slammed my fist into Stevie's balls as hard as I could.

He staggered back, his mouth hanging open, his hands cupping his nuts. I grabbed the nunchucks off his neck and bolted for the door. My cuts burned and I felt a little faint, but I pushed myself up the stairs. Below me, I heard Stevie shouting and the rumble of pursuing footsteps.

At the top of the stairs, I crashed through a door marked "Roof." The sky had grown dark with gray rippling clouds. In the distance, a universe of lights glowed across the bay. Beneath me was a six-story drop to the parking lot.

"Nowhere to go, asshole!"

I turned around. Stevie had the .38 in his hand. Beside him were 3-D, Charlie Brown, and Sello.

I held up my hands as Stevie pointed the gun at me. He pulled back the hammer and licked his lips.

Hollow points are nasty bullets. They're designed to explode, spreading like shrapnel, inflicting massive tissue damage.

It helps if you put them in the right gun.

When Stevie pulled the trigger on the .38 there was a loud bang and a flash of flame. He fell to his knees, the fingers he had left dangled by strands of skin.

I twirled the nunchucks like a buzz saw and flung myself at them, inflicting maximum damage.

After a while, my arm got tired.

On the roof around me, Sello and his gang moaned, clutching at broken arms and fractured ribs. Stevie had gotten it worse.

His face was a wheezing red pulp and his limbs all extended at odd, broken angles. I dragged him to the ledge and pulled him up on my shoulders. My cuts roared with pain, but I pressed him over my head and howled.

Stevie fell face-first into his Corvette, crumpling the roof and blasting the glass from the windows.

In the distance, sirens cut through the night. I walked past Sello and his gang and limped down the stairs.

I kept in the shadows and staggered north. At Victory Boulevard, I climbed a fire escape of a clothing warehouse and waited for the next train to rumble past. Twenty minutes later, I was on the other side of the island.

In the morning, Milo picked me up and brought me back to the arcade. He didn't ask any questions, just sewed up my cuts and made me chicken noodle soup.

I spent a few weeks in bed, until Milo accused me of being a lazy hippy. My ear is fucked up and I've got some nice new scars. But honestly, it only makes me look more wicked.

The pigs never came to question me, so I figured Sello and his gang had kept their mouths shut. Besides, they had enough problems with the cops finding shit in their apartment.

I kept expecting to see Hector again. I thought he'd tell me how he had learned to stand on his own and how life was better, but he never came back to the arcade. I had almost forgotten about him, until one Sunday a couple months later, I was on 98th Street grabbing a slice from Rose's Pizzeria.

Right down the street was Sello's friend in the 3-D glasses. He saw me and crossed the street, but I followed. After a half a block, he wheeled around and held up his hands.

"Jesus, man. What do you want?"

I said, "Where's that kid Hector?"

3-D looked down at his shoes, absent-mindedly rubbing at the arm I had broken.

"He's in ICU at Saint Vincent's. Can't talk or move. They say he's got brain damage."

I grabbed him with both hands and shoved him against the wall.

"Was it Sello? Was it you?"

"It wasn't us, man! We were trying to help him!" 3-D squeaked. "He fell. Hit his head or something."

"Fell?"

"My homeboy said it was Hector's old man. Said he's a total hard ass. My homie told me people heard Hector's dad screaming at him for coming home late. I know Hector was afraid of his dad. That's why he wanted to join the Threats. Sello said that if he passed initiation, we would take care of things for him."

I let 3-D go.

He shrugged his shoulders. "The pigs don't give a shit. Why should they? Just another beaner to them. Hector's father didn't even get questioned."

I put a hand over my eyes and pushed the darkness deep into my gut.

"You OK?" 3-D asked.

I had him follow me back to the arcade and told him to wait outside. I threw some duct tape and road flares into a backpack. At the bottom of the stairs, Milo asked where I was going. I told him I was going to do some repairs, fix something that was broke.

When I came outside, 3-D was still waiting.

I asked, "You know where I can find Hector's dad?"

"Yeah."

"Show me."

THE END

Not all men's adventure books of the mid–1980s were Reagan-era paranoia combined with liberal doses of gun porn (and borderline actual porn). Some authors used the freedom of the genre to make social commentary and show the grit and grime of the world they themselves lived in. The Cruel series was short-lived but has been cited as an influence on many writers' work, including discoverer FRANK LARNERD.

L.A.N.D.B.O.A.T. (THE BOAT THAT GOES ON LAND)

in

L.A.N.D.B.O.A.T. (THE BOAT THAT GOES ON LAND)

by Chase Verdugo

(discovered by Oren Brimer)

RED. ORANGE. YELLOW. Green. Blue. Indigo. Violet. Boat fuel painted a refracted spectrum onto the surface of the cool Caribbean water. But the gasoline rainbow only had one to one-and-three-quarters moments to play in the sun before it was dashed by the wake of a matte-black speedboat. A speedboat named L.A.N.D.B.O.A.T.

Brick Argus' sun-bleached shoulder-length hair whipped behind him as his wrap-around polarized Oakley® sunglasses expertly shielded his eyes from the mist and also the UV rays. He adeptly guided the steering wheel of L.A.N.D.B.O.A.T., weaving the vessel through the chop like some sort of weaving machine, a loom maybe, set to fast.

"L.A.N.D.B.O.A.T., proximity?" Brick asked his boat.

"Thirty-seven meters until contact with the target. The target being drug runners smuggling drugs." said a robotic voice from ultra-sonic projection speakers.

Brick commanded, "Activate thrusters, initiate high-velocity rudder."

L.A.N.D.B.O.A.T. calculated. "Ocean current analytics calculate that we have a ninety-five percent chance of capsize if we hyper-thrust."

Brick smiled. "I like those odds."

A small screen in the dashboard crackled awake. "Don't even think about it, Argus!" said the angry, eye-patched man on the screen.

"Ferce," Brick spat.

"The eXperimental Yachting Laboratory Organized to Promote Heroism and Operations in Nautical Equality didn't spend three decades building that boat to have some hotshot destroy it on its first mission."

"It sounds like the head of X.Y.L.O.P.H.O.N.E. prefers that these drug runners get away." Brick said defiantly.

"You and I both know that's hooey," Ferce cursed. "Don't turn your rage into stupidity, Argus. I know what you're going through."

"How could you? How could you know what it's like to have amnesia, to not remember anything before a year ago, except for the occasional memory which comes flooding back at the most inopportune times?" Brick foreshadowed.

"Don't forget who's in charge here," Ferce countered. "Me. I am in charge."

"Well, last I checked, drugs still flow into America nonstop and until our nation's leaders wake up and enact tough legislation, it's my job to stop these drug runners the old-fashioned way: with a talking boat."

Ferce hesitated, then spoke. "You're right, Argus. You're a true American—"

The screen blinked off, Brick's hand on the "screen off" switch.

"Whatever," said Brick. "Activate thrusters, L-B." A panel on the aft of the boat slid open and a class-6 jet propulsion hyper-engine slid out smoothly. Brick got a semi. "It's drug stopping time."

Blue flame burped out of the jet engine. L.A.N.D.B.O.A.T. sliced through the water like a samurai sword through water. Brick's trained hands conducted a symphony of speed in the key of fast, the drug runners' cigarette boat growing in size. It wasn't actually growing in size, but as they got closer, the perspective made it seem like it was getting larger. That could only mean one thing: they were getting closer.

The drug runners' boat was a shiny white number with chrome detailing to match the white suits and silver guns of the criminals onboard. One fat drug runner drove and the other, skinny, sat on a pile of black duffel bags surely filled with addictive drugs. As L.A.N.D.B.O.A.T. neared, the drug runners' boat screeched to a halt.

L.A.N.D.B.O.A.T. slowed and Brick eyed the criminals. Beneath their cheaply constructed aviator sunglasses, which lacked even the most basic scratch-resistant coating (standard on every pair of Oakleys®), they wore smiles.

Scientists have concluded that there are five senses: smell, sight, sound, taste, and touch. Brick had a sixth: the sense of danger. A blessing and a curse, the sharp realization that danger had reared its dangerous face could save your life or make you want to take a long nap. Longer than two hours, even. A forever nap.

Brick felt this sixth sense, the danger one, stab him in the gut as two more cigarette boats closed in. They looked dangerous; each piloted by a crew of maniacal gun-toting drug runners and equipped with a machine gun turret ready to clear its throat of lead phlegm. And, unfortunately, the machine guns had just come down with a cold. And they were all out of tissues. Brick, on the other hand, had plenty of tissues, a box of Kleenex® Puffs™ he kept under the dash whenever he needed soft comfort.

Brick steeled himself. "Thanks for coming, gents. Let me slip into something...more comfortable."

"Like a pair of Champion® sweatpants?" The drug runner called out.

"No," Brick responded. "Nothing is that comfortable."

With the whir of servos, L.A.N.D.B.O.A.T.'s arsenal presented itself. Two high-capacity sub-structure Gatling guns shot forth from the fore. A liquid fire launcher, complete with indo-destructor fuel cells, erected itself from the stern. Turbo-steel mesh plating clanked all around. Then, a section of the deck slid away, and out rose a laser-guided helix missile rack loaded with ultra-infrared guided hollow-core warheads.

"Is that a laser-guided helix missile rack loaded with ultra-infrared guided hollow-core warheads?" the skinny drug runner asked in slack-jawed awe as a cigarette dropped from his mouth.

"Is it?" Brick asked L.A.N.D.B.O.A.T.

"It is," L.A.N.D.B.O.A.T. said to Brick.

"It is," Brick said to the drug runner.

"YAAAAAAAAAH!" The drug runner fired his chrome AK-47 at L.A.N.D.B.O.A.T., each bullet ricocheting off the turbo mesh steel plating. The flanking boats tore off, circling, preparing to attack. L.A.N.D.B.O.A.T. rotated towards the stationary boat. Two lasers found their home on the fat and skinny drug runners.

"You guys seem like fish out of water." Brick grunted through gritted teeth. "Let's fix that."

Gatling guns whirred a metal storm, replacing the drug runners' bodies with red Swiss cheese. There was no time to pair the cheese with wine, maybe a Boone's Farm® Bordeaux or a Chianti depending on what dish followed the cheese (although Boone's Farm® wines were delicious with any meal). One of the other cigarette boats was approaching fast, the silver-toothed drug runner onboard aiming an RPG straight at L.A.N.D.B.O.A.T. He wasn't only aiming it; he was also shooting it.

The rocket rocketed towards L.A.N.D.B.O.A.T., and with aquacatlike reflexes, Brick roared the super-thrust fuel-cell hydro injection engine and turned one hundred and eighty degrees, sending a huge plume of water into the air, knocking the RPG off its path and into the deep.

"Thanks, water," Brick said.

Facing the oncoming boat, Brick manned the liquid fire launcher and fired fire, a hot melty stream of napalm arcing in an arc of pain towards the boat. The cigarette boat ground to a halt, the napalm landing on the surface of the water in front of it, burning harmlessly.

The silver-toothed drug runner laughed. "What's the use of a fancy boat that shoots fire that burns on water if you can't aim? Huh? What's the use?"

Brick scoffed at the drug runner's ignorance. Of course he was ignorant. He did drugs. He hit a large red switch.

A muted pop filled the air. Then, silence.

"Is that it?" screamed the drug runner. And then he and the driver laughed. It would be their last. Yet, Brick was the one having the last laugh. And he wasn't even laughing.

Suddenly, a giant wave rose and freight-trained through the napalm. The wave mixed with the fire-liquid, causing what was once a simple wave of water to transform into a not-so-simple wave of flame.

The drug runners' cigarettes dropped from their mouths as hellfire charged them like a bull seeing all the kinds of red. Dark red, light red, middle red, and maybe even a pink or two. The criminals were instantly melted. The duffel bags of drugs exploded, releasing a cloud of drug smoke into the air.

"It's not the size of the boat, but the motion of the ocean," Brick whispered to himself and any psychics listening in.

He turned to the final boat, whose occupants stared slack-jawed at the carnage, their cigarettes falling from their mouths. The driver cranked the engine and fled the scene.

L.A.N.D.B.O.A.T. and Brick gave chase, quickly gaining. The fleeing boat's motor was no match for the pure power of hyper-jet propulsion.

Brick thought of his amnesia. "I hate my amnesia. I have amazing boat-driving and combat skills, yet I don't know where, or even how, I got them. Hopefully," he hoped, "these clouds will part and my memory will return."

Brick's thoughts were interrupted by L.A.N.D.B.O.A.T.'s digi-voice. "Brick! They are surrendering!" The boat that goes on land was right. The fleeing drug runners' boat had stopped and their hands were raised to the sky.

"Surrendering, huh?" Brick asked rhetorically. The laser guided helix missile rack loaded with ultra-infrared guided hollow-core warheads swiveled towards the drug runners. "What about the countless children who have surrendered to the ravages of the drugs you provide?"

"We are just filling a niche created by the failure of your government to crack down on the flow of illegal drugs into your country," said the drug runner.

"I agree with you there," Brick responded. "But until the day where our nation's leaders wake up, which is why we're paying them with our hard-earned tax dollars, it's missile time."

L.A.N.D.B.O.A.T. gave Brick a status update. "Missiles engaged, ready to fire."

"I was born ready," said Brick.

Brick looked up to the drug runners one last time. Something was amiss. There were those smiles again. Their cigarettes were still in their mouths.

A cruise ship flickered into existence, its cloaking shield deactivating. A deck-mounted electromagnetic pulse cannon pointed straight at L.A.N.D.B.O.A.T. and a sound cannon straight at Brick. L.A.N.D.B.O.A.T. went dark, Brick seconds later.

Single frames raced through Brick's unconscious mind. A beautiful island. A beautiful island woman. Beautiful island sex. Oh, no. Guns. Guns. More guns. Bullets from those guns. Screams of pain. Screams of rage. Generic screams. The deep roar of a motorcycle engine from the sky.

The zip of a nylon rope around Brick's wrists truncated his nightmare. "Memories," Brick thought as his consciousness awakened. His eyes opened to discover that he was tied to a chair in a cruise ship cabin.

The clean lines, the Airsoft™ bed with thousand-thread-count sheets and modern, yet sophisticated décor; it had to be a Carnival® cruise ship. Brick could recognize its elevated luxury and style anywhere. And while the cabin could fit a family of four comfortably or act as a luxurious escape for a solo traveler, two people occupied the room in this instance: Brick and a wiry, leather-skinned man in a lab coat. Brick had seen his file at X.Y.L.O.P.H.O.N.E. H.Q. This was Doctor Death.

"I am Dr. Death," said Dr. Death.

"I know who you are," Brick croaked, mouth dry. If only he could reach the complimentary Fiji® water bottle that came standard in every Carnival® room.

"Thank you for delivering the Land Able Neo Destructor-class Boat (with) Optimized Automated Tech, Mr. Argus," Dr. Death said. "It will be a boon for our drug trade."

"His name is L.A.N.D.B.O.A.T.," Brick said defensively. "And his loyalty protocols are octo-quadruple encrypted. He'll never work for you."

Dr. Death positioned an IV stand above Brick's head. "I've broken the wills of countless men, Mr. Argus. I don't think a boat will be that difficult. My will-breaking talent is the reason your old friend The Captain hired me."

Brick stared into Dr. Death's dead eyes. "I don't know any The Captain." Brick turned away, recalling his amnesia. "But then again, I don't know much of anything, anymore."

Dr. Death placed an IV bag filled with liquid onto the stand. "Do you know what Chinese water torture is, Mr. Argus?"

"Yes, but I hate to break it to you, Dr. Death—you aren't Chinese. You're Korean," Brick said, calling forth his impeccably accurate ability to discern Asian races. "So this isn't officially Chinese water torture."

Dr. Death smiled out of the corner of his mouth. "You're right. Mr. Argus." His corner-mouth smile dropped. "I'm also using acid."

Dr. Death turned the nozzle, and a drop of acid dropped. Brick leaned over and the acid burned into his shoulder, sizzling. Brick gritted his teeth but released no sound.

"Well, that won't do," Dr. Death tsked. Dr. Death's tulle-skinned hands gripped the sides of Brick's head, keeping it still. The next drop fell towards Brick's eye.

At the last possible millisecond, Brick tilted his head back and let the acid land in his mouth. He swished it around and spat at Dr. Death's face. The thin man emitted a fat scream. Brick flung his legs back, kicking Dr. Death into the rich mahogany walls of the perfectly arranged cabin. Brick's bound hands reached into his boot and retrieved an SPR-422 compact hand spear gun. He quickly calculated trajectory and velocity, as was his way, and fired. The harpoon whizzed through Dr. Death's eye socket and didn't stop until it hit brain cavity. Brick scooped his arms under his legs and spat at his bonds, the nylon melting. Brick tore his bonds away like they were acid-melted nylon ropes.

Brick went to the adjoining bathroom and gargled the complimentary Crest® mouthwash. It refreshed him with Winterfresh™ goodness. He loaded another spear into the SPR-418 compact spear gun and left Dr. Death's face to its melting.

Brick dashed onto the deck and tactically maneuvered past the fun for the whole family Family Fun Time™ Waterslides. He spoke into his wrist communicator, which Dr. Death stupidly forgot to remove. Stupid Dr. Death. "L-B. What's your status?"

"I electrocuted two gear-monkeys trying to tinker with me, so my electro-shielding works. Hyper-weaponry inactive, self-repair protocol at fifty-three percent, mega-engines functional, but they won't do me any good where I am."

"And that would be?"

"Suspended in a lifeboat rig, alongside plenty of lifeboats, enough for everyone on the ship plus backup, as is Carnival®'s way."

"Of course." Brick said, already mentally planning his next vacation as he moved through the ship like a one-man SWAT team. "I have a plan. We rig your thermo-induced hyper thruster engine to blow, and when we're safely off the ship...blamo, we destroy the ship, the drugs, and the bad guys."

L.A.N.D.B.O.A.T. processed the statistics of success. "Good plan."

Brick peeked into the dining hall and immediately changed his mind about the goodness of the plan. Right beside the plentiful buffet of steak, lobster, and chicken fingers for the kids was another buffet. A buffet of problems. And it was all-you-can-eat. Just like the other buffet, which was also all-you-can-eat. There, bound and gagged, sat the cruise ship's staff and passengers. They were guarded by guards who fingered their guns' triggers like twelve-year-olds at camp.

"Abort plan," Brick whispered into his communicator.

"But it's a statistically perfect plan!"

"Add this variable to the equation, L-B. Hostages."

"It's no longer a good plan, Brick."

"We have to take over the ship," Brick deduced.

"By force?"

"That's the only way I know how."

The guard looked down at the protruding polycarbonate meta-barbed projectile that had just thunked into his chest. He tried to gasp, but instead he fell. The other guard did a double take: one take, then the other, then opened his mouth to produce a warning cry, but no air escaped his throat.

Brick, still reloading his SP-480 compact spear gun, looked up to find a twenty-one-year-old raven beauty strangling the silent guard from behind with zip-tied hands. There was fire in her eyes. Almost as much fire as in Brick's loins. A sex fire. And that fire was big enough to take out a five-acre swath of unsexed forest. Brick watched in erotic appreciation as the girl waited for the guard's death rattle.

Brick pulled the spear out of the other guard and cut the girl's bonds. "Who are you and what happened?"

"Well, I..."

"Make it quick, sister, we don't have all day," Brick interrupted.

"We were..."

"There are sure to be more guards on their way. Spit it out," Brick said, becoming annoyed.

The girl smiled at Brick, enjoying his forcefulness. "Lily Kershaw. My family and I were taking a Carnival® cruise. A perfect vacation for any family, whether you're on a budget or not."

Brick nodded in agreement. "Well, you made a great choice. The best, actually."

She rubbed her raw wrists. "Then these criminals took over the ship."

Brick eyed Lily from head to toe and then eyed all of her non-head and non-toe parts. "You look like you can take care of yourself. Can you use an SPV-437 compact spear gun?" Brick said as he tossed her his side-spear-arm.

"Of course," Lily said, catching it.

Brick grabbed the guards' machine guns and turned to Lily. "Come with me."

Lily winked at Brick. "Yes, I will, eventually."

Brick cocked his head quizzically. "What do you mean, 'eventually'? I need you to come with me now."

"Right, but 'come with you.' You know, it could mean two things, depending on the context."

"I don't follow. Are you coming with me now or not?"

"I am. But I'll also come with you later. In a very different way."

Ten seconds of silence passed.

Finally, Brick spoke. "So...you're coming with me now..."

Lily dropped her head. "Yes."

"Good. We have to act fast. If the guards find out I escaped, they'll come, quickly and all over the place."

Lily looked at Brick deadpan. "So you *did* get the double entendre."

"I have no idea what you're talking about, baby. Never learned French. But time's a-wastin' and we don't want to lose the element of surprise."

"Surprise is the best weapon," Lily added.

"Well, it's the second best," Brick retorted.

"What's the first?"

"The best weapon," Brick said, "is two machine guns."

Brick and Lily fought upstream through a river of hench towards the boat's steering room, drug runners falling at the snap, crackle, and pop of Brick's machine guns and the silent whispers of Lily's spears. They reached the steering room, a Hansel-and-Gretel trail of blood behind them should they ever want to get back. But there was no going back. Unless back meant forward, into danger.

Brick punched open the door and stepped into the steering room. It was dark. Too dark. Which made it the very definition of dark.

"Bravo, Argus," said a manhole cover scraping concrete.

A name shot through Brick's amnesia.

"Grid!" Brick growled.

"I'm happy you could be here to see this historic collaboration: the drug runners and the tech cartel, working together to get drugs into your country. For a healthy profit, of course."

Lily scowled. "I'm going to spear him like an hors d'oeuvre."

"Cocktail hour hasn't started yet, baby," Brick said, holding his arm out. "I need answers first. About my past."

"Oh, you'll get answers, Brick," Grid seethed. "Gun-answers!"

The lights slammed on, blinding Brick and Lily. But not seeing wasn't something that ever stopped Brick from firing a gun. He opened dual-fire while Lily snapped spears towards the voice. When their eyes adjusted, they saw a plush chair riddled with holes and spears and a speaker lying on the seat.

Brick squinted at the unoccupied chair. "I may have amnesia, but I know that's not Grid."

A voice from behind them scraped, "You're telling me."

The butt of a gun slammed against Brick's temple, shooting sparks, comets, and shooting stars through his corneas. These weren't the delicious kind you find in every box of iron-fortified Lucky Charms® cereal, but the concussiony kind. Grid appeared behind Lily, a vicious Bowie knife sliding around her neck.

Grid had an expressionist painting of a face, clearly made in the artist's Ugly Period. Four facial scars created a tic-tac-toe grid, but in this game, the only outcome was ugly. He was ugly. Grid lifted an enormous hand-cannon towards Brick. "Oh, Brick. Will you never learn that I always win?"

"What do you mean, always?" Brick said, quizzically, staring down the nose of the housecat-sized revolver.

"Hahahaha!" Grid ha-ha'd. "You really don't remember! What do you have, amnesia?"

"Yes. I have amnesia." Brick said, remembering the words necessary to form the response, but not his past.

Grid harrumphed. "Killing you won't be nearly as sweet if you don't remember who I am and what I did..."

"WHO ARE YOU? WHAT DID YOU DO?" Brick roared.

"I think I'll leave that mystery"—Grid cocked his industrial heater—"a mystery."

He squeezed the trigger.

A spear snapped into Grid's foot. Lily had covertly loaded her spear gun and waited for the perfect time to fire it. Which was then. Grid's shot fired errantly into the ceiling as Brick lunged. With the power of a front-kick, Brick punched Grid, causing the antagonist to fall back and drop his pocket-mortar.

"Don't mind if I do," Brick said as he lifted the wrist-breaker, giving it a couple cowboy spins. Brick aimed the handheld-Howitzer at Grid but only found Lily in his sights. Grid was using her as a shield. A shield made of human.

Grid dragged Lily out of the steering room and down the deck. Brick followed, keeping his distance, the really, really big gun trained on Grid. He wouldn't dare take the shot, for risk of leaving a football-sized hole in one of Lily's football-sized breasts.

Brick followed them down the starboard side of the Fiesta Deck, with its comfortable lounge chairs and endless supply of Martha Stewart Signature™ towels, and up to a helicopter pad. Brick was impressed. "A helicopter pad," he thought. "For mid-voyage resupplies, flown-in entertainment, and flying island tours. What *hasn't* Carnival® thought of?" Brick refocused on the task at hand: killing Grid with his bare hands then putting those same hands all over Lily's body.

Grid dragged Lily towards a large, jet-black motorcycle that lay dormant in the middle of the helicopter pad. Brick had been briefed on the Aeronautical Intelligent Robobike Built for Immediate Killing and Extermination. Oscilli-rotor slug cannons framed either side of its spiked front wheel, a laser-guided Mach rail gun shone in the moonlight, and installed between the handlebars was a cyclone sensor hydro-vacuum launcher. It also had a sidecar, for passengers.

Grid sat backwards on the bike, slinging Lily onto the seat in front of him like a sack of hamburger meat. Brick grimaced. He knew she was a prime cut of USDA Choice Angus steak. He wanted to put her in his mouth and taste her juices. But the steak would have to be for desert, because the main course was revenge. And that meal was about to be served. Cold. Like a chef salad or some other cold entrée.

Brick approached. "You got nowhere to go. Except a grave. And I hope you like your graves watery. Because we're on a boat. Your account has run dry, Grid, and I'm the debt collector."

"Oh, are you?" Grid retorted.

"Yes," Brick seethed. "And I don't take kindly to late payments. And my interest rates? They'll kill you. And also, so will my guns."

Grid waited for Brick to finish, then spoke. "Remember that first part, where you said I had nowhere to go?"

"Of course. I may have amnesia, but when it comes to threats, I'm like an elephant. I never forget. To destroy my enemies. With my guns. And I'm still sure that you have nowhere to go."

"Nowhere to go but up!" Grid turned his head. "A.I.R.B.I.K.E., activate!"

The motorcycle lit up like a Christmas tree plugged into a nuclear power plant. As the weapons whirred awake, an all-too-familiar roar screamed out of the exhaust pipes and straight up Brick's spine and into his memory.

"Ow! My memory!" Brick said.

Then, the motorcycle spoke. "Ready to engage."

As the motorcycle lifted into the air, life became slow motion. Lily let out a deep scream, her hands clutching the sides of the motorcycle for dear life as the bike flew farther into the air. A sidewinder missile erupted from the bike towards the cruise ship, exploding into the lower hull and ripping a giant hole into the beautiful curves of the ship. Water rushed in. The cruise ship began a slow descent into the dark blue.

"What a shame," Brick thought to himself. "This cruise liner could have taken countless families on vacations to the Bahamas, Trinidad, or many other affordable destinations. Fortunately, Carnival® has the largest fleet on the market. And the most advanced."

Brick's lamentation was interrupted by the formal introduction of a steel-mesh motorcycle tire going eighty miles an hour to his face. The force sent the back of his head against the immaculately clean deck. And in the case of Deck v. Head, Head was guilty of being softer than Deck. Brick saw airborne motorcycle taillights disappear. Then the stars faded, leaving him in simple black space.

Brick woke up in bed, soft floral sheets a haphazard knot that could only mean one thing: wild, passionate lovemaking. He looked to the thatched roof of his hut, turned, and smiled. There was Dalia. Her naked D-cup breasts lay flat against her chest; they were natural. She blinked herself awake and smiled at Brick. Brick closed his eyes and kissed her, his tongue making its way all the way into her mouth.

When Brick's eyes opened, he found himself on his fishing boat, mending a net that had been cut by the local youth. They were good kids, but they needed guidance, as their fathers chose to work jobs far less noble than fishing. Unless, of course, you consider drugs fish, which they aren't. Brick looked to shore to see Dalia waving at him. They played a long-distance game of peek-a-boo; a game that had brought them together before Brick learned her island language. She laughed and blew him a kiss.

Brick woke with a start to the deep, bassy throb of an engine. Brick could aurally identify every boat on the island, and this definitely wasn't a boat. Brick took his harpoon off the wall—the one he used to fight the great whites that sneaked into his nets—and stepped out of his hut.

Outside, the frogs croaked, the crickets chirped, and the wabu bird let out its soft nighttime lullaby. But no engine. Maybe it had been a dream. Brick turned back to his hut, excited at the prospect of eating a midnight snack, the snack being Dalia. Then the island went silent. The wind stopped whispering, the air grew still, and all the animals fell quiet, even the wabu bird. And you know how wabu birds are.

The vacuum was broken by the hiss of a missile snaking past Brick. It flew directly into the hut and exploded in an explosion of fire and other, smaller explosions. Then, the gunfire began, Dalia's screams somehow rising above the cacophony. Brick's mind was blank, his new realities causing a neural traffic jam and bottlenecking his paralyzed psyche.

Out of the fire, a form formed, forming the form of a man riding a motorcycle. It was a man with tic-tac-toe face scars. And he was laughing. It was a guttural, bassy, machine-gun laugh. Much like the engine of the motorcycle he was flying.

"GRID!" Brick screamed as he woke, the cool deck of the cruise ship cradling his face. He rose wincing. If only he has some Tylenol® Extra Strength™, it could help him with his headache and the pain of rediscovered memories. And while the generic brands were cheaper, he just felt better buying a name he trusted: Tylenol®.

Brick remembered his life before X.Y.L.O.P.H.O.N.E. He remembered learning the ways of the sea. He remembered meeting

Dalia at the tiki bar where she served drinks and danced the hula. And he remembered all the way back to his arrival on the island, a broken man struggling with amnesia.

"Darn," Brick cursed. "Double amnesia. I've heard about this... somewhere...but where, I can't remember. Because of the other amnesia."

It seemed Brick had another mysterious past to uncover. But that could wait. Brick had a hankering for a game of tic-tac-toe, but he had never learned the game's rules. He only knew the rules of war. And there was only one rule: kill and destroy. And also, noncombatants should be protected for any unnecessary suffering, as per the Geneva Convention.

Brick dashed along the top deck, looking down the port side. He found L.A.N.D.B.O.A.T.

"L.A.N.D.B.O.A.T.!" Brick shouted.

"Brick! My Aura-sonic multisensor is picking up A.I.R.B.I.K.E. to the west."

"Are you repaired?" Brick asked.

"One hundred percent functionality, Brick."

Brick leapt off the deck, landing in the driver's seat. The impact broke the tethers holding L.A.N.D.B.O.A.T., dropping them into the water. Brick gritted his teeth. "Well, let's make it one hundred and ten percent, L-B. We have a flying motorcycle to catch."

With a roar, L.A.N.D.B.O.A.T. pounced through the water at breakneck knots. Much like the delicious and refreshing cranberry juice of the same name, the cold ocean spray snapped Brick into laser-focus. He looked back and saw all the hostages safely on the lifeboats as the cruise ship sank deeper into the water. They must have freed themselves. That was fortunate.

The Eastern horizon lightened as L.A.N.D.B.O.A.T. neared A.I.R.B.I.K.E. Grid grimaced at the Land Able Neo Destructor-class Boat (with) Optimized Automated Tech and rained depth charge after depth charge down into the ocean. Brick grabbed the steering wheel and swung it to the right, causing L.A.N.D.B.O.A.T. to stop on a water-dime. One second later and ten feet ahead of them, a plume of water spiked up.

"That was close," Brick said, his voice deep with adrenaline, "but not close enough to hurt us, which is good."

Brick snaked L.A.N.D.B.O.A.T. through the water, avoiding the depth charges.

"Arm laser-guided helix missile rack load with ultra-infrared guided hollow-core warheads!" Brick ordered.

"L.G.H.M.R.L.W.U.I.G.H.C.W. armed," L.A.N.D.B.O.A.T. responded.

"Aim them at a point which will stop the bike, yet fling Lily off safely."

Lily called from the seat of A.I.R.B.I.K.E. "I trust you, Brick!"

"I don't care!" Brick called out. "Fire!"

Two rockets leapt from the missile launcher. Like thoroughbreds, they vied for lead position in the race to the explosion-line. A rain of flares shot from beneath A.I.R.B.I.K.E., confusing the rockets like thoroughbreds that just saw the first-place horse explode at the explosion-line. The rockets slammed into each other, exploding harmlessly, except for maybe some birds or flying bugs in the area.

Brick perused his mental catalogue of weaponry. "Arm water pulse barrage cannon!"

With a whir and a click, a gun rose from the aft. It was a like a Hasbro® Super Soaker™ that was somehow given a circulatory system, injected with steroids, then turned back into a gun without a circulatory system.

"Set PSI to one million," Brick said. "Let's drown this bird."

The water that L.A.N.D.B.O.A.T. rode on dropped away, its mass sucked into the cannon and fired into the sky. As the jet of seawater neared the flying motorcycle, it dispersed into millions of tiny droplets.

Grid shouted down to Brick, now directly below him. "How do you like my hyper-tronic wind disrupter, Argus?"

Brick scoffed. "I know how much you blow, Talon. But I never knew how hard."

The insult stung Grid, who growled over the collective roars of the two ultra-vehicles' engines. "How did you like it when I killed your wife, Argus?"

Lily's eyes widened. She shouted down to Brick. "You had a wife?"

"I did," Brick shouted back. "She was the love of my life. And Grid killed her. I will never love again until I have my revenge."

Brick was interrupted by Grid. "I guess that means you'll never love again. Or breathe!" Grid slammed a large red button on A.I.R.B.I.K.E.'s dash. The sidecar disengaged.

Brick looked up, curious. "Why would he drop his sidecar?"

"That's not a sidecar," L.A.N.D.B.O.A.T. said, a semblance of fear in his robotic voice. "That's a sidecar-sized bomb!!!!!"

Lily's jaw went slack, the cigarette dropping from her mouth. "NOOOOOOOOoooooo!" she wailed.

Brick reached under his seat and retrieved the harpoon he brought with him wherever he went. With the strength of an American Gladiator, he hucked it at the bomb. The harpoon met the bomb, piercing through the thick metal shell and poking the warhead inside. The bomb exploded midair, the blast blasting A.I.R.B.I.K.E. forward, upside-down, and over.

Lily flew from the aeromotorcycle and plunged into the ocean. She rose for air and was immediately plucked from the salty water and onto the deck of L.A.N.D.B.O.A.T. Brick's hands were around her. He kissed her face.

"I thought you could never love again," she protested.

Brick looked into her eyes. "My love was extinguished years ago by a bucket of liquid death. And bullets. And a missile. But this isn't love. This is survival."

She swooned into Brick's arms, which glistened from the ocean spray (once again, not to be confused with the delicious beverages from Ocean Spray®. Did you know that cranberry juice is great for urinary infections?). Brick laid her down and manned the helm once again. He lowered his sleek, Oakley® wraparounds with their one-year warranty over his eyes and locked onto the now-smoking A.I.R.B.I.K.E. which careened towards a seaside road. When the flight bike's wheels met the earth, Brick's face dropped.

"Damn! Land!" Brick exclaimed, smashing his hand against the metal steering wheel.

"Brick," said L.A.N.D.B.O.A.T.

"Yeah?" Brick asked.

"They don't call me L.A.N.D.B.O.A.T. for nothing," said L.A.N.D.B.O.A.T.

L.A.N.D.B.O.A.T.'s jet engine spat fire like a dragon with an engine and blasted towards land. A.I.R.B.I.K.E. puttered down the seaside road.

Then, with the ferocity of a lion and the rage of a bull, L.A.N.D.B.O.A.T. went on land.

L.A.N.D.B.O.A.T.'s glimmering black hull knocked Grid from his seat. A.I.R.B.I.K.E. toppled and fell, the sand etching its name into the motorcycle's paint job. Brick deboated L.A.N.D.B.O.A.T., grabbed Grid by his greasy hair, and dragged him to the ocean.

Grid screamed, "It wasn't me! I didn't do it!"

Brick spoke calmly, the surf churning around them. "You should know that no amount of land can stop me or my boat. My boat that goes on land." Brick brought his face close to Grid's. "Did you know the human body is made up of seventy percent water?"

Grid shuddered in the surf. "It wasn't me! I was being controlled!"

Brick ignored Grid. "Let's see what happens when that percentage becomes one hundred."

Brick extended his arms, submerging Grid's game board face into the brine. Grid clawed at Brick futilely. Brick's unblinking eyes refused to close until the eyes of his enemy did. After two minutes, Brick blinked.

Brick walked ashore and into Lily's arms. "It's over," he whispered. They kissed passionately, with tongues and everything.

"Ha. Ha. Ha. Ha," a robotic voice chimed.

Brick turned to see A.I.R.B.I.K.E. upright, lights glowing. "Glad to see you have your memory back, Argus," it croaked in monotone. "Thank you for disposing of my puppet. He was growing tiresome. I like your new girl. I can't wait to kill her too."

Brick's eyes widened. Grid was telling the truth. It had been A.I.R.B.I.K.E. all along. Brick screamed, "L.A.N.D.B.O.A.T. FIRE!"

A.I.R.B.I.K.E. rose vertically, evading the stream of bullets. Its guttural engine rumbled its staccato laugh. "HA. HA. HA. HA. HA."

Brick embraced Lily as they watched A.I.R.B.I.K.E. disappear. "It looks like I have a new enemy to destroy. And a more distant past to uncover."

Lily joined his stare into the sunrise. "Since you killed Grid, does that mean that you can love again? Or does the fact that your true nemesis is that flying motorcycle mean that you still can't love?"

"Yes...one of those," Brick said.

They embraced, falling to the sand. Brick looked to L.A.N.D.B.O.A.T. "You may want to turn off your high-compression ultra-infrared sensors, L-B."

L.A.N.D.B.O.A.T. chirped quizzically, "Why would I?...Oh, gotcha." The boat's lights dimmed.

As Brick and Lily embarked on a naval voyage of passion, the spray from the surf rose up to the sky where the rising sun caught it just right, creating an arc of glorious color: Red. Orange. Yellow. Green. Blue. Indigo. Violet.

Just like in the beginning.

THE END

Chase Verdugo never shied from hot-button issues, and with subtlety and nuance, he weaved his opinio-facts into a tale where boats can talk and crime lives on the high seas. At the beginning of his career, Verdugo struggled to find a publisher. Yet, always resilient, he refused to take no, "Hell no!" and "Why would we ever publish this crap?" for an answer. Instead he got creative, as creative writers do, turning to corporate sponsorship to get his novels out to the public.

OREN BRIMER found L.A.N.D.B.O.A.T. in the desk drawer of a Carnival® cruise line cabin, right next to the Bible and a brochure for Nicaraguan timeshares.

MAJOR MCCALL & THE WIFE
in
FRAGGED
by Stephen Mertz

Vietnam. 1970. Quang Ngai Province, north of Saigon.

THE HUEY GUNSHIP banked in over Firebase Tiger, a clearing carved from the jungle hilltop. The woman, who was calling herself Tara Carpenter, snapped pictures from the open side door of the helicopter, from behind the shoulder of the door gunner and his big, mounted M-60 machine gun.

The landing zone was a barren five acres. After the stark green carpet of jungle they'd flown over from Saigon, the base was drab and squalid. There were no trees, no color except for the coating of dust that blanketed everything: bunkers, vehicles and personnel. Machine gun emplacements were at intervals along the perimeter. Artillery and mortars were inside the compound. The sun, like an angry red ball seen through the gauze of a humid haze, arced low in the west, painting the horizon a brilliant red. This all vanished behind a veil of red dust, a sandstorm kicked up by the chopper's backwash as the pilot touched the Huey down gently and initiated systems shutdown.

Tara's fellow passenger stood beside her.

He said, "Getting enough pretty pictures for the war protestors back home?"

He didn't wait for a response, leaving the gunship and striding toward a welcoming committee of three waiting soldiers.

His name was Cord McCall. He was an investigator assigned to a special operations unit of the Joint Services Criminal Investigation Division. Death was naturally commonplace in a war zone, but there were other crimes perpetrated within military ranks—homicide, desertion, robbery—that fell under the CID's jurisdiction. McCall, a Major, was forty years old, dark-haired, heavily muscled. His fatigues were sharply pressed even in the three-digit heat and suffocating humidity. He wore an Army issue Colt .45 automatic in a shoulder holster.

Tara caught up with him. She was seven years his junior, a redhead with intelligent green eyes that glittered like those of a mischievous cat. The GI fatigues she wore did nothing to conceal a trim, shapely figure. She chose not to respond to McCall's sarcasm because, McCall knew, she well understood and appreciated its source.

He was not overjoyed in the first place about being assigned the dual task of performing his duties in addition to nurse-maiding an embedded journalist. But there was another, more significant reason for his displeasure with the presence of Tara "Carpenter" in Vietnam, and she and he were the only two people in country or anywhere else who could appreciate the undercurrent of tension that crackled between them.

They were husband and wife.

Therein lay one hell of a tale, somehow as simple as it was complex. She'd been his wife for three years before he volunteered for Nam. Tara had never been your average military base wife. She'd been freelancing her photographs to wire services and news magazines before they met. During their separation while Cord was in Vietnam, she had continued to rise through the ranks of professional news photographers.

But he had been dumbstruck when he showed up that morning at the Saigon airport, not having the slightest idea that the photojournalist assigned to him was his own wife.

Tara had brazenly confided in him, with only a trace of smugness, that it had taken considerable finagling on her part, including coming up with a cockamamie story for her editor about the need for a cover name, but she pulled it off. Wars were the stuff Pulitzer Prizes were made of but ambition and self-interest were not the only reasons she'd hustled up this assignment. She'd grown impatient, sitting on the sidelines in the States. She wanted to learn for herself what was going on in Vietnam. Her voice softened when she explained to McCall that she wanted to experience his world. She would not have interfered under normal circumstances but this war was hardly normal. As his wife, she well knew his strength, his self-confidence. Now, she explained that morning at the airport, she yearned to know the source of that strength that she had decided could only be forged in sharing the fires of war with him.

Well, hell.

He had agreed to maintain the secret that she was his spouse as much to avoid complications as to avoid appearing the fool, but he'd made no secret of his displeasure during the drive to CID HQ and had protested adamantly, in her presence, to his commanding officer. Colonel Conglose had proceeded to not-so-patiently re-explain to McCall how this was part of an important PR campaign being waged on the home front by the Pentagon. McCall would obey orders and allow Miss Carpenter to accompany him during duty hours until further notice. That said, McCall was handed his assignment to Firebase Tiger.

He and Tara crossed from the Huey to the trio of waiting soldiers.

The ranking man stepped forward. He had the build and the leathery features of a farmer, thirtyish, with a sunburned crew cut and flinty eyes. He did not salute. Enemy snipers loved to disrupt the chain of command, and seeing who was saluted made selecting targets easy. Saluting was avoided in the field.

"Major, I'm Captain Larson, Executive Officer in Charge. Welcome to Firebase Tiger, though I imagine you'd rather be someplace else."

The man next to Larson was a strapping man with a caffè latte complexion and E-6 stripes on his sleeve. "That goes for every mother's son in this hell hole, sir."

Larson said, "Easy, Top. Major, this is Sergeant Hines. He's my top shirt."

"I know," said McCall. "I studied your personnel files on the flight in."

Hines kept shifting his attention between them and scanning the darkening jungle beyond the perimeter.

The third man was a first lieutenant named Grey and everything about him matched his name. Blond-haired, in his late twenties, there was paleness to the junior officer that was almost albino-like except for the empurpled, swollen area around a bandage at his right temple.

Grey said, "Sergeant Hines speaks the truth. I wish I'd never heard of Firebase Tiger."

McCall said, "You have a colonel who was fragged."

Larson nodded. "Lieutenant Colonel Emmett, 13th Infantry Battalion. Someone tossed a hand grenade into his hooch just before dawn and splashed the walls with his guts."

"Hooch" was GI slang for makeshift living quarters. "Fragging" was another recently coined term. Bad command decisions by an officer too often got good soldiers killed. Sometimes an officer's own men—considering it more an act of survival than murder—would toss a grenade into the officer's hooch, blowing the officer into itty bitty officer parts—"frag" him, in other words—before the officer got anyone else killed.

"Where's the body now?"

Larson said, "What was left of it was tagged and bagged and sent to Saigon on the daily chopper run."

Grey cleared his throat and nodded at Tara. "Uh, if you don't mind, Major, who is she?"

"Her? Name's Carpenter. Pretend she's not here. Okay, Captain, show me where the fragging took place."

Larson led them toward a squalid, dust covered pile of sandbags that was somewhat bigger than the other hooches.

"The colonel's hooch was next to the main bunker."

Tara commenced taking pictures.

Activity swirled around them; a world of coarse language, exhaust fumes and the clicking and clanking of engines, equipment, and weaponry. Nearly every soldier in sight was toting an M-16 and a wary attitude. The shadows of encroaching night deepened by the minute.

The colonel's hooch was a low, ten-by-twelve, makeshift structure of timber and plywood beneath a shell of sandbags. Its entrance was charred, misshapen from the outward force of the murderous blast. McCall stooped and entered while the others grouped behind him outside.

Walls were splashed with gore. Flies buzzed, thick and loud. The sickly sweet smell of death was almost overpowering in the enclosed space.

"Did anyone see anything?"

Larson shook his head, negative. "Everyone heard the blast but Security was paying attention to outside the perimeter. The nearest personnel when it happened were me and Sergeant Hines and the lieutenant."

Grey indicated his bandage. "I caught this when my patrol was ambushed the other night. I was laid up in my hooch, woozy on pain pills the medic gave me. But we compared notes. No one saw anything. It wasn't the VC. They'd never breach our perimeter."

Hines indicated the Tactical Operations command bunker.

"The captain and I were sprucing up the files for the Inspector General's visit day after tomorrow. If it hadn't been for a couple of walls between the colonel's hooch and the TOC, we'd have been hamburger too."

"Any ideas about who'd want the colonel dead bad enough to frag him?"

Larson said, "Suspects?" The flint was cold in his eyes. "Yeah, I could think of a few."

Grey cleared his throat. "You might as well go ahead and tell him, Cap."

Tara said, "Tell us what, Captain Larson?"

This got McCall's goat.

"Not us, ma'am. Me." He spoke to the men. "I take it the colonel was not well liked."

Hines chuckled. "I'll bet you're saying that just because someone fragged his ass to hell."

McCall said, "Emmett was assigned here just last month. A new CO always shakes up a command to put his own brand on it. The troops never like it, but it usually settles into a mutual respect."

Hines regarded the damaged hooch with no visible sign of emotion.

"You want a list of suspects, Major? You could start with every man on this base."

Grey stared at the ground as if looking at something far, far away. "Eight men who were stationed here went home yesterday in body bags."

"A platoon from Bravo company," said Larson. "Ambushed. Heavy casualties."

"Wiped out by one of our own bombs," said Hines. His eyes kept shifting back to the jungle tree line. "The VC find our dud shells, rig them up and use them against us."

"Let me guess," said McCall. "Saigon promised replacements today but they're not here."

Larson nodded. "The green machine. Efficient as hell, ain't it? And until those new men get here, I'm way short of manpower. I'm hoping Charlie hasn't figured that out yet."

"Issue me an M-l6," said McCall. "You've got one replacement."

"Two, actually," Tara volunteered.

They ignored her.

McCall didn't miss the flash of anger that made Tara's eyes turn a deeper shade of green.

He went around to the entrance of the command center and glanced inside. Tactical maps were spread out upon folding tables. Ammo crates served as chairs. A clerk was busy at a typewriter. A radio man monitored mostly static from a small receiver.

Grey said, "Colonel Emmett should never have ordered me and my men out on that patrol."

Larson told McCall, "The firebase is assigned two companies of light infantry. One supports the other. The line company conducts recon patrols around the base, and it was Bravo Company's turn on the rotation schedule. The other company provides mortar and artillery support from here."

"The colonel should have never ordered my platoon into that area after dark," said Grey. "I'm not some wet-behind-the-ears cherry. That ambush wasn't my fault. Me and Sergeant Williams always brought our guys home. Right, Captain?

Larson nodded. "Right, Lieutenant."

Hines said, not unkindly, "You need to relax, Lieutenant, if you don't mind my saying so, sir. You, uh, haven't been right since, well, since it happened. Maybe you ought to lay down in your hooch, sir. I'll have a medic check in with you."

A sideways glance told McCall that an impulse within Tara was trying to dissuade her from capturing on film, for posterity, Lieutenant Grey's vulnerability and emotional unbalance; a poignant portrait of the ravages of war on a trained, competent man. She grimaced, lifted her camera and snapped the picture.

Grey said, "The sergeant who died in the ambush, Sergeant Williams, he served way back in the Korean War and until two nights ago he was keeping alive a good bunch of guys who should have been back home drinking beer. Every man on the base respected him. The sarge was our teacher, our preacher, the one we looked up to. And I owed him a personal debt. That's why I wish to God that *I'd* been one of the dead in that VC ambush, not him."

"Lieutenant," said Larson, "you are not responsible for what happened."

McCall said, "What sort of personal debt?"

"My dad served with Sergeant Williams in Korea," said Grey. "He saved Dad's life. Sarge greased a Red Chinese who was about to run Dad through with a bayonet. They stayed in touch after the war. They were both lifers. I must have heard the story a hundred times growing up. I never got tired of it. Cancer got Dad last year. I was raised to be a soldier. I couldn't believe my luck when I got assigned to Sergeant Williams. I was supposed to be the platoon leader, but we all knew who kept us alive." Grey's lower lip trembled.

Tara stepped forward. She rested a hand gently on Grey's shoulder.

"Lieutenant, listen to your captain and to Sergeant Hines. There is a thing called survivor's guilt. You must maintain. That is what you owe Sergeant Williams and your dad and yourself."

Grey's lower lip stopped trembling.

"Yes ma'am. You're right." He drew himself to his full height, his shoulders back. "I'm not doing anybody any good, pissing and whining, am I? I've got to regroup and be ready for whatever's coming next."

Tara nodded with a smile. "1 couldn't have said it better myself."

Grey turned to Larson. "Captain, uh, I guess maybe I should try and get some rest."

"I think you're right, Lieutenant. You're dismissed."

"Thank you, sir." Grey added to Tara, "And thank you, ma'am." He lowered his eyes from theirs and walked away.

When Grey was out of earshot, Larson said, "There goes a fine soldier, wearing a hair shirt from hell."

"He'll make it," said Hines. "That kid's got a lot to offer this man's army, but he was on the razor's edge of losing it. Miss Carpenter, I believe you helped steer that soldier back in the right direction."

Tara started to say something.

McCall spoke before she could.

"Yes, ma'am. That was a humane and noble gesture. But now I must ask you to allow me to proceed without distraction. You're a non-participating observer, Miss Carpenter. Captain, I'd like to take a look as Sergeant Williams' hooch."

"This way," said Larson. He started them toward a line of hooches near a row of mortar placements. "Mind if I ask, Major, what are we looking for in Williams' hooch?"

Striding apace with them, Tara said, "The lieutenant said the men on the base looked up to Sergeant Williams like a hero."

Hines nodded. "That's as good a word as any, ma'am, and that's why everyone hated the colonel after Sergeant Williams died on a patrol that never should have been sent out." A bleak smile creased his coffee latte features. "And that's the connection. I get it. Lady, you're a Sherlock Holmes."

McCall tried hard not to yield to his building irritation.

He said, "She's a civilian." This wasn't going to work, having Tara tagging along every step of the way. He would just lay it all out for Conglose when they got back to HQ. They had a war to win. He had a murder to solve. What the hell was Tara thinking? What the hell was she doing here? Cool it, he told himself. He said, "And I'll thank you, Miss Carpenter, to just zip it and take your pictures, okay?"

"Understood, General."

McCall sighed. "Sarcasm yet. I'll be lucky to stay a major with you bird-dogging me." He barely caught the man-to-man grin that passed between Larson and the first sergeant at this verbal sparring. Damn. The electricity between him and this sassy redhead was so obvious that anyone who witnessed it would catch on even if they didn't know exactly what they were seeing. To change the subject, he nodded to the row of mortars near Williams' hooch. "Not the quietest neighborhood."

"No such thing as a quiet neighborhood in this sector," said Hines. "We're surrounded by bogey land. It's a free fire zone beyond that perimeter."

"The first change Colonel Emmett made when he took command," said Larson, "was to send out patrols after dark. It was unnecessary. Too risky. Everyone except the colonel knew it. The mission for this firebase is recon. You can't recon in the jungle at night."

Hines spat. "We have an outstanding record for targeting VC for the flyboys. We do our job. But doing our job wasn't good enough for the colonel. He wanted a higher enemy body count so he could get himself a general's star and he didn't give a damn about sacrificing good men like Sergeant Williams for a promotion."

Tara lifted her camera and snapped a picture of Hines.

They reached Williams' hooch.

McCall entered the hooch alone. Tara lowered her camera and positioned herself between Hines and Larson in the entrance. Their grouped presence in the doorway deepened the interior gloom. The hooch was of uniform furnishings: cot, foot locker, a makeshift desk. McCall knelt on one knee to conduct a thorough search of the foot locker.

"Uh *huh,*" he said.

He rose, letting the lid of the locker snap shut. He exited the hooch, leafing through a small bound-leather volume.

Captain Larson craned his neck to try to make out the printing on the book.

"What did you find, Major?"

Hines guessed, "A Bible?"

McCall shook his head, snapping the book shut. "Not even close."

Tara studied the book's dimensions and appearance. "A diary."

"When men keep one, it's called a journal."

Larson ran a broad palm across the bristle of his crew cut. "Why would Sergeant Williams keep a journal?"

"Why the hell wouldn't he?" growled Hines. "I'll bet he had plenty of stories to tell, going back to Korea."

"Too bad he kept them to himself." Larson extended his hand, palm up. "Mind if I take a look, Major? Maybe he wrote something that will help us."

Tara said, "You could make bet on that."

McCall slid the book into a pocket. "Sorry, Captain. First I'll have a look for myself."

Tara studied him. "You think that diary—excuse me, journal— holds a clue to who fragged the colonel?"

"That's what I intend to find out." McCall patted the book in his pocket. "Something tells me this is going to make for an interesting read, and I want to get started."

Sergeant Hines said, "I'll show you to the guest billets, for what they're worth." He glanced at his watch. "And it's past chow time."

Tara let herself into one of the guest billets—not her own—without announcing her arrival.

McCall sat at a makeshift desk, a slab of plywood resting across two empty oil drums. Remaining seated, he pivoted with incredible speed, a blur of movement, freezing with the .45 in straight-armed target acquisition, its muzzle inches away from the center of Tara's forehead.

She froze, lovely mouth agape, her green eyes wide, holding her breath in astonishment.

McCall sighed mightily, flicked on the safety and returned the .45 to its shoulder holster.

"Now there was a real temptation." He returned to the material spread across the desk. "I thought we were going to avoid personal contact, Miss Carpenter."

She stood beside him. She rested a hand on his shoulder. Her touch had always had its intended affect on him. He felt that humanizing affirmation borne of the touch of woman, of grace and beauty so uncommon, practically unknown in the harshness of war except as memories nursed by those who fought. She glimpsed the paperwork he'd been poring over: three personnel files, a yellow pad full of his notations, and the slim leather volume, folded open with the spine up.

She read aloud the names off the personnel files.

"Captain Larson, Lieutenant Grey, Sergeant Hines. I'm glad I don't have to guess which one of those three fragged the colonel."

McCall decided that he could either blow up or give up. This woman had a backbone of steel coupled with a tenacity that could wear down stone.

"And what makes you think the killer is one of them or that I'm guessing? It's called investigating. What the hell am I going to do with you?"

An impish smile curved her lips, and with one graceful, impudent motion she was straddling his lap, her fingers entwined behind his neck, mischievous green eyes glistening, her lips, inviting, only inches away.

She whispered huskily in his ear, "I've got an idea what you could do about me."

"You're a vexatious wench."

"Vexatious?"

"Sometimes I wish you were more of a nag. That would be easier to deal with."

Realizing that he was serious, she lost some of her good humor. She withdrew from his lap.

"So what about the journal? Was it interesting?"

"What journal?"

At that instant, someone outside yelled, *"Incoming!"*

Then everything became drowned out by a startling, eerie whistling that increased in pitch and then was itself drowned out by a deafening explosion, an impacting blast that shook the hooch violently. Dust and red dirt powdered down upon them.

McCall grabbed the M-16 he'd been issued and rushed outside.

A night fog had fallen. A bursting flare overhead cast the base in surreal daylight. The first explosion had been a direct hit on the Huey that had brought them here, now nothing but an unrecognizable, flaming ruin. Everywhere on the base, soldiers were responding to the attack, some firing their M-16s on the run, firing the weapons on full auto into the darkness beyond the perimeter. The artillery and the mortars and machine guns opened up, shredding the night with thunder and fury.

A whistling round missed McCall by inches, chipping off a chunk of the hooch doorframe. He felt a trickle of blood from a flying splinter, razor-thin along his cheek.

The next incoming mortar shell struck the main bunker. The Tactical Operations Command evaporated in a copper-red eruption of flame.

Then Tara was with him.

She said, "Damn but I wish they'd issued me a weapon. Don't suppose I could borrow one of yours?"

McCall grabbed her wrist. "First let's get you to cover. They're targeting the hooches."

They stormed into the battle, dodging strobe-like explosions. Shouts filled the air along with the stench of destruction, of burnt gunpowder, of killing and dying. McCall led her to a nearby pile of debris somewhat in the shadows; empty oil drums and discarded machine parts. A good place to stash a troublesome wife until the fighting was over. A round pinged off an overhanging piece of metal. She was right. He could not leave her unarmed.

He handed her his M-16. "Here. You qualified with one of these on the range back home. Time for practical application. Keep your head down. You are a non-combatant." He unleathered the .45 from its shoulder holster and flicked off the safety. "I've got to keep moving, to help out."

She took hold of the rifle, wholly comfortable with it. Then her eyes were distracted by something.

"Cord, look."

He whirled, half knowing what to expect. Then he saw it too.

Through the disorganized melee of battle, a soldier, whose features were obscured, darted through the tumultuous firefight with determined haste, staying low to avoid incoming fire, one hand steadying his helmet as he ran, appearing to McCall to be somehow disengaged from the battle, particularly when he gained the hooch the McCalls had just vacated. The soldier entered the guest billet.

"Wait here," said McCall, and he bolted.

"Right," Tara said to herself.

She gave McCall a ten-count. Then she slung the M-16 over her shoulder by its strap and followed him.

McCall hesitated at the entrance to the hooch, the .45 automatic held down at his side, his presence undetected by the man inside because of the ferocious battle raging around them and because the soldier was preoccupied, in the process of reaching for the slim black book on the desk.

McCall said, "It's not a journal."

Larson whirled. His expression struggled between surprise and panic.

"Major, I can explain."

They had to raise their voices to be heard above the cacophony outside.

"Captain, I'm arresting you," said McCall. "You murdered Colonel Emmett. You fragged a fellow officer."

Larson drew his broad, farmer's body up straight, doing his best to reassert command even if he was outranked.

"Arrest me? On the strength of what? Every man on this base wanted to see that bastard dead."

"Yeah, but you're the one who went for the bait." McCall nodded to the black book. "That's no journal. It's a notebook that I always carry. I had it on me when I knelt down to search Williams' foot locker, and with the dim lighting inside the hooch and a little sleight of hand I had everyone thinking I'd found it there. I wanted to see if I could smoke out someone with a guilty conscience, and it looks like I succeeded. You wanted to see if Williams incriminated you in a journal after you confided in him that you were going to frag the colonel. Maybe I hadn't gotten to that page yet and you could steal the book before I did. It was a crazy long shot, but it was the only chance you saw, so you went for it. A soldier like Sergeant Williams would tell you to bite your tongue and follow orders."

A jolt of raw, bitter emotion erupted from Larson. "That's exactly what he told me. Let it alone, Williams said. Follow orders. Right, follow orders. Sounds real honorable but look what it got the sarge and those other men of Bravo Company. Emmett was killing my men, goddammit. He had to be stopped, and I stopped him."

A shell struck the next hooch over with a thunderous *crack!* like a lightning strike. Shouts for *"Medic! Medic!"* could be heard.

Larson lunged at McCall. *"Bastard!"*

McCall had hoped that sight of the .45 would discourage something like this, but Larson wasn't about to be taken easily. McCall brought up the .45.

The *snap!* of a camera flashbulb came from close behind his ear.

Tara had crept up from outside and eavesdropped. The white flash seared the interior of the hooch, not impairing McCall's vision because it came from behind him. The flash startled, stunned and stopped Larson. He reflexively threw his arms up to cover his eyes.

Tara said, "Gotcha!"

McCall brought his .45 around in a swipe that cracked the side of Larson's head. Larson's knees buckled and he collapsed. McCall pinned Larson with a boot to his back. He holstered the .45 and reached for the handcuffs attached to his belt. He spared a quick glance over his shoulder.

The beauty of his wife's face was smudged with grime. Her red hair was tangled. She looked stunning.

He said, "Thanks, hon."

Larson's face, against the earthen floor, was an emotionless mask.

"You've got this all wrong, Major. Yeah, I thought it was Williams' journal that you found. I came for a look to see if he thought anyone on base killed Emmett, to see if he wrote that down. I didn't frag anybody."

"Sergeant Hines will fess up," said McCall. "He gave you your alibi when he said you and he were together prepping for the IG inspection. But Sergeant Hines is lying because he hated Emmett too. You weren't in the TOC bunker with your First Sergeant when Emmett was killed. I'll go to work on Top's conscience and his duty under the Uniform Code of Military Justice, and when he breaks, Captain, I'll have the proof I need."

Larson sneered. "What the hell kind of a soldier are you? Whose side are you on, McCall? I'm on the side of *our* troops. That's more important than any VC body count so some fat-assed colonel can advance his career. You think I could let that go on? *Our* body count is my concern. Emmett got what he deserved. You know that, in your heart."

"You're out of luck, Captain. It's my job to take you in."

Someone outside yelled, *"Incoming!"* and again the air was split by that fast-approaching, ear-piercing whistle.

McCall sprang at Tara without hesitation, yelling to the man on the floor, "Move, Larson! Save yourself!

Larson got to his feet but made no effort to move.

He said in a calm voice, "Up yours, Major."

With the incoming whistle growing impossibly loud, McCall plowed into Tara with enough force to knock her off her feet, sending them both airborne, pitching them outside of the hooch and onto ground. They landed together. Cord's arms were around her. They rolled a few times before coming to a stop with Cord on top.

Again lightning and thunder struck. The ground trembled beneath them as a direct hit demolished the hooch. McCall pinned his wife, shielding her from a pelting shower of falling debris.

Then they lifted their heads.

The battle was winding down. Three Huey gunships had rotored in to commence pulverizing the surrounding jungle, making the night sky a fire show of tracer bullets, rocket fire, and multiple explosions. There was no more incoming fire. The mortars and artillery were quieting down. The primary activity on the base now was tending to the wounded, regrouping, assessing.

Tara arched her neck for a view of the smoldering remains of the hooch they had just vacated.

"Captain Larson..."

"It's better this way," said McCall. "He died in combat. That's better for his family back in the world."

"You're not going to report that he fragged a colonel?"

McCall said nothing.

She stared up at him for a long moment. Then she kissed the thin red line of dried blood that crossed his cheek and for one stolen moment there on the battle-scarred ground, they shared a prolonged embrace.

"Know what?' whispered Tara.

"What?"

"It's been so long, I wouldn't even mind being on the bottom."

"You," said McCall, "are impossible."

"And that's only one of the reasons you're crazy about me, right?"

"Yeah, I guess so. Crazy is definitely the word. I must be out of my mind." Two figures were hurrying in their direction. "Here come Sergeant Hines and Lieutenant Grey. I've got some explaining to do." He got up off her, extending a courtly hand. Tara accepted, rising to her feet, and he said for her ears alone, "Now stow the personal stuff, okay, hon? I mean it, Tara."

He turned to greet the approaching men.

"Right," Tara said to herself, and hurried to join them.

THE END

All kidding aside, Blood & Tacos *is honored to have STEPHEN MERTZ included. While we poke fun at the genre here and there, we've always viewed our stories as loving homage and the writers of the originals with respect and admiration. Having Mr. Mertz included in* Blood & Tacos *definitely forces all of us young pups to raise our game.*

If you don't know who Stephen Mertz is, you know nothing of men's adventure books. Wikipedia him if you have to. But what you should really do is buy. If you need a place to start, try Hank & Muddy. *In men's adventure, he wrote at least nine Executioner novels, possibly more. He created Stone: MIA Hunter and Cody's Army, as well as the Tunnel Rats—an accomplished writer who deserves to be discovered and rediscovered. Check out a pro at work.*

AUTHORS

Andrew Nette is a writer based in Melbourne, Australia. He is one of the editors of the on-line magazine, *Crime Factory*. His short fiction has appeared in *Crime Factory: The First Shift* by New Pulp Press and *The One That Got Away*, an anthology of crime stories released in 2012 by Australian independent publisher Dark Prints Press. His debut crime novel *Ghost Money* was published by Snubnose Press in 2012. His blog, www.pulpcurry.com explores crime film and literature, particularly from Asia and Australia.

Bart Lessard is the fake name of a cranky loner. Here he has adopted a cranky loner persona through the use of a fake name. He is the author of *Rakehell* and *The Danse Joyeuse at Murderer's Corner*, both out on Kindle.

Brad Mengel works in Australia's criminal justice system. His book *Serial Vigilantes of Paperback Fiction: An Encyclopedia from Able Team to Z-Comm* (McFarland 2009) was the first book to examine vigilante fiction of the '70s and '80s. He has also contributed stories to *Tales of the Shadowmen, Pro Se Presents,* and *Pulp Obscura* anthologies.

Cameron Ashley is the editor in chief of *Crime Factory*. His most recent fiction can be found in *D*cked, Noir at the Bar* and upcoming in *The One That Got Away*. He lives in Brunswick, Melbourne.

Chris La Tray is a rocker, a writer, and a wannabe adventurer. His nonfiction writing has appeared in the *Missoula Independent, Vintage Guitar* magazine, and *World Explorer* magazine. His short fiction has appeared at *Beat to a Pulp*; *Pulp Modern*; the Crimefactory special edition, *Kung Fu Factory*; *Noir at the Bar*; *Needle: A Magazine of Noir*, and the charity anthology *Off the Record*. His story "Run for the Roses" was the winner of the 2011 Watery Graves Invitational story competition, while his story "Genny Bow" won the 2012 Watery Graves Invitational story competition as well. He lives and travels from Missoula, MT, where folks seem overly impressed by how loud his obnoxious rock band, American Falcon, is. Obviously none of them have aurally experienced High on Fire.

Christopher Blair is a teacher, freelance writer, and former crime reporter. In addition to being raised on ten-for-a-dollar used paperbacks, he grew up on a nutritious diet of comic books, Stephen King stories, and pure cane sugar.

Frank Larnerd is currently a student at West Virginia State University, where he has received multiple awards for fiction and non-fiction. His first anthology as editor, *Hills of Fire: Bare-Knuckle Yarns of Appalachia* was released in the fall of 2012 from Woodland Press. Frank lives in Putnam County, West Virginia.

Garnett Elliott lives and works in Tucson, Arizona. Recent stories have appeared or are slated to appear in *Alfred Hitchcock's Mystery Magazine, Beat to a Pulp: Round Two, Needle Magazine, Pulp Modern*, and *Battling Boxing Stories*. Look for his novellas "Vin of Venus" from Beat to a Pulp publishing, and "The Shunned Highway" in Alec Cizak's anthology *Uncle B's Drive-In*, due out later this summer. You can follow Garnett on Twitter @TonyAmtrak.

Among **Gary Phillips**' latest is another short story, "Feathersmith's Excellent Plan," in the *Dead of Winter* e-anthology, and a collection of his previously published short stories, *Treacherous: Grifters, Ruffians and Killers*, out from Perfect Crime Books.

Jimmy Callaway lives and works in San Diego, CA. He is the underboss of *Criminal Complex* and overboss of *Attention, Children* and *Let's Kill Everybody!*

Along with his role as editor of Blood & Tacos, **Johnny Shaw** is a screenwriter, playwright, and the author of the novels *Dove Season: A Jimmy Veeder Fiasco* and *Big Maria*.

Beautiful, Naked & Dead, **Josh Stallings'** first novel, is garnering great notice from readers and reviewers alike. Its sequel, *Out There Bad*, has met with equally stunning reviews. He is busy working on the third Moses McGuire crime novel, *One More Body*. In addition to his fiction, his noir memoir *All The Wild Children* will be published by Snubnose Press. He lives in Los Angeles with his wife Erika, two dogs and a cat named Riddle.

Matthew C. Funk is an editor of *Needle Magazine*, editor of the genre section of the critically acclaimed zine, *FictionDaily*, and a staff writer for *Planet Fury* and *Criminal Complex*. Winner of the 2010 Spinetingler Award for Best Short Story on the Web, Funk has online work indexed on his web domain and printed work in *Needle, Speedloader, Off the Record, Pulp Ink* and *D*CKED*.

Nick Slosser works at Murder by the Book in Portland, Oregon, where he lives with his wife and daughter. He prefers cats to dogs, waffles to pancakes, samurais to ninjas, and Joan Jett to Lita Ford. Nick recently had a story published at Shotgun Honey.

Oren Brimer is a writer, director, and comedian. He has produced field segments for *The Daily Show with Jon Stewart* and directs/co-writes CollegeHumor's popular Dark Knight parody series, Badman. Currently, he is a supervising producer on the forthcoming Conan companion show starring Pete Holmes, which will premiere on TBS this fall. "L.A.N.D.B.O.A.T." is his first published short story.

Ray Banks shares his birthday with Chuck Barris and Curtis Mayfield and screeched into the world on the same day that Roberto Rossellini took his leave. He has worked as a wedding singer, double-glazing salesman, croupier, dole monkey, and various degrees of disgruntled temp. He writes novels (like the Cal Innes series) and short stories (like this one) and keeps a fairly clean online abode at www.thesaturdayboy.com.

Rob Kroese is the author of the Mercury trilogy: *Mercury Falls, Mercury Rises,* and *Mercury Rests.*

Stephen Mertz is one of the architects of the men's action/ adventure series genre. His two landmark series from the 1980s, *Stone: M.I.A. Hunter* and *Cody's Army* (as by Jim Case), have been reissued in e-book format. Under his own name Stephen has written a number of highly praised novels. The most recent of these, *Hank & Muddy* (2011) and *The Castro Directive* (2012), are also available as e-books. He lives and writes in Arizona.

Thomas Pluck writes unflinching fiction with heart. His work has appeared in *The Utne Reader, Needle: A Magazine of Noir, Burnt Bridge, PANK Magazine, McSweeney's, The Morning News, Beat to a Pulp,* and numerous anthologies. He is also the editor of *Protectors: Stories to Benefit PROTECT.* You can find him on the web at www.thomaspluck.com and as @tommysalami on Twitter.

Todd Robinson is the creator and Chief Editor of the award-winning 'zine THUGLIT.COM. His writing has appeared in *Plots With Guns, Needle Magazine, Shotgun Honey, Strange, Weird, and Wonderful, Out of the Gutter, Pulp Pusher, Grift, Demolition Magazine, CrimeFactory* and *Danger City.* He has been nominated for a Derringer Award, short-listed for Best American Mystery Stories, selected for Writers Digest's Year's Best Writing 2003 and won the inaugural Bullet Award in June 2011. The first collection of his short stories, *Dirty Words*, is now available as an E-book and his debut novel *The Hard Bounce* was released in January 2013 from Tyrus Books.